RE

The Ang

Louisa Young was born in London and read history at Trinity College, Cambridge. She lives in London with her daughter, with whom she co-wrote the best-selling *Lionboy* trilogy, and is the author of eleven previous books including the bestselling novel *My Dear, I Wanted to Tell You*, which was shortlisted for the Costa Novel Award and the Wellcome Book Prize, was a Richard and Judy Book Club choice, and the first ever winner of the Galaxy Audiobook of the Year.

Praise for *The Angeline Gower Trilogy*:

'Funny, sexy and tender' ESTHER FREUD

'Spectacularly worth reading' *The Times*

'A stylishly literate thriller' *Marie Claire*

'You will keep coming back to this book when you should be doing something else' LOUIS DE BERNIÈRES

'Exciting, compelling and tense' *Time Out*

'Funny and scary. In writing honestly and unsentimentally, Young celebrates the unequivocal nature of parental love with verve and style' *Mail on Sunday*

'Wry, perky, entertaining' *Observer*

'Engaging, wise-cracking, likeable, brilliantly sustained . . . funny, humane and utterly readable' *Good Housekeeping*

Also by Louisa Young

FICTION
Baby Love
Desiring Cairo
My Dear, I Wanted to Tell You
The Heroes' Welcome

NON-FICTION
A Great Task of Happiness: The Life of Kathleen Scott
The Book of the Heart

TREE OF PEARLS

The Angeline Gower Trilogy

Louisa Young

THE BOROUGH PRESS

The Borough Press
An imprint of HarperCollins*Publishers*
1 London Bridge Street
London
SE1 9GF

www.harpercollins.co.uk

This paperback edition 2015
1

First published by Flamingo, an imprint of HarperCollins*Publishers* 2000

A catalogue record for this book
is available from the British Library

ISBN: 978-0-00-757800-9

For Amira Ghazalla, the friend at the surface of the water

Introduction

I wrote these novels a long time ago. I spent my days correcting the grammar at the *Sunday Times*, and my nights writing. I could no longer travel the world doing features about born-again Christian bike gangs in New Jersey, or women salt-miners in Gujarat, or the Mr and Mrs Perfect Couple of America Pageant in Galveston, Texas, which was the sort of thing I had been doing up until then. I had to stay still. I had a baby. Babies focus the mind admirably: any speck of time free has to be made the most of.

I had £300 saved up, so I put the baby and the manuscript in the back of a small car and drove to Italy, where we lived in some rooms attached to a tiny church in a village which was largely abandoned, other than for some horses and some aristocrats. A nice girl groom took the baby to the sea each day in my car while I stared at the pages thinking: 'If I don't demonstrate some belief in this whole notion of novels, and me as a novelist, then why should anyone else?'

Re-reading these books now, I think, 'Christ! Such energy!' I was so young – so full of beans. I described the plot to my father, who wrote novels and was briefly, in his day, the new Virginia Woolf. After about five minutes he said, 'Yes, that all sounds good' – and I said, 'Dad, that's just chapter one'.

It was only about twenty years ago, and a different world. Answerphones not mobiles, no internet. Tickets and conductors on the bus. And it was before 9/11, and the mass collapse of international innocence which 9/11 and George Bush's reaction to it dragged in their miserable, brutalising wake. Could I write a story now, where an English girl and her Egyptian lover meet at the surface of the water? Yes, of course – but it could not be this story.

Anyway, I have grown up too thoughtful to write like this now. I exhaust myself even reading it.

I see too that these, my first novels, were the first pressing of thoughts and obsessions which have cropped up again and again in things I've written since. It seems I only really care about love and death and surgery and history and motorbikes and music and damage and babies, and the man I was in love with most of my life, who has appeared in various guises in every book I have ever written. I realise I continue to plagiarise myself all the time, emotionally and subject-wise. And I see the roots of other patterns – *Baby Love*, my first novel, turned into a trilogy all of its own accord. Since then, I've written another two novels that accidentally turned into trilogies – and one of those trilogies is showing signs of becoming a quartet.

People ask, oh, are they autobiographical? I do see, in these pages, my old friends when we were younger, their jokes and habits, places I used to live, lives I used to live. I glimpse, with a slight shock, garments I owned, a bed, a phrase . . . To be honest I made myself cry once or twice.

But, though much is undigested and autobiographical, in the way of a young person's writing, I can say this: be careful what you write. When I started these novels I was not a single mother, I didn't live in Shepherds Bush, I didn't have a bad leg and I wasn't going out with a policeman. By the time they were finished, all these things had come about. However as god is my witness to this day I never have never belly danced, nor hit anyone over the head with a poker.

Louisa Young
London 2015

ONE

Winning the peace

I was in the bath when trouble came for me for the third and, pray god, the last time.

My habit in winter when I have nothing better to do is to lie in the bath, keeping warm, reading ancient novels, steamed fat from previous sessions. Comfort reading. I've done it since childhood: it makes me feel safe. Georgette Heyer, *Catcher in the Rye*, Raymond Chandler, Naguib Mahfouz, *Madame Bovary*. That's where I was, one Tuesday morning in early December 1997, taking comfort after a time of turbulence; settling down and attending to the correct healing of wounds and to the immense and profound change which had come over my life. Out of all that the past months had thrown at me – and there was plenty, let me tell you – one thing stood out: I had discovered that my daughter had a father.

You may think that unsurprising – that she has one. Or surprising – that I didn't know. You may have a point. But in my life many things are inside out or upside down. Here in the bath, I lie safe and warm with my hair swirling round me and only the tip of my nose out of the water, and think about them, think about the shape and nature of our life to come.

I raised my head from its underwater reverie because I could hear, through some strange relationship of vibrations between the telephone and the floorboards and the water, the ring of the telephone and the formal tones of a voice on the machine. Through the rush of water down from my hair and over my ears as I rose, I could hear that it was not a voice I knew. This made me a little nervous, because unexpected and unwelcome phone calls had been something of a feature of the recent . . . turbulence. Not the domestic turbulence. Another part. Anyway, I wouldn't be getting out of the bath for whoever it was, so I turned on some more hot water, removed one of Lily's sponge letters of the alphabet (G, purple) from under my arse where it had fallen, and resubsided, putting from my mind echoes of the dangers I had come through. It wasn't Eddie Bates's voice, and that's all that mattered.

I lie, actually. It wasn't Sa'id el Araby's either. But I wasn't even entertaining that thought. (Hey, thought, please don't go, I'll put on a floorshow for you . . .)

*

Three quarters of an hour later I trailed into the study, wrapped in a bath towel, and listened to my messages. My message. Simon Preston Oliver, please could Evangeline Gower return his call without delay, phone number on which to do so. Formal, polite, authoritative. No explanation, no introduction beyond his name. He could have been a fitted-kitchen salesman, except that he obviously wasn't. Or someone from the accounts department ringing to cut off my electricity. I sniffed and pulled my towel up and went to turn up the heating, and I forgot all about him. I don't want anything new.

First I'm just going to tell you what you need to know for any of the rest of it to make sense.

I'll start with Janie, my sister, because I did start with Janie. I only ever had eleven months of my life without her – we were true Irish twins – until she died, and since then I've had her memory, and her child. My child now, since her birth and her mother's death, five years ago. Lily, the light of my life and the most beautiful, kind, intelligent, magical creature God ever made, bar none, and no, that's not bias.

Janie died in a crash. I used to think I killed her because I was riding the motorcycle she was on the back of, but I accept now that I didn't. It's taken a little while to realize that. In fact I'm still so . . . satisfied . . . with accepting it that I'll say it again: I didn't kill Janie.

Before the crash ruined my leg I was a bellydancer. I loved four things: bellydancing, motorbikes, Harry Makins and Janie. A year or two ago, I found things out about

Janie which I don't so much hold against her any more, though I did then. There's no reason to withhold it though it's not my favourite subject.

OK. She was a prostitute and a pornographer. I didn't know until after she was dead. She lied to me. She used film of me dancing in her dirty movies. She wore my costumes while selling sex to my admirers, pretending to be me. Then she died, and left me alone with all that to deal with.

I've put all that down and my heart is not beating faster, my belly is unclouded. I don't hate her any more.

Harry thought I knew about her . . . activities, and condoned them. This misunderstanding contributed to his throwing a chair out of the window at me, and me absconding to the Maghreb and Egypt for a couple of years to get over it. That was, oh, about ten years ago now.

Then a year and a half ago Janie's hitherto absent boyfriend appeared, wanting Lily. He didn't get her (that's another story) but in the middle of this – not a good time for my family – a mad bastard called Eddie Bates turned up, with a psychotic crush on me, which had first blossomed without my knowledge twelve years ago, when I was a table-hopping bellydancer in the Arab clubs and Levantine restaurants of the West End of London, and he was a diner, a stage-door Johnnie who never – as far as I knew – approached me. Eddie – I am being deliberately light here, just giving the facts – did me wrong in many ways, and ended up in prison, though not for anything to do with me. Just because he was a rather successful drug baron and vice lord. Harry helped put him away. Harry, who when I used to know him had been a wideboy biker, had grown up into a policeman. Not that I knew, until it was all over.

I'm sorry if this is confusing. It confused me too.

Then Harry told me that Eddie had died in gaol, and I thought I was free. As free as I could be.

But then. Then I started getting curious and unpleasant letters and phone calls. I thought they were from Eddie's wife, Chrissie. And then – well Eddie wasn't dead, after all. He was alive, if you please, and in Cairo, having turned evidence on his nasty cronies and won himself in return a secret new life, from which he decided it would be fun to carry on tormenting me. By a peculiarly unpleasant and clever trick he got me out there. I went, and ended up saving him, maybe saving his life, by mistake I can assure you. I believed – and believe – sincerely and with good reason that as a result, he is granting me freedom from his attentions.

All these things seemed more or less resolved by November 1997. I had learnt something about Eddie, a realization and a resolution: I could ignore him. I could deal with him. I wouldn't want to, but if I had to I could. I had done before. Twice. Three times – god, you see, I lose count. The time he pretended to have kidnapped Lily; the time he did kidnap me; and the time in Cairo. So now, if he wants to tweak my chain, as Sa'id said, so what? I have taken the chain off.

And Janie's secrets were known and settling in the slow, drifting, mumbling way that revealed secrets do settle, finally joining the pile of family history like autumn leaves. Mum and I had talked.

And Lily, my little darling, my honey-gold curly-haired loud-mouthed sweetheart, had a father. And that was the future.

The father?

Oh.

It's Harry.

He had slept with Janie, drunk, six years ago, under the impression she was me, apparently. Well after he and I broke up. She and I are (were?) very alike, physically. She'd been in his bed when he got home. Well, yes.

He wasn't altogether a surprise. He'd told me it might be him. In fact he was something of a relief, given the other contenders – Eddie Bates (one of her regulars); a pimp-cum-policeman called Ben Cooper . . . but even so, yes. My old love is my child's father. Exactly.

So all we had to do now was learn how to do it. How to have a father in our lives at all, our lives that had been just us for five years. In our flat. In our daily routines. In our priorities. He was keen, in a fairly tactful way, to do the right thing. The prospect was, quite frankly, terrifying.

But there he was, and he was Harry. Decent, responsible, handsome, funny, long tall Harry. DI Makins. Who I'd known so long. Since he was louche, disreputable, handsome, funny long tall Harry, wideboy biker. The one I used to fight with all the time. The one with my name tattooed on his long, rope-muscled, milk-white right arm.

Is any of this clear? To me it is. This is just the story of my life. I am so accustomed to melodramatic absurdity by now that I forget how strange it must sound to other people. One fruit of it, though, is that I am reluctant to take things at face value; reluctant to believe that every little thing is going to be all right, unless I personally make sure of it. Which is one reason why I am so interested in whether I can just let Harry be Dad in his own way. Trust him, is I think what I am talking about. Not so much whether he is trustworthy as whether I am capable of trust.

The other question, of course, was Harry and me.

Twice, since we parted, he has offered.

Twelve years ago, in that bar in Soho, I'd said: 'Yes, and then not for a month.'

A year and a half ago after our last bout of chaos, I'd said no.

Two weeks ago I managed maybe.

'OK,' he said, his face quite steady, untroubled. 'OK.' And ordered a curry instead. And the moment had passed.

I wasn't even sure it had happened at all.

Waiting for the curry to come he went and looked at Lily as she slept. Then when the silver-foil boxes were laid out on the kitchen table, we sat opposite each other

7

to eat and I just stared at him. Letting it sink in. Lily's father.

'What *do* we do now then?' he said. 'If not fuck?'

For a moment I thought I was getting a second chance, but I wasn't. He was just being . . . humorous. Cheerful. Open. Sarky.

It's not that I turn him down because he's not sexy. Sometimes, when we were together, I used to have to have words with girls who would become irrational in his presence. It was the combination of the cheekbones and the louche cockiness that did it. The cheekbones are, if anything, better, older; the cynical trickster boy has retreated though, in the face of something, as a grown man, which – well, he thinks it's to do with Gary Cooper. Which side you are on. He decided, at some stage during the time when we weren't seeing each other, that the villain's black hat was all very well but he preferred a kind of lonesome maverick white hat. It suits him.

'We . . . oh god,' I said.

You'd think after my adventures I could deal with all sorts of things, but sitting at my kitchen table eating a prawn dhansak with this man I'd known a third of my life was proving to be too much.

He leant across the table and put his cool and gnarled hand on my temple, saying, 'Sorry, darling. Impossible question.' His 'darling' is more cabbie than Harvey Nichols. Harry's not posh. He's from Acton.

'We eat,' he said. 'Let's just eat.'

So we ate. Then we watched telly. For a while I shot him little sideways looks, to see if he'd changed in the course of the evening. Father of the child. Here and present. Sticking around, one way or another. He had changed, actually. He looked happier.

Then I fell asleep. Later he put me to bed, barefoot but clothed.

Lily came into my bed in the small hours, the child who for five years had been mine and now, suddenly, was his. She talks in her sleep; tonight she wanted me to help her because there were too many bananas. I murmured, 'Of course I will, honey,' and she rolled over and wrapped her arms round my neck and put her feet between my knees, and then woke up complaining that my hair was tickling her nose.

I couldn't get back to sleep. I disentangled myself from my five-year-old octopus of love and wandered into the kitchen. There was Harry asleep on the sofa, all six foot four of him, oddly folded and sprawled, his arms crossed across his chest like an Egyptian mummy clutching his flail. His face was impassive, showing his age. He manages – even his face – to be both scrawny and muscular at the same time. What's the word? Lean. He has those lines that cowboys have, the deep ones around the mouth, the ones that women take to indicate humour, natural intelligence and the ability to make a woman feel good. Of course he has those qualities too.

We have no streetlights up here, but by the light from

the hall I could see, just visible where the sleeve of his ancient t-shirt ended, part of the curling tattooed wave that broke under the prow of the fully rigged HMS *Victory* on his left bicep, with the guiding compass-point star above it and the name in a furling banner beneath. Every eldest Makins son had had the *Victory* on his bicep since an early-eighteenth-century Harry Makins had served on board, as powder monkey or something, no one could quite remember what. Harry's dad had wanted to break the tradition, and forbade all his sons from having any tattoos at all. Harry, with his historical loyalties and his rebellious nature, had celebrated his eighteenth birthday with *Victory* on his left arm and his twenty-first with the opening line of *The Rights of Man* like a bracelet round his right. For his twenty-eighth I had given him a tattoo of his choice. He had said he wanted a rose as he was getting soft, but he wouldn't let me come with him to the parlour and he had come out with my name, damn him, in a curled tattooed banner wrapped around his arm beneath the bracelet of Thomas Paine.

I looked at him for a while as he slept. I used to kiss him, I thought. And shook my head violently, and went back to the child.

*

Lily, god bless her, took it entirely in her stride. As daddies are the men that live with children, so if Harry is her daddy of course he would be there for breakfast. Her logic is simple.

Mine isn't. The reality of sitting round the breakfast table with them shook me about. Will she want him here for breakfast every day? My sole purpose in life is to look after her, to love her and save her from fear and shock, of which she had quite enough at her birth. She is innocence walking, and I am her minder. I make good. That's my purpose. I make good for Lily. But for all the time Harry and I have had to wonder about how Harry As Dad, Us With Dad would be – before deciding to do the DNA test, since waiting for the results – for some things there is no possibility of preparation. We can't know. We have no role models. No instructions. No guidance. Even less than people usually do. But this morning we have a masquerade of domesticity. (I put from my mind an image of a version of man woman child that was briefly here a few weeks before: Sa'id, Lily and I. Sitting about the breakfast table during the tiny moment when it seemed that anything could happen, and be all right.)

Now, here is Harry, having to go to work.

He had woken early and calling my name.

'I'm here,' I called, trying to call quietly not to wake her just as I realized she wasn't in with me. I got up and went through to the kitchen.

Lily was there beside the sofa, blinking and smiling, with her curls all ruffled up and her eyes gleaming. She didn't even look at me. 'Dada,' she said, in the sweetest little voice.

'Oh god, hello,' he said, with his hair all ruffled up too

and confused amazement in his normally so steady green eyes. He looked back at me, and back at her, and shook his head as if in disbelief and said 'oh god' again. I thought Lily would make one of her clever comments about God, like why are you talking to God when you've only just met me, or something, but she didn't. She just stood there in the puddle of her too-long pyjama legs and looked up at him with the sweetest little expression on her face. 'Dada,' she said again. Where the hell did she get 'Dada' from?

Harry wanted to hug her. He was embarrassed to because he was horizontal, in yesterday's clothes, and half asleep. His limbs are so long and he didn't know what to do with them. He is unaccustomed to hugging children. She reached over to him and patted his cheek. He looked at her, staring at her eyes. He sat up and leaned forward, his long back arching. He looked as if he might be going to howl with amazement and tenderness.

'Hello, you little darling,' he said. As he said it I realized how he had been holding himself back from her until now, now that his role is accredited.

She curled into herself. 'Dada,' she said. Coy as cherry pie. Inarticulate as a two-year-old. But getting her message across just fine.

He pushed back the blankets and swung his legs over the side of the sofa, squinting at his boots and shaking his head. He looked up at me. I had my face in my hand and was thinking about weeping. Or laughing. Something involuntary and physical, anyway.

'Do you want some breakfast?' he said to her.

'First I go to the loo,' said Lily, 'and then I have breakfast.' Ha ha! Letting him know how things are, how things work around here.

'What do you have?' he said, standing up, not knowing whether or not he was to go into the bathroom with her.

'You can come in if you like,' she said. In he went, and she started to explain about cereal, porridge, pancakes on highdays and holidays, melon that we had on holiday once and a naughty little horse came and tried to eat it.

I sat on the sofa. I had an image of a great big tiny girl's little finger, with raggy nails and the remains of sparkly pink nail polish from a birthday party, and wrapped spiralled all around the length of it was long tall Harry. There could be worse ways for it to go, I knew. It was . . . all right. For them to be in love with each other.

The sofa was warm where he had been sleeping, but behind my neck there was a coldness. A sad little coldness, all the sadder for knowing it was absurd. But it was there. If you love each other then what about me? And they are blood. Blood closer than me. It's Janie's blood in there with them. Not mine.

I pulled the little feeling round from behind me and placed it square on my lap. 'Don't be daft,' I said to it, not harshly, but it looked me square in the eyes and I knew it had a point, and that I would have to bear it in mind. Sitting there with his warmth under me, thinking about love, I wondered whether, if I had said yes, sex would have crowned us and saved us and thrown us to the top of the mountain whence we would have surveyed our glorious new future, clear-eyed and confident like Soviet youngsters saluting a five-year plan. Maybe. Maybe.

I could hear Lily instructing Harry in how to get her dressed and make her breakfast, and I felt very, very odd.

*

Harry went to work. As men do. Rise, kiss children, and go to work. God but it felt weird. A little version of normality suddenly and weirdly come to sit on my head. There hasn't been a boyfriend in my life – my domestic life – for years. The last one, actually, was Harry. Then the years of travelling and running wild, then the years of just me and Lily.

Except Sa'id. But I'm not thinking about Sa'id.

And now here is Harry going to work.

As soon as he left, Lily and I looked each other and said, 'well?' At least I did. She didn't. It was as if she knew everything, and didn't need to talk to me about it. Didn't need gossip, or discussion, or analysis, or reassurance.

'Well, sweetheart?' I asked.

'What?' she said.

Part of me yelled out, 'Jesus fuck, five years of love and devotion and total non-verbal understanding gone, just like that, just because love has gone multilateral . . .' A silent part, of course.

'About the daddy?' I said. The daddy we've been talking

14

about so long, the daddy I promised you, the daddy you longed for and I wasn't sure I could provide and now I have — what about him?

'Why are you calling him the daddy? He's just Daddy. Not the daddy.'

He's just Daddy. She spoke as if she's known him all her life.

'Are you . . . is he OK? Are you pleased?'

'Doesn't matter if he's OK,' she said. 'He's my daddy so I love him.'

'Oh,' I said. How very easy this seems to be for her. How very misleading that impression might be.

'You know, Mummy,' she said. 'Because it was his little sperm so he's part of me and so we love each other.'

I don't feel left out and I am not jealous. I'm really not. I can accept that I might feel these things briefly but they're not . . . how I really feel. I really feel really happy that she is being so uncannily together about this. And I'm not sure I believe it. But she is looking at me, so straight and clear and young, and I find myself thinking, my god, maybe it is possible that she just is this well-balanced, maybe between her own natural self and my long devotion to her security she is capable of happily and harmoniously swanning into having a father after all.

But swans paddle furiously under the water.

No, go with it girl. Don't look for grief. If there's to be any you'll notice soon enough.

'Of course,' I said.

'Don't worry,' she said. 'You're still my mummy even if it wasn't your little egg.'

I was ridiculously pleased to hear it, and we walked to school as if nothing had happened, as if it was still just us, and then I came home and got in the bath.

*

Dressed again after my bath, I was staring out of my study window, looking out over the grey and yellow mouldy plum December skies and the chilling, battening-down rows of west London winter roofs, not applying myself to some negligible piece of work, wondering about Harry. It had been a few weeks since he had produced the official certificate of his right and duty to be around. He leaves nothing here. No detritus for me to clear away, nothing to suggest he's coming back. Physically, he might as well never have been here. But he does come back. He's been coming back for a while.

So now we arrange a semi-detached homelife for Lily, from scratch. I was hugely alert to what we could slip into. We needed to talk, and yet when we did there was so little to say. Perhaps we just needed to do. Perhaps I should, as Fontella Bass recommends, 'Leave it in the Hands of Love'.

The phone rang. I stared at it a bit dopily, then answered. A stranger's voice, a man, asking for me by my full name. Something put my hackles up. I am a most defensive and protective person. But I was prepared to admit that I was me.

'This is Simon Preston Oliver,' he said.

I was none the wiser, and implied it. And then remembered his name from the message.

'Scotland Yard,' he said.

Immediately I had a flood of the feeling I get when the school rings: they know parents and their first words are always 'don't worry, nothing's happened to Lily'. I wanted this man to say these words of Harry. Why would Scotland Yard ring me, if not . . . ?

'Why?' I said, not very intelligently.

'I need to talk to you, Ms Gower, and . . .'

'Is Harry all right?' I interrupted.

There was a pause. 'DI Makins is fine,' he said.

'Of course,' I said. Still hurtling up the wrong track. 'Isn't that . . .'

'I'm not calling about him, no. I need to talk to you about another matter. I could call on you later this afternoon, or tomorrow . . .'

I'm not having him here. I had enough of that in the old days with Bent Copper Ben Cooper calling round at all hours trying to blackmail me and ruining my life, before I knew Janie's secrets and before . . . oh, before so many things.

'Why?' I said again. If it wasn't about Harry, if Harry was all right, then there was nothing I could possibly want to know about lurking anywhere down this line of talk. This means disruption and I am trying to settle.

'In person would be better,' he said, cajolingly, setting my hackles right on edge.

'Why?' I said again. Using the weapons of a three-year-old, and leaving him sitting in the silence.

After a while he said, 'We want to ask you some questions.'

Well, that's subtly and fundamentally different from wanting to talk to me. But it doesn't answer *my* question.

'What about?'

'Angeline,' he said – which was wrong of him, and set my hackles flying from the ramparts. I object to chumminess in people I don't know, particularly if we are obviously not getting on. I also knew I would have to talk to him. I knew I was being obstructive and silly. But that's how I felt. He would have to tell me sooner or later, why not now? Why this secretive big-willy stuff? He *did* remind me of Ben.

'Just what's it about?' I said, interrupting.

I could hear him thinking for a moment, and I heard his decision the moment before the answer popped out.

'Cairo,' he said.

Cairo.

El-Qahira, the victorious. People who know it call it Kie-ear-oh, one long swooping melting of vowels in the middle. People who don't call it Kie Roh. As he did. This was quietly reassuring. It meant that he didn't know the city or, probably, anyone in it. But the reassurance was small next to my main reaction.

I have no desire to talk about Cairo. There is nothing about Cairo that bodes any joy for me and Lily.

'I have nothing to say about Cairo,' I said pompously. Breathing shallow.

'Well let's see, shall we? I'll come to you at five tomorrow,' he said, and the sod hung up.

I resolved to be in the park.

TWO

Beware policemen in pubs

By five the next day I had seen sense, though part of me still thought it a shame that I had. Lily had come out of school begging to be allowed to go home with her friend Adjoa, so that was easy, and I was free to lurk like Marlene under the streetlight at the bottom of my staircase until he appeared. He was not coming to my flat, whatever he might think. I had to see him, but I didn't have to welcome him.

It was such a wintry evening that no one was hanging around the stairwells or the strips of park and path that lie between the blocks of the estate, which is rare, because the estate is a very sociable place, what with the teenagers and the crackheads and the men yelling up at the windows of the women who have thrown them out, and just as well because people round here have a strong sense of plod. Enough of my neighbours break the law on a regular basis to be able to smell it when it comes calling. (I prefer to associate myself with the mothers and the kids still too young to be running round with wraps of god knows what for their big brothers. You know, the three-year-olds.) But what with the weather and the dark, no one but me saw the dark car rolling up quietly through the dingy Shepherd's Bush dusk, and stopping, and its passenger door swinging open.

'Get in,' came the voice, the figure leaning over from having opened the door. I ignored it. How did he know I was me, anyway? Presumably they had bothered to acquire a photograph of me, somewhere down the line. I don't like the idea, but neither do I imagine there is anything I can do about it.

'Get in!' Louder.

I rubbed my mouth, and looked this way and that up and down the road, and then went round to the driver's side. He wound down the window. Very pale face. Putty-coloured. Very dark brows, very arched.

I said: 'How would you, as a police officer, encourage your wife or daughters to respond to a stranger in a car who shouts "get in" at them?'

For a moment I thought he was going to tell me to grow up, but he didn't. He sighed, and said, 'Where do you want to go?' There was something so tired in it that I gave up. I got in the car, and directed him to a done-up pub down by Ravenscourt Park where they have a wood fire and nice food and good coffee. I yearn for comfort.

I chose an upright little table and ordered what Lily still calls a cup of chino. He had a lime juice cordial thing, and

I realized he was an alcoholic. Don't know how. It was just apparent. We sat in silence for few moments, and I thought: 'I don't want this to start up again. I don't want any more of this. Not again.' I know that I am strong, that I can deal with it. But.

'Cairo,' he said. I felt my insides begin to subside. Like all the lovely crunchy fluffy individual concrete ingredients in a food mixer – switch the button and they turn to low gloop. 'You know more or less what this is about.'

I didn't answer. A slow burning anger was running along a fuseline direct to my heart.

What, through the gloop? The absurdity of mixed metaphors always cheers me up, makes me sharpen up.

Cairo meant only two things to me now. Not the time I spent there in my previous life, nine or so years ago, though it seems like a lifetime (well, it is a lifetime – Lily's lifetime, and more), living in the big block off Talat Haarb that we called Château Champollion, and dancing for my living in the clubs and on the Nile boats. When I saw every dawn and not a single midday. Not the friends I'd made then, the girls of all nations, the musicians of all Arab nations, the ex-pats and chatterboxes at the Grillon. Not the aromatic light and shade of the Old City, or the view from the roof of the mosque of Ibn Tulun, not the taste of cardamom in coffee or the flavour of dust. No . . . Cairo, now, only means Sa'id. And this could not be about Sa'id. So it had to be about Eddie Bates.

'You flew to Cairo on Friday October 17th, on October

20th you continued to Luxor, and you returned to London via Cairo on October 24th. Is that right?'

He pronounced it Lux-Or. Not Looksr. Definitely not an Egyptophile. Well, why would he be?

'Yes,' I said.

'Can you tell me about your visit?'

'Can you tell me why you want to know?'

It's not that I don't trust the police. I'd say not more than half of them are any worse than anyone else in life, which given their opportunities is probably a miracle. It's just that last time I sat in a pub with a policeman he ended up blackmailing me into spying on Eddie Bates in a stupid effort to save his own corrupt arse, and that was the beginning of the whole hijacking of my life and Lily's by these absurd people. So I am wary.

He looked at me under his sad eyebrows. 'Have you ever heard of obstructing a police officer in the course of his duty?' he said.

'Have you ever heard of taking the trouble to gain a witness's trust before expecting them to tell you all their business?'

He squinted at me.

'Or aren't I a witness?' I said. The food mixer went again in my belly. 'All I want to know,' I said, tetchily, 'is what this is about.' Not quite true. What I really wanted was for it not to be happening.

'How many things have you got going on in Cairo that might be of interest to the police then?' he replied.

I wasn't going to tell him anything. Not unless he told me first. As I can't remember which country and western singer said, in big hair and blue eyeshadow: 'I've been to the circus and I've seen the clowns, this ain't my first rodeo.'

'Nothing that I know of,' I said. 'That's why I'm asking.'

He looked disappointed in me.

'Eddie Bates,' he said.

'Eddie Bates is dead,' I replied. That's the official version and there is no reason for me to know any different. 'He died in prison,' I said. I even managed to look a little puzzled.

'François du Berry, then,' he said. 'Could we just get on?'

'I don't know what you mean,' I lied. I knew exactly what he meant.

It was Harry who had told me that Eddie was not dead, but living in Cairo under an assumed name. What I didn't know was whether Preston Oliver knew that Harry had told me – risking his career and maybe saving my life by doing so. I'm not telling any big policeman who I don't know anything about this.

'What were you doing in Egypt?' he said.

'I was on holiday,' I said.

He just looked at me.

Sooner or later one of us was going to lose our temper, and I was afraid it was going to be me. I decided to do it the controlled way. Like the angry posh lady hectoring the Harrods shop assistant.

'I think you'll find,' I said, 'that asking the same question over and over is going to get you nowhere. I have no desire whatsoever to hamper you in the course of your duties, indeed I am happy to tell you anything that may be of use to you, but it is not unreasonable of me to want to know why. Do you think I am a witness to something? Do you suspect me of something? I have to insist that you be specific, because otherwise I'm afraid I can't help you. You can think about it. I'll be back in a moment.'

'I think you'll find.' What a great phrase. And as for 'I have to insist' . . .

I found the public telephone, snatched up the receiver and rang Harry at work. Not there. Rang his mobile.

'Harry?'

'What is it?' he said. He can smell urgency. Logically, I would be calling about our domestic and emotional situation, and he would have no business saying 'What is it?' to me in that tone. But he could tell.

'Simon Preston Oliver – mean anything to you?'

'Why?' he said.

'He's here. Not right here – you know. He wants to know about Cairo.'

Harry knew about Cairo. Harry knows it all, pretty much. Well . . . most.

A moment passed.

'Tell him,' he said.

'Everything?'

'Everything you told me.'

25

'Does he know you told me about Eddie?'

'Not . . . not as such. I mean yes, he does, he must do. But we haven't talked about it.'

'So —'

'I think he's cool with it, but. But. Slide by it if you can.'

'Do you think he'll let me?'

'He wouldn't usually. He's a snake – he's brilliant. But in this case, yes – well, he loves me. I think. Shit.'

Well that was reassuring.

'What's it about, Harry?' I asked.

'I don't know. I've heard nothing since you've been back. Which may be because he's put two and two together – you and me.'

The phrase hung between us. You and me. Its other context glowing slightly down the line.

I wrenched back on course. I'm going to have to get used to this. 'Is he the bloke you talked to about me before I left?' I asked. Harry had told me that a senior colleague, doubtful about the wisdom of putting Eddie on witness protection, had told Harry about it, specifically so that someone near to me could know, and remain aware.

'Yes,' he said. 'He's all right. He's not Ben Cooper.'

'Thank you,' I said. Meaning it.

*

Back at the table, Preston Oliver greeted me with 'And how's Harry?'

I laughed.

26

'You can't blame me,' I said.

'I thought you would have spoken to him earlier,' he said.

'There's a lot on my mind,' I said.

'So I would imagine,' he said, eyeing me. He probably thinks I trust him now, I thought. Well . . . he's not top of the list of people I don't trust.

'So,' he said. 'In your own words.'

I reckoned quickly. He knows a certain amount about me. There's nothing to be lost by him knowing my version. And perhaps he will be nice and leave me alone if he feels that I am cooperating. So I briefly ran through for him some of the things that had been keeping me busy over the past few months.

'A few months ago,' I said, 'I started to receive letters – anonymous letters, threatening. I worked out that they were from Chrissie Bates – Eddie's wife. Then some purporting to be from Eddie. Who I knew to be dead. I'd been to his funeral.' I had. And I'd met Chrissie for the first time, and it had been very mad, though not as mad as later when Eddie turned out to be not dead at all.

'One said . . . let me get this right,' I said. 'One said that he had put money in an account for my daughter in Cairo, and I was to go and fetch it, and if I didn't his lawyer was under instructions to give it to the BNP.'

He raised his eyebrows.

'I don't like the BNP,' I said. Understating it rather. You

don't live my life, live where I do (where the premises on the main road go: Irish laundromat, Lebanese grocery, Turkish cab firm, Armenian deli, Irish snooker club, Syrian grocery, Trinidadian travel agent, Syrian butcher, Lebanese café, Jamaican take-away, Chinese take-away, Indian fabric store, Nepalese restaurant, Thai restaurant, Italian restaurant, Ghanaian fabric store, Nigerian telephone agency, Australian bar, Polish restaurant, Pakistani newsagent, Irish café which turns Thai in the evenings, mosque, Brazilian film-makers' collective, Ukrainian cab firm, Serbian internet café, Greek restaurant and something called the Ay Turki Locali, which may well be Turkish but whatever else it is I've never worked out), without developing rather strong views about racism. Mine is that it's both the most ludicrous and the most evil of injustices. 'So I went out there, and got the money, and came back.'

He just looked at me. And then made a little gesture, a little twitching of the fingers: more.

'Your turn,' I said.

'Did you meet François du Berry?'

Ah, very good. What a delicate way of doing it. Slipping from the 'dead' man to his new identity without a word.

'Yes,' I said.

'And?'

It's not just Harry. I have a couple of other people to protect here, none of whom have done anything wrong, but who could get in trouble, and who did it for me.

'He, um, he was there to meet us when we collected

the money, and then later I saw him at a show, in a hotel. Bellydancing.'

'We?' said Preston Oliver.

'What?'

Oh bugger.

'You said "we".'

'Oh . . . yes, a friend came with me.' Please don't drag him in. Please don't drag him in. I could see him as he was that day: so cool, so beautiful, so protective, so funny. That fantastical scene in the foyer of the Nile Hilton, carrying £100,000 in a case, and Eddie eyeing him up with a view to group sex . . .

Preston Oliver was looking knowing. 'And do you know two brothers called . . .' Oh god '. . . Sa'id and Hakim el Araby?' he was asking.

Just hearing his name said out loud in a stranger's voice gave me a frisson. He exists! He's real!

Yes, but his name is in the wrong mouth, the wrong context.

And anyway, you left him. So sharpen up.

Pointless not to.

Ha ha. Pointless.

Preston Oliver was looking at me.

I tried to think how to put it.

'We know . . .' he said, but I interrupted him.

'They're old friends of mine,' I said. 'I knew their father when I lived in Egypt before. They are from a good family.' I realized I was justifying them as I might to an Egyptian policeman, rather than an English one. 'Their mother is an English academic. They were staying with me in London before I went out to Cairo; Sa'id came with me to the bank that day . . .'

'And where is the money now?'

I didn't want to tell him. 'Why, are you going to do me for tax evasion?' It was a joke, but of course he could. Except that I don't have the money. I hate the fucking money. To me that money means only manipulation and blackmail and Eddie Bates tweaking my chain. And god only knows how he made it in the first place. From mugged old ladies via ten-year-old junkies, probably.

'Why, do you have it?' he was asking.

I don't have it. I left it with Sa'id.

'I gave it to charity,' I said. Which was more or less true. I gave it to Sa'id to give to a children's charity in Cairo, because that was the only way I could think of to make dirty money clean again.

He looked disbelieving. As indeed you might. I'd be disbelieving myself – £100,000 given to charity by a semi-employed single mother from Shepherd's Bush? But that's what I did.

'Why are you asking about them?' I said.

He sniffed. 'Sorry,' he said. 'Cold.'

I said nothing.

'Thing is,' he said, 'du Berry has gone awol.'

'Awol?' I said.

'Absent without leave,' he said.

'I know what it means,' I snapped. 'I just . . . I don't think I'm very interested.'

And I wasn't. I had put Eddie away from me. He has been what he has been but he is no longer. He is nothing to do with me now. Yeah, and hasn't been for seven whole weeks, said an inner voice. You think you're getting off that lightly? He's history, I told it. History. Don't drag me into this.

'He's disappeared,' said Preston Oliver. 'The Egyptians don't seem to give a damn, but they have been polite enough to mention the el Araby brothers.'

Of course history does have a way of affecting the present.

How very sinister they sound, described that way. Sweet young hothead Hakim, and beautiful Sa'id, alabaster merchant, economist, Sorbonne graduate, singer of love songs, speaker of five languages, Nile boatman, holder of my heart. Sa'id who I left.

'Why?' I asked.

'Something about a fight in a hotel in Cairo,' he said. 'I believe you were there.'

Oh.

'Well, they're not criminals,' I said. 'It's ridiculous. If Eddie's decided to abscond, that's his business . . . probably he just threw out some accusations to muddy the water.'

'That's what I thought,' he said. I was pleased. 'Now tell me about the fight.'

I love the way people throw out questions as if they

were nothing. 'How are you?' is a good one. This was another. Six words. It sounds so easy. I was silent a moment, thinking, collating. Oh yes, the fight, that old thing. How will I choose to tell him about that? Given that I am telling him. And I was silent a moment longer, wondering if I could resist some more.

I could. But I wouldn't, and I knew if I tried to I would be pretending.

He was watching, eyebrows tragically calm. He looked as if he had heard a thousand and one stories.

'Eddie and I had a disagreement in a hotel corridor,' I said. 'Hakim had followed us because he feared for my safety, and when Eddie . . . attacked me, Hakim pulled him off.'

The 'more' gesture again, the eyebrows in repose at once calm, tragic and receptive.

'That's it, really.' I don't need to mention the knife, or say that Hakim had been working for Eddie, naif little fool that he is, nor that Eddie had been attacking me with a sexual purpose. I don't think he needs to know that. And I felt the shameful ripples of Eddie and sex run over my shoulders and down my back.

'What was the disagreement about?'

I didn't answer. He didn't push it, but he didn't retreat either. All I wanted was to know that Sa'id and Hakkim were all right. But Sa'id and Hakim are not my business any more.

'Are you in touch with the el Arabys?' he asked.

'No.'

'Hakim el Araby has been questioned. He's not a problem. But Sa'id has not made himself available. Do you know where he is?'

'No.'

I was thinking about Sa'id's family: Abu Sa'id, Mariam, Madame Amina. Oh god, all these decent people. Caught up. I *told* him I shouldn't have gone to stay at his aunt's while I was dealing with Eddie.

'He took a flight to Athens ten days ago. Have you heard from him?'

'No.'

'Despite their being such good friends of yours? Staying with you and all that?'

My heart was falling, slowly, gently. I am just at the beginning of my days of healing and rebuilding. What's it to me if Sa'id goes to Athens? If Eddie moves on? Leave me alone. My old enemy and my old lover. They're not mine.

'We were hoping you could help. If either of them gets in touch with you,' he went on, 'you must let us know.'

I gave him a long low look. Does he have the slightest idea what he is asking of me here? What he is doing to me? What either of these men has been to me? How Eddie, despite the quick, spontaneous, devilish pact we made that night when I prevented Hakim from knifing him, has never been anything but my enemy, my complex enemy, on many many levels? The serious enemy – the one who brings out from your own depths your own worst faults, your weaknesses? It was to Eddie that I did the worst thing I have ever done, and I hate him for it.

It's part of the story. There's no avoiding it. A year and half ago, when he kidnapped me in London . . . I'll put it simply – he was trying to fuck me, I resisting. I hit him with a poker, knocked him out. Then as he lay unconcious and, due to the workings of the autonomic nervous system (I looked it up later), still hard, I fucked him back. Did to him the bad thing he had been trying to do to me. Out of anger and revenge, I gave him what he wanted in a way he could never enjoy. And my worst self enjoyed it very much. So I hate him.

There. Very simple.

And Sa'id? Sa'id taught me to leave the dead alone, showed me how forgiveness works, made me capable, in myself, of seeing off Eddie and his frightful attachment. And, if I am honest, mine. My frightful . . . not attachment. My . . . interest. Something.

'I don't imagine,' I said, staring at him, 'that either of them will.' Don't you stir this up, you. I'm trying to win the peace here. I have a child to look after. Leave me alone.

'If they do,' said Preston Oliver.

'Sure,' I said. Easily, because they wouldn't, and if they did – well, I lied.

*

Then it was time for me to fetch Lily. She and I ambled home in the dark, unable to hear each other speak for the

34

traffic heading west on the Uxbridge Road. We cut into the small streets as soon as we could, and admired other people's lives glowing through their bay windows: their televisions and their teas. Lily wondered why we don't live in a house.

'Because we live in a flat,' I said, interestingly. I was tired.

She said she'd like to live in a house. I concurred in a non-committal grunting fashion.

Then felt bad about my lack of interest. 'Why?' I asked.

'So that when you die I can bury you in the garden and you'll still be near me.'

'Oh sweetheart,' I said. 'Oh.'

'I know it won't really be you,' she said. 'I know it'll just be your body, and worms will eat it, even your eyes, and your lovely little nose.'

I looked down at her, and she reached up, and touched the tip of my nose tenderly.

Oh sweetheart,' I said.

'But what I really want is a leopard that can read my mind, and knows where to go.'

Oh my god, I thought. And said: 'So do I.'

THREE

I'm not Canute

It was seven by the time we got home – time Lily should be getting ready for bed. Harry was sitting on the doorstep, up at the end of the long red-brick balcony that leads to my flat, reading the *Independent* and ignoring the cold. He looked to Lily first. She seemed to have forgotten all about him – and then remembered.

'Dada!' she trilled, blinking at him. He stood – unfolding himself as he does, like a camel or a telescope – and picked her up, and her legs hung down as if she were a puppet on his hand. Long dangly big-girl legs. She's five now. A creature of playgrounds and reading books and the girls' gang, no more the plump little dimpled thing I used to know. My girl.

He smiled at me over her shoulder. As you see dads do. Dads in coats carrying big girls in coats. In the park, at the playground. Girls climb up on their dads. My girl, her dad.

I opened the door and they followed me in. The hallway seemed smaller than usual. So did the kitchen. What with this new identity spreading out all over the place. Of course Harry's been there many a time before, but Lily's father hasn't. And he seems to take up space.

I'm not complaining.

I started to make an omelette, automatically. It wouldn't be a very nice one because I was rather too weary to whisk it up properly the way she likes. I tried to do a little yoga breathing as I whisked. Just because a policeman asks you some questions it doesn't mean your life has to be upended again. It came out as a sigh.

'Can I do it?' Harry said.

I just stared at him.

'Why not?' he said.

No reason at all.

'Make up for lost time,' I said. I have cooked tea for his child seven nights a week for five years; he has never.

'Can I put her to bed too?' he said.

'You don't have to ask,' I said. 'At least you don't have to ask me.'

'No you can't,' said Lily. 'But you can read me a story.'

Harry eyed her.

'You know what?' he said.

'What?'

'You don't boss your father.'

She thought about it. I observed, interested.

She changed the subject. Enquired about the omelette,

wanted milk, carried on with normal business. Much like I'm doing myself, now I come to think of it. My normal business of my family. Of Lily. Of incorporating Harry. And this is going to be such an interesting business. I must keep my mouth shut and let them work it out for themselves even though I know everything much better than they do. She can tell him what she wants; he can learn. I'll just stand by. Or lie in wait. Or bite my tongue. Or something.

But I won't be thinking about Cairo.

*

When she was asleep we sat at the kitchen table. Again. This could be turning into a routine.

'Was it OK with Oliver?' he said.

I could feel my face falling back into itself. When the child is awake and with you, you tend to the child. And then the moment she crosses the school gate, or sleeps, everything else floods back.

Of course you can't keep things in boxes. Of course they must be dealt with.

'Waah – he was OK,' I said. 'I think.' I didn't want to talk about it. Talking about it affirms it, makes it truer. And me talking about it makes it my business. But Harry has a right to know. I could feel it getting more tangible by the second. And I added, 'But *it* isn't OK.'

'How so?'

'Eddie's left Cairo. Well, gone off. Disappeared.'

'Off the scheme?' cried Harry.

'Think so. Assume so. Don't know how it works.'

Harry stared at me. Not aghast, but –

'Why didn't he tell me?' he said.

'Don't know,' I said. Why *did* he tell me?

'But I'm meant to be . . . fuck,' he said. 'Oh fuck.' I could see what he was thinking. Not informed equals left out. Why? To what end? Fearing.

'Do you think it's because of me?' I said.

'Could be,' he replied. 'I don't know. But to tell you and not me – Jesus. How long ago?'

'I don't know.'

He was rubbing his forehead, adding information to what he already knew, computing visibly. Suddenly he snorted an angry noise and started to walk about.

So it's true, it's happening, it's affecting things. Am I Canute to try to hold back the tide?

'Apart from what it means for your career,' I said, 'and your position on the case, what does it mean?'

'It means he's a fucking lunatic . . .'

'We already know that,' I pointed out.

'. . . because when he was there, he was safe. He had his ID and a few of the Egyptians keeping an eye on him. But if he goes off, he's at risk. And he is a risk. Fuck! How did it happen? Do you know any . . . fucking Oliver. Fuck him.'

I could understand that he was pissed off at having to ask me. But I wanted his opinion of the situation as a whole – well I did. An idea had occurred to me – 'Eddie's done this on purpose to wind me up'. But you see if I entertain thoughts like that, I'm doing Eddie's job for him. Nurturing seeds of mindfuck. I need Harry to remind me that Eddie is in the past and that none of this means anything to me.

Yes. And bears shit in the Vatican. What I promised myself, what Sa'id told me, was that if Eddie reappeared I could deal with it. Nobody said deny it, we said deal with it. So deal. Eddie's actions are touching those who touch me. So.

It hadn't been a long respite, had it? What? Six, seven weeks off from him?

Harry was looking at me. 'So?' he said.

'Would you understand,' I said, 'if I were to say that I want nothing, ever, to do with Eddie again, to such a degree that I don't even want to talk to you about this now? Because it's not me he's having a go at . . . Would you understand if I just backed off completely, and said look, you and Oliver do what you have to do but this is not my business? Would you think me disloyal? Would you . . . ?'

He kept on looking. His eyes took on a narrowed flatness. Thinking.

'You put yourself at risk going to Cairo to face him off for the sake of multicultural society, to stop the BNP getting that money,' he said, fairly mildly. 'All I'm asking is a question or two.'

'I'm very keen on multiculturalism,' I said.

'I would have thought you might also be quite keen on our . . . friendship.'

'And I would have thought you would be quite keen on my safety and preservation.'

Stop it, stop it. This is the kind of argument we used to have. We don't do this any more.

'I am,' he said. 'But I think you're probably up to thinking about him for five minutes. For my sake. For the sake of my career, and stuff, if that means anything to you.'

'It does,' I said.

'I understand your reluctance,' he said, 'but don't hide. Hiding won't help.'

Well, he was right.

'We're getting there, Harry, aren't we?' I said.

'What? Where?' He looked very slightly irritated.

'Not arguing,' I said.

He frowned and wished I'd shut up, though he didn't say so, so I did for a moment, to be kind.

'The Egyptian police put Oliver on to Hakim and Sa'id,' I said after the moment was over. I said Hakim's name first in case Harry felt delicate about Sa'id. Which he has done on occasion.

'Why?'

'Because of the fight – the hotel thing I told you about – when Hakim was defending me.' (Sa'id had not been defending me. He'd been on the loo. When he had re-appeared and realized what was going on he'd been angry.)

'What about the money?'

'I told Oliver about it. That I'd given it to charity.'

I'd told Harry what I had done with the money. He had thought I was mad. He had said, 'What reason do you have to trust him? There's plenty of poverty in Egypt, you know. Jesus.' I saw in his eyes now that he was thinking the same thing now. I didn't mind him thinking it. He didn't know that Sa'id was not like that. It's very much to Harry's credit that he has any faith in human nature at all – he spends so much time dealing with crime, and he knows too well what poverty does even to people who were decent in the first place. And yes, poverty is strong in Egypt. I may be in love with the place but I'm not blind. I may have a weakness for minarets but that doesn't mean I don't see the flies.

I think Harry had feared that Eddie would want the money back. He underestimated quite how batty Eddie actually is. Eddie got a kick out of giving me money. He had a big psychological confusion around dancing and whoring. I'd refused everything he had ever offered me and he was happy as pie to be able to force me to accept something. Made him feel big. Bigger than me. The more money it cost him to do it, the bigger that made me, and the bigger he'd feel about vanquishing me. He would only want his money back if he thought he hadn't got his money's worth. Which he had, because the more it cost him the more he valued it. If I'd just let him pick me up all those years ago when he used to come and watch me dance in the restaurants on Charlotte Street he would never have got so obsessive about me and none of this would have happened.

So it is all my fault. All my fault for having some virtue.

'So what's happening now?' Harry was asking.

'Now I'm stopping pretending that this hasn't happened, and that it doesn't mean anything, and anyway it's nothing to do with me.'

He smiled.

'I'm sorry,' he said. 'I'm really fucking sorry.'

'So am I,' I said, and I was glad he was there.

'Well,' I went on. 'I assume there are people looking for Eddie. And the Egyptians have questioned Hakim. And Sa'id has left the country.' I don't know why he should have gone to Athens. Business, perhaps. The family is in alabaster. Always has been. So perhaps he has been selling alabaster. Or buying marble, or arranging for malachite and lapis lazuli to traverse the world. But that is not my business. My business has been to put distance between us.

But I want to know he's OK.

I could ring Sarah. Their mother. Two months ago, when Hakim had been staying with me in London, Sa'id had sent him back to Cairo, and neither Sarah nor I knew where he was. We had been worried.

Sarah is English. She lives in Brighton – she's an academic. I like her but she . . . has reservations. She was married to Abu Sa'id for some years. Lived in Luxor with him. Bore his sons. Walked out when Sa'id was ten and Hakim five. Couldn't take it – I don't know, we've never

talked about it in detail. I know a little about the complex-
ities of an Englishwoman married to a man in a provincial
Egyptian town. Expectations, confusions, culture, religion,
habit, communication . . . but she and I never got close
enough for me to know the details of her own story, because
Sa'id didn't forgive her and when she realized what was
happening with him and me her past came down over her
in clouds of disapproval and irresolution.

The plan was, she and Sa'id were going to make up. I
left them all in Egypt, and that seemed to be the next step.
But by then I was out of the picture. Out out out. No
Angeline in that family. I had just exposed them to all the
mayhem with which Eddie is so generous, and then jumped
ship. Though it's true Hakim had managed to find Eddie
on his own, and make his own mayhem.

But I could call Sarah. I supposed she would be back in
Brighton. And I could call Madame Amina, the aunt, Abu
Sa'id's sister-in-law. Abu Sa'id is the father. It's a village
custom – you're called after your first-born. His actual
name is Ismail. He's not particularly a village man but he
prefers simplicity; he stayed in Luxor while the boys went
to school in Cairo, spending time with Madame Amina,
and becoming cosmopolitan.

If the police have been round they might, of course, be
angry with me about it.

'Left the country,' Harry was saying, slowly. 'Where's
he gone?'

Harry knows I was in love with Sa'id. Harry told me I

was a life-avoiding coward for leaving him. Harry told me I'd been a life-avoiding coward ever since I came so near alongside death with Janie. Harry thought I should get a grip. Harry was right.

'Athens, apparently,' I said.

'You haven't heard from him?' he asked.

'Not since I left Luxor,' I said. Not since he wrapped me in his big white scarf at dusk on the dusty landing stage on the west bank of the Nile, and didn't try to stop me going.

I'd rung when the news came through of the massacre at the Temple of Hatshepsut. Only weeks before we'd looked down on it by moonlight when we snuck out at night on to the flank of the great sphinx-shaped desert mountain behind his village. Sixty-two people killed, practically on his doorstep. Sarah had said he looked like death. (He doesn't look like death. He looks like life.) But that's all I knew.

Harry put his hand across and lifted my chin. I'm always amazed by how far he can reach. 'Eddie won't come to Britain. He can't . . .'

'He can do any mad thing he likes . . .' I said, but Harry cut in.

'He can't. Immigration or customs would have him in two seconds. François du Berry is a man with a very circumscribed life. Are you scared?'

'No. I just want to get on with my life.'

'What do you want to do about Sa'id?'

'Just know he's ok.' I had brought trouble to their family. Remember when Hakim had first arrived in London, out of the blue, claiming that he was bringing trouble to my family. Little did he know. I was ashamed to ring them. Would they curse me and throw down the telephone?

I left him. Why unleave him now?

'Would you like me to find out?' Harry said at last. 'If you don't want to be involved . . . what with everything. I could see what's happening for you. Even if I'm out of favour. I mean — as far as I knew it wasn't an active case anyway. But there we go — let me see what I can see. Shall I?'

'So you spend your days looking for my lover and your nights looking after my child?' I asked with a smile.

'Our child,' he said. 'And ex-lover.'

Uncomfortable phrases — but absolutely the shape of my world. Absolutely. I laid my head on the table, and after a while the mists of Egypt retreated from my mind. I got out the vodka, and proved my strength against Eddie by turning resolutely to my life and asking Harry if he thought we needed to make any plans or decisions or anything about Lily. And how it was going to be. He said no. 'Let it roll,' he said. 'We're doing all right, aren't we? Am I behaving? And we can tell each other anything we don't like.'

'Do me a favour,' I said.

'What?'

'Tell us what you do like as well.'

He grinned.

'No, I'm serious. It's a root of good childcare. Love and reward their goodness, and pay as little attention as possible to badness. And make sure they know that you love them however bad they might be. You have to tell them. They're always thinking that everything is their fault, because they think they're the centre of the world. So you have to reassure them a lot, and . . .'

He was looking at me.

'It's important,' I said. 'I'm not going to tell you how to do it, I promise you, but there are a couple of things . . .'

'I know,' he said. 'I like you telling me. And I'll tell you if I don't.'

It made me happy. Thinking about Lily and her family life. Happy, in the heart of what matters.

'Oh,' he said. 'Umm – Lily's invited me for Christmas.' He paused. 'She says you're going to cook a turkey.'

It's a logical development. It's bound to happen. It's cool.

'We go to Mum and Dad's usually,' I said. 'Oh. Would you . . .'

'I probably should,' he said. 'I mean, if you . . .'

'Of course,' I said. 'Of course.'

'OK then,' he said.

'Right,' I said.

We smiled at each other. Family Christmas. Crikey.

'I hate Christmas,' he said, musingly.

'I remember,' I said.

47

Soon after, he left, and as he left he kissed me unlingeringly on the mouth, which seemed to me to be both firm and ambiguous, an interesting combination. For a moment I wondered what he meant by it, then shook off the thought. It was too brief to touch me but . . . But nothing.

FOUR

Answering the phone to Chrissie Bates

For the next week or so I behaved completely normally. Lily and I opened the doors of our advent calendar each morning, and at the weekend we went to the market and bought a tiny Christmas tree, which she covered with hairclips and doll's clothes; while she was at school I copyedited most of an Iranian carpet magazine, which included re-translating someone else's translation (from Farsi into nonsense) into decent English, hurrying to get it done before the school holidays. I got so involved with to-and-fro clarificatory telephone conversations with the translator that I forgot to screen my calls. And that is how on Friday afternoon I found myself answering the phone to Chrissie Bates.

'Don't hang up,' she said. 'Please. Please don't. Please do this for me – oh lord. I'm not calling to ask you for anything. I just want to say something to you. Oh!' And then she hung up on me.

Well, I didn't like it one bit. Her previous phone calls had been . . . unpleasant, to say the least. So had the razorblade in the post, and the screaming heebie-jeebies when she had burst into my bathroom that time. Admittedly even now it was a little hard to work out which of the unsolicited letters and calls and acts of aggression had been from her and which from Eddie, but overall my view of Chrissie was that she was a nasty little thing who had been married to an even nastier one. Either way I didn't want her around. Plus . . . there was the minor item that she had at one stage seemed very pissed off that Eddie was trying to give me so much money, and I had rung her and left a message saying she could have the bloody stuff, and stick it up her arse for all I cared, or words to that effect.

So maybe she wants it.

But she didn't sound angry, or aggressive. For a moment I hadn't been sure it was her, because I have only ever heard her voice drunk and furious before, unless you count the funeral where she was drunk, furious and tragic.

And anyway, she can't have it, because Sa'id has fed it to the hungry children and bought them all new shoes so nyaaah.

The phone rang again.

'I'm sorry about that,' Chrissie said. 'I'm not very good at this but I really want to do it and get it right. I'm sorry. There. I'm sorry.'

'What?' I said.

'Sorry,' she said again.

'You're ringing to say sorry for ringing?'

'No. For . . . for everything. Look, can I visit you? I'd like to do this face to face, it gives it more . . .'

'No,' I said.

'Oh. All right.'

She sounded very small. Very accepting. Completely different.

Actually she didn't sound drunk either.

'OK,' she said. 'Then I'd like to say this. Oh. Bother. I dropped the piece of paper.' She rustled around a bit, and I held on, waiting.

'What is this?' I said.

'Hang on – I'm nearly there. OK. Right. Angeline, It's Chrissie.'

'I know,' I said.

'And you haven't hung up. Oh thank you!'

'No, but I might yet. What is it?'

'I have to apologize to you,' she said. 'Want to, sorry. Not have to. I did some terrible things and I have a list here and I want to apologize for each one.'

Each one?

'Please, don't,' I said. 'Please.'

'Please,' she said.

So we pleaded with each other a little. Then 'Why?' I asked.

'Just let me do it then I'll explain. Please?'

Don't plead. Please.

I let her.

'Angeline, this is Chrissie. I am apologizing to you. I am sorry for the letters. For the phone calls. For the scene at the funeral – I think. I'm not sure what happened but I think I probably should apologize. And for coming in on your bath and passing out on your bath mat and upsetting your friend. And for all the shouting and everything and for thinking what I did about you and Eddie. I want you to know that I am very very sorry.'

I was gobsmacked.

'And I would like to apologize to your friend in the bathroom who got me the taxi.' (That was Sarah.) 'And if you know where Harry can be found now because I haven't seen him since Eddie . . . passed away . . . since he went to gaol, actually, and nobody knows where he is now but I know you and he were friends and I have a lot to apologize to him for too.'

Whoa.

Of course she would think Eddie was dead. But going back suddenly to the days when Harry was Eddie's employee, running his fancy garage for him . . . Chrissie doesn't know Harry's a cop. Of course not. Unless Eddie told her, when she visited him in prison. If Eddie knows, that is.

Does Eddie know? No, of course not. Eddie is the main man Harry was undercover from, for god's sake.

Oh, fuck the lot of them. I only want a quiet life.

Not a helpful declaration. I am one of them. In my quiet way.

'Why, Chrissie?' I asked.

'Oh!' She has this slightly breathy squeak. She must be going on fifty but she still wears what Fergus the crime correspondent calls her heyday hairdo, which is sub-Bardot, and very high heels. 'I can tell you. You know I was drunk – well I was. Now I'm not. My name is Chrissie and I'm an alcoholic. And I'm not a criminal's wife any more. I'm – something else. I don't know what yet.'

'So?' I said, not quite so unkindly.

'Do you want to know? No, of course not. I'll give you the short version. You probably know about it. It's the twelve steps. One of the steps is that you apologize to everybody you did wrong to while you were drunk. You were quite high up my list actually. I had to go through people a lot because I kept thinking I should be apologizing for stuff which was Eddie's. Couldn't tell whose was whose, if you see what I mean. But with you it was quite clear, and recent, and so you were a good person to start with. I did my mother first. But I'm going to have to go back to her. Several times, actually, I should think. But I thought I could get you under my belt – sorry! I know that sounds rather . . . because of course you don't want to have anything to do with me, and that's absolutely fair and right. But you know it's terribly embarrassing. Thank you for not, you know, laughing or anything.'

'That's OK,' I found myself saying.

'So that's what I'm doing and thank you for listening

and . . . if you wanted to talk about any of it I'm here. I know that might sound rather mad. But you see I'm trying to think of myself as a normal person now and that's the kind of thing I would want to say if I was a normal person – you know, if Eddie hadn't hijacked me and I hadn't turned to the booze to protect myself from him. If I'd just met some nice man. Or if Eddie had been ugly or something, or poor, then I wouldn't have fallen for him. Because I wouldn't have, I don't think. I was so stupid when I was young. But I'm not going to be any more. And it's quite a challenge. Anyway I don't want to go on and bore you. Well I do, but I don't want you to be bored. I want you to forgive me, and if you do, you know, in your own time, I'd really like it if you could let me know, because it will just make all the difference. It will be like fuel for my redemption rocket, you know? And it would be awfully good karma for you. Not that I mean to try to bribe you or anything. But forgiveness is good, isn't it? And I know my husband caused you grief, and while I know that's not my fault, if I had been a different woman, not so weak, everything might have been different, even that, so I don't feel responsible for you but I do feel for you. I'm sorry, they do feed us an awful lot of rubbish at this place but it's terribly good. I do hope I'm not talking like a Californian. Oh look. I'm peeing in your ear and you've got better things to do – but I would like to talk to you. Any time. You've got my number, haven't you. Here it is again. Or e-mail me – Chrissie@newchris.demon.com.

Are you on e-mail? It is fabulous . . . sorry I'm going on. Look. Any time.'

'Chrissie,' I said.

'Yes,' she said.

'A word.'

'Yes?'

'While reinventing yourself, it might be worth putting in the gene that lets other people get a word in edgeways.'

'Nervous,' she said. 'Very nervous. Not a drop for six weeks. Sorry.'

'OK. Listen. I am all for redemption. I wish you well. I hope you succeed but I don't want to talk to you.'

'It would be a wonderful bonus for me if you did, very good for my recovery,' she said, 'though of course I know that recovery is within the individual, you can't look to anyone else to do it for you.'

'I owe you no bonus,' I said.

'No, nor any £100,000!' she cried. 'I'm living off what he left me because I have to eat but I tell you, this is genuine. I'm going to be redeeming left right and centre. I won't bother you. If you wish me luck that's all I need. Thank you. But if you forgive me, let me know. God bless you.'

God bless me.

Blimey.

And that was it.

I sat back, rather exhausted, after she rang off. I didn't know what to make of it so I left it lying on the side of my mind like an unanswered letter. At least Preston Oliver hadn't rung me. Nor anybody else.

*

Harry came round that night to put Lily to bed. He'd rung during the day to say was it all right. And to say maybe I might like to go out, or something – should he babysit? I was pleased, but I didn't want to go out. I watched the news, amazed to have the hours between six and eight to myself. There were TV programmes I'd never heard of that had presumably been going on all this time between six and eight, never watched by mothers of young children.

I must get a job. I don't know anything about the real world any more. I just sit here and pretend things aren't happening.

I could hear them giggling in Lily's bedroom. He was telling her the wide-mouth frog joke. Doing voices. It squeezed my heart.

Lily dismissed Harry, and I went to read to her. Climbed into bed with her.

'Does he stay forever?' she asked.

'Who, Paddington Bear?' I asked, because that was who I was reading about.

'No. Daddy.'

'He's your dad forever, yes,' I said.

'Good,' she said. 'When are you getting married?'

Blank. Help!

'We're not,' I said. Have I led her to believe that we were?

'Oh, all right,' she said.

'What?'

'I thought you were. I thought that's what parents did. Adjoa's parents are going to get married. She's going to be a bridesmaid. And lots of parents are already married. You know. Like yours. Were you a bridesmaid for them? You and Mummy? Dead mummy? Not you and you. You couldn't be two bridesmaids. And anyway Mummy would have felt left out. Dead mummy.' She was asleep.

Dead mummy. She accepts stuff now. How will we explain Harry having shagged Janie though?

Well we will.

We. That is such an alarming word.

*

Harry had waited for me. He wanted to talk about Eddie. I stopped him.

'Do babysit,' I said. 'For an hour or so. I want to clear my head.'

And I jumped in my car and went down to Hammersmith, where I bought half a pint of cider from the Blue Anchor and climbed over the river wall on to the pontoon, stranded on the mud at low tide, and sat, looking across to the playing fields in Barnes, down river to the bridge, spangled with lights, and up river towards Brentford where the gryphon lives, and the herons, past the curve of

Chiswick, as Turner a view as you can find now in London, over the roofs of the house boats, their paint tins and geranium pots wonky as their hulls settled diagonally on the Thames sludge, their little portholes throwing gleaming coins of yellow electricity out on to the dark slimy mud surface. It was shiveringly cold, and I sat huddled in my coat. Artificial light and natural dark, water and late birds. You get more night on the river than anywhere else in the city. The largest expanse of dark without a light of its own. In Upper Egypt the trees are full of egrets, who hang at dusk like handkerchiefs, and say buggle buggle da, buggle da, burbling like shishas. Written down the words even look like Arabic. And the sky is striped, green and rose and gold, the colours of alabaster, and the moon lies on its back.

A couple of late scullers called across the pewter water. Mad people.

I hadn't intended to think of the night on the Corniche el Nil when Sa'id and I began to fall apart, but sitting by one river you can't but think of others you have known. It made me too sad and the soothing effect of the night river, which has been a favourite of mine since I was old enough to stay out late, stopped working, so I went home.

On the way back I stopped at a phone box and rang Sarah. My fingers moving independently of my will. Unable to stop myself. It's for her to decide if she doesn't want to talk to me.

'Sarah?'

'Yes?'

'Angeline.'

'Oh. Hello.'

'Hello.'

The trouble with the spur of the moment is that unless some fluke leaps to your aid, you don't know what to say. I didn't. The irresistible urge which had guided my fingers had no interest in helping my voicebox now that I had got through. Plus I had developed this habit of discretion. I am constantly aware that I might say something that will get Harry into trouble.

'How's Sa'id?' I asked. What else could I say? There's nothing else I want to know.

There was a silence. The line breathed, from London down to the sea where she lives.

'Fine,' she said. In that English way which could mean anything. That cold way.

'Is he back from Greece?'

'Yes. Why?'

'Don't be . . .' I started to say, and stopped.

'Don't tell me what to be,' she said.

'Are you . . .'

I couldn't talk to her.

'Listen,' she said. 'You've forfeited your right to know. I'm not unsympathetic. I forfeited my right too once. I'm working on getting it back. You are not popular in that family. I want to know my sons now. I'm not taking you up.'

I winced, even down the phone.

'Everyone is all right. The police have gone. For now. I dare say you feel the burden of what you brought on the family but again . . . I'm working on getting my children back. They don't want you.'

And I didn't believe her. Her excuse made sense – that if she tried to rehabilitate me at the same time as herself it would be too much. But I didn't believe her. They may not want me – I don't want them either. But they wouldn't object to my expressing concern, to my wanting to know that the problems I introduced them to are passing, to my sympathetic interest in how Hakim, for example, who had found Eddie quite without my involvement after all, was dealing with the fallout from our shared psychopath.

She doesn't want them to want me. She's still confused – oh, say it. She's jealous because Sa'id loved me and didn't want to love her. And because I told him he had to, because she's his mother, she resents me. And because she loved an Egyptian and it failed, and she wanted us to fail. And we did! So what's the problem?

'Please convey my affection and respect to Abu Sa'id and to Madame Amina,' I said. 'If my name should be mentioned. I mean the family nothing but well, and I greatly regret that my misfortunes have overflowed on to them.' I don't know why I bothered saying all this to her. But sometimes you just need to say things. It doesn't matter if they're heard.

'OK. Well,' she said.

'Yeah. Goodbye.'

But he's OK. She said so.

*

Back in the kitchen Harry was drinking a beer that he had brought in a plastic bag, and reading the paper, with his feet up on the table. He looked deeply at home. I tried to remember him in the kitchens of our shared past. Sitting on the draining board in Clerkenwell. Bike boots steaming on the boiler. Those huge woolly council-issue socks we all wore: cream-coloured, ribbed, up over your knee before you rolled them down. Not wearing them when I was going to work because they left red marks on my calves and ankles: no good for my beautiful dancing feet. Harry climbing in the bath with me that time with all his gear on; he'd just come in from despatching all day and said he was soaked through anyway. His leathers smelt of my bath oil for weeks. Ylang-ylang and WD-40.

The past is blurry.

He looked up, hesitating, before folding away the expanse of newspaper, elbows wide like a pelican's wingspan.

'Beer?' he said, and reached out to give me a bottle. I took it and sat down across from him.

'I've been talking to Oliver,' he said. 'Trying to.'

'And?'

'He doesn't want to talk to me. He's been avoiding me all week.'

'Oh. Does that mean —'

'It means he wants me out of the way. I was a little insistent with him. He said — well, he confirmed what he'd told you, that Eddie has absconded from the scheme, that Interpol are upset about it, the Egyptians are doing what they can but they're very taken up with the anti-terrorist stuff since the massacre at Luxor, and as it appears that he's left the country they are quite pleased not to be bothered. He said your boys seem to be in the clear. Everybody in Luxor knows they're OK, and they're all in shock there anyway and not knowing where their next crust is coming from because the tourists have just disappeared. And he said I was not to worry my pretty little head about it, but get on with this insurance fraud like a good boy.'

I pictured Luxor, empty of visitors. How we put ourselves in other people's hands. How we suffer when they leave.

'What insurance fraud?' I asked, absently.

'My job. You know. What I do. This complicated boring bloody insurance thing. You don't want to know.'

It's true. I didn't.

'But if you were working all that time on Eddie, why are you off it now?'

'Because it's out of our hands, anyway — we're the regional crime squad. Witness protection is nothing to do with us. Oliver's just keeping track of it. It's bureau-cracy. And pride. No one can quite let go of a catch like

Eddie. And resentment. It was a fucking insult when he got cut this deal, actually. Those who knew – Oliver, and me – were insulted on behalf of the other lads, too, because a lot of work went into this, as well as a lot of taxpayers' money. Though of course I shouldn't know anyway. So I can't complain, or have an opinion. Except to Oliver.'

'But why is he cutting you out?'

'That I don't know. That I don't know.'

We sat in silence for a moment.

Big bony hands wrapped round the beer bottle. I spend half my life round this table.

'Does he . . . does he think that you're too closely involved with me, and I'm too closely involved with *it*, if you see what I mean?'

'Maybe,' he said. 'Could be.'

I would be sorry if that were the case. I don't like to see Harry feeling sidelined; I wouldn't want it to be because of me. And I want to be uninvolved. I was becoming uninvolved. I thought I had done so well. But now it's back, but it's all so intangible, I don't know what to do. Live with it? Is that the moral of the story? Learn to live with it?

'I rang Sarah,' I said.

'I thought you weren't going to,' he said. Not unkindly.

'I wasn't.'

'What did she say?'

'That everyone's fine and the police have gone. But she didn't want to talk to me.'

'Do you mind?'

'No. I don't need to talk to her. She says they're OK, Oliver says they're ok, so I don't need to worry. It's only them I felt bad about.'

So why do I still feel bad?

Because I'm disappointed. Because if Sa'id had been in trouble I could have gone and rescued him and . . .

Oh shut up.

And because I can feel Eddie tweaking. He may not be tweaking me directly, the chain may not be round my neck, but it's on the floor beside me, I can hear it tripping up people I love. He's still out there.

'Chrissie rang me,' I said.

'Yikes,' said Harry. 'The mad lady. How is she?'

I told him. He laughed. 'Oliver did that too. But he's too proud to admit that that's what he was doing. Just went round saying to everybody: "I haven't always been very . . . well anyway sorry."'

'She was kind of sweet,' I said.

'Well, off the booze, away from Eddie, who knows.'

'Still mad though. Wanted me to confide in her.'

He laughed and laughed. 'Doesn't know you very well then,' he said.

'What's that meant to mean?'

'Oh, you know.'

'No, I don't.'

'Mrs Do-it-Yourself,' he said.

'Well who the hell else is going to do it?' I said, crossly.

It pisses me off, when people castigate my naturally independent cast of mind, when they should know full well that I have nothing else to depend on anyway.

'Yeah. Anyway you're getting better.'

Then I got a bit crosser, because I don't like to be judged, specially not by an emotional fuck-up like Harry (though actually he is getting better too). But we cheered up again, then it was time for him to go, and as he stood up he put an envelope on the table, and looked at it, and looked up at me.

'What's that?' I said.

'Five hundred quid,' he said.

I raised an eyebrow.

'I'm getting it estimated properly – there's a proportion of my salary that is, umm, the proper amount. But in the meantime.'

I hadn't even thought about money. Jesus, he's going to support us. Well, her.

Ha ha. I'm being helped.

'Thanks,' I said. There was a tiny voice inside that said, 'What, you think I can't do it alone? I've done it without you for years and I don't need your bloody money thank you very much . . .' but that was some other voice, nothing to do with anything. 'Do you want to back-date it?'

For a moment he looked worried. 'Well,' he said, 'Yeah. I mean – I don't want to barge in. But whatever you need. Do you need more? Have you got debts? Because I can, absolutely. I mean, up to a point.'

'Fuck off,' I said, kindly. 'I'm not telling you about my financial situation.'

'Exactly,' he said. 'But I mean it.'

'Thank you,' I said. And meant it.

If I'd ever imagined this scene I would have imagined that Harry would look sheepish. But he didn't, not in the slightest. He looked everything a man should under such circumstances. Courteous, firm, a little proud. Decent. But the word made me laugh, because I remembered very clearly how very indecent he can be when he wants.

FIVE

Kicking

I was kicking a rotten cauliflower in the middle of Portobello Road, shopping bags on one hand and Lily on the other, feeling weak, trying to get through the crowd to go down to Ladbroke Grove and catch the tube home. Serve me right for coming out on the Saturday before Christmas. Should've gone to Shepherd's Bush Market, but Lily said she was bored of Shepherd's Bush and wanted to eat prawns at the tapas bar on Golborne Road, so after I gave her a swift and sweet lecture on what a useless word (indeed concept) boring was, and feeling flush with child support, we came up here, even though I don't really like to any more. Because before there was Agnès B and Paul Smith on Westbourne Grove, when the pubs were still called the Elgin and the Rose, not Tuscany or the Ferret and Foreskin or Phoney McPaddy's, when the Italian restaurants were run by Italians, not by people called Alastair who charge ten quid for a plate of pasta and pesto in a room which ten years ago was a squat . . . before all that, I lived here.

A gust of incense came from a shopfront hung about with paper lanterns. Indeed they all seemed to be hung about with paper lanterns, star-shaped with holes cut in like a child's paper snowflakes, cut from white A4 on a rainy afternoon. Except that on rainy afternoons when I was a child I used to come up here and hang around with Fred the Flowerman (his name wasn't Fred), who had a faceful of florescent broken veins, and let me think I was helping out on the stall. 'Oh no, here comes trouble,' he'd say when I appeared, and pretend to hide from me. I'd learn the prices of all the bunches and tell the customers, and I'd roll up what they bought in cheap printed paper. Five salmon-pink tulips in cellophane; daffs, the powdered yellowness of their petals, no leaves, milky stickiness from their short-cut stems. Rain or shine, when I was about eight. His son was a cabbie, and sometimes he would appear in his cab on the corner of Blenheim Crescent and yell down to his dad.

The groovy stalls crawl further up into the vegetable market every year. Well, I don't know, I haven't lived around here for years now. I've been priced out of my childhood neighbourhood, like so many Londoners, by people who think they can buy what my neighbourhood was, and who, by their very arrival, change it. My neighbourhood was mixed, funny, bohemian, black, Irish, liberal intellectual, Greek, Polish, hippy, posh, full of cherry blossom and rotten cauliflowers; now it is full of bankers who go round moaning about the Carnival and congratulating each other on how mixed, liberal, intellectual, bohemian, funny etc. they are. But they're not. It's gone. It's too fucking expensive for those things to survive.

But I don't care. I was there when it was good, and today we had been in a remnant of it, and we'd had our tapas, bought our vegetables, and fulfilled our purpose. Breaking away into Lancaster Road, losing the cauliflower, I sat down on someone's stoop for a moment to rationalize the plastic bags that were garrotting my wrist. I felt odd. Lily was looking at me, her big intelligent eyes, her day-before-yesterday plaits with aureoles of fluff from the wind and damp. I must redo them.

'Mum?' she said.

I couldn't stand up. Neither my good leg nor my not-so-good leg wanted to. So I didn't. Unbelievably weak. I felt as if I had some wasting disease. Maybe I'd caught something in Egypt. No. Too long ago, eight weeks or more.

During which time.

I hadn't menstruated.

Now I come to think of it.

So perhaps I am ill.

Or perhaps not.

'Mum?' she said.

Yes, I thought.

'OK,' I said. OK Lily, my love, my darling, I'm still here. I'm just sitting down having a little rest.

Was it possible?

Sa'id was the king of condoms – the most elegant, efficient user of condoms that woman has ever witnessed. We had had no noticeable leakages or spillages or splits. We had had no . . . I looked back up the road to the market.

We had, of course, had that moment when he had thought that I had thought that he was becoming caught up in his traditional, formal conventionality, and had decided to disabuse me of the notion by fucking me swiftly and beautifully in a doorway in the alley beside Mahmoud's Fancy Dresses, in the heart of Khan el-Khalili, under the wooden scaffolding, behind the braid seller and left at the oil drums, wrapped in his big scarf, with a scrawny cat looking on and the bazaar chuntering along within feet of us. We had.

'Mum?'

'Come on, honey, we must go to the chemist,' I said, and dragged my legs back to themselves.

*

I loved Lily that afternoon. Fed her, read to her, bathed with her, talked to her, held her, tickled her, loved her. Stared at her. Flesh not quite of my flesh, child but not of my loins. My child. In the bath she blew bubbles on my belly, and scrubbed my back, and sang a song about broad beans sleeping in their blankety beds. She used to have an imaginary baby brother called Nippyhead.

She wanted *The Happy Prince* so I read her *The Happy*

Prince. 'I am waited for in Egypt,' said the Swallow, describing the cataracts of the Nile, the hippos and crocodiles, the gods and mummies, things that exist no longer, that never existed, that exist still, unchanged after all.

'Mama wants to go to Egypt,' she said, half asleep. 'I'll come with you. We'll be swallows and then I won't die and be put on the rubbish dump.'

Bloody story always makes me cry at the best of times.

'Tell me about Egypt,' she said. 'Tell me about cataracts.'

Sitting on an island, on a mass of pink granite, the Nile the liquid child of obsidian and malachite lapping twenty feet beneath us. It moves like oil. Granite gleams up from beneath the surface of the water before disappearing into the depths – are the rocky outcrops knee deep, or ankle deep, or up to their necks? We can't tell. The sails of feluccas glide by, in front, behind, sliding like theatre flats. Tips of sails appear and disappear behind low islands, Elephantine, Ile d'Amoun. Date palms arch and wave. Turtle doves – *hamam* in Arabic, *minneh* in that Nubian language whose name I never remember. A gentle cooing and chattering of birds carries from one island to the next: wagtails, ibis, egrets, herons, kingfishers, swallows. There is eucalyptus, bougainvillaea – pink, scarlet, crimson and purple – high shaggy pampas grass, and sixty-foot pebbles, sitting there. A primeval landscape. It is easy to see the hippopotami and crocodiles wallowing by the banks, beneath hieroglyphs carved in the rock. Pink granite, very like every statue of Ramses you see. We could be sitting on his massive knee, this vast and trunkless leg of stone. The rock looks as if it were melting, and you couldn't blame it if it did. Hard sun. The swirls of water against the rock beneath us make patterns like Greek friezes, like mosaic sea, folding over and over itself. Where it's calm, amber-green weed floats like Ophelia's hair. Above, the clouds are a stippled pattern, a melting *mashrabiyya* screen between us and the pale lapis sky; beneath it the leaves and branches of eucalyptus make another screen, foliate like a beautiful script, the curved blades of the leaves like each ligature and flourish, *bismillah*. Behind us, low-swaying branches of mimosa like soft yellow pearls. Patterns in repetition and constant movement. Beyond, ranges of apricot-yellow Sahara, layer upon layer shaped by the winds into lagoons and plateaus, baboon's brows and natural sphinxes.

But the cataracts have been drowned by the High Dam. What I am remembering is a different thing. Half real, half dreamed. Oh lordy, Sa'id.

I lay with her until she fell asleep, and then I lay there a while longer, and then I got up and went and pissed on the stick, and then I waited, and then I looked.

Blue dot or no blue dot?

Oh – which means which?

Look at the instructions again.

Ah.

So I went and lay down with Lily again, and hugged her to me and remembered how she had felt as a tiny baby in my arms, her hair then, her face, changing shape every time you looked at it; her little boneless arms, her growing strength, her words, her tongue, her belly button and the creases of her neck, her sweet greedy mouth, her lengthening limbs. This long girl-child, whose feet now kick my knees when we lie down together, where once they only reached my ribs. She had learned to walk at the same time as I had learned to walk again after breaking myself in the accident, hobbling and wobbling together at Mum and Dad's when we were staying there, stumbling together, seeing each other through. Coming back to the flat together for the first time, on our own four feet. Not now my only child.

I didn't think that I could love this new thing as much as I love Lily. I didn't think it was entirely right to grow my own-flesh-child when I had Lily. It might make her sad. She might feel left out.

And at the same time, despite that, I was very profoundly happy.

*

On Sunday I sat very still. Lily played around me, my satellite. I was actually in a trance of some kind. I stared a lot. Lily was gentle with me. Brigid called with the children and took her to the park. I declined, in favour of sleep. Brigid gave me a long look but I said nothing. Brigid, my friend and neighbour, mother of four, knows me well. I was afraid to speak to her because she would guess.

Zeinab, my Egyptian friend from our schooldays, rang to see if we wanted to go and play. I let the machine take it.

While they were out, Chrissie turned up on my doorstep, standing on the communal balcony looking like a rich person who has strayed from her red carpet by mistake into some grubby area of reality, beyond the limelight of money.

'Oh no,' I said. 'What are you doing here?'

She was carrying a handbag and wearing big hair and sunglasses, which she took off immediately I answered the door. I could see she had been crying.

'Are you drunk?' I said.

'Absolutely not,' she replied. 'Still clean and planning to remain so but, please, I need your help.'

Oh no. No no no.

'What?' I said. Now why did I say that? Something in her face made me. Something in my heart. I didn't say fuck off, madwoman. I said, 'What?'

'I want to tell you something because I can't think of anyone else to tell. I don't know what to do. I am going out of my mind. I terribly don't want to. I want to be normal and I – can I come in?'

I let her in. I don't have much truck with words like normal – either we're all normal or we're all strange. In which case it's perfectly normal to be strange – indeed it might be strange to be normal. None of which is any help to anything – so why bother to mention it? But I knew what she meant. I knew about desiring the safety you perceive other people's lives to contain. We went through to the kitchen.

'I see in you that you like to be normal too,' she said. 'But you're not. So I thought you might understand. And you might tell me if I'm crazy. Which I might be anyway because of the drying out but I cannot tell the people at the clinic about this because it is the kind of thing they section you for. I would, if I was them.'

'What.' I said.

I was still standing.

'I've been visiting Eddie's grave,' she said.

I said nothing.

'Well his – filing cabinet. Like they have in Italy. Little cupboard, for his urn.'

'Yes,' I said.

'A few times.'

I let her breathe for a while.

'Quite often actually.'

Fair enough.

'Can I sit down?'

You can't say no.

She sat on my old sofa, her knees together and her ankles splayed and taut with their high-heeled shoes.

'To begin with, I was drunk – well, I'd go up there and drink. I miss him, you know. In a way. In a funny way.' She didn't start crying again. 'And I'd sit, and drink. Then later I'd go up sober and sit and think. Trying to work things out, and talking to him and so on. And . . .'

I didn't like this.

'There's a gravedigger up there, George. We got chatting – he's nice. Well accustomed to widows, he says. Sympathetic. Likes a drink too. So we'd drink together. On Eddie's doorstep. And then. Oh god.'

I was sure I didn't like it.

'Angeline, he says there's nothing in Eddie's grave.'

She looked at me, mascara wide as sunrays round her eyes. Like a picture by a child who has just noticed eyelashes.

'In his cupboard,' she said. 'He says he was the one who sealed it up, and that the urn in there was empty, and he swears it. He said he wasn't meant to know, but that the urn was too light and he checked in case he had the wrong one, but the undertaker said to him, yes, he'd been given that one sealed up, even though it was usually his job to get the ashes together and put them in, and he could tell by the weight that it was empty, so he'd checked it, and there were a few ashes but not, you know, human ashes, and he thought it was really odd but didn't say anything. The gravedigger was drunk when he said it and later he tried to say he didn't mean it but he did, I know he did because why else would he say it? Why would he say it if he didn't mean it? And how could he mean it? So I shouted at him not to lie, and he said yes it was true, and then I didn't believe him, but later I was sober and I could see he was telling the truth. He was so upset. He said he couldn't bear the sight of me weeping day after day at an empty grave. He's a nice man. Kind. And he said, he said: "You ask around. You ask some of those people. Someone'll tell you." But I daren't because I don't know what it means. I wanted to ask the undertaker but the gravedigger wouldn't tell me his name; he didn't want anyone getting into trouble. What can it mean, Angeline? Do you know?'

'No,' I said. Without a flicker. 'I haven't: a clue. It sounds like nonsense.'

Her shoulders went down a little. They must have been up. Tension. Not that she looked relaxed now. More — disappointed.

'But why would he say——?'

'I don't know. People are strange. I don't know.' I was very blank with her. Very Teflon. This is nothing to do with me.

'Are you all right?' she asked suddenly. Her head went to one side for a moment and for that moment I could see what she must have looked like as a girl. Gymkhanas, Fergus had said. County military girl. Boarding school, and gone wild at an early age. I could see her, fifteen and boy-crazy, full of semi-educated English self-confidence. In a previous generation she would have been the backbone-of-the-empire's wife, until she had a nervous breakdown on a verandah in Malaya. She had a very English profile. Pretty little nose. Fine fine lines on dry dry skin telling of late late nights and a lot of gin and tonics.

'Fine,' I said. In that English way.

'You're not pregnant, are you?' she demanded.

Teflon slid off me. I was totally confused. Why was she asking me that? What the hell do I say? I can lie about Eddie's death but I can't —

'Why?' I asked.

'You look it.'

Don't say, 'How can you tell?'

I didn't have to.

'It shows,' she said, and I looked to my belly and gave it away.

'Not there,' she said. 'In your face.' She was smiling at me, a warm, lovely smile.

I couldn't look at my face. But my face looked at her, and she knew.

'How marvellous,' she said, with complete sincerity and kindness, and she was the first person to say so, the first person to know, and even though she was her, I kind of loved her for it. Then she jumped up and hugged me. Taken aback? Yes I was.

'How many weeks are you?' she asked.

The phrase confused me for a moment. What does it mean? Then I worked it out. 'Nine,' I said. 'Or . . . no, nine.'

'Oh wow,' she said. 'It doesn't usually show at all so early. Maybe it's twins. How long have you known? Oh . . .' And I thought she was going to cry again.

I remembered her in the back of the ambulance that Harry and I called to take her away after Eddie's funeral, in her big fur and stilettos, her over-sized black sunglasses, shouting and calling about abortions that he'd made her have. No children, wanted children, had children, had children taken from her.

What does she mean, twins?

I don't know about pregnant. Pregnant is new to me.

Oh god, Sa'id.

*

Chrissie and I were still talking when Brigid came back with Lily. I didn't want to. But I didn't not want to. She told me what I didn't know – that after the abortions (four) she had got pregnant again, which she considered something of a miracle, and gone away on a cruise, and not come back till she was eight months gone, and produced a daughter, for whom he hired full-time nannies, and who he had sent to boarding school from the age of four. She's sixteen now, and Chrissie was going to see her at Christmas though she was spending the holidays with a schoolfriend because she (Chrissie) didn't trust herself yet. Eddie hadn't seen her for three years when he . . . died. She told me about scans and Braxton Hicks, about evening primrose and pethidine, about yoga and pools and the perineum, about hot curry to bring on labour. About clary sage and pre-eclampsia and BabyGap and Kamillosan and the Natural Childbirth Trust and the importance of letting the umbilical cord stop pulsing before it is cut. I didn't mind. I told her that I had only known for twenty-four hours. I told her that I was amazed and terrified. She said that was normal.

She made me laugh several times, and didn't ask who the father was. She told me about foetal alcohol syndrome. I didn't tell her her husband was still alive. She left when Lily came back, and ruffled her hair as she went.

Then Harry came to put Lily to bed. 'I was thinking I'd like to have her for weekends sometimes,' he said, 'but actually I'd rather be with both of you.'

'You'll be wanting parental responsibility, anyway,' I said.

'Yes,' he said. 'I will. Better write to the court. When we get back the new birth certificate.'

New birth certificate.

I didn't tell him.

That night I lay in bed thinking of the tiny Egyptian inside me, and I dreamt of a painting I'd seen in one of the tombs outside Cairo, where the occupant – Ptah Hotep – is portrayed with a tiny adult-proportioned daughter, just tall enough to reach his knee, holding on to his calf with one outstretched hand and striding along with him, between his knees, as he strides that Egyptian tomb-carving stride. If I remember rightly he was the Pharoah's Official Keeper of Secrets, and hairdresser. Or maybe that was Ti. Anyway, *plus ça change*.

*

On Monday Preston Oliver rang during breakfast: well, while Lily was letting her porridge get cold and I was wondering why I didn't feel like drinking coffee.

'Can you make it down here for 9.45?' he said.

'No,' I said, on principle.

'Try,' he suggested.

'I'm not available,' I said.

'Make yourself available,' he said. 'Seventh floor. They'll tell you at reception.'

So I rang Zeinab and took Lily round there to play with Hassan and Omar, school having broken up, and climbed on a number 94 from the Green, changed at Oxford Circus and read the paper all the way in self-defence against Christmas shopping and rucksacks and loden coats and swinging cameras and Selfridges bags and all the rest of the battery of the tourist in London. And got off at Westminster, and ambled down Victoria Street, and approached our national centre of law enforcement at about five to ten. I was glad to be late. It made me feel free.

I'd never been inside before. It just looks like an office. Computer screens everywhere. Could have been a news-paper office, or an insurance office, or anything. Noticeboards, big rooms divided into little ones by unconvincing screens. Photocopiers. Someone had put up some half-arsed paper-chains. I hate offices more than almost anything. My sweat smells different in office buildings. I come over all metallic.

Oliver's office was not big, not small. I know people set store by this stuff. Status and so on. But I wouldn't know where to begin. He had a window, though, so he can't be that lowdown. And a desk of his own.

'Glad you could make it,' he said.

'Yes, well,' I replied.

He looked at me.

'Coffee?'

Visions of Nescafe floated up on the smell of central heating. 'No thanks,' I said. I haven't been sick at all, I realized. Aren't you meant to be sick? Maybe I wasn't pregnant. I was going to the doctor that afternoon.

'Harry will be joining us in a moment,' he said, 'but before he does I want to talk to you.'

I grunted.

'You're going to have to help us, Angeline.'

Bollocks I am, I thought. And just gazed at him, as a cow might. A nice fat pretty cow called Bluebell.

'You're a freelance, aren't you? Consultations and what-have-you? I'm hiring you.'

Oh yes? I almost laughed.

'I'll give it to you straight. We have to find him. And we can't. The Egyptians have lost him. And there's no point us sending anyone there, unless they know something more than we do at present. And you have been volunteered.'

I blinked. Slowly. As if I had very long, very heavy lashes. Hard to lift up again.

'You can pick up where he left off in Cairo. You know the city, you know people who knew him as du Berry, you know where he went when he was there, you speak Arabic. And you won't be going for long . . .'

'I won't be going at all,' I said.

'Yes you will,' he replied. Very straight, very sure of himself.

'No I won't.' What I should have said when Ben Cooper first lured me into Eddie's orbit in the first place. No.

'Yes.'

'Why?' I said.

'Because it is your civic duty.'

I didn't laugh. Funnily enough if there had been one reason why I might have gone, that would have been it. Because I do have this honourable brave and public-minded streak. But no.

'It is not my civic duty to put myself in the line of a maniac who has threatened me, attacked me, kidnapped me, tried to rape me, pretended to kidnap my daughter. It is my civic duty to go nowhere near him.'

'You won't be going anywhere near him,' he said. 'That's the whole point. He's not there. All you will be doing is looking for footsteps. Then when you find some, you come home. No harm done.'

'I don't think you have a clue what you're suggesting,' I said. 'I have no training for this, not a clue how to do it, I don't want to do it, it would be dangerous – it's a completely stupid idea. Dangerously stupid.'

'What is?' said Harry's voice behind me. Cold. I hadn't heard him come in.

'Sending me to Cairo to find out where Eddie's gone,' I said.

I looked up at him. He was looking at Preston Oliver.

'No,' he said. Very simple.

'Yes,' said Oliver.

'Why?' said Harry. 'Haven't we got any coppers? No detectives? No professionals? No one but a young woman to do our dirty work for us? The one person in the world most at risk from this crazy fuck who would be safely inside if it hadn't been for someone's clever idea?'

'That's why she'll go,' he said.

'What are you talking about?' said Harry.

'She knows she'll never be safe till he's sorted out. Don't you?' And he turned to me, and gave me a look so smug I could have jumped out of the window.

I stared back at him levelly, then looked across to Harry.

'I thought you said he wasn't Ben Cooper,' I said.

'He wasn't,' said Harry.

Oliver sat, pale and still, on his grey plastic chair behind his grey metal desk on its grey plastic carpet.

'It's true though, isn't it?' he said. For a moment I couldn't remember if it was or not. Then I thought, 'No!'

'If I could think of a better way, believe me I would,' he said, and sighed and turned as if to produce the contract that he had ready-drawn-up all along, waiting to get over my paltry objections before getting me to sign.

'But I'm pregnant,' I heard myself say.

Silence.

I heard only the sound of Harry staring at me.

'All the more reason to get him sorted out then,' said Oliver seamlessly. And smiled up at Harry. 'Congratulations.'

But Harry was still staring.

'Oh,' said Oliver. 'Or not?'

I said nothing.

'It's not Eddie's, is it?' said Oliver. Almost laughing.

'No, it's not,' I said. Furiously but calm.

Harry came back to life.

'You're not sending an unqualified pregnant girl to find Eddie Bates. I don't believe that you can do this. It's stupid and it is *too dangerous*.'

'No, it's not,' repeated Oliver patiently. 'As I was explaining, she won't be going anywhere near him. She's going to Cairo precisely because Eddie is not there. OK? And can I remind you Harry that you are here as a courtesy? Your objections have been noted. She's going.'

'No, I'm not,' I said.

'You are going, because if you don't, we will not see Bates again until *he* chooses to reappear. Which he will. I leave it – as he does – to your imagination where, when and how that might be. Your pregnancy simply means you will have to go soon. Which we want you to do anyway. You'll be going as a dancer. Look for work, and while doing so find footsteps. That's all. For goodness sake,' he said, 'you're a perfectly intelligent girl. Just go to Cairo, ask around a bit, and then come home. You can manage that, can't you? I don't know why you're making such a fuss.'

I didn't like being called a girl. But I liked everything else less.

'I can't get work. I don't dance any more.'

'You don't have to. Just tell people that's what you're doing if they ask.'

'They won't believe me. There is no work. It's all Russian girls now. Anyway there are no tourists since . . .' I didn't want to say it.

'That doesn't matter. You don't need work, you only need an excuse to be there. And anyway, there's plenty. No Egyptian girls are dancing now. They're scared. So are the Europeans, everybody. There'll be plenty of work on offer, and everyone will be delighted to see you.'

'And I have a daughter,' I said, 'who needs looking after.'

'Yes, of course,' he said. 'Well, DI Makins hasn't had his paternity leave yet. Have you, Harry? You can start as soon as you like. She'll be leaving this week.'

Harry's face.

'No, I won't,' I said. 'Anyway, it's Christmas.'

'If she goes I must go,' Harry said finally.

'No.'

I looked from one to the other. Make decisions for and about me, why don't you. Ignore what I say, why not?

'I'm going home,' I said. Harry made to leave with me. As we left he turned and said to Oliver, not as a threat but as a quiet statement of fact: 'You *will* regret this.'

'I shouldn't think so,' said Oliver, calmly.

SIX

Yes, I am

I stormed down the corridor to get out of that place as fast as I could. Harry followed me, steering me past sharp-edged filing cabinets and ugly, bloodless men in shirt sleeves. We burst out on to Victoria Street, mid-morning full of taxis and buses, limp rain and London life. Each of these people no doubt was carrying their own drama. The volume of human activity. I am beginning to hate cities.

'I'm not going,' I said, as soon as we were outside. I said it warningly, as if I thought he were going to try to persuade me. Traffic noise drowned me anyway.

He took my arm and stared about, as if searching for an island of peace. 'Pub?' he said to me. 'Café?'

'No,' I said. 'I hate places.'

'You're pregnant,' he said.

I shot him a look. I don't know what I meant by it or what he read into it. It was, I think, imploring, silencing. We seemed to be walking west, and after a few moments we cut north towards St James's Park, up the beautiful little Queen Anne streets, red brick and white stone steps, where dandies and countesses used to live. Government offices, mainly, now. Crossing Birdcage Walk he was still with me, silent. We stepped over a low iron fence, and found a bench, and sat, and gazed out over the lake, the flamingoes, the mandarin ducks, the fountain, the willows. Pretty as a picture.

'You're pregnant,' he said again.

'Yes,' I replied. And again saying it out loud made it truer. 'I believe so.'

'Why didn't you tell me?'

'I didn't know,' I said, automatically, but not pleased. Is that his first reaction? Why didn't I tell *him*?

'When did you find out?' he said. I wasn't sure that I didn't feel a little interrogated. He's checking for his basis and then he's going to judge me. Find me wanting, or not.

'Saturday,' I said. 'I'm seeing the doctor today.'

Someone was feeding the ducks, who were making a big racket, pecking and splashing. Duck dramas.

'I don't know much more than you, you see,' I said. What I meant was, 'I desperately need you to be nice here.' I think he sensed that, but we're only human. He didn't know what to do.

'It's Sa'id's, I suppose,' he said.

'I suppose so,' I said. Meaning it to sound like a jocular confirmation, not like a reluctant acknowledgement, but I don't know how it came out. Anyway, what did he mean by supposing? Of course it's Sa'id's. Who else's?

And what's this 'it'? 'It' is not a friendly term.

'What are you going to do?'

For a moment I read that as 'Are you going to keep it?' – that great euphemism – and I nearly told him to fuck off. Just in time I reminded myself that that's not what he said, and therefore not what I should respond to. It may have been what he meant. But I can give him the benefit of the doubt here. If I thought he was suggesting that I might want an abortion . . . Jesus, my skin curls up at the idea. No judgement – no judgement – on a woman who needs to do that. But I don't, and I won't. And I couldn't bear to hear Harry suggest it because how could I forgive him? This is a baby. One of those small innocent sweet-smelling things that love us. Like Lily was. Like he was, and me.

I remember from somewhere that before three months you don't tell anybody. Don't know why, or where I heard it. Perhaps because most miscarriages are during that period. A blue dot on a strip of plastic.

'I'm going to have a baby, god willing,' I said. And smiled at him. As I did I felt the smile grow wider and wider till it nearly fell off the edges of my face. It grew from right inside me, and blossomed all over my mush like an immense flower. Harry felt its force.

'So you are,' he said. And gave a funny, sad, little desperate sighing laugh.

'So what do you think?' I asked, in safety, now that he knew exactly what he was not allowed to think.

'I don't know what to think,' he said. 'I'm in shock.'

'So am I,' I said.

'I mean . . .'

'What?'

He was silent.

'Let's talk about it when you've been to the doctor,' he said. I could see he was buying time, and I thought that maybe – yes, probably – he was hoping, quietly, that perhaps I was mistaken. But I knew I wasn't. Some non-cerebral, non-logical part of me knew perfectly well. You don't dance for years without getting to know your own body. You don't nearly die in a road smash without recognizing life when it's kicking around inside you. However young and tiny; however shrimplike, translucent. However few cells.

Still, he can have time.

I didn't know what was in his heart. He wasn't telling me. Well, he can have time.

'OK,' I said. We sat in silence for a few minutes. It wasn't that cold. I love to look out over water. Even an urban ornamental lake.

'And what about Oliver's plan, then?' he said.

'I'm not going. It's all mouth, isn't it? It's up to me how scared I am of Eddie. He's not going to be coming to Britain, you said so yourself, so why should I care where he is? There's no good reason why I should go except that Oliver wants me to, and is trying to spook me. So I won't be spooked.'

'He won't like it,' said Harry. Looking quite pleased at the prospect.

'Not as much as I wouldn't like going,' I said.

He took my hand and patted it. 'Attagirl,' he said, mildly.

*

The doctor, a camp black man with Lionel Richie curls and a tweed jacket, made me lie down, palpated my belly, asked me the date of the start of my last period, gave me a number to make an appointment at the hospital, three leaflets on the dangers of smoking and alcohol during pregnancy, and a certificate. It certified I was pregnant. According to him, it was ten weeks, because according to him it is counted from the date of the last period. According to him. But I knew exactly.

'Congratulations,' said the nurse, when I went in to be weighed and measured. 'You can pee in a policeman's helmet now, if you need to.'

'Why would I need to?' I asked. Which wasn't quite the question I meant, but I had to ask something.

'If you're taken short,' she said. 'You're allowed to pee anywhere, and a policeman would have to offer you his helmet. So I've heard. It's probably like taxis having to carry a bale of hay for the horse. But you could try it.'

'Thanks,' I said. And got weighed. First time in years. She said a number in kilos, which meant nothing to me, which is just as well because I have a strong natural aversion to thinking about my weight. Biggest waste of energy. Think what women could do with all the time they spend worrying about their weight.

'You'll need to eat well,' she was saying, 'but don't put on too much because it's harder to get rid of afterwards. Pregnancy isn't very good for the body, you know. This is your first? Well . . .'

She took my blood pressure. It took me back to the time after the accident, the bad time, Janie dead, Lily in intensive care, Mum and Dad in shock, me in traction. Long nights with the black rubber bandage expanding and contracting, sighing like the tide, breathing slowly and regularly around my arm, the powdery feel against my flesh and the strong slow squeeze. All night, those long hospital nights. When they took it off I missed it.

My body was so hijacked then. Immobilized, bound up, suspended, drugged – I still feel in some way more resentful of the doctors than the accident. The accident just did what it had to do – smashed up my leg and killed my sister. But at least it did it quickly. The doctors and the healing took so long. Back in this nurse's hands, I felt that immobilizing force of medicine coming down on me again. Please don't start telling me what to do, I can't bear it.

The thing is, having Lily, I think that I know all about babies. But in reality pregnancy is a new world to me. I thought of Janie: how happy she was to be pregnant, how happy we all were, even though we hated Jim, with his bullying insecurities – this was the first grandchild, who would shift the balances of our family and provoke love simply by being. And Janie never got that love. Never got beyond pregnancy.

Our bodies. Our poor dear bodies. Up to their own things.

I resolved to start dancing. Gently but frequently. Bellydancing always was the woman's dance, the fertility and pregnancy and childbirth dance. And if my body is going to do this thing, this thing which seems to have nothing to do with my brain or my thoughts or my decision-making faculties, then I had better open up those channels of communication that I used to have with my body. Sex and dancing – those are the links. And this is where sex has got me. So I will dance again. I will dance as a damaged woman can dance.

I remember once going to an extravagant *baladi* wedding in the City of the Dead in Cairo. The family that lived there (it's not unusual to move in with your dead relatives, or someone else's, among the tombs and mausoleums; Cairo's a very crowded city) had put up a *sheder* between two tombs, a huge tent lined with canvas hangings decorated with curls and arabesques in black and white and red and blue, patterns that look like the love-child of a classical Arabic script and a bank of lotus flowers. Everyone seemed very stoned; hashish and frankincense hung on the air. And, of course, there were dancers: men doing the stick dance (the one which ended up over here as Morris dancing, Morris from Moorish – it's rather more dashing the way they do it in Cairo), and four big vulgar bellydancers, great fake blondes with shining eyeshadow and wicked tongues. There was an old tradition of verbal abuse called *radh:*

when a working-class Cairo matron really wanted to insult someone, she would throw her shawl on the ground, put one hand on her hip, cock the other at her temple, and let rip a diatribe in rhyme. I could just picture these babes doing that. Swagger? God could they swagger. I ended up hunkering down next to an old woman, as stoned as everybody else but unimpressed by the dancers. 'You don't need all this to dance,' she muttered, sitting like a cobbler and gesturing to the sequins and the flash. 'You don't need anything.' And with that she took my hand, and put it on her black-clad belly — and danced. Without standing, without it showing, without an outwardly visible movement she moved her muscles and her flesh, under my hand, in a dance as interesting and entertaining and passionate as any I have ever seen. I thought of her a lot when I gave up dancing for a living, after I left the perfect youthful strength and alacrity of my leg there on the roadside with Janie; I thought of her now.

The nurse was talking about share care, home birth, St Mary's, Queen Charlotte's. 'You won't need to decide yet,' she said, 'but if you can get the home midwives I can tell you they're very nice, the ones here, they're a lovely lot. Oh, you won't know what's hit you!' she said, with a sudden spurt of pleasure. It occurred to me that for them, medical staff, dealing constantly with death and disease, a newborn baby must be their professional antidote. Their nice thing.

*

I went straight to Zeinab's to get Lily. She was in a sulk, about what was unclear. Probably it would all come out at bedtime, when we lie and talk between stories. And one of these bedtimes I was going to tell her that she's going to have a real Nippyhead.

It's such a lot to take on. A father she's only had for a couple of weeks, and now a sibling. Well, not now, but soon enough. I resolved to tell her quite late, to give her time to settle with Harry. In a few months. As late as possible, but before she notices, because she hates to feel left out. She will be happy about it in principle – but how will it be in practice?

I remembered something she said ages ago. 'If you have a new baby will it have a daddy?' And when I said yes, she said, 'Can I borrow its daddy?'

It's that word normal again. It's normal to have a daddy. It's also normal to go to work every day, and to think Chris Evans is funny. So I'm not normal. Well, we find our own level. And then we destroy it again. Just as I start to set up something approaching a version of liveable normality with Lily and Harry, something else crops up. Nippyhead.

And of course Nippyhead does have a daddy. And so does Lily. From no daddy to two, in a few weeks.

And what am I going to do about Nippyhead's daddy? Wait a few a months? As late as possible? How would he feel about being left out?

When Jim was accepted as Lily's father, I was righteous for his cause even though I despised him. A father is a father, I said. Whatever we think of him, it's his blood and he has the right. The fact that he never exercised it for three years, and then when he did it turned out he wasn't the father, and had no rights anyway, made it easier for me to be so righteous.

And now?

Well. I will have to tell him.

There on the Uxbridge Road, coming home, in the chill of a small soft winter rain, a flood of joy came over me. I have to tell him – it's right to do so. I have to contact him. I will see him, or speak to him, again. God it made me happy. For that split illogical second. Then I remembered that it would come to no good, so . . . And I allowed myself a moment to fantasize . . . maybe it could come good. Maybe . . .

And then Lily and I had our daily 'no-we're-not-going-to-the-sweet-shop' session, followed by one of our regular 'what do you think I mean when I say no? Do you think I mean that if you whine and go on about it I'll say yes in the end? Or do you think I mean no? On account of how I have never in your life changed a no to a yes on account of whining and going on?' sessions. She played it just long enough for real irritation to be on the verge of getting the upper hand ('How many times do I have to say the same thing? Why don't you listen? Why don't you remember, for god's sake? Haven't you noticed that if you go on and on I get cross and then you get upset and then it's all horrible? Why not just drop it, and we can be happy and nice? It's your choice') but I caught the irritation just as it was about to jump out, and threw it under a bus, and started tickling her instead, and it was all right. Then she wanted me to tell her about the little bugs that would try to eat her teeth if she ate too many sweets, and how the toothpaste soldiers would fight them off because they have to protect the buried treasure, which is her new grown-up teeth that she will get when she's six. Then we had the usual problem with the tooth thing, which is, why is it that we have to brush our teeth to stop them falling out, when they're going to fall out anyway and that's a really exciting thing, to be looked forward to and the fairies bring us money? When we got home we drew pictures, and then she told me that Omar was meant to be the baby in their game but he wouldn't go to sleep, so Hassan had frightened him to sleep with a rotten plum. I was musing on how the rotten plum had escaped me as a sleep aid for restless babies when she started reading me a schoolbook about a dragon, and she could read. 'Look here. Look. Here. Here. Look!'

'It's not very interesting, is it Mummy?' she said, and started reading the milk carton ('Pure dairy milk. Homo. Homog. What's that?') and the blue stencilled writing on the bread bin ('Bread. That says bread!') and then she got a book she loves called *Amazing Grace* and had a go at that. 'Once upon a time there was a girl called Grace who loved stories.'

She must have been building it up inside, and now out it spills. Accumulated knowledge becoming a useable skill.

Reading. All that singing the alphabet song, all that Lucy Lamp Lady and Harry the Hairy Hat Man (she'd laughed about that when she first met Harry). Paying off. I hugged her a lot.

While she was eating her tea Chrissie rang.

'How are you feeling?' she said. 'I was thinking if you haven't been sick so far you probably won't be, which some people say means it's a boy. How was it at the doctor's?' And I found myself telling her, quietly, from the study, because I didn't want Lily picking up on anything. I found myself telling her how irritating it was people being such know-alls, and how I didn't like the feeling that I was entering some kind of production line of people who did this every day. Not the nurse, but the doctor. I told her I hated hospitals, and she said if I did share care then I wouldn't have to go to the hospital more than a couple of times, and anyway what about a home birth, and I said that the doctor had said I was elderly (if you please) and didn't advise it, and she said I shouldn't really listen to him on things like that, because if I didn't feel he was sympathetic probably I was right, and he would just be trying to arrange things to his own convenience, which plenty of them still do, and I should just remember that it's my business, my baby, my body, and do what I want. I found myself telling her that I didn't really know what I wanted. And she said not to worry, everybody I spoke to would tell me what they wanted, and I could pick and choose from the options everybody else would give me. Including her, she said, and that made me laugh. Had I told people yet, she wanted to know, and I said no, not really. I thought of her going off for six months and telling nobody. And I asked her how the wagon was going, and she said it was rattling along, not that comfortable, but a nice view. It felt funny to like her but I did.

*

Tuesday morning I rang Oliver.

'I've considered everything you've said,' I told him, 'and it adds up to nothing. I won't be going.'

There was silence at the other end.

'I hope you find him,' I said. 'If there's anything I can do that doesn't put me at risk, I'd be glad to do it. If I hear from him, I'll let you know. I wish you luck.' I paused a moment more, and as he didn't seem to be saying anything I was about to say goodbye and put the phone down when I heard a sigh.

'I'm sorry to hear that,' he said.

'Well, I'm sure you understand my position,' I said.

'Sadly yes,' he said. 'Better than you.'

I had no time really to wonder what he meant by that.

'I didn't want to do it this way,' he said.

I said nothing.

'But if you insist.'

I said nothing.

'I have on file,' he said. And stopped, waiting for me to twig, or stop him, or something. I must have been a bit dim that day because I didn't twig. 'Some unpressed charges,' he said.

I began to twig.

'Drink driving, and so on. And attempting to bribe a police officer.'

'Succeeding,' I pointed out, saying the obvious while the actual nub of what he was saying sat there like a lump I couldn't bear to look at.

'Whatever,' he said. 'Makes no difference.'

No.

He let me mull on it for a moment.

Two years ago, during the time when Jim had been laying claim to Lily and I was concerned to keep my reputation utterly clean, in order not to seem unsuitable at any custody hearing, through no fault of my own (my designated driver having stomped out during a row, in the middle of Piccadilly Circus) I got done for drunken driving. Ben Cooper offered to lose the charges – OK, I asked him to. It seemed worth it. And he did, and proceeded to blackmail me over it, making me chum up (lord, how the phrases come back) with Eddie Bates, who he knew to have a thing about me. He didn't tell me that bit. Just shoved me into danger for his own purposes. He knew Eddie Bates was about to go down, and didn't want to go with him. They'd been in the vice business together. With my sister. You know. All that. So Ben thought perhaps I could find out something to save his skin. I was the straw he clutched at. But in the end they all sank and I swam, except that they came bobbing up again – Cooper on perpetual sick leave, claiming to be too ill and upset to face trial, and Bates bouncing around Egypt sending me letters and bribes and trying to carry me off up the Nile.

And now up from the depths floats the old original drink-driving charge that Cooper put in a file and lost two years ago, and one he must have added on the side – trying to bribe him. Funny old thing that he is. Laying it up like wine, for use when he needed it. Only it's not him using it, it's Oliver.

'So?' I said. Trying to face it out. If he is going to try and use what I think he is then I want to hear him say it.

However good a mother I've been to her, I am not her mother, and thanks to Jim and his custody bid social services know about us. I remember Harry saying to that woman, the court welfare officer, 'It would be a shame if Ms Gower has to lose her good reputation just through being a witness to criminal behaviour.' Something like that.

'So if the charges were reactivated, social services might be interested,' said Oliver.

My turn to be silent.

'Of course, apart from that it's quite nebulous,' he continued, 'but there's a possible assault charge, on Eddie Bates, there's the abduction you mentioned, now why didn't you report it, not to mention the goings-on in Egypt a few weeks ago. Why *did* a convicted criminal give you £100,000? And there's your connection with those young men wanted by the Egyptian police . . .'

'He was dead all along and they're in the clear,' I said.

'I thought you were going to let me know if you heard anything about them,' he snapped. 'Anyway. As I was saying. All this could be investigated. The welfare of your child could become an issue.'

He gave me a moment or two to think about that. Then continued.

'However, I believe you to be an innocent person caught up in some bad events. All I need is for you to prove it to me.'

Oh yes.

'By doing your civic duty.'

Bastard.

'You wouldn't go through with it,' I said. Rather pathetically, because I knew it didn't matter if he did or not. He could, and that was all the leverage he needed.

'Yes I would. Just start it off, set it going. It would take forever.'

'Nothing would stick.'

'So what? It could ruin your life anyway. And Lily's.'

'You unutterable bastard,' I said.

'Yes, well, I dare say. You'll need to go soon. My secretary will be in touch.'

*

Unutterable, unutterable bastard. The whole point of anything, ever, had been to protect Lily, to keep her safe, with me. Years ago, I saw Jim, violent boyfriend, father as we thought of the child, as the enemy whose rights I respected, and I tried to arm myself against him. Now, again, my own weapons rise up to get me. I did one wrong thing, for all the right reasons. And here I am.

I went out on to my balcony and looked out over the A40, watching the cars creeping under the rain, and felt panic rising in my throat.

I have to go. And if I go, I will see Sa'id.

SEVEN

Making friends

Chrissie rang again that night, while I was in the bath with Lily. She left a message: she was feeling a bit . . . a bit down, and did I want to go to the pictures? I rang her back, saying I couldn't because of babysitting – 'Oh stupid me!' she said – and I found myself inviting her over. She said would I mind if she brought her pregnant lady yoga book, it was way out of date probably but she'd found it so useful, but she didn't want, you know, to be one of those bossy friends who give you stuff all the time . . . I said, no, bring it, I'd be interested.

Then I did a doubletake on the word friend.

I sat and thought about it for a moment.

Then I called Fergus Droyle. Fergus is a semi-divorced Irish Catholic crime correspondent with a taste for Russian literature, and he drinks too much. We met in a holiday camp in Algeria, of all ridiculous places. His line was on voicemail – leaving a pager number, a mobile number and the number of a secretary. Or I could leave a message. Or fax him. Or e-mail him. All numbers given. I decided that today I would honour the pager.

He rang me back almost immediately.

'Droyle, you rang,' he said. I thought he probably hadn't recognized my number and thought I was some hot informant or policeman or something. I let him know that I was me.

'Finally!' he said. Fergus was always wanting the full Eddie Bates story from me; I am always ringing him for confirmation and information and refusing to tell him anything. 'You picked one of the worst moments though,' he said.

'What are you doing?'

'Trying to get off with a teenager,' he said. 'She ordered green Chartreuse and it's only eight o'clock. Should I give up on her?'

'How old is she?'

'Oh, twenty-five. I don't know.'

'Twenty-five's OK,' I said. Depending, of course, on the twenty-five-year-old. Sa'id is twenty-five. Well, twenty-six. And nobody would call him a teenager.

'Yippee!' he cried. 'But she won't want me. I'm a fat balding self-pitying drunken slob — what are you doing? I'll lose her and take you out instead.'

'Ah well,' I said. 'That's what I wanted to talk to you about . . .' For a moment I heard him wondering if he'd heard right, and translating what I'd said as a come-on, so I talked over it.

'Mrs Bates,' I said.

'Oh, lord, not Madame again. Is she apologizing to you now for the letters and that? Yeah, I know. She's on the twelve steps. She's – Jesus, I feel sorry for her, I do.' (Fergus attempted the twelve steps once but got stuck on the fact that they kept going on about a superior being: 'I'm a fucking Catholic,' he'd say. 'Do you mind if I call him God?')

'She wants to be my friend,' I said.

'She was always flakey as fuck,' he said. 'I'd've thought you had enough flakey friends already. But you know, she had a time of it with that man – he put her through it. And she loved him! The way she loved that man was a crime. The lies he told her. You remember her at the funeral? Of course you do.' He laughed. He'd introduced us there – our first meeting. He'd been pissed off with me because I wouldn't be quoted for his valedictory piece on Eddie. So he'd pitched me into the drunken Chrissie's den.

'How much did she know about him?' I asked.

'To be honest, I think not that much. About what he did, you mean? I think she just thought he was a businessman. She's not what you would call stringent in the brains department. Not rigorous. Listen – can I call you in the morning? You're not going away for Christmas, are you? Or tonight, you know, if I don't achieve my teenage nirvana with this wench. Wish me luck. I'll speak to you.'

I hung up thinking about age gaps. Thinking about Sa'id. Trying to fix him in my mind. In practical terms.

He is nine and a half years younger than me. Despite his English blood, his five languages, his time at the Sorbonne, he is specifically Egyptian. He uses a phrase like 'my Arab brothers' without a touch of the self-consciousness that other educated, cosmopolitan young Egyptians might bring to it, at least in front of Europeans. He pretty much runs the family business, though his father is there, and Hakim. When he sails a felucca on the Nile he steers with his foot, as Nile boatmen have for thousands of years. He is intelligent, political, patient, funny. Better read than me. He will happily haggle over mint tea for hours with an amusing customer, haggle to the last five Egyptian pounds, flirting and joshing in various languages and currencies, pouring handfuls of cheap turquoise scarabs into their pockets for souvenirs, and then go and read George Soros on solutions to the crisis of the Third World Debt. His grandmother calls him *damu sharbaat*: sugar blood. It means, so sweet, so funny. I don't know what he plans to do with his life. With his brain, with his inclinations. His habit of trailing clarity and understanding in his wake.

Sa'id is perfect. My perfection. My golden heaven.

So why did I leave?

I have wondered about this. It wasn't just that half term was over and Lily expected me and I had a ticket booked. You don't leave a man like Sa'id for everyday reasons of practicality and administration. The truth is I don't know why I left him.

I thought of Chrissie, weeping on the empty grave of a man she knew nothing about.

This is my child's father. I know him, and yet, and yet . . . There is plenty I don't know. Of course mystery is magnificent, because it has all its potential forever, as long as it remains mysterious. A conversation came back to me: Sa'id and me at Fishawy's, a café in Khan el-Khalili in Cairo. Under the sunbleached awnings in a narrow medi-aeval street, talking about Orientalism, about whether we had attached any racial or cultural ideals to each other – was he my Rudy Valentino, was I his Ice Queen? So much of my dream life has been Egyptian, so many of my yearn-ings and desires, through the physical joy of the dancing and the haunting humanity of the music, let alone, when I actually got there, the architecture and the fabulous Nile and the ruins and the desert and the taste of the air and the friends and the generosity and honour and, of course, the ancient English tradition of being enchanted by the East (I could hardly claim immunity from that). So had I fallen in love with the country and taken this man as its personification? I said no, I was well acquainted with Egypt, with Egyptians, and if I had been going to do that I had had plenty of opportunity before, when I lived there. And I'd fallen in love with him in London. I hadn't even been in Egypt for years. He could have been just another Arab lad trying to build a life in Shepherd's Bush. There was nothing special about him, except himself. I'd asked if he thought I orientalized him. (What did we mean by that?

Glamorized him, yearned for him, played that game of so desiring the beautiful mystery that you keep reinforcing its mysteriousness, in order to continue to desire it, while ignoring what it truly is, refusing to know it truly, because if you did the potential would be lost.) He said he just wondered. He had shaken his head, looked at me sideways.

Gérard de Nerval, as well as walking a lobster on a lead in Kensington Gardens, had a good line about dreams and memories *vis à vis* the Orient, and whether the romantic and poetically inclined late-nineteenth-century European mightn't do better not to go there at all. Something about how when you swap the dream for the memory you don't always get a good deal.

Am I saying I left him in case he was going to prove to have feet of clay? Was it that simple? Teenage idealist ruin-your-life romanticism?

But I know reality can come up with more and better stuff than my dreams. I know that my imagination is not all the world has to offer; I don't construct, alone, the best that there could ever be. I don't not go places because I prefer my own version of them to the reality. I may be arrogant, I may like to be in charge, but not that much. Sa'id was in every way lovelier than I could have invented.

He had been perfect to me. And if you think someone is perfect, you don't know them. And if you're having their child you have to know.

*

Chrissie brought two little trout with her and some vegetables, and cooked us a lovely little cordon bleu cookery-course meal (that genteel upbringing again), even down to the finely chopped parsley sprinkled on boiled new potatoes and the flaked almonds on the trout. Flakes from a flake.

'You need good food,' she said.

It was curious not to have a bottle of wine with it, but there you go: her on her wagon, me breeding. I had no urge to drink at all. Didn't want to. She, on the other hand, did. Big time. She had tried out every damned potentially interesting non-alcoholic drink on the market, from camomile to Aqua Libra, and had settled on nettle cordial. 'It tastes OK,' she said. 'You have to drink dock-leaf cordial afterwards.'

But you don't need *vino* for *Veritas*.

'I was wondering,' she said, 'why I married him. Do you know why? Shall I tell you?'

I was still wondering if I wanted to know when she started telling me.

'Sex,' she said. 'Fatal to a well-brought-up girl, you know. I just fancied him so much, and I thought that if we were sleeping together that meant I had to marry him, and of course if I was to marry him I had to be in love with him . . . a vicious circle of total misunderstanding. Never loved him at all. Except – well you kind of do, just by sleeping with them, don't you? Making love – ha ha! So yes, I made all that love, and then assumed I was in it. God, I was young.'

I thought of what Fergus had said: 'The way she loved that man was a crime.' Now, as she distanced herself from her own past love and youthful self, I could see that they were both right, truths overlapping like layers of ice on a frozen pond . . . ready to shatter at any moment.

She was crazy for him – then. Passion was all – then. Now, in order to remain sane, she has to invent a distance, put all that passion away down the other end of that distance, and pretend it had been there all along. In the hope that it will stay there. I liked the making love theory. Harry had a similar one, warning against promiscuity. 'Fucking leads to kissing,' he'd say. 'You have to be careful.' I never let myself think about him kissing Janie.

Chrissie was still talking. 'I'm so glad he's dead,' she was saying. 'I can't believe I said that. But I am. Only way I could really get out of him. I tried to before – tried to leave him. Drinking was a way of leaving him. Of just being elsewhere from him. And Darla! Poor little Darla carries the whole burden, the whole thing . . .'

Darla is the daughter.

'I know, I know. But what can I do for her now? She needs so much, and I'm just going to make myself strong and then start making it up to her. I don't blame myself, because my position was impossible, but I am the only person who can do anything for her. And I'm going to. When I'm well.'

She didn't look well, to tell the truth. She did look better than I'd seen her look before. But that isn't saying much.

She was staring at her nettle cordial.

'You probably don't want to talk about him,' she said.

'No, not really.'

A silence settled over us briefly, a soft dusting of it.

'I didn't know what he did. He was a businessman. I didn't know what businessmen do. I hadn't a clue. Was that stupid of me? Was that stupid? I never thought. Is that stupid or bad, never to think? And Darl . . .'

I could see which way she was heading. All that trouble to have a child, and this is the heritage you give it, selfish to have had it at all, selfish bad weak drunk blame bad guilt bad bad . . . well I felt for her, but I could not play mother confessor in Eddie territory. It was not safe. Eddie should not be in my head at all, under any pretext, and I should not be listening to this when I know he's not dead and she doesn't.

She started to cry, and because I couldn't give her brandy I gave her chocolate. She dried up and started apologizing. I hugged her and said never mind, never mind. She was wearing less scent since she'd sobered up.

'I'm so sorry about what I did to you,' she said. 'Those letters. This isn't a duty apology, for the programme. Really. I'm so sorry.'

'Yes, well, flowers, razorblades – at least you were imaginative,' I said, in a jocular fashion, hoping to jolly her out of it.

She froze.

There was one of those silent moments before something comes crashing down.

'I never sent you a razorblade,' she said.

A pause.

'Well,' I said, mildly, non-committally.

She was staring at me.

'And I didn't send you any flowers,' she said, 'because I've been sent those things myself by my husband, sent them in anger, I mean, in sadism really. The dead flowers, the nasty poems, the notes that sound so innocent but deny your very existence; I'll give you one, it was, "Darling how I long for our happy little family to be together again", sent to the clinic after my second abortion, with two dozen pink roses. The razorblade was before the first. Just to make it clear. So no, I didn't send you any razorblade. If someone did, it wasn't me.'

I tried hard to think of something to say but there was nothing I could say. Either she'll get there or she won't. I can't say a thing.

'How curious that two people should be sending you unpleasant things at the same time,' she said. 'Very confusing, of course, I see that. It was at the same time? Of course, or you wouldn't have thought it was me. And did you get flowers? Poems? Did you?'

Those bloody men. Oliver, whoever. Thinking this fake death was a good way to do things. And Eddie. Look at the state of this woman.

I watched her, and I saw her working it out, putting it together with the empty urn, disbelieving, believing. There is a fairly strong human tradition of not believing in death anyway: look at the ancients, at Christianity, at plastic surgery, at cryonicists, at Osiris. Look at Gilgamish, the first written story: he went to find a flower at the bottom of the sea to bring his dead friend back. Look at me, with Janie. Look at Chrissie, looking at me, realizing that for her the timeless human dream is about to come true. Here, at least, death shall have no dominion.

What had her question been? Did I get flowers and poems?

'Yes,' I said.

'Oh,' she said.

Then: 'So, what . . . ?'

'He is alive,' I said. She knew anyway, but I wanted her to think I'd told her, so that she would be loyal to me. Or at least not hate me. I felt that this might help, at some unspecified time in the future. I felt that Chrissie's reaction to her husband's treachery might be volcanic, and that my position in relation to both the explosion and the lava flow would benefit from a little . . . positioning.

What would her first reaction be? Relief or anger? Which is bigger, her love or her sense of betrayal?

The look that came into her eyes was gentle and light.

'Oh, is he,' she almost whispered.

Jesus, it's love, I thought. Then saw clearer. It wasn't just love. Or not just love of him. It was, perhaps, love of the fight she was going to have with him now. Or something.

*

I knew I shouldn't have told her. I knew it could be risky to Harry – but now that Oliver knew I knew, and was using that, and given that the gravedigger had told her anyway, I felt covered. Plus I had a sense of the unavoidability of meltdown – it wasn't working, this protection racket. It had gone wrong anyway, so why not add to the chaos in the interests of bringing on the ultimate conflagration, to be followed by settlement and sweet rest? Why not indeed. Like the fundamentalist Christians who wanted to go and shoot up Jerusalem for the millenium, to encourage the second coming. Good thinking, boys.

But I was glad I had told her. Because I like truth. And I think she has a right to know. And I don't like men messing around with women's lives. And I hoped it would give Oliver a headache because he was a bully.

Of course once she knew the fact of it, she wanted the details. Like how did I know? I told her I had gone to the police with the wild communications, and that when he had started trying to manipulate me into going somewhere they had, as a final resort, told me why I should under no circumstances go. (I didn't tell her that the policeman in question was Harry, nor that I had ignored his advice.) She wanted to know where he had tried to get me to go, where he was. I reverted to Teflon, told her it wasn't known. I didn't mention Egypt – of course I didn't! I didn't want her knowing that I knew anything about it. But by this stage I was tripping over myself. How could I have not known where he was trying to make me go? No-one would fall for that.

And then she said: 'What about Egypt?'

And I said: 'What about it?'

And she said: 'He always wanted to go there and he never did. He loves Tangiers but he's known there. I bet he'd go to Egypt. I *bet* he would.'

And then she said: 'It's one of your places, isn't it? With the bellydancing and everything? Aren't you going to Egypt soon?'

Surely I hadn't told her. Had I?

She said, why was I going? I said – and of course this was true too – to tell the father of his incipient child. She didn't ask about him. Of course not. She was in her own drama now. She was buzzing, glittering. Little glints of energy pinged off her as her specks of realization connected up into a web of knowledge.

And then she said: 'Can I come with you? If he *has* been there, maybe I can find out where he's gone. I can ask the police, and go to those bellydancing clubs and things. You can help me,' she said. Looking happy. 'And I can help you, and look after you.'

'No,' I said.

'Why not?'

'Because it's stupid, he's not there, there'll be nothing to find out, you don't . . . there's no point.'

'No harm done then,' she said brightly. 'No reason not to. And I have to. Please help me. It'll be much better than me doing it alone.'

'But Chrissie – why do you need to know where he is?'

Stupid question.

'Have to,' she said, simply, which made a kind of sense.

'Think about it,' I said. 'You've had a terrible shock.'

'Oh, I will. I'll probably think of nothing else,' she said.

'You may change your mind,' I said. 'Don't do anything in a hurry. After all, as far as he's concerned you think he's dead, so you're safe from him, so . . .'

She looked at me. 'Safe isn't the point,' she said.

That, of course, is where we differ.

I looked at her. Tear-stained, deep-cleavaged, manically sober, only very precariously attached to her rocker. I could just imagine her stravaiging Cairo looking for her former late husband. I could just imagine what good it would do her, and I could just imagine the effect she would have on my plans to get hold quickly of one quiet, small piece of information and bring it back to Oliver like a good dog.

Safe?

Oh fuck.

'OK,' I said. 'I'll help.'

Fuck her bloody perspicacity. Fuck fuck fuck.

*

The thought of seeing Sa'id was constant at the back of my mind. It made my heart leap and flex like a fish.

*

Harry came over again the next day. I was surprised by how much time he seemed to have but, the way he talked about it, it seemed that half the force was pulling sickies every five minutes, and those who didn't – like him – were allowed a little leeway. The everyday, small-scale, low-level corruption he talked about was hideously depressing: officers making every assault racially aggravated or sexual, so they could claim to be cleaning up in those areas; chucking extra charges at the last minute on people who had said they would be pleading guilty and not seeing a lawyer; going out and pulling twenty prostitutes because at least ten of them will be guilty of something, and that's a 50 per cent clean-up rate. 'Too many of my colleagues,' he said, 'have what you might call a statistics-led attitude. As long as an offence happened on paper they don't always care that it didn't happen anywhere else.' He told me about a fantasy he used to have about leaving the force and becoming a security advisor to eco-warriors. It was getting harder and harder, he said, to tell who was the villain. Which was why he liked Eddie – no question there. But when he saw demonstrators against the arms trade being arrested, he said . . . and then he went quiet. I'd never heard him say anything remotely disloyal about the police before.

It was Christmas Eve: a dingy, grey, mild Christmas Eve, a dull milky London winter day like any other. Looking at the trees, you'd find it hard to believe they had ever had leaves. Hard to imagine there really was a sun behind that great grey plain of cloud. Every window of every house was shut; people inside preparing for the glut of food, booze, squandered money and TV into which the celebration of the fleshly manifestation of god has descended. I do like Christmas – the private aspects. Family, candles, warmth in midwinter.

It's the public face that makes me boggle. The advertising, the crass consumption: OK, the commercialization.

We all went to the park – Harry, Lily, Adjoa and me. The little girls were jumping at Harry like puppies, and trying to pick his pockets because he'd told them he had a magic ant in there which could turn them blue or green or yellow. Then he picked them both up at the same time and put them in the dustbin. Shrieks of delight tore across the drab winter lawns; gaiety like summer. He promised to put them down the loo when we got home. They formed themselves into a small marching troop and stamped off in time yelling, 'Hurray for Harry! Hurray for Harry!' A little later I overheard Adjoa say to Lily, 'It would be rather an interesting experience, wouldn't it,' and Lily replying, 'Yes, it would – seeing all the poos.'

Later he was telling them the story of the Frog Prince and halfway through it became apparent that the frog in question was the wide-mouth frog. Their joy as they realized made them quiver.

'Now you finish the story,' he said.

'We don't know how this version ends,' they said.

'Nor do I,' he replied.

Some things are Dad things.

I didn't tell him about Chrissie, about going. I was happy just to be able to exchange so-far-so-good glances with him, and smile at the antics of children. I was happy, too, on Christmas Day, sitting with my parents, Harry and Lily, everything being all right, the unorthodox family getting used to itself with turkey and tact. I was pleased when Harry gave Lily a bicycle, pleased to be annoyed because it would be me having to lug it up and down stairs when the lift wasn't working, pleased because this was such a nice little everyday family thing to be annoyed by. Pleased with Mum and Dad's semi-detached courteous acceptance of Harry. There have been times when I have felt frustrated by their lack of involvement in my life, their seeming lack of concern; now I was happy that they respected what we were doing and didn't ask questions or tread, even lightly, on tender points. And Lily climbed on Harry all day, and he only told her to get off twice; and I was happy to keep my secrets wrapped up – even from myself – and sample this new normality.

*

Oliver wanted me to go and see him on Boxing Day, but I refused. I talked to him instead on the Saturday, having had a chance to think. I told him I wanted £300 a day plus expenses including childcare and insurance. I told him I would not spend more than a week away, and expected to be paid for preparation and for the time we had spent discussing it so far. He agreed too easily to everything and I wished I had made it more. I intended to do as little as possible, and come back as soon as possible. I also intended Oliver to believe that having capitulated to his blackmail I was indeed going to do my duty. He said he felt I was somebody who did not have it in her to do a job badly. I smiled.

Then I had to tell Lily.

She didn't like it.

'We were both going to be swallows,' she said. It took me a moment to realize what she was talking about: *The Happy Prince*. 'My friends are waiting for me at the Second Cataract . . .', but the second cataract is drowned now, along with so much else, under Lake Nasser, since the High Dam was built at Aswan. I hate that damn dam.

'Can I come?' she said, after a moment of quiet.

Bugger. I don't want her thinking god is going to send an angel to pick up her little corpse off the municipal dump, if she doesn't fly south. (This is what happens to the swallow – it ends up in the garden of paradise, but that's not the point.)

'Next time,' I said. I am not the kind of mother who says next time without meaning it. Lily knows that.

'You always go. You went last time,' she said. True, I had. I resolved to take her somewhere very nice, very soon. Oliver's money – call it three grand – could buy some nice time at the seaside. Maybe Sinai, Dahab perhaps . . . Alternatively I could pay off my overdraft.

'I know.'

'I want to see the yellow lions with eyes like green perils and the king of the mountains of the moon and the river horse on a couch among the bulrushes and the great green snake eating honeycakes and the pygmies at war with the butterflies,' she said, quoting Oscar Wilde, sort of.

'It's not entirely like that any more,' I said.

'I know,' she said. 'I still want to go.'

'Next time,' I said, and thanked myself for all the effort I had ever put into keeping my word to her, so that at moments like this I am trusted, and she accepts it.

'Who will look after me?' was the next question.

'Who would you like?' I answered. 'You could stay with Grandma and Grandpa, maybe, or we could see if you might go and stay with Brigid, or with Zeinab and the boys, or . . .' (I wasn't sure about this. But I had to suggest it) '. . . if you liked, you could maybe be with Harry. Your dad.'

Her face went scarlet.

'With Daddy?' she said.

'Yes,' I replied tentatively. Was this fabulous or terrible? She was blinking.

'Would he like that?' she said.

'Of course.'

'Does he know how to look after children?'

'You can tell him,' I suggested.

'And anyway, he is a daddy so he should,' she said. 'Oh Mum,' she said. 'Oh Mum.'

It was joy. It was incredulous joy. She hadn't thought that such a blessing could be hers. I wished Harry could have seen it.

'We'll talk to him about it,' I said. But in her mind it was already happening.

I had to talk to him anyway. Tell him about Oliver, about Chrissie. He was going to be pissed off.

*

'I thought you weren't going,' he said.

I told him what Oliver had said. How he had pulled the Ben Cooper line.

'Bastard,' said Harry.

'My sentiments,' I said. 'But Harry . . .' and this too had been on my mind '. . . say they track him down, then what? How can you arrest a dead man? Or do they somehow arrest du Berry instead? Or how could they gaol him? Or do they just keep on keeping tabs on him? It's becoming somehow surreal . . .'

'That's what I've been thinking about,' said Harry. 'And I suspect . . . well, I'll tell you. I don't know if I'm right. But you know it was a senior officer who arranged this whole scheme with Eddie, giving him the fake death and the new identity in exchange for shopping those Colombians, and that Oliver didn't want it?'

'Yes.'

'I suspect. I suspect . . . that Oliver is going to pull the plug on it, and the superior. Bring Eddie in, flush the whole thing out. Which'll just mean another couple of corrupt officers on eternal sick leave, but they'll be out of our hair, and that's got to be good. I think he's doing it for the right reasons.'

I didn't quite follow.

'The whole scheme was only a little bit official,' he said. 'I thought you knew that.'

I gulped.

'No.'

'The superior officer – I don't even know who it was – was not necessarily acting entirely legally when he did this. There are a lot of grey areas around this, and people don't like it. You remember there was a Yardie brought over from Jamaica to give information, and he murdered someone? While under police protection? Well, exactly. So perhaps Oliver wants to get Eddie back in and clear out the . . . the superior. If that's what he's doing it's extremely brave of him actually. And also it might be why he's cutting me out – he might be . . . um . . . protecting me from involvement, if it all goes wrong. No one likes to admit this stuff goes on, you know, and if this goes public it is going to be a fucking racket, I can tell you.'

I liked this idea. Being part of something that was going to clean up corruption and put Eddie in prison was much more appealing than being bullied and blackmailed into a wild-goose chase the only possible benefit of which would be to continue the protection of my enemy. And I liked there being an alternative to me being the reason why Harry's mentor was coldshouldering him. And I liked the idea of Oliver being a goodie, even if he was being an utter bastard to me. Why? Because it made me feel safer.

'I wish he'd told me,' I said.

'Yeah, I wish he'd told me,' said Harry. 'I may be completely wrong, anyway.'

'So what about Lily?'

'But honey, if you're going I've got to . . .'

'What?'

'You can't go alone. I know he's not there but – you can't.'

'I'm not. Chrissie Bates is coming.'

There was a silence.

'Now I'm lost,' he said.

'She knows he's alive.'

'Jesus fuck – how the—'

'The gravedigger told her.' Well he did. It wasn't a lie. 'She was up there getting slaughtered on the grave every day and the gravedigger joined her and told her – *in vino Veritas* – this little urn is empty. She hasn't had a drink for six weeks, she's pretty wobbly, and if I don't help her track Eddie's footprints through Cairo she's going to do it herself, thank you. Leaving, for example, now.'

'If it's a party booking I am definitely coming too,' he said.

'What about Lily?'

'She can stay with your parents.'

I was silent.

'Some schoolfriend,' he said.

I paused a moment. It wasn't that I didn't want Harry around on this . . . escapade. Harry is a good safe man to have by your side.

'Harry,' I said. 'Listen. She wants you. If you had seen her face when she asked for you. She's only known about you for three weeks. It would not be good to – I'm sorry the word is too strong but I can't think of another – abandon her. I mean, it would be incredibly good if you didn't. If you were able to be there now, when I'm not, it would be of huge benefit. It would prove things for her here and now which you will never get the same opportunity to prove. It would be unspeakably marvellous and you should do it. Take that paternity leave, and be with her. You will never regret it.'

'But I must go with you.'

'Welcome to parenthood, Harry. You can't always do what you want.'

'But . . .'

'Jesus, boy! When they talk about parental sacrifices they don't mean you only have to sacrifice things you don't mind about. They mean this. Difficult choices. And I know this is difficult from where you stand but from where I stand it's easy. You sacrifice your desire to protect me, for Lily's sake. And I sacrifice having your help and support, for Lily's sake. You appearing is one of the biggest things ever to have happened in her tiny little life and she does not need both of us buggering off a week later. Evidently, I *must* go. So you must stay. End of story. *Khalas*.'

'What?'

'What what?'

'What did you say?'

'Oh. *Khalas*. It's Arabic. Means finished. End of story.'

He was silent a moment. I imagined torch beams flicking into the various sections of his mind, looking for an alternative, a reason, a way out. But I was right.

'OK,' he said.

Also, in the back of *my* mind, if I flashed a torch in there, was the fact that I didn't want Harry around when I was seeing Sa'id.

EIGHT

Yalla, *let's go*

We left on New Year's Day. The plane was delayed three hours before we even took off from Heathrow. We were given meal vouchers to make up for this: we spent the vouchers on chocolate and the time in a Japanese restaurant, where I ordered two platters of sushi and two glasses of champagne before remembering that I couldn't eat raw fish and neither of us should be drinking. So Chrissie ate the sushi – and only the salmon and yellowfin and tuna, squandering squid because there was so much – and I drank the champagne. I can't imagine that champagne could possibly hurt my child. My Egyptian child. Well . . . I won't be bringing him (her) up as a Muslim. Ha ha! The gaiety with which I assume that. But I won't. Anyway Sa'id is not devout in that way. He drinks sometimes. He's half English. (No I'm not, he said, laughing, when I had mentioned it once. But he is.) And anyway he . . .

There we go, you see. I don't know what he is, or what

he is to be, to me. To us. But I am already doing things, deciding things. The seeping and tangling beginnings of potential confusions and assumptions are already seeping and tangling in. I am assuming things. I am beginning to see the great volume of work that one way or another this is going to involve.

I'd never been on expenses before. Well, not my own. In itself, it was fun.

The flight was long and dull, but at least it was direct. I listened to Qur'anic chanting on the headphones to counteract the champagne and to start the job of giving Nippyhead a balanced view of his bi-cultural heritage. Flicking the channels, I found Barry Manilow, some energetic German-sounding classical music, an opera I didn't know, something quite indecipherable which may have been in Japanese, and then – oh glorious joy – Umm Khalthoum singing '*Enta 'Omri*,' You Are My Life. Our song. I know – it's the whole of Egypt's song too. It's like having 'We'll Meet Again' for your song. Mixed with 'And Did Those Feet', 'Respect', 'Cwm Rhondda', 'You'll Never Walk Alone', Beethoven's Ninth and '*Che Gelida Manina*'. Famous, yes, but so fucking gorgeous. She is Aretha Franklin, Edith Piaf, Frank Sinatra, Puccini, Callas and Elvis, she is . . . oh lord. Patsy Cline and Gladys Knight, Victoria de los Angeles and Miriam Makeba. Do you know how Gladys Knight can sing 'uh huh'? How James Brown grunts? You know how Patsy has a teardrop in every note? You know how sometimes, just occasionally, even the best

American things seem a little bit facile and obvious; and you know how sometimes when you watch the Muslim demonstrators walk down Bayswater Road, striking their hearts with such fervour and you think, 'Oh, that faith, *such* faith, where do they get that . . .'? When Umm Khalthoum sings 'Ahh . . .' I have broken wine glasses I thought I was just holding in my hand listening to this woman sing 'ahh'. And when she starts in with the *Ya habibi* . . .

'*Enta 'Omri*' is about redemption through love. Is there any better subject? It is also a dream to dance to. It's one of the first Egyptian songs I ever knew, all those years ago, when I was a dancer, and when I ran away after breaking up with Harry, in my old life, before Lily. Whenever I hear it my backbone grows longer and my foot arches, my ribcage starts to move around on the stalk of my spine, I begin to sway and to feel a mild but definite yearning for the weight of a heavy sequined band around my hips.

Umm Khalthoum. The Nightingale of the Nile. The Star of the East. For thirty-seven years she broadcast live from the Qasr el-Nil cinema on the first Thursday of every month, and the whole Arab world tuned in. There's an Umm Khalthoum radio station in Cairo, every evening from five till ten. Her funeral was bigger than Nasser's: two million people on the streets of Cairo. Her mourners stole her body and carried it from Midan el-Tahrir, downtown, three miles to Midan el-Hussayn, wanting to bury her next to the head of Hussayn, the prophet's grandson.

There it was on channel 12. Our verse: *'Elli shuftu, elli shuftu, abl ma teshoufak enaya . . . enta 'omri.'* 'What I saw before my eyes saw you is a lost age — you are my life'. I haven't been listening to it lately. Sa'id sang it for me at dawn on the flyover down to al-Azhar, in the old city, not so long ago. It was one of the completely perfect moments of my life.

Next on the headphones came *'Fakkarunt'*, They Made Me Remember. 'They spoke to me again of you, reminded me, reminded me . . . They woke the fire of longing in my heart and in my eyes . . . they took me back to the past, with its ease, with its joys and its sweetness . . . and its pain and harshness, and I remembered how happy I was with you, and oh my soul I remembered how we came apart.'

Chrissie looked at me oddly and passed me a handkerchief. So I was crying and I hadn't noticed. I didn't think that boded well.

*

Cairo was chaos. Even I found it so. It wasn't that I had forgotten that it was Ramadan, I just hadn't remembered. We arrived in the late afternoon and everybody was hungry and ratty having fasted all day, and rushing around trying to get home in time for *Iftar*, desperate for the first cigarette since five that morning.

Chrissie took one look and wanted to go home. I said

I hoped she wasn't going to be wet. She said she hoped I wasn't going to be mean. We both burst out laughing and I dragged her through the crowd. She had no experience with which to make sense of a Third World airport. By the time I had baksheeshed us through the queues, sassed a couple of heavily armed teenagers masquerading as soldiers and let a pair of total strangers (aged about eight) carry off our baggage, she was almost gibbering.

'Don't worry,' I said, sitting her down in the back of Farag's cab, which I had rung him to ask for the night before. 'Everything's cool. Don't worry.' What I had forgotten, in my initial reluctance to come, was what I forget every time. That being here just gives me pleasure. I am happy to be here. Today I was happy in a new way: happy to have Egypt in my womb and in my life forever. It is mine and I am its. I looked out, as at a new land, through new eyes, fed by the Arab blood swapping nutrients with mine, inside me.

What I had noticed, in the airport, was that Chrissie and I were almost the only *khawagaat* there. (*Khawagaat? Gringo*, *obroni*, *gweiloh*. You know – paleface.) The usual crowds of slighty bemused looking Swiss/American/ Japanese/German tourists in shorts and cameras, with their guardian tourguides and dragomen, and their aircon coaches to ride around in, were just . . . not there. How Nadia and I used to laugh at them, in our independent pride. Oh let us avoid the Great God Tour-Group, we would say, with his High Priest Charabanc and his terrible hymns of Constant Comment through his spokesman Megaphone, and his hordes of devotees in their awful outfits. Let us find out the hours of their devotions (which was easy: any taxi driver would tell you when the coaches came in, and when they left) and avoid them. But they weren't here, and I knew why they weren't.

On the way into town the trees were garlanded with fairy lights, and the buildings festooned with little model mosques, made of paper and card and cloth and ribbons, lit up from within with a lightbulb. Like me, I thought. I'm lit up from within, by Nippyhead, happy to be here.

I'd made Oliver book me into the Oberoi out by the pyramids. At least I could see the pyramids over breakfast, and rest in relative elegant simplicity. I thought Chrissie would like it, too. Really I wanted to stay at the Marriott as it was years ago, before they filled it with shops and Mexican theme restaurants, and chopped the beautiful garden into barbecue corners and swimming pools. It used to be a lovely pile of nineteenth-century marble and *mashrabiyya* gorgeousness, with brass lamps and padding servants and doves to sing you to sleep. Khedive Ismail built it for Empress Eugénie, in 1869, for the opening of the Suez Canal. That's how gorgeous it was. In my previous life in Cairo, whenever I was feeling a bit five-star, I'd get Orlando from the Château and we'd go up there and drink champagne. But like so much, it's not the same any more.

I left Chrissie cooing at the bathroom fittings, and started to telephone. I had sorted out my plan of action, and it was very simple. I would track down the Turkish dancer who I had seen with Eddie in London, and again ten weeks or so ago, here, at the Semiramis. The girl whose announcement that I ('Madame Angelina! Not seen in Cairo since eight years!') was going to get up on stage and dance had made me lose my temper. The one who had been there the night in London when Eddie drugged me. His pet dancer. That one. And I would see if she was around, or where she'd gone, and what she knew. And I would find a useful nugget or two for Oliver, and then I would go up the river and see.

So I called the Semiramis (it's a hotel, named after the ancient queen of Babylon, noted for her beauty, power and licentiousness), and asked could I come and see the entertainments manager. I told them all the grand places I had danced before, and dropped a few names. I said I was not sure when I would be free but I would so like to meet him and introduce myself. I said of course they would not be engaging dancers during Ramadan. I would call tomorrow. Not before noon, they said. No problem. Fine. *Shukran, masalaamah*. Thank you, bye.

Back upstairs, Chrissie was abluting. She had more accoutrements for her toilette than a tranvestite. (I speak advisedly. I briefly shared a flat with one.) She was steaming up an aromatic storm in the bathroom and I sat on her bed, being amused by the labels. Amused by my amusement, she told me how during one excitable phase she had experimented with applying them randomly: 'Hair conditioner on my face, moisturizer in my armpits, leg balm on my hands, hand cream in my hair: it worked OK, except the facepack on my bikini line which I did just after waxing . . . foolish really. I thought I was going to take notes on it all and send them to the *laboratories* that these people go on about – you know, the manufacturers. Point out to them that it's not to do with beauty, it's a mental health issue. If I was the government I would tax beauty care and fashion advertisers, to subsidize the National Health, for paying for treatment for mad, anorexic, bulimic, alcoholic, depressed, paranoid women, most of whom would be just fine if they didn't have this – this *stuff* – imposed on them all the time.'

'So why do you use so much of it?' I wondered. She was slathering herself with an anti-pollution, free-radical-type facial treatment as we spoke.

'Just because I know what's wrong doesn't mean I can put it right,' she said. 'I'm susceptible, me. And this is a cheaper addiction than many.' She smiled at me, a woman at home with her weaknesses, strong among her debris, regrowth coming up fine. I distrusted it. It's too soon. She's funny and tough and she's got all kinds of phrases and maybe all kinds of genuine understanding, too, but it's too soon. Remembering her piling into my bathroom only a couple of months ago, how wild and disconnected she was, I found myself glad that we were in a pretty dry country. Wondering even whether we should perhaps be in a cheaper hotel, where it would be harder to get a drink, should she . . . fall under pressure. Decided no, there shouldn't be that much pressure – for her at least. Me, that was another matter. If I hadn't had a strong pregnancy-induced aversion to liquor of any kind, plus the basic Egyptian thing of not drinking . . . in many ways, a double Dutch courage would have done me fine.

There was an ancient tribe – the Lydians? The Lacedaemonians? – who would get formally drunk any time they had an important decision to make. Then the next day they would think about it again, sober. If by some mischance a decision was made sober, everybody would have to get drunk and agree on it again.

I made Chrissie come out with me, and we walked across to the pyramids, basking under the tiny sliver of silvery *hillel* moon. It's good luck to look at the new moon with someone you love. It's shining on Qurnah, this moon. Maybe he's looking at it.

The evening air seeming warm after London although it was not warm. Chrissie gasped quietly as the great tombs slid into view, silver and black in the silver and black night. It was the height of the tourist season, but no one was there, taking the southern air or wondering at the glory of the ancestors. A handful of restless tourist police stared at us, surprised, relieved, to see that there were some *khawagaat* at least willing to be here, to come out. I found it spooky, strange. The Egypt I knew was safe, familiar and friendly to me. Here another feeling lurked. Those policemen feared for me, feared for me in their land, and took it personally. It made me sad and we wandered back.

'Come on,' I said. Grabbing that mood and shaking it, I found a cab and took her back into town. I wanted to go down to the Old City and see what was going on. There'd be the Ramadan tables of mercy – free meals laid on by the prosperous for the poor – smells of meat and frankincense, festivities, holy and beautiful goings-on. Singing, sufis, a *Zikr,* crowds and music and the inversion of night and day . . . but we were tired and I could see that Chrissie might quite easily get overloaded by the sensation of this city, and have to lie down in a darkened room. Stendhal syndrome: English ladies get it in Florence, and Jerusalem. Collapse of stout party due to too much beauty. Or just too much. Of course this might be a good idea – keep her out of trouble. I considered, briefly, sabotaging her in some way, but a spiked drink (anyway, spiked with what?) seemed too cruel to a recovering alcoholic.

So we stopped at the river, and walked along by the Nile, gleaming beneath us, streaky and stripey with light shimmering on the black, and I thought, not for the first time, how many colours eau de Nil can be. I looked across to the Corniche on the further side and remembered Sa'id and I having our first – well, our first serious – moment of true difference of understanding. After I had lost my temper with the dancer, I had confronted Eddie – on my own – and had that fight, and Sa'id had understood for the first time how profoundly, immutably independent I was. Which he felt dishonoured him, because he was protecting me, and I had run off from within his protection. So I had unmanned him, which is a bad thing for a woman to do. I think that's what was going on. And that was the beginning of the end. We had pretended it was not, and gone to Luxor together for a few days of mutual self-deception.

This river is flowing down from his town. These lights recall the lights of Luxor, seen from the west bank. Gleaming, and undulating over the ripples of black water. Like stripes of coloured silk on a dancer's black dress, or beacons of hope in a dark future. Nebulous.

Back at the hotel, I attempted to fob her off by saying that I would ask my old friend Mr Hamadi, entertainments manager of the Semiramis, who knew all about everything in the nightclub world, if anyone of Eddie's description had been around.

'I'll come with you,' she said. As she would. Luckily I had thought of that, and a way round it. 'You can't, I'm afraid. Because it's Ramadan, men can only see women if they have a business reason to do so. Nothing social. And you wouldn't count as business . . . it would make it complicated.' Ridiculous, I know. Luckily she knows nothing of Islam.

'But it is business, in a way,' she went on.

'But we don't want to explain that to him,' I said. 'Do we? Do we want to explain all our business to him?'

She thought it was ridiculous, and said so. Coming all

this way, and then not even going . . . I told her she was welcome to go back, but if she wanted my help she must do it my way. And she was nervous in this foreign city, so in the end she accepted it. I was glad, and nervous, because I didn't want her having another of her flurries of sudden comprehension.

So we decided that the next morning I would either take her to the Egyptian Museum or leave her by the pool (though it was probably too cold for that) while I went to see Mr Hamadi.

Who when I walked into his office turned out to be the manager who had arrived in the aftermath of the Eddie/me/Hakim fight which had been the result of my losing my temper with the Turkish girl. How very fortunate that Chrissie was not with me. I didn't know if he recognized me.

He squinted at me as if he might. A small plump man, well looked after. I imagined a wife who fussed over him and fed him tiny pastries.

'*Saba al'khir,* Mr Hamadi.' Good morning, I said, holding out my hand and behaving not at all like a woman who wears a veil and gets in a fight and is taken off in disgrace by her cross husband.

'Madame,' he said. 'How are you?' The formalities rolled on. Then, 'So, you danced in Cairo before, some years ago? You are the same Angelina?'

'Yes,' I said.

'Ahh . . .' He looked worried. 'Excuse me. Perhaps I

make a mistake, you know. But were you here before? Not so long ago?' Which way to go?

'I was,' I said, because I liked his eyes. Round, brown, resourceful, patient.

He sat down, and motioned me to sit.

'Excuse me. This thing. When Hafla says you will dance, and then outside, with Monsieur du Berry. Do you mind that I ask?'

Well, it wasn't what I had in mind, but if I answered when he asked perhaps he would be more inclined to answer when I asked. I gestured that I didn't mind at all.

'So, you are friend of Sa'id el Araby? Or . . . wife?' But he said it very doubtfully.

'Friend,' I said. 'You know him?'

'All the stone for my hotel bathrooms, all my ashtrays, some bowls, some lights. Not this hotel. Other one. He's a good man, you know.' He paused. 'But he said that day wife.'

It took me a moment to work out. Why would he mind whether or not I was married to Sa'id? Then I saw that he didn't, he was upset because Sa'id may have lied to him about it.

'Mr Hamadi,' I said. 'I was Sa'id's guest, and when Monsieur du Berry attacked me Sa'id was embarrassed. He just wanted to take me away, and to have no fuss. It was simpler, with the officials, if I was his wife. I am sorry.'

He thought about this for a moment.

'I am angry too,' he said. 'You were my guest, *hena*, in

my hotel.' *Hena*, right here, in his hotel. Such a Cairene usage, such a Cairene (*masri,* as they say in Cairo) sentiment. Pride and hospitality combined.

'Thank you,' I said. 'You are kind.'

I noted that he said angry, not embarrassed. Though of course the two are closely related.

There was another silence.

'So, why did Monsieur du Berry attack you?' he said finally. A little nervously.

It's a long story, I didn't say. I smiled, and shrugged, and shook my head, and tried to look stoical.

'Where is he now?' I asked, as if in passing.

'I heard he left. I hope so. I do not like men to attack in the hotel, you know. Someone said he left to Damasc, you know, Syria. Why, you want him?'

'I want to know where he is, so that I don't go there,' I said, a little jocular, a little rueful.

He smiled. 'Ahh,' he said. *Masri* that he is. That Cairo 'ahh' that punctuates every conversation.

'Maybe Hafla knows. You want to talk to Hafla?'

'Maybe. Is she here?'

'Now no. She went to Upper Egypt for Ramadan. Maybe Luxor, maybe Aswan. I find out, I can tell you. Everything very quiet now, Ramadan, and . . .' Here he fell silent. I knew he was talking – or not talking – about Hatshepsut. About what happened. That thing for which there doesn't seem to be a name, because it is too terrible, in every way, from every direction.

'I am so sorry,' I said.

He was silent.

'Is business very bad?'

'Here not so much – is more business, government. But for the other hotels, for the taximen and so on. There is nothing. Nobody. They were not Egyptian, the men who made this. Not Egyptian.' He was emphatic. Angry. 'It will get better. *Insha'Allah. Insha'Allah.*'

There is a sadness and a desperation about this. A whole country held to ransom, a people who live with routine poverty knocked about by fanatics who claim the love of God. Just more children with not enough to eat because there's no one to hire their dad's felucca. And if the feeling is this strong in Cairo, how will it be in Luxor?

'*Malesh,*' he said. Never mind. 'So, I will find where Hafla stays and I will telephone to you. Where do you stay?'

I told him, and we exchanged courtesies, and he sent his respects to Sa'id, which reminded me of all the other things I had to say to Sa'id, and as I came down the marble steps and left the hotel trepidation took me by the hand and promised not to leave me.

*

Chrissie was in a state of bliss back at the Oberoi, having discovered the hotel masseur (from the Arabic: *masaha*, massage). Luxury became her. (Luxury, from the Arabic: *el qusur*, the palaces – like Luxor.) I was glad – I couldn't continue indefinitely to juggle what she knew and what

she couldn't know with what I was trying to get done.
And I couldn't rely for long on her nerves about being in
a new country. Any minute now some of Egypt's trailing
charms would hook her, and she'd be off getting into trouble
– or creating it.

Mr Hamadi rang within the hour. Hafla was staying
outside Luxor, at the house of a German couple. She was
giving lessons to the wife, and would be there until the
end of Ramadan. He gave me the number. I considered
ringing. I was going to, but when I picked up the phone I
found myself asking instead for the hotel travel agent, and
booking us on the next flight to Luxor. I was on the same
landmass as my beloved, and the pull was too strong.

The flights were cut right back because there were no
tourists, but there was one tomorrow.

But he is not my beloved.

*

When Osiris was murdered for the second time by his
jealous brother Set, Set chopped him into pieces and scattered the bits up and down the Nile. Isis, Osiris's sister
and wife, searched Egypt looking for them, and found
them, and brought him back to life, and conceived Horus,
the hawk-headed god. This is curious because, in several
versions, she found all of him except his penis, which may
or may not have been eaten by a Nile crab. But in several
other versions she conceived Horus after the first murder.
Some even concede that Osiris may have been alive when

he fathered his child. I have seen family similarities in this: Harry being blind drunk when Janie conceived Lily, Isis's sister Nephthys seducing Osiris and bearing a child, Anubis, which she then gave to Isis to bring up . . . I do identify in various ways with this ancient sacred soap opera.

Isis found Osiris's head at Abydos, where Seti built one of the most beautiful of temples. The carvings there are the sweetest: hardly any smiting of enemies, as is the pharaonic norm, just people in fine muslin skirts (you can see their legs through the cloth, even though it's all carved in stone) laying their hands tenderly on each others' shoulders, patting each other, and offering each other eggs, and incense, and the *ankh*, the breath of life. Lying in my gorgeous bed that night, cool and clean on cotton sheets, it occured to me that Chrissie and I were a pair of northern Isises, searching for their men up and down the Nile. Hers previously dead, and now come back to life. Mine . . . I didn't know. Alive, but alive to me? Or maybe as dead as only the past can be. And Horus already conceived. I dreamt of hawks over the desert. (From the Arabic, *dsrt*. Meaning desert. Actually it's not, it's from the Latin, desertus, left waste. An early example of Orientalism: a western/ northern judgment on a southern/eastern thing. There's nothing left or wasted about the desert to the Bedouin. Or there wasn't, for thousands of years. I'm thinking of Palestine, Israel, land rights – don't let me start.)

On the plane I gave Chrissie a simple account of Sa'id. That he lived there, and that I would need to spend some time with him. She seemed to assume that he was some hunky illiterate camel-driver (she asked me, god forgive her, whether he was *clean*, whether I was, you know, *worried*. God knows I've never met a cleaner man in my life), and was keen for a full girly chat about the situation. I wasn't.

NINE

The palaces

We arrived at dusk, just as the blue sky turns to stripes of green and gold, pink and amber, and the golden desert turns indigo. As we came out into the car park, the warmth of the south slipping up my skirt and round the back of my neck, there was a muffled explosion, and Chrissie looked at me, eyes wild. I calmed her: no terrorism, just the cannon announcing *Iftar*. All around men pulled out cigarettes and started smoking like – well, like Egyptians.

It was the colour of the palm trees that rattled my heart. The silvery turquoise in the last rays of the departed sun, gleaming in the dusk. Sa'id's eyes are that colour.

Well they are. I didn't design him.

Abu was waiting for us. Abu was the man who had first taken Nadia and me to Abu Sa'id's shop, ten years ago. He had taken us to Dendara, to Abydos, to wherever we wanted. He was calm and quiet and clever. He had two children now, *alhamdulilleh*. My driver in Luxor. Last time

I hadn't seen him. I'd been a guest, why would I need a driver? (I'd had Sa'id, Hakim and the old dusty powder-blue Mercedes with its box of cassettes: Khaled, Umm Khalthoum, Edith Piaf and Satie. Sa'id had driven like a shark through the dark nights, gliding down wide, empty roads, sand blowing up from the desert. The road seems nearer at night, rising up on the strange dips and looms of rock desert. Dogs roaming about. People only put on their headlamps once they've seen you.)

Along the roadside into town, men were cooking over small fires, and starting to eat, beckoning to Abu to join them. He wouldn't stop: he had brought a small paper package of dates, and offered them. Melt-in-the-mouth sweetness. Chrissie looked horrified. I think it was the Arabic writing on the newspaper they were wrapped in that did it for her. But I was pleased with her; she was being quiet, and doing as she was told.

By the time we arrived at the Old Winter Palace the sun was gone and it was cold. The Corniche was so beautiful with its extra Ramadan fairy lights, twining the tree trunks so densely, arranged on the trunks in shapes of flowers and leaves and arabesques. The tall palms had as many rings as the giraffe-necked women of Borneo, pink and yellow, green and blue, powered by the cheap electricity which is the gift of the High Dam. The new moon lay on its back to the east. A few late *calèches* waited for custom, their ponies' heads hanging low, their fancy bridles and the carriages' ornamented hoods muted in the dusk.

The drivers sat with their feet up, smoking and calling half-heartedly to the even fewer passers-by. And there was the Nile, dim and immutable. Beyond it, between me and the gold and green remnant stripes of sunset, on the other side, was the sand and scrabble village of Qurnah, among the tombs, and there, over the traffic lights, past the colossi of Memnon, go right at the fork towards the Valley of the Kings and up and it's on the left, is the *El Amr el Misri* (Full Moon of Egypt) Alabaster Factory, and there on one of the divans in the courtyard, eating bread and salty cheese and green and crimson pickles from communal plates on huge tin trays, or perhaps in his empty marble-floored sitting room above the showroom, maybe doing the accounts, maybe reading, or half watching an absurd soap called *The Woman of Garden City* (for which Hakim has a weakness) was the father of my child.

Habibti, el falous mish naga, el hob quel naga! My darling, money is nothing, love is everything . . . the ubiquitous Arab soap opera line. How we laughed about that. Worked out equivalents in every language. *Senza di te, dentro di me,* without you inside me, a line which appears in 90 per cent of Italian pop songs. Why, cry, die, goodbye. *Ne me quitte pas. Recuerda me un poco tan lejos estoy.* All around the world. He'd tried to explain the plot to me: 'This one went to Switzerland for an operation on her leg. That one is her husband, they have a son. She wants to divorce him but he is a doctor so of course she can't. This one is mad. His mother is the one we saw in the hospital, weeping at his brother's bed – the soldier. He wants to marry the one with the eyes. The sad one. She has a daughter of seven, her husband stole her; she loves her very much. These are her friends, they are helping her to get the girl back. These ones are cousins, married to each other. They come from such a good family, they could only marry each other.' This very drily.

Chrissie was halfway up the Winter Palace's semi-circular staircase, exclaiming at the fact of carpets on steps outside. I looked up after her, about to disappear through the revolving doors, and I looked across the river. I cannot be here and not be with him.

I stood like an idiot in the drive. Ilexes and palms around me, fairy lights flashing.

'One moment, Chrissie!' I called up to her. She leant over the balustrade and I called up: 'Check us in! I won't be a moment.' And I ran down, and across the Corniche, through the flowerbeds on the middle, across the pavement, down the steps to the bank, past the half-built (or is it ruined?) floating house that used to be (or will be, one day) a restaurant, and out on to a long rusty pontoon, feluccas sleeping quietly to one side, curiously dark flotels moored beyond, and I climbed over a boat or two at the end, and found myself on board I think it was *Bob Marley,* one of the long iron boats with cushioned seats, and a tented shade, and a little engine, that takes people across, or up and down. A little Nile barge.

No one was around. I sat on its metal deck at the gap

in the rail amidships, and hung my legs over the edge, among the orange-painted bicycle tyres that served as buffers. The mist rose around me, smelling of cool, depth and darkness. The rivery smell, like a Lorelei's embrace. It was cold. Looking out I thought I could make out the warm orange spark of a small fire at the public ferry landing place way over on the other side. The mass of the mountains was just visible, black against the sky. He is there, on the other side, between the river and the mountains. I stared and stared, though I could see nothing. I just stared, and breathed the river mist smell until my lungs were cold within my ribcage.

A soft voice at my shoulder.

'Madame,' it said. 'You want go other side?'

I was silent. I realized my body was swaying, almost as if I was going to tip myself in, and swim. Perhaps the boat boy feared I would.

'*Bokra*,' I said. Tomorrow.

And I let him help me up, and I climbed back over the boats, and walked back down the pontoon, and across the bank, and up the steps, and across the Corniche, and in to the drive, and up the movie-star stairs, out of Egyptian Egypt and into the light and warm and welcoming foyer of the beautiful Old Winter Palace, bastion of reformed colonialism, with its absurd crimson Venetian chandelier, under which Chrissie was sitting with a plump and clean man of about fifty, in a blazer, who was trying to persuade her into the bar. She was resisting admirably, in a courteous way. A hotel factotum had a cool eye on the situation, as did Byron, *en orientale*, from a portrait on the pale wall. You are never alone.

I wanted to go out into the night, to find the country, connect with it, love it. Find a felafal stand or a coffee house, and feel the dust, the rattle and smooch of the language, the smell of hot oil and fresh mint. I wanted to absorb and be absorbed. But I didn't. I stayed inside the hotel, in *khawaga* paradise, because I thought that I couldn't go back into the country until I had found the man.

*

I had taken a room on the Nile automatically because it was the most expensive, and now I wished I hadn't. I lay between my cool sheets, flat and useless, unsleeping, unthinking, just a receptacle for a mass of unknowingness. At times during the night I found myself holding on to my bones: my collar bones, the strong girdle of my pelvis. Just to know their strength and solidity. Towards dawn, in the darkest of the night, I heard a distant *musahourati*, the public waker calling the time for *sahour*, the last meal before *Imsaak*, the resumption of the fast. *Ramadan karim, Ramadan karim*, he sang, beating his drum, way over yonder. Ramadan is generous, Ramadan is sweet. Then descended a calm: all over town there is eating, washing, smoking. (If you are truly devout, you do not even swallow your own spit during daylight in Ramadan. You don't shout, you don't have sex.) And of course there is some sleeping through. But however devout you are or are not, Ramadan is around you, affecting you with its sounds and its smells, its intensity. Even if your own senses are not heightened by the physical fast, everyone else's are. Everybody does it, knows it, feels it. Everybody can be meditative, calm, harmonious. Everyone can renounce a little, according to their own way.

I called room service and ordered a coffee. *Ahwa turky, ariha.* A little sweet, not too much. Like you, he'd said. The room service person said, 'Madame make Ramadan? You want before *Imsaak?*' No, I said. No, Or maybe I do. I just . . . I just. I didn't know. I want.

I'm not a Muslim and have never wanted to be − well, not often, and never for a very good reason. Only for the architecture, really: the domes, the courtyards, the fountains and the minarets. And the play of light and shade around and through them. And for the glorious communality of the call to prayer. Across the nation, across the Arab and Muslim world, five times a day, in time with the rising and setting of the sun, in unison, in stripes of unison across the time zones from Casablanca to Indonesia, the voices and the words rolling out over deserts and cities and jungles and slums, reminding every Muslim that God is great. And I like Ramadan. Ramadan is not a Vic and Bob TV special, a pile of shopping, Santa at Selfridges. It's a living thing.

Twenty minutes after *Imsaak* came the dawn muezzin: *Allah u Akbar*, God is great, it is better to pray than to sleep. How well I knew this sound from coming home from work in Cairo, night after night, years ago. As the muezzins started, one by one across the town, I was standing on the crumbly sand-coloured balcony, cold as can be, looking out, thinking: today I am going to change your life. Today, you become a father. This is the last morning you wake as a free young man. And you don't know.

Ramadan is not, of course, the ideal time to land this on a man.

Dawn emerged from night as if the muezzin's voice were calling up the colours, summoning the changes, choreographing. How the colours shift. Before dawn the red mountains are invisible, smudges of indigo that you know are there, inchoate against the indigo sky. Then floating peaks in the darkness, visible only because there is the most delicate of pale mists, looking Japanese, showing them up – but not quite. Then the sky behind the mountain suffuses crimson – why? This is west, and dawn. And stage by stage the dance of light continues, shifting in a different pattern of crimson and gold, lilac and the palest silvery blue, as it has every morning since Ramses, since chaos, since the sacred mound first rose out of nothing at Heliopolis and Atum masturbated and cast his seed on the world to make it live, before it settles into this particular day's regular horizontal stripes of full daylight: blue sky, red desert mountains, verdant valley, mud bank, blue Nile. Stripes pierced only by the graceful silver fronds of palms, minarets, and the painted wood and canvas of the masts and lateen sails of the feluccas. Arching.

The morning chorus was beginning. Chattering. Banging. Working. The day begins.

I was so sad. So scared. I didn't know what he would say. Jesus, I didn't even know what I would say.

*

Chrissie came in at about eight thirty, to find me back in bed, lying like some mummy, immobilized for three thousand years.

'Sleep well?' she said. 'No sickness?'

'No,' I said, to the latter not the former, but that was OK because she didn't distinguish.

'Are you coming down for breakfast?' she asked. (I had a moment's overconsciousness of the word: break fast. As if we ever had a fast to break. As if it counted.) 'Only that guy, Helmut, last night – he's taking some friends down to the Karnak Temples this morning, and said would we like to go? They're going to go quite early before it gets hot – I don't know, what do you think? If you had plans, or . . . Would you like to come?'

It's a curious thing to ponder one of the wonders of the world, a complex of temples as glorious as anything in the world, and not want to go there, even though it's only half an hour down the road. But I didn't want to go.

'You go,' I said. 'It's fabulous. Huge. Look out for the Temple of Khonsu, and the little Temple of Opet just by it. She's a hippopotamus. Osiris's mother. It may be closed but you can peer in through the rusty wire. Say a prayer for me.'

'Will you be OK on your own?' she asked.

'Yes,' I smiled at her. I was pleased to be asked. 'Take a jacket,' I said, 'it's not that warm. And remember to give baksheesh. Just do. It's part of the system, like tipping the waitress.'

'I used to be a waitress,' she said, with that look which women who used to be waitresses get when they recall the indignities they suffered. Then, 'Gosh I must run, he said he'd come by at quarter to nine.'

I was glad. Kept her out of trouble, left me free.

*

How do I do this? Do I ring him? Do I turn up?

*

I couldn't do it. I was incapable. I lay in bed all day. I slept a little. I marked the muezzins, the movement of the sun, the shifting of the breeze, the murmuring of the voices. Somebody came and asked for laundry. Somebody came to make the bed and change the towels. Somebody came to bring sweet basil and a sprig of jasmine in a little vase. Somebody came to turn down the bed and leave a small chocolate. I put it in my bag for Lily, and thought it would squash. I dreamt of Lily. I dreamt I had lost my voice, and Horus was sitting on my shoulder in his guise of a hawk, talking for me. I dreamt that a flock of egrets had come from Nubia to visit me, and were saying to me *witighiree, witighiree, sabah al'khir, witighiree,* in low southern voices. More, more, good morning, more. But *witighiree* is not

Arabic, it's —I can't remember the name of the language. A Nubian language. The one not drowned with Nubia under Lake Nasser, beyond the High Dam. I hate that fucking lake too. A huge spooky, wet, murderous thing. Look down through the wide blank surface and remember what lay below, what lies there still. Nubia, its people, its villages, its life. And Abu Simbel and Philae, how can you dig them up and transport them out of the way of the artificial water that is rising up around them, and just put them somewhere else, and expect them to sit happily there? How could the shape and topography of the huge surrounding stone and desert, the *sine qua non* of this whole land, not mean something to the nature of these temples, carved out of the self-same stone and desert? How could their position within their own substance mean nothing? How could the gods not be offended?

I dreamt I was with Sa'id in the City of the Dead in Cairo and I had told him, and he had said, '*Ya habibi*', in Umm Khalthoum's voice, and when I woke that time I was so happy because it was all going to be all right. Then I realized it was a dream.

Every now and then I stood up and I looked out. The streets were quiet, almost empty. No tourists. Vendors, felucca men, *calèche* drivers, not bothering to hustle after the custom that was not there. I had never seen it like this: everything available, and no one to take it up. This town has been *bit*, I thought. Smacked in the belly and winded. It's reeling. I looked over to the other side. The sphinx mountain, riddled with the tombs of dead kings, just gazed away to the west, unconcerned with me, with the emptiness, with the men who live on its flank. I murmured *el-Fatha*, the opening verses of the Qur'an, in a kind of useless, yearning way. But mostly I lay, with my hands across my belly.

Tomorrow, I said. *Bokra.*

Chrissie came back around five. They'd had such fun. They'd gone to Karnak, then they'd gone on a felucca, they'd seen kingfishers and had a lovely meal moored on a sort of sandbank island, she was so glad I'd told her to take a jacket. Tomorrow they were going to Abydos and Dendara, taking a car, they'd invited her – and me, of course. These temples were just fantastic. And so empty! It's an ill wind – of course everybody was talking about it, and it's a dreadful thing, but a marvellous opportunity too, in a way, to see things in peace – Gosh what a selfish outlook. Awful for these poor people. But the carving! And the styles are so different, in London you just think they all look the same, but when you see them in the flesh, so to speak, the variety is marvellous – though of course eighteen dynasties is a bloody long time, and you wouldn't expect European art to stand still for thousands of years, would you? She was glittery with pleasure. I suspected it wasn't just the art, I suspected she had been flirted with, that Egypt had nibbled her earlobe with its kind manners and warm breezes, and that maybe a handsome policeman had made eyes at her and called her ballerina. She was exhausted from so much fun, and went for a rest before dinner.

I'd like to go to Dendara. Hathor smiles down on you from the capitals of six times six great columns, four goddess faces – time- and vandal-ravaged as they are – to each capital, and you can climb up on the roof and listen to the call to prayer rolling away across the empty red desert, and think how much older are the gods on whose roof you stand than the prophet whose call you listen to. But I am not here as a lady traveller.

How amazed the lady travellers would be to see Luxor now. Lucie Duff-Gordon, a Victorian invalid sent south for her health and abandoned here, used to live in a little house built on top of the Luxor temple. Everything was still awash with desert then, and when Thomas Cook started to bring a few visitors sailing up the Nile in the big, graceful *dahabeyyas* it was tremendously shocking and rather vulgar. Later, rich visitors might be invited to a grand dinner served on the top of a pylon: white table cloths, silver cutlery, Princess Marta Bibescu in evening dress, with gloves; servants gliding about with dinner among the sphinxes and the colossi, Ramses looking on, no doubt in approval, extravagant and grandiose as he was. The full moon sailing above; candles scarcely flickering in the light air, scent of mimosa on the Nile breeze. The whole regiment of lady travellers visited Luxor: cheerful Mrs Colonel Elwood, knowledgeable Annie Quibell, Constance Sitwell, bossy Florence Nightingale, Harriet Martineau to whom everything was interesting, clever Amelia B. Edwards, sensible Sophia Poole. And all of them regretted, yearned, in their various ways, in their different times, the loss of something which they perceived had been here before, but was now gone.

They knew nothing of what we can regret in our time – the dams, the modern hotels (the Old Winter Palace itself was an architectural outrage), the concrete embankments and the bridge. Bit by bit the beauty, the glory of the ancients, is falling apart. It is said . . . I don't know about this. It is said that the changes in the water table following the building of the dams and the consequent control of the Nile's annual inundation have caused changes to the chemical composition of the ground; certain salts are creeping in where there were none before. The tombs and the temples, it is said, will not survive. They are being eaten, it is said, from within, by the very land of which they have been part for thousands of years.

*

I was a little surprised that people were being allowed to go out into the countryside. Normally in moments of tension freedom of movement is the first casualty and, even at the best of times, foreigners going through the countryside had to go as part of a convoy, police escorted, and be ticked off at every road block: ten Swiss and an Italian in a minibus, two English ladies in a cab. A memory came back to me: Abu driving Nadia and me back from – yes – Dendara, and there was a fat American lady who wanted to go via Naqquada, because that's where you'll find the biggest dovecot you ever saw, with room for twenty-five thousand pigeons. (A note on pigeons: a tenth-century Fatimid Caliph of Cairo, Al-Aziz, when he wanted cherries, would have his vizier send a message by pigeon to Lebanon; the governor of Lebanon would send, by return, flocks of doves with cherries tied to their feet, which would arrive in time for breakfast.) Naqquada and its pigeon castle is on one bank, the approved and protected route is on the other. Security is expensive: you take the approved route. She – fat lady from the land of the free, based in Cairo and thinking she knew everything – wanted to take the Naqquada route. The policeman of our convoy said she couldn't. She insisted. Her thinner friend giggled and encouraged her. The police made courteous radio calls, enquired of their regional chief. No, she may not go, we must all go home. She stepped out of her cab like a deposed queen and began to walk, determined fat hips swaying along the dusty road, palms swaying way above her fat head. (I'm not being fattist here, I'm being . . . anti-imperialist.) The little policeman begged her to get back in the car: 'You're just a small man with a big gun, think it makes you important,' she said. Her friend continued to giggle, excited by the discourtesy and the possibility of conflict. 'How you gonna stop me,' she said. 'Shoot me? So shoot me! Shoot a tourist in the back, why doncha!' The big handsome policeman tried to joke with her. 'Look at them playing soldiers,' she said, her scorn so out of place it made me wince. The rest of us — two more cars of foreigners, and a lost Japanese man hitching a lift with a jeep — waited, and crawled snailpace along behind her, and waited, and crawled, along the banks of the eau-de-Nil Nile. The small policeman walked alongside her, cracking jokes, paying compliments, and pleading. Nadia and I kept our sunglasses on and smoked and listened to Abu's tapes of Hakim, singing along. The handsome policeman came to apologize to us, bending down to look through the car window, leaning his weight on his two hands on the roof and peering in.

'The big lady makes a big problem,' he said. He had been on duty since five. It would be getting dark in an hour or so.

I told him that she was getting lots of attention from young men, and was probably terribly happy. He laughed, and sent a policeboy on to the stand at the junction to order tea for all of us. *Shay koshari*. With fresh mint, in glasses, sweet as can be.

Abu told us that a few months before people had been killed here, and that if the policemen didn't get us back to Luxor before dark they would be in big trouble. Abu's son's name was Ramadan.

The big lady was telling the little policeman that he might as well paint a great big target on her and an arrow saying 'tourist, shoot here'. The little one turned away, ramrod stiff with self-control. Her skinny friend came and told us what she had said, inviting us to laugh along at her wit and free-spirited cuteness. We declined. Some camels loped by in the distance.

Later, when we were finally able to drive off, and were about to do so, the handsome policeman hesitated as he walked past our car. Pausing a few feet off, and looking at me, he kissed the pad of his thumb, a firm and giving kiss, then stepped up to the car and pressed it, swiped it slowly down the glass of my window. I am more than accustomed to unsolicited attentions from men, but this thumb print placed, and then swooping slowly down, and the glass pane between me and it, at arm's length, has stayed in my mind.

We got home late. She did see the pigeon castle. No one was shot – that time. I don't know what happened to the policemen. I mentioned it to Abu Sa'id and he shrugged. Later I ran into the little one; when I asked him about it he shrugged too. I was not to be bothered by it. Strict instructions.

This was years before the Hatshepsut . . . massacre.

So that time it was all all right, but as we know now it isn't always.

Lying in bed.

I should ring Hafla. I didn't want to.

After my day of dreaming I felt somehow prepared and purified for talking to Sa'id.

I pictured them sitting on the green-cushioned divans in the courtyard, the workmen with their dusty feet clearing up the alabaster debris, putting away the iron hooks and files and tools of the trade. Bread and pickles and salty white cheese laid out on the wide tin trays, on the mats, waiting for the cannon. Remembered how he had broken off bread, scooped up meat and fed me from his own hand.

Abu Sa'id is my child's grandfather. Sarah its grandmother. Oh lord.

There it goes.

Silence falls on the town. On the whole of Egypt, on the Arab world.

Twenty minutes to eat. Ten minutes for tea and a cigarette.

I called at ten to six.

TEN

Ya habibi, *oh my darling*

'Hello?'

'Hello . . . Is Sa'id there?'

'Mr Sa'id? OK. You wait. Who is?'

It was one of the boys; one of the workshop boys who helps in the house too. Sa'id is such a pasha at home. Doesn't even change the TV channel himself.

Pasha is an everyday greeting up here. *'Ya besha!'* the young men call to each other. Hey, my Prince!

'Angeline,' I said. Be still my beating heart. Fuck it, it's not a joke.

'Angelina?' he said. Surprise. Amazement even. 'Angelina!'

The phone was out of his hand in a second.

'Hello?'

His voice.

His voice, in my ear, by electricity or however. His voice.

'Hello,' I said.

Silence.

It was quite a long silence.

'Where are you?' he said.

'Here.'

An intake of breath. His breath. Sweet Jesus, breathe it out into me.

'Where?'

'Winter Palace.'

Silence.

'Ten minutes,' he said.

He didn't sound in the least bit pleased.

I thought I might die.

*

Ten minutes wasn't long enough for him to come round by the new bridge at Dayyaba. He'd come by boat. I shaved my legs – why? What was I thinking? – and brushed my hair and stuck a note for Chrissie under her door (Gone out, back soon. Eat without me if I'm not – love) and wrapped a cloth around me. Not his big white-on-white Luxori paisley one. I had it with me. But it wouldn't be right. It was that cloth he wrapped round me in the bazaar when Nippyhead was conceived, and it was that cloth that he wrapped round me for the journey when I left him. Too damn symbolic.

Then I went out to the landing place, and waited.

When he stepped off the boat at the river end of the pontoon I was leaning against the wall under the Corniche. I remembered, suddenly, when I had first seen him in

London. I'd been out, and he was waiting for me outside the door of my flat. I'd walked the length of the red-brick London balcony, with him leaning against the wall, watching me. I'd tried to prevent my hips from swaying. He had lounged, as I walked before his gaze.

Now he walked before mine, picking his way among ropes and gangplanks, in harmony with them because harmony is his constant companion.

He stopped a few paces in front of me.

Elegant, is what he is. Too fucking elegant for words. He stands, and it is just exactly as a man should stand. He is the height a man should be. His shoulders cannot help the perfection of the angle at which they hang. His nose is straight and his mouth is pharaonic, this I know, and can see. His eyes are pale, and not happy.

He has a cloth – the colour of dark lapis – folded and wrapped around his head and neck in the Luxori way, against the evening chill, which makes his demeanour more Arab and his face darker. (More Arab than what? Darker than what? Than I remember?)

I remembered wishing, when I first met him, that his voice would be squeaky, so that I would have at least half a chance of not falling completely in love with him. But it wasn't. And I did. Did I?

Then why did I leave him?

'Where do you want to go?' he said. In his far-from-squeaky voice. You never normally notice how incredibly intimate this thing speech is. This sound comes out from within them, inside their body, borne on their breath, and enters into your ear, conveying their thoughts right inside you.

'Other side,' I said, without thinking.

He shook his head, and started walking up to the road.

Well, OK. His father would be there, Mariam, Hakim. Maybe I wouldn't be so welcome. Maybe it wouldn't be so simple. But I didn't mean his house necessarily. Just . . . I like the other side. The emptiness of the dust and the tombs after the conviviality and bustle of the East Bank. It's like crossing the Styx.

I followed him. He started walking up the Corniche. I hated it, it reminded me of the Night of the First Disagreement, in Cairo. I never want to see him walking away from me under trees and streetlights beside the river. Never never.

'Grand hotel, or coffee shop? Your choice,' he said. Still in this cold way.

'Why are you so angry with me?' I asked. I couldn't bear it.

He broke into a grin. For a moment I thought – but it wasn't his beautiful grin. It was a coyote's grin. It was horrid.

'You left me,' he said. And turned and started walking again.

I stood where I was and called out, 'You didn't stop me going.'

'You're an Englishwoman, you do what you like,' he called back.

'Where are you going?'

He stopped immediately.

'Oh, sorry. Wherever. Where would you like?' He was not being polite. He was being sarcastic. I had never seen this. He was being 'oh, you're in charge, of course.'

We could go to the bar at the hotel, I thought, because I couldn't think of anywhere else. The bar is beautiful, in a colonial kind of way. Black marble, brass rails, vodka martinis made very badly, pianist playing 'Michelle', 'Send in the Clowns' and 'Für Elise'. Prints of Nubia and *mashrabiyya* screens from Fatimid Cairo. Of course it's a ridiculous place to go with a Luxori – like two Londoners going on the Round London Sightseeing Tour on the open-topped bus.

'You want me to go to a bar in Ramadan?' he said.

'Since when were you so bloody religious?' I asked. Which was rude of me.

He just stared at me.

At that moment a child of about eight came up, carrying a plastic bucket with roses in it. He wanted to sell one to Sa'id, presumably for him to give to me. I winced at his unfortunate timing. For a moment Sa'id looked at him as one might at a mosquito, then again, on recognizing humanity. He spoke to the boy in swift, soft Luxori Arabic, much gentler than the hard Cairene, with soft Js instead of hard Gs, and a slinkier rhythm. Greeted him by name.

'Were you at school today?'

'*Aiwa,*' said the boy. Yes.

'Have you finished your schoolwork?'

'*La-ah.*' No.

Sa'id looked at the flowers, and the boy shrugged. Even I could tell that he could not go home until he had sold them all. Which he could not possibly do, as there were no tourists.

Sa'id looked at me and I turned away. This was not to do with me. He turned his back to me, told the boy to remember him to his father, and bought the whole lot. I turned back the moment he had turned away, in order to see.

It floored me, to tell the truth. His doing it, his slight embarrassment at me seeing him do it, his slight pride too, that the embarrassment wouldn't stop him doing what he had to do. Some men, you'd know they only did it to impress the girl – but even that wouldn't matter, because the child would still get home at a decent hour – yes, and his dad would probably send him out with another bucket . . . though not, I think, when Sa'id had sent his greetings, by name . . . ah but most of this was probably in my head. He was just doing what he did. I was just floored by it.

He rejoined me.

Does he love me? Will he soften at the sight of me as I do at him?

No.

'Come on, we'll go to my flat,' he said, and turned to stride on, the roses in his hand with their heads hanging down.

'What flat?'

'My flat on this side.'

I didn't know he had a flat on this side.

'Where I take the tourist girls to fuck them,' he called, over his shoulder, striding ahead.

Now that was bad. That was really unpleasant for the obvious reasons and because we had talked about this, about how the economic situation makes it hard for people to marry until later than is sexually comfortable, about the hungry tourist women and the desperate Egyptian men, the middle-aged ladies, the camel boys, who is exploiting who, and how, and why, and does it matter, and to whom . . . what the Luxori women think of it, about the politics and economics of it, about Flaubert on his travels and his interlude with the dancer, Kutchuk Hanem, comparing nineteenth- and twentieth-century sexual tourism, and sentimental exoticism, about all kinds of things. We had never had to mention that that was entirely what we were not.

So his saying that was, exactly, like a slap in the face. Just like they say. Splat. Ow.

So I stopped walking for a moment, to think.

And I thought: my god he must be hurt. To punish so strong.

Which means there's hope.

Hang on – hope of what?

Of something good coming of this, I told myself. Still not defining what I meant by 'something good'.

He is being cruel, but he is not dishonest. He knows I know he doesn't fuck tourist girls.

So I skipped up behind him, and kept up with him though he kept a few paces between us as we crossed some streets and went in from the river. And I skipped through the dusty ill-fitting iron gate when he unlocked it, under the ratty dusty hibiscus, and skipped up the dusty concrete stairs behind him, and into a darkened flat where no one had been for months.

'Well, clearly you haven't fucked any recently,' I said, peering into the gloom, and tripping over an empty Baraka bottle (the Evian of Egypt, though the very name – it means blessing – tells you that clean water in a bottle is something other here than it is in Europe). The flat stank of old ashtrays, and the rugs had fallen off the sofas.

'Only one,' he said. 'She didn't come here.'

'Watch it,' I said. But this was a comforting logic. The nastier he is, the more it means he loves me.

A sick logic too. Along the lines of the old song: he hit me, and it felt like a kiss. But we're in a moment of crisis here. It's not as if this is a horrible old rut into which we've fallen.

He was picking about in the dark interior of the flat.

'Why don't you turn the light on?' I said.

He coughed. There was a thick layer of dust, and lots more empty bottles on a coffee table. Not alcohol though. I think he hadn't realized how horrid it was, and now didn't want to illuminate it.

'Anyway,' he said. 'There haven't been any tourists.'

'Don't use that, Sa'id,' I said.

'I don't tell you what to do, so don't tell me what to do,' he said.

I didn't like it. No one likes punishment. Well, I didn't like it.

'Can you stop it now please?' I asked.

'No,' he said. But perhaps he said it a little sadly.

'Please,' I said.

A moment's silence.

'I don't think I can,' he said.

'Do you want to?'

Silence.

'Do I want to what?' he said, turning to look at me.

Gradations of subtleties of cruelty. He knows what I mean. He knows I know he knows. He is withholding understanding, our sweetest gift.

'To stop being unkind,' I said.

He took out a cigarette, and lit it, then holding it between his teeth he picked up a bottle of Baraka and took the lid off and passed it to me.

'Sit down,' he said. 'Have a drink, and tell me what you've come here for.'

I sat, and I had a drink, but I didn't tell him what I was here for. Some specialized part of me needed us to be friendly before I told him. I wasn't going to use the child as a bridge. I was sad already: the first my foetus had heard of his father's voice was in anger and pain.

Did I say his? Or hers. Aisha el Araby Gower. Nippyhead Horus Gower el Araby. Or Omar: Life. Or Tariq: the Path. Amira: Princess. Noor: light. Shagaratt ad Durr: Tree of Pearls. Such beautiful names.

There's Sa'id, across from me, leaning back on the sofa, wary, angry. A bit of streetlight shone in between the curtains, enough to show the furrow in his brow. He looks older. I want him to be older because he is too young for me. Yes, and he hates me. Never mind.

'The British police want to find Eddie,' I said, finally.

'Him again!' he said.

I hate this. This sarcasm and coldness. This is so unlike anything I have ever seen in him before. I said nothing.

'Have they lost him?' he said. 'How foolish.'

I said nothing.

'And, what, so you've come to get him? Or to warn him off?' he said.

'No,' I said, defensively, crossly. 'I mean – he's not here, so, that's just the point. I'm just meant to be finding out where he might have gone. That dancer is here, from the Semiramis, and . . .' And. There is something else.

'He *is* here,' said Sa'id.

I stared at him.

'He's here in Luxor.'

And stared. Shock moving through me, and doubling back, and doubling back.

He watched me, observing my shock.

'Didn't you know?'

'All God's angels couldn't drag me to where he was,' I whispered, beginning to shake. 'Sa'id, I must leave. Help me.'

His face was changing shape in the darkness.

'You want my help,' he said, still leaning back, still unmoving.

'Yes,' I said.

'Do you want my love?' he asked.

'Yes,' I said. Why not say it, when it's true?

'Do you want to marry me and have my babies?' he said, with a smile beginning to curl one side of his mouth.

And I started to laugh. I remember thinking, 'I must remember to answer that,' and then, funnily enough, I fainted.

*

I woke up in another room, on a dusty bed. It was cold – deep night. Sa'id was asleep beside me. One of his black curls was wrapped around my little finger, my hand lying on the pillow. And there was his face. Harsh, even in sleep. Not as it should be.

That's what Sa'id means. The Happy One.

Last week Harry, on my sofa, chaste but loved. This week Sa'id. My men putting me to bed at moments of stress.

*

A while later I was half woken by hands on my flesh, an arm under my waist and a gentle lifting of my hips. But it didn't come. I felt him, sensed him. Smelt him, the clean leather smell. Breathed his breath, and lay immobile. I could feel his mouth not kissing me. Hear him listening to my breath, making sure I was all right. But it didn't come.

*

I woke again to the sound of the *musahourati*, awaking the faithful to another day of discretion and harmony, of moderation and of prayer, of the non-indulgence of appetites. Of renunciation. Ramadan is not the time to bring a crisis of love on to a Muslim head. Not the time for a passionate reunion, for a terrified flight, *hejira* from a foreign gangster, for an announcement of pregnancy, the fruits of fornication with a *khawageyya*. No mind that he's half English, that there's no devout bruise on his forehead. Even if you don't pray, you pray during Ramadan. Ramadan is generous, Ramadan is sweet, Ramadan is universal, cultural as well as religious. And this was Ramadan after a great sin, a great tragedy, which took place almost on his doorstep.

He wasn't there. Just a dusty dark empty room, with a too-big, white, curly Louis Farouk wardrobe and a tiled floor. I was rolled in a blanket, from which I disentangled myself. I walked through to the living room, feet bare, head low. He was lying on his back on the sofa, his eyes open. He looked up and we just gazed at each other for a while.

'Are you all right?' he said.

I nodded.

'You fainted.'

I shrugged.

'Then you woke, then you went to sleep.'

I went and sat. On the other sofa. Pulling a tangled-up rug straight as I did so. I couldn't sit near him.

'It's not very nice, your flat,' I said.

'No.' He cast his eye around. 'I got it when I thought I wanted somewhere to be away from my family. Then I found that I didn't really want to be away from them at all. So it is neglected.'

I was glad. Neglected meant no girls.

There were some dishes on the coffee table, beside the roses wilting where he had dumped them. Seventeen roses. The remains of some meat, bread and tomatoes. The turtle-shaped bread of Luxor: fat body, four little blobs like feet. 'Are you fasting?' I asked.

'Of course,' he said. Of course.

He glanced at the dishes and said: 'I got food last night, while you were asleep. Are you hungry?'

'No.'

I drank some water though. I would have smoked. But not on my child.

'I have to leave,' I said, gently.

'Again, so soon,' he murmured, and then he saw my face, and he looked at it in the pre-dawn light, and he moved from the path he had been on.

'I am angry with you,' he said. 'Do you want to know why?'

I knew why. Because of leaving, because of coming back, because of Eddie.

'Yes,' I said, and pulled the rug around me.

'I thought you were here to play with your dangerous toy. To play those games again, where somebody makes you do what you know is wrong and dangerous, but you let them make you. Some people go for Russian roulette; you go for Eddie. I thought you were here to do that again. Do you know why that made me so angry?'

'You know I do,' I said.

'What we knew has been broken,' he said. 'Tell me why.' He picked up one of the dying roses, and looked at it absently. I remembered a night in a club on the Pyramids road, when I danced and he sang, and we cast rose petals and jasmine over each other as Cairenes do in approbation of a performance,

'Don't test me,' I said. 'It's all still there. I know, you know, we understand.'

He smiled at me.

'It's broken,' he said.

'So mend it. Bind it up and let it heal. It's still here.'

He turned away, putting down the rose, looked at his watch, and pulled himself up to take a long drink of water. 'Ten minutes till *Imsaak,*' he said. Darkness was dissolving around us. I didn't want it to go, because it gave us an intimacy. Being here was intimate. The day might make us separate. It might bring abstinence.

'Do you want to get some food?' I asked.

'Too late,' he said. Then: 'It was my gift to you: set you free from him. Even if you didn't want me, I wanted you to have that gift. To keep my gift.'

'I have kept it,' I said. 'I didn't know he was here. I came because . . . yes, because they made me. Because of Lily – they were going to drag it all up, all these things, and make life difficult, maybe take her away . . .' My voice went odd as I said those words. I know he heard it. He might want to pretend that we don't understand one another but that doesn't make it true. He can't help understanding me. It's in his nature. 'I let them make me because . . .' and here I remembered that I cannot lie to this man, or keep truth from him. And I was filled with joy. 'Because I wanted to come here. To see you.'

And he smiled, and it was nearer to right.

'Why not just come?' he said.

'Because I left,' I said. 'Scared,' I said.

'Oh,' he murmured.

I went over and sat on the floor beside his feet, my back to the sofa. He didn't react. We sat there a long time. I fell asleep again.

I woke turned towards him with a stiff neck and my arm over his thigh, my cheek pressed against his jeans. He was lying back again, still looking at the ceiling. Still, or again. I pretended I hadn't woken and tried not to stroke my cheek against him, embrace his leg. Impossible. I was about to start kissing his denim seam and taking his belt between my teeth, so I pulled myself away.

And why? What would have happened if I had?

Oh, he might have rejected me. And anyway it was past *Imsaak*. Sex during Ramadan is one of those questions – but if you're going to do it at all you certainly do it at night. And with your spouse.

I sat up, and ran my hands through my own hair instead, and rubbed my own face.

Part of me felt that I could stay in this dingy flat forever. But something in me that was not lovelorn reminded me that where Eddie was, I could not ever be.

'I have to leave,' I said again.

Sa'id scrunched his face and shook his head. It hadn't been what you might call a good night's sleep.

Oh shit. Chrissie.

She's going to Abydos today.

I must ring her. Tell her we're leaving. And ring Oliver. And sign off.

'Sa'id, *habibi*,' I whispered.

'Yes,' he said.

I hadn't realized how much I like the fact that he says yes. Not yeah, yes.

'I must leave. If he is here I must go.'

He opened one eye.

'There is . . . there is some stuff,' I said.

'Isn't there always,' he said, and unfurled himself from

the sofa, and went to wash his face. The tap didn't work; I heard it clattering and burping. He came back in with a bottle of Baraka and passed it to me.

'What?' he said. Stretching.

Does he want to know? To help? Can I involve him again?

'I'm not here alone,' I said. 'My friend – it's Eddie's wife. Chrissie.'

'The mad woman?'

'We all would be, married to him.'

'Oh!' he said. 'Is she redeemed?'

'On the way. Maybe. But – are you awake?'

'Yes,' he said.

Well, I will offer him the chance, the chance he took for himself last time without even asking.

'She found out he's not dead,' I said. 'She wants to find him – don't look at me like that, she said she'd come anyway. If I hadn't let her come she would've just – oh, caused mayhem, I don't know. I don't know what she might have done. Marauded around Cairo getting me into trouble. I thought she would be safer close to me. Safer for her and for me. She's OK but she's flakey.' Every now and then a word is not of his vocabulary. I was sure he'd have learned flakey from me now, because there is some flakiness around me. 'Damaged. Given to random acts of idiocy. Not to be trusted, but not because she is bad.'

'*Marousha?*' he said.

'Yes, sure.'

He smiled at me. Pure smile.

'I must take her too. It's not part of the plan that she should be near him. I only let her come because everyone said he wasn't in Egypt. They said he left. They said he'd gone to Damascus.'

'He's been here a week.'

'Didn't you know the police wanted him?'

'I only knew they wanted me and Hakim,' he said mildly.

I apologized. A lot. I said I wanted to apologize to Abu Sa'id and Madame Amina and everybody.

'How is Hakim?' I asked.

'Better. Chastened by our experiences, and sent to Aswan to be sensible. I am pleased with him.'

'What happened with the police?'

'All the police here are my friends. We went to school together, did national service together. There's a bunch of them coming for *Iftar*. I am a good citizen, they are not going to give trouble to my family because of some *khawaga* who changes nationality every month.'

'Do they know he's here?'

'I don't know.'

I thought for a bit.

'The British police really want him. They said he'd left the country, in the confusion after . . .'

He looked at me. 'You can say it,' he said.

I didn't want to say it.

'I wept for you,' I said.

'For the tourists, surely.'

'Stop it,' I said. Almost shouted. Then more gently: 'Stop it. I'm here. I can't help it. I'm sorry. I'm sorry to bring this on you in Ramadan. I wanted to see you. Stop sulking.' We looked straight at each other for a moment before I continued. 'Please,' I said more gently still. 'Please be your good self.'

He just looked at me, but his eyes were full of something.

'In the British papers they kept saying fifty-eight tourists killed, not mentioning the Egyptians,' I said. 'I wept for everybody.'

He lowered his eyes, and looked up at me again.

'Sorry,' he said.

He gave me his hand for a moment. I had such an urge to put it to my belly. Resisted it.

'Were you . . .' I said.

'At the *fabrique*. We heard the gunfire, went up there. I'll tell you about it. Some day.' He left the room again, and I heard him in the kitchen, murmuring. *Bismillah el rahman el rahim, el rahman el rahim, el rahman el rahim.* The merciful, the merciful, the merciful.

'So where is your friend?' he said on his return.

'At the hotel. She said she was going to Abydos today with these people she met . . .'

'Abydos! If it's going, the convoy leaves at eight – we should get her before she goes.'

It was seven forty-five.

'Do you have a phone here?'

He gave me a look, and took out the mobile. Call one

told us that the convoy was going today, yes at eight. Call two said Chrissie had already left the hotel.

Shit.

'Let's get down there, get her out before it leaves,' he said.

Ya habibi. He's going to do it.

ELEVEN

Convoy

For a moment outside the flat the Merc sat in its cold dusty parking place and refused to start, to the amusement of a couple of small children. Sa'id called them over and made them laugh some more, and gave them a bit of money, and then it started.

'God's blessings are not always so immediate,' he murmured. I just curled up in the front seat with my cloth pulled round me and felt happy, safe and beautiful, in this crappy old car, in this crappy parking lot, unwashed and unbrushed, on this cold morning, among these dusty concrete houses, all sprouting thick twists of steel wire for when the owners' children got married and they needed to build an extra storey for the newly-weds to live in. I leant forward to rattle through the tapes, and found Khaled, and put it on, and hummed. There's a line in one song where he sings the word *sa'id*, I don't know what he's singing about because it's an Algerian Arabic that's beyond me. But the word is there. I smooched with myself a little, next to the man. Happy as a hummingbird. Just because I was with him, and he hadn't chucked me out, saying you're on your own, *habibi*.

It was our — joke. He'd call me *habibi*, for a man, rather than *habibti*, for a woman. It was a little personal/political thing, for when I was being all independent. It was a *kind* of joke.

When we got to the street from which the convoy leaves, the sun was a quarter of the way up the sky, and the cold and strangeness of the night and the dawn had left us. The river was swift and limpid as we came back down the Corniche, the fairy lights off. The town looked even more unlike itself in daylight. Empty. No fat bums in inappropriate shorts; no small boys shouting, 'Welcome to Alaska! Lovely Jubbly!' and equivalent jokes in French, Italian, Spanish, Japanese and German. No business, basically. Deserted.

The convoy was small. Four cars, to be precise, a minibus and a police jeep. Usually what they do is stick a policeman in the leading car as well. The minibus had diving stickers all over it and was presumably on its way to the Red Sea, to Hurghada.

More significantly, it was setting off. We were able to slot in just in front of the police van drawing up the rear. Sa'id waved cheerily to the driver and mouthed something as he cut in front. It seemed to work. Great thing, community.

Actually, it's not just community, it's him. He knows

everyone here. Knows everything that's going on. *Ga'dda* is what he is. A big man. A good old boy. Strong in his community. I've seen it in the way the children know him, and in the respectful way he treats his elders, in his giving money and receiving blessings. In that thing with the roses. When I was here before he was always having to talk to people who wanted him to solve things for them. So young and yet so wise. Half the town seemed to be his *ezwah*, his — oh, how to explain it? *Ezwah* is a . . . a belonging thing. A homeboy thing. A favour bank, a loyalty, a protection. Your *ezwah* will look out for you among strangers, help you in time of need, see you all right if he can, know that you will do the same for him. 'Long as I got a biscuit, you got half' is Texan for *ezwah*. Harry, perhaps, is the nearest I have to *ezwah*.

I think that Sa'id does it on purpose, despite — no, because of — going to Paris, and being half English. It's his stake. For all he is so educated, multilingual and cosmopolitan, when he is home he wants to be the heart of his home.

But now we were going somewhere. Which hadn't been the plan. Not that I minded. It meant that he couldn't walk out on me.

Sa'id said never mind, we could jump out at Qus or Qift, and speak to her then, see if we could hang out with the road block, and come back with the next convoy. I said I was sorry, he must have had things he was meant to be doing that day. I made some kind of facile and idiotic suggestions about how he should be getting back to work.

He ignored them, and he drove, and I hummed. The little carts rattled along on the hard shoulder, young lads bounced along perched on the coccyxes of their trotting donkeys, and the layers of countryside glided by: sky, mountain, valley, mud, Nile, mud, valley, mountain, sky. Like puppet-show scenery: sliding by at different speeds, depending on the distance. I felt what I feel every half hour: why don't I live here? Warmth seeped into the car, and we opened the windows a little. The smell was green: sugar cane coming to ripeness. Greenness burst out of the pink earth; shades of beautiful rolling green covered the plain as fertility crowded in upon itself. Burgeoning puddles of green and puddles of irrigation. Tight rows of vegetables in beautiful little packed vegetable gardens served by tiny irrigation channels, leading from bigger canals, leading from the illustrious Nile. Years ago someone said to me: 'Is it true in your country your Nile falls from the sky?' We passed villages. 'Hello! Hello!' shout the children, barefoot, smiley, girls in pink and yellow, boys in *gallabeyas*. Lots of them had shiny rucksacks on their backs: going to school. God bless them all.

I'm not going anywhere without Lily ever again. Anywhere Lily can't go, I'm not interested in. Except to bed with Sa'id. And maybe to the cinema. If there was a Fellini season at the Riverside Studio . . . I was off on a *La Strada* fantasy, with me as the girl and Sa'id as the lover, chanting under my breath, '*E arrivato – Zampano!*' which for some reason is my favourite line from the film, the tender uselessness of her as she tries to do what he wants, beating the drum and announcing his show, and fails so sweetly, so completely . . . and wondering when Lily will be old enough to enjoy Fellini.

I wanted to put my hand over his on the gearstick. I wanted to gaze at him. I wanted, I wanted. But I can't. He hasn't taken me back. He has only not thrown me out. It's not the same thing.

I hadn't really noticed how it had crept up on me. When I had thought, last night, that there was hope, I hadn't identified it. But now, god, it was simple. Him, me, together, anywhere, somehow, no matter what. Please. All I wanted was for him to love me. I think perhaps it was Nippyhead, calling out to his own flesh through the medium of mine, calling to his own blood out there in the world, pulling the father to the mother. Or my pregnant hormones, designed to want *that* man, so that he would guard the cave door and fight off the mastodons when I go into labour. Some ancient animal thing.

I also felt a bit foolish that during these moments of emotional delicacy and potential danger, it was lust that rippled through me. My breasts were growing by the minute, my backbone melting. My arms ached for him – they did! And as for my belly, his child, all that – all I can say is I felt it, physically. I felt magnetic and immoveable. If he didn't make love to me within twelve hours then Hathor, Mother Nature and the lot of them would give up and go home.

And why wouldn't I make love to him, earth goddess that I was?

Because, and because. Something to do with dignity. His, rather than mine.

'How is your mother?' I asked. Meaning, how are you about her, tell me your heart, confide in me, talk to me on this unexpected journey, come back to me.

'We've been talking a lot,' he said. 'E-mailing. She is coming back here, soon. She wants me to go to her university and do a research project there. With her. She wants to make up for lost time. Send me to school, boss me around.'

'What's the project?' I said. Buying time. Sa'id in Brighton. Oh.

'On *gam'iyyaat*,' he said.

I'd heard the word, but couldn't place it.

'The financial networks in the communities,' he said. 'The savings associations. A form of micro-banking. Do you know about them?' I didn't, really.

He was just starting to tell me when I noticed something.

What I noticed was that in the shifting of the order of the cars in the traffic, we had ended up behind a blue and white Luxor taxi which had, in the back seat, Chrissie. Beside her was a man. I noticed that it wasn't the German from the Winter Palace. It was her husband.

I closed my eyes, pulled my scarf up around my head and interrupted him, said, 'I think we should fall back one car.'

'We can't,' said Sa'id. 'It's the police van behind us.'

'Can we let someone overtake?'

'If they want to, of course.'

'Don't you want to know why?'

'I know why. I've been trying to. For the same reason.'

'Why didn't you say?' I squeaked.

'Would it have helped? Made any difference?'

No. Of course not.

'This is bizarre,' I said. 'This is utterly bizarre. What the fuck is going on?'

'I don't know,' he said. 'Can you explain to me a bit please? Just, what you know?'

'I'm beginning to think I don't know anything,' I said. 'Excuse me.' A very sedate panic was making me try to climb into the back seat. Fear had taken me. I just did not want to be sitting in a car behind Eddie. I wanted, as I had pointed out, to be as far from him as possible. Into the back seat seemed like a move in the right direction, albeit a small and useless one. Only it wasn't possible.

'What are you doing?' he said.

'Trying to escape.'

'Fil mish mish,' he murmured. In the time of the apricots. Like, you should be so lucky. Because the apricots are not in season for very long.

I sat back, and endeavoured to go into total purdah, there and then, under my scarf. It was hot, but it was better.

'Open the window, would you?'

He did.

'Has he noticed us?' I asked.

'No. Nor has she. They are what you might call engrossed.'

'Are they now.' An easy comment, to cover. Why cover? Who would be convinced? Not me. Not Sa'id.

Where the hell had she found him?

'It's a small town,' said Sa'id, reading my mind as he is apt to do.

'It's bizarre. Where are the Germans? And why the hell is Eddie tooling about the countryside with a police escort, when the British police have been told he's left the country?'

Sa'id laughed.

'What?'

'Well, probably, because of baksheesh, *habibti*.'

Sometimes I feel very young.

'But this is serious, this is Interpol and stuff.'

'And money is serious. And these boys are very busy with their duties here now. And the big boys are very caught up with the terrorism, and very pissed off with the English because of your asylum laws. They think London is crawling with *el Jama'at el Islamiyya*. They may be right. Why should they give up your villain when you won't give up ours? Specially if your villain is paying well.'

'Fucker,' I murmured, admiringly. About Eddie, or the notion, or police morals, or something.

Then: 'What do we do now?'

'We can only drive. If the convoy stops . . . I don't know. It's about twenty minutes to Qus. Let's think of something.'

I could only think of hiding in the back seat. He agreed that was a good idea, but mentioned also that it wouldn't get us very far.

'But–'

There was still a big problem.

'What the hell is she doing with him?'

'Reuniting, by the look of it.'

'I don't understand! I don't understand!'

'Have a cigarette and mull it over,' he suggested. He seemed so deliciously unperturbed.

'I stopped smoking,' I said.

'Good.'

We sat in silence for about three minutes. I could have told him then. I've stopped smoking, and this is why. I should have. It would have saved trouble later on.

'If she's reuniting,' I said, 'she won't want to be taken away.'

'Probably not. If that is what she's doing.'

'So there's no point our being here. We should just turn round when we can, and I'll just leave, and . . .' The other ramifications of my words twinkled quietly in a row along the dashboard like a taxi driver's fairy lights. 'Just leave' was not really an available phrase in my current vocabulary. 'I'll rephrase that,' I said, shooting him a kind look. 'You will just take me somewhere, and . . .' And I'll just tell you about your child and then we'll go and live happily ever after. Somewhere. Somehow.

He was smiling again.

Five minutes later I found I was humming 'There's a place for us' from *West Side Story*, and he was laughing out loud, his beautiful teeth gleaming.

Ten minutes after that he said, 'But you don't want to leave her here with him.'

'No,' I said. Funny thing, loyalty. How it pops up.

I didn't think she was reuniting. Remembered all that she had said on the subject. But I didn't know.

We were coming in to Qus: more donkeys, more children. A donkey cart was waiting at a petrol pump. No one was sticking the hose up the donkey's bum. Or in its ear. Then a man brought it a pile of greenery – clover, something like that. It stood there by the pump and ate.

'I think,' I said, 'that I haven't a clue what's going on. I know that she's a flake. A vulnerable person. She gave up drinking, only a few weeks ago.' Do they have alcoholism in Egypt? Can this restrained, when it comes to the booze, nation (and man) understand the seriousness and precariousness of her position? 'And she said she hates him. She's hated him a long time. And been in love with him too. God, I wonder what he said when he saw her . . .'

'Don't,' said Sa'id. 'Don't wonder.'

'And I feel,' I said, continuing on, because he was right, 'that no good can come of this. And I brought her.'

A wobbly bicycle cut us up, and then ran into a goat. Sa'id swerved around the ensuing small fracas. Fracas must be an Arabic word.

'So we follow, at a polite distance?'

'Are you happy to do that?'

After a while he said, 'Till we think of something better.'

*

We didn't think of anything better. We followed them all the way to Abydos. At Qus, at Qft, at Qena and at Dendara they stayed in their car, so we had to stay in ours, because we didn't know when they might get out, and because we hoped and believed that they had not seen us. At least soon after Qena a truck came in between us and them, and I stopped having to worry quite so virulently about whether or not Eddie would recognize Sa'id, who he had met twice, after all, if in very strange circumstances both times. Luckily he is the kind of man to whom all Arabs would look the same, or at least stereotypical: the handsome ones and the fat ones. The ones in scarves and *gallabeyas* or the ones in pleat-fronted trousers and patterned shirts. But then Sa'id had held a knife to his throat, back in the beige marble halls of the Nile Hilton in Cairo all of seven weeks ago, and maybe you would always recognize someone who did that to you. And – whoops, my belly didn't like this memory at all – Eddie had kissed him. In that bare-throated sacrificial moment. His way of claiming something back from a situation where he was losing. Sa'id had been about to walk out with the money and the girl. So Eddie just – oh fuck him. Fuck Eddie and what he does, how he plays.

Hafla staying with Germans. German guy in the bar. Small town. And Hafla is often where Eddie is.

We still hadn't seen the Germans or Hafla. If they were all on the trip together surely someone would have got out of the car and strolled over to the other car for a chat, on one of these long boring stops? If they're not here, does that make a difference? I didn't know. My head was getting hot.

'Does your phone do international?' I asked.

'Yes,' he said, and passed it.

Bugger. I didn't know Oliver's number. My address book was at the hotel. 222 1234, for Scotland Yard? Or is that London Transport Enquiries? Or should I dial 0044 171 999, and ask to be put through?

It was 8.45. 10.45 in London.

I rang Harry.

'Makins,' he said.

'Harry . . .'

'Where are you?' Alert, not worried. These calm men. I am less calm when they are around to be calm.

'Outside Qena.' Oh lord, that means nothing to him. 'In the countryside. Near Luxor.'

'What's going on? Why's the line so bad?'

'I'm on a mobile . . .' I swear at any given moment 60 per cent of all conversations on mobile phones are people telling other people that they're on a mobile.

'Why? What's . . .'

It was curious to hear him. So incredibly out of place. It was slightly cruel, too. Cruel of me to be speaking to him when he was powerless. In a way.

'Can you put me through to Oliver?' I said.

'No, I can't. Talk to me. What's happening?'

'Eddie's here, Harry. He's in Luxor, has been for a week. I have a number back at the hotel, where he's staying. He's not staying at the hotel, sorry – he's staying with some Germans, and I have their number. Or if he's not staying there he's in contact with them. The Turkish girl is there. But I can't get you the number yet. I'll call you later . . .'

'Do you know where the place is?'

I asked Sa'id. He said, yes, by the river, north end of town on the way out, past the airport road. I repeated this to Harry.

'Fat lot of good,' he said. 'Where will you be?'

'I don't know,' I said, uselessly. Then with more energy: 'Listen, Harry, Chrissie has hooked up with him . . .'

He started talking.

'Wait – no, he hasn't seen me. I don't know if he knows I'm here. I don't know if she told him, I haven't spoken to her . . . yes, . . .' I couldn't make it clear without explaining my immediate situation, and I didn't want to, because I didn't want him worried, because what good would that do?

'Look,' I said, 'I'll be leaving as soon as I can, I'm not staying, don't worry. There's not that many flights in and out at the moment, or trains, but I'll go straight back to Cairo, and get the flight the day after tomorrow. I just don't want to leave Chri . . .' He began to speak very quickly and angrily. 'Yes, I know,' I said. 'But I can't leave her.'

'Yes, you can,' he said. 'Just get out. Leave. You've done your bit.'

We went silent: a humming through the distance, electronic nothing over the miles.

Suddenly I missed him, sudden and hard. I looked across at Sa'id, driving, inscrutable. Sa'id. Harry. I was biting my lip with a deeper fear than my fear of Eddie.

'How's Lily?' I asked. Oh lord, my other world.

'Exactly,' he said. 'She's fine, she's at school, she misses you but we're doing OK. She's looking forward to you getting back.' He put a little emphasis on it. Just a little.

'Don't tell her I rang. Just tell her I love her.'

'OK,' he said. 'Give me the mobile number — who's is it?'

'Sa'id's,' I said.

'Can't he drive you to Cairo?'

'It's not that simple.'

'Bollocks, either he can or he can't.'

'Foreigners can't just roam around the country, Harry, there are security measures . . .'

'Well, get on to the Luxor police and arrange some then. Or Sa'id can. Or I will.'

'Harry—'

'What?'

'I will leave as soon as I can.'

'Let me talk to Sa'id,' he replied.

What, and let the pair of you decide what I should do? I don't think so.

I said nothing.

'Angel!'

'Please. Harry. I'm not an idiot.' Another empty electronic pause.

'Have you told him yet?'

'No.'

More emptiness.

Sa'id just drove. Looking nothing, saying nothing, following.

'Not the time to talk, I suppose.'

'No,' I said, and disliked the deception involved even in that.

I asked Sa'id the number, and repeated it for Harry to stop his line of enquiry. Sa'id gave me a sideways glance.

'I'll be in touch,' Harry said. 'Don't do anything. Let me know when and how you'll be leaving. Make it soon. Like, immediately. And don't do anything. Please.'

We rang off, and I put my head on the dashboard.

Sa'id said: 'He's right, you know.'

'Of course he is,' I said. 'But I'm not leaving her with Eddie.'

We drove in silence.

'How is Lily?' he said, after a while.

'He is her father,' I said.

'Oh,' he said. Nothing more.

Before long we were drawing into the car park down the hill from the Temple of Seti at Abydos, where Isis found Osiris's head. Years ago I lost a pearl earring here, and left it, happily, as an offering. This is the sweetest temple. Full of love. All the carvings giving each other lemons, and flower pots, and life. Osiris sat on Isis's lap. Apart, that is, from the strange sunken temple round the back, the Osireion. It's low, like a stone-lined tank, open to the sky, made of slabs of Aswan granite, grey and massy as the dawn of time, and surrounded by lone and unlevel mounds of desert. The water table has risen since it was built (because of the High Dam) and it stands ankle deep in green immobile water, with feather-topped reeds growing, an occasional wind-ripple moving across the surface, the stone pavement visible beneath the shallow water. Darkened doorways lead off the main chamber, but you can't go there; it is chained off. Last time I was there there was nothing but some chattering sparrows and a lone grey-black catfish gliding along the floor to give it semblance of life. It is a very dim and mysterious place.

One of the policemen came over to have a chat with Sa'id. I curled up like a good reticent woman, and left them to it. The plastic interior was hot now that we had stopped, and the dust swirled up by our arrival began to settle. Chrissie and Eddie's car had drawn up to the left of us: to go to the entrance of the temple they wouldn't walk past us. I tried to peer past Sa'id's head and the leaning policeman's bum to see if they were getting out yet.

There they go. Walking over to the gateway, and up towards the ramp. Eddie tall and elegant, in typical well-dressed European gentleman clothes. Including a panama hat. You could almost see the copy of Herodotus in his baggy linen pocket. I laughed at the image. Herodotus held that the origin of all East/West divisions was a bout of ancient tit-for-tat woman-stealing between various Greeks and various occupants of Asia Minor, and that the Greeks overreacted terribly to Paris's theft of Helen, because it was impossible, he held, for a woman to be stolen against her will. Right up Eddie's street. Plus all that stuff about the Lacedaemonians: every Lacedaemonian woman had at some stage of her life to go to a particular temple and sell herself to whatever man selected her. Tall handsome women, he observed, would last only about five minutes, but plain women could wait outside for up to three years, waiting for someone to take pity on them, chuck them a coin and fuck them so they could go home again and lead a decent life.

Lovely place names though. The plain of Magnesia, the Ceramic gulf and the river Meander. Stuck in my mind from all those years ago when I was getting my education.

I realized that I had hardly ever seen Eddie out of doors. Not since the day we went to the exhibition of Islamic Art at the Royal Academy in London, and he had shoved me into his car with a pad of God knows what over my mouth, and taken me off. Oliver's question reverberated in my mind: why hadn't I reported any of the things Eddie had done to me to the police? Because of Ben Cooper, I told myself, as good an example of why you shouldn't trust a copper as any girl ever needed. Because of that clean nose

I wanted, in case of any risk of losing Lily. And because I was complicit: in bribing Ben, in lurking around Eddie, and in my own curious revenge on him.

I have never seen him in sunlight. It didn't suit him. Maybe the back of a motorboat might, some gin-palace-type sunlight, cast green by the shade of a smoked wind-shield, but this pure Egyptian sun showed him up as the lizard he is, even from here. May it shine on his head and burn up his brain. Take him, Amun Ra, he's all yours.

And Chrissie? Dammit I should have paid more atten-tion. Oh, how could I? This was the one place he wasn't meant to be. I couldn't have known. But why didn't she tell me that she had found him? Did she see him yesterday? A rivulet of chill ran down my back as these questions followed each other through. When she invited me to come on this trip, did she know he was coming? Had she, and the chill settled in the small of my back, been setting me up?

I tried to remember how she had been last night. Excited. I had thought it was Egypt that had done it to her. But perhaps it was her husband. I ran through the possibilities: he's got her again, and she's going away with him, happily reunited. She's warning him off – but then he would have left already. They're plotting together, some badness for me. She knew all along, arranged to meet him here and deliver me to him. She's been lying all along. Or she saw him for the first time this morning; she's a rabbit under his spell, she hasn't told him I'm here, and she wants and needs me to save her. It was just possible. And as long as it was possible, I had a responsibility.

Could she have spent the best part of a day with the German and his friends, and Eddie not have been mentioned? Oh. The Germans, of course, know someone called François du Berry. Perhaps he heard that they had a Mrs Bates visiting, and chose to join the party. So where are the Germans now?

It's surreal. After all this, Chrissie and her dead husband are going sightseeing.

Sparrows were hopping around the car. One of them could have eaten my little pearl.

Only she knows what's going on, and I can't ask her. I can't trust her. Even though somehow I do.

Yeah – trust her to do what, exactly?

Say I got to her, away from him, she could still just go back and tell him – and then what? I could try and seize her – oh, please, Angeline, you're pregnant, you're surrounded by police.

If I told these police that he was wanted, would they hold him? And then what?

But the police here know he's wanted, and they have chosen to do nothing about it.

There's nothing I can do until something changes.

Pantarea. A Greek word my mum taught me. It means: everything flows. Sit, while it flows. I leaned my head back and tried to breathe better.

Sa'id's policeman went on his way.

'The convoy leaves in an hour and a half,' he said.

I looked up at him. His eyes were steady. That steady pale look. I said: 'I'm not happy leaving them alone. It frightens me.'

'They are alone now,' he said.

'I know.'

'Do you want me to ask the boys to keep an eye out? Do you fear for her safety?'

'Maybe . . . what could you tell them? I don't want it to become chaotic. Chaos would not be good.'

'Do you want to drink tea? They won't come out for a while.'

I looked up towards the temple, its long low steps, and long low frontage, with the scattered bits of town around it and the desert wide and huge beyond.

'OK.'

And the knowledge flowed into me: bollocks to feeling responsible for Chrissie, I was just happy to have a reason to be near Sa'id.

TWELVE

Abydos

We sat inside the teashop, at the back. If they came out, they would have to walk past the proscenium arch of the front of the café; we would see them, they would not see us. I had sweet black tea, *shay koshari*, in a heavy glass. The fresh mint that came with it was astoundingly green and lustrous in this dusty place: an oasis in the middle of a tin table. Sa'id sat with the stoicism of Ramadan. I realized that I couldn't drink, now, with him beside me. Stupid: the pregnant, the sick and travellers are excused fasting anyway. And anyway I'm not Muslim. But I never said I wasn't confused.

Meanwhile the tea sat and grew cold.

'Aren't you drinking?' he said, after a while.

I shook my head.

He gave a little snort. 'It's not that simple,' he said.

'I know.'

'I know you know,' he said. 'I mean altogether.'

I sat for a moment saying nothing. Is he talking about

our future? That future that we may – or may not – have?

'I don't for one moment imagine that anything is simple,' I said.

A tiredness washed over me. Here I am. I have found him, and seen him, and spent the night with him, we have misunderstood each other and come through it, and here we are, sitting. No magical impulse has thrown us together. He has stopped sulking but he has not melted. I have, but he is taking no notice. It's all gone wrong. Here I am in a teashop, unable to go into my favourite temple, unable to kiss my lover, if he is my lover, unable to understand or protect my new friend, if she is my friend, far from my child, unable to impede my enemy. I am powerless. And yes, it really has all started up again. That bloody man, Eddie Bates, root of all and constant disturbance in my life.

I wondered about what Sa'id had said about Russian roulette. Is it true? My . . . connection, shall we call it, with Eddie. Was that it?

Well, maybe it was. But was is the important word there.

Certainly I hate him. But hate is not enough. I want to feel nothing for him; to feel no hate, and no fear.

A big-eyed child was peering round the doorway from the kitchen, checking me out. I greeted her and she ran away. Two minutes later she was back, with her mother, who looked about eighteen. I greeted her, too, and she ran away. Then back they came, with two more small children and another young mother. Rows of black eyes like olives, eyeing me. I smiled.

The old man in charge asked Sa'id if there was anything wrong with the tea. He said no, I had just become suddenly devout. The man eyed me too. What am I? I saw myself through their eyes for a moment and it made no more sense. I don't know. I'm not a dancer any more. My child is not with me. I never became an archaeologist or an anthropologist, despite my studies. I am . . . pregnant. Thirty-five. And here.

One of the young mothers beckoned to me. Relieved to do anything, I went with her into the back, where she wanted to show me her oven: a great clay beehive, hot and fragrant. She showed me her bread, and her tiny baby, a red-faced amoeba in a grubby shawl. I took it and held it. Samira. She blinked, and I smiled, and the other children brought me their schoolbooks one by one, and I said how clever they all were. They were amazed and delighted that I spoke to them in Arabic. One boy – deaf and dumb – was learning English. Here is a cat, he has written, in pencil, in a book with a picture of a cat, its belly fat and its tail curling, like a capital Q, black on white. The little girls billowed in their efforts to hide behind each other. An old woman appeared, and I told her, in the roundabout way necessary, that her daughters were beautiful. They said my dress was beautiful, and gave me a loaf of bread. I sat on a low caked-earth wall, in the half room half yard of their kitchen, and felt the baby's breath against my body, and smelt the bread and goat smell. The girls *were* beautiful. All eyes and cheekbones. You don't want to go on about it though because it makes the gods jealous, and they may send bad luck. Amasis – a Pharoah, a very cool one by all accounts – had a friend who was so fortunate that even when he tried to make his own bad luck (to avoid afore-mentioned jealousy, on Amasis's advice) by throwing away a ring that he valued above everything, the ring came back to him, in the belly of a fish delivered to his kitchen. At that Amasis said, sorry, mate, I can't be your friend any more because I will not be able to bear the terrible tragedies which are undoubtedly going to come to you to pay you back for all this luck.

They wanted me to eat the bread but I said no, and they thought I was really making Ramadan, and covered me with blessings. How many children did I have, they wanted to know. *Bint, wahda*, I said, just the one daughter. *Alhamdulilleh.* Showed them the picture in my wallet. Oh! Beautiful. *Masha'Allah.* Your husband is a fine man and you are young, you will have many more, *insha'Allah.*

I joined in the chorus. *Insha'Allah.* I felt very much in the lap of the gods. Whose lap would I prefer? None of those men gods. Got to be Isis, like Osiris in the painting inside the temple. Beautiful clever Isis, who tricked Amun Ra into telling her his secret name, who saved Osiris and fought Set and bore Horus and did every damn thing on her own, yet clever enough to bring in help when she needed. When she went to Syria, and Osiris's body was in the tree trunk, and the king had made a column of it, and the wood smelt so fabulous. Isis was always the one for me.

And Hathor, smiling cow-headed Hathor, with her horns made for garlands, her calmness, and deep strength. Mother and lover Hathor. I'll sit in the lap of the goddesses.

The kitchen soothed me, even though the flies buzzed around and the smell of goatshit wafted in from behind. I felt safe in there, as I do in my own. I thought of Harry, sitting in kitchens, bottles of beer small in his big gnarly hands. London Harry, with his London intonations and his London wit. Imagined an Egyptian woman falling for Harry because she had fallen for London, for the angle of fine rain under a streetlight at night, for suburban roses turning from yellow to pink to orange over red-brick walls, for walking from Notting Hill to Westminster all through parks. For cherry blossom against white stucco against biscuit-blue sky. Quite possible, quite possible.

I didn't want to sit with Sa'id. He scared me. Eddie and Chrissie scared me. I wanted only to be put to bed. The tiredness which hijacked my legs that day in Portobello was returning, coiling me in its tendrils, wrapping me in its cloak, leaving me dark with inability.

What am I calling inability? Twelfth week, I'm making a central nervous system in here. I'm busy. Busy within. Inability is only external. But, fuck me, is external unable. I closed my eyes, and leant against the wall, and listened to the women murmuring, and the heat hum. Lap of the goddesses.

*

I woke from my doze to an adjustment in the murmuring. A different noise. New? Yes. But not only new. I awoke, in fact, to Eddie's voice.

I had not expected ever again to have that particular voice do that particularly intimate thing of making itself heard by me. Piercing the fearful hollow of my own ear. It was speaking French. Saying: *'Sa'id el Araby – quel surprise! Qu'est-ce que tu fais ici? Pas de tourisme, non, ça n'est pas pour toi . . .'*

It recalled the first moment I met him, in his Pelham Crescent drawing room, with his Chagall and his Degas, and he spoke my name, and I thought, 'This is why my parents gave me this name: for him to speak it.' How it rolled off his tongue then, like honey; how Sa'id's rolls off now. Patrician, Shakespearean. Evangeline. Patronizing, cosmopolitan, Sa'id el Araby. *Tutoying* him, even.

'Bonjour, monsieur,' said Sa'id. My mind's eye saw him, looking up, otherwise unmoving. I didn't want Eddie to witness that cool pale-eyed look. I wanted it. Not aimed at me, but – I wanted to witness it.

'Lovely temple you've got here,' Eddie was saying. Speaking the English an educated cosmopolitan patronizing Frenchman would use to a foreigner who he assumed didn't know French. 'I have just been to the Osireion. Very spooky down there. Do you know it? Of course you do – I'm forgetting my manners, it's your heritage, isn't it? Though in fact I've never been to the Arc de Triomphe. A great many Parisians haven't. Like the English and the Tower of

London. They are too busy going to Florida and Majorca. There's a big fish down there, in the floodwater, a big grey one like a submarine, rather like those golden carp in Shanghai – have you been to Shanghai? The hotel filled the lake with them and they all turned grey again, through exposure to normal conditions – they returned to their natural dullness. All the special breeding and glamour was gone. Like a woman when she takes her party frock off! Ha Ha!'

He chats, he laughs, he does his French thing though he knows that Sa'id knows he's English. God, how I can read him. I don't have to see him. He's sitting there, insulting Sa'id without missing a beat, insulting women – did he give Sa'id a look when he said that? A look to say yes, I have seen that woman we both know without her dancer's glad rags? If Chrissie is with them – is she? – does he even notice now the pain he flicks out, or has it become so much second nature, so minor in comparison with his real crimes, the crimes he does – or did – for a living, that he doesn't even register it?

If she's not with him, I could try to find her. Where would she be. Toilet. Where. Oh yes; new little concrete block, down the front. I could go out the back, intercept her. Except that I am frozen in place. Melted with inability, frozen with fear.

He was still talking. Small talk from hell.

'*Enfin*, Sa'id – have you heard from . . . our mutual friend?' he was saying.

He doesn't know I'm here. Chrissie hasn't told him.

He doesn't know I can hear him. He may scare me but he doesn't scare me to death and he has never won. He's never beaten me. Hold on to that, and keep breathing.

A pause.

'I don't believe we have one,' said Sa'id. I smiled despite everything.

Eddie tutted.

'My wife has been seeing her,' he said, and my heart lurched, 'in London.' Unlurched again. Comparatively. 'Have you met my wife?' said Eddie. 'Christina, this is Sa'id el Araby.'

So much for the interception.

'How are you?' said Sa'id. Giving it a little weight, as if he wanted to know.

'Hello,' said Chrissie. 'Angeline's told me all about you.' Giving nothing. I couldn't tell.

This is some new kind of hell. Some new way of sitting helpless. Trapped under a web of unknowingness, possibilities singing around me. Will either of them give away that I am here? Will Chrissie give away to Sa'id that I am pregnant? Has she told Eddie that I am pregnant? Will Eddie say something? Between them, I was immobilized. Say nothing, I prayed. Stop this chitchat.

I sent out little tendrils towards her, like a vine to creep up her leg and into her mind: Chrissie, what's going on? What do you want, Chrissie?

And to Sa'id: 'Read her. Read her. Do we rescue her? Or can we run away now?'

'She tells me they get on well,' Eddie was saying. 'Tells me it was Angeline who told her I was not dead at all. Irresponsible really, don't you think? Loose talk costs lives, don't you know.' I was so glad I couldn't see his face as he said that. And anyway he's so fucking cavalier with his secrecy . . . 'I'm sorry, that's an English reference. From the war. Was Egypt in the war? I can't remember. Were you still part of the Empire then? I remember you were under Napoleon – my history is shockingly bad . . .' Of course there is no reason why Eddie should know that after Egypt won independence in the 1920s the British pretty much – in effect – refused to leave; that there were 140,000 Commonwealth troops stationed in Cairo in 1941. That the British ambassador openly referred to King Farouk as 'The Boy', and British soldiers would sing along to the Egyptian national anthem thus: 'King Farouk, King Farouk, Hang his bollocks from a hook . . .'. Cairo practically burnt itself to the ground rioting against the British in 1952, just before the Revolution. But why would Eddie know that? Why would he care?

'Not that I mind seeing my wife,' he was saying. 'There's something pleasant in a familiar fuck. Alongside everything so very unpleasant. I haven't decided yet whether I'll indulge her.'

With most men, you might imagine that this meant his wife was not present. With Eddie it meant nothing. He could perfectly well be giving her his cruel little look. Or not bothering to.

My back was melded to the dusty wall. The family had disappeared.

'Really, Eddie.' It was Chrissie.

And I could not judge her voice. Was it a familiar little, slightly flirty, slightly ticking-off voice, the habit she has had for years for getting through living with him? Or was it a new and separate voice, just a way of getting through this moment?

And then Eddie said, very quietly, in his ordinary old English voice: 'And how's my money, Sa'id? Making the most of my generosity, are you? Because if you need some more, you know, my offer is still open. There's plenty to be made, and it's up to you, of course, how you spend your share. Be plenty for those good works of yours. I just need somebody with a business here, an infrastructure, a brain . . . And we'd only be selling to nastier, greedier even more corrupt people than me, making a profit out of them. No conscience problems, I promise . . . A little straightforward manufacturing, a little import/export. As I said, nothing you couldn't handle . . .'

As I said? Offer still open?

Sa'id hasn't told me about this.

And fear sneaks down my spine. Is Eddie doing to Sa'id what he has done to all of us? Is he corrupting him, too? Is Eddie's money, which I gave Sa'id, turning him to the bad? Sa'id likes money. He's good at it. It's one of his strengths, and his weakness. I remembered Harry's doubts, and my own. Remembered how Eddie made Chrissie abort the children she wanted, how he made Janie do all those things she did, how he made me . . . How he makes us do the worst things.

Two thoughts. One: why is he trying to corrupt Sa'id? Hasn't he noticed that he is a very pure man?

Oh – stupid. He's trying to buy what is not for sale. As he did with me.

Two: maybe he has succeeded in his purchase. Maybe that contributes to why Sa'id is *so* not happy to see me.

He got me, after all, didn't he?

And then I remembered, very vividly, fucking Eddie, and how wild that was, and how wrong, and I went quickly out the back of the kitchen, out into the empty land beyond, and was sick, by a thorn bush. One of the women appeared. Samira's mother. I had the presence of mind to hiss: 'Don't tell my husband.' God bless the sisterhood of women. She said nothing. Brought me water. The sick, after all, are excused.

Then I washed my face and mouth, wrapped my scarf around me in complete purdah, took Samira's mother by the arm and walked round to the front of the café. Just two female figures, wrapped in cloth, at a little distance in an Arab landscape. I couldn't really see the three of them sitting, in the dimness right at the back, framed by the arch that Sa'id and I had thought would protect us. I stared at where they would be, knowing he would feel me, look up and see me, and respond. I wasn't wrong. I was glad – hard gladness. It was a victory against Eddie that it

was Sa'id who felt my stare and not him. After a moment
or two Sa'id rose and after another moment moved away
from the table and towards me. I held on to Samira's
mother's arm.

'What's your name?' I asked her.

She was Aisha. Lovely name. Evening, life, bread. Leila
is night. Beautiful names. If Nippyhead is a girl I can call
her garden of nightingales, beloved of the prophet, morning
star, tree of pearls. Though Shagaratt ad Durr had the most
dreadful story. She was a slave, thirteenth-century, married
the Sultan, who died of a fever. She kept his death secret
for two months, long enough to call back his son from
Syria, and took up with the head of the Mamluk guard.
But the son was no good, and demanded that she give up
her jewels: the Mamluks murdered him, and for eighty
days the Tree of Pearls ruled as sultana. Then she married
her Mamluk captain, made him divorce his wife (Umm
Ali, after whom the delicious pudding is named) and made
him Sultan, if only in name. But then, seven years later,
he decided to take a Turkish princess as his wife, and so
she had him killed, whereupon Umm Ali's son (Ali) roused
his father's troops and delivered Shagaratt ad Durr to his
mother, who had her beaten to death with wooden clogs
and thrown into the moat, where she was left for three
days, wearing only her crimson sash with pearls on it.
Somebody came and stole it. It smelt of musk. In the end
she was buried in the beautiful tomb she had had the
foresight to build in the City of the Dead. It's there now,

dusty and neglected, ask for Mr Nabil at the green house to the right if you want to go inside. A glass mosaic of a tree bears fruit of inlaid mother of pearl: 'Oh ye who stand by my grave, show not surprise at my condition,' says the folded and beautiful text: 'Yesterday I was as you. Tomorrow you will be as me.' When she knew it was all up for her she ground up her jewels in a mortar, to stop anyone else from getting them. While waiting for her stepson to come and take his revenge. Just another soap opera.

Written Arabic, the flowery fioriate and leafy foliate, the ordinary print and the neon signs, handwriting and the logo on a packet of twenty Cleopatras, makes patterns as beautiful as any artificial thing in the world. The language, Arabic, is built on patterns: from a root (usually three consonants) come words meaning everything to do with that root, including, often enough, its own opposites. Hence: *ktb*. Simplest form: *kataba*, to write. And thence: *kattaba*, to make someone write. *Takaataba*, to write to each other. *Istaktaba*: to dictate. *Kitaab*, book. *Maktab*, office. *Maktaba*, library or bookshop. *Kaatib*, clerk. *Mukaataba,* correspondent. *Miktaab*, typewriter . . . and so on.

Why was I thinking all this? Because there is always a pattern, from a root; because patterns can mystify, because trees grow from roots and bear fruit, because the right word is a pearl, and the Arabic language is a tree of pearls, and Sylvia Plath wrote a poem about sitting up a fig tree, admiring the beautiful figs that hung at the end of each branch, unable to choose which one she wanted the most, and one by one the figs dried up and dropped off and she sat there, hungry. Because any of us could end up in the moat in a crimson sash. Particularly if they go after *everything* they want. And at the same time anyone could end up stuck up a fig tree, watching the pearls drop off. And because I had had a shock, and too much sun, and it was about time someone took me and made me lie down in a darkened room.

Sa'id was approaching.

Aisha glided off as he arrived.

For a moment, when he came alongside me, I was going to turn around, stride back to the café, take Eddie's head and tear it from his neck. I was going to seize the flimsy café knives and strike him dead. I was going to laugh at him and spit and dance on his corpse before I flung it over the walls of the citadel and left it to the hyenas.

I never used to understand why sex and violence were always bracketed together in talk of what was bad, from a censorship point of view, in films or books. I thought that sex was good and violence was bad, so why should they be associated? That was before adrenaline entered my life. Looking back towards the café now, hating Eddie, I realized it's just excitement. Adrenaline. It's just a chemical in my blood. That's all. I saved his life when I could have let him be knifed. My heart and honour are bigger than my fear and hatred. They were, they are.

Then Sa'id was at my shoulder, pregnancy flooded out adrenaline, my strength drained off and it was all I could do to stand. I could have leant on him, climbed into his pocket. I could have hidden behind his ear. *Ya habibi*, take me to a darkened room.

'Come,' he said, 'They'll be coming out soon.'

Semi-conscious, I walked back to the car, trying to address my brain, but it wasn't answering. Now that he was here the soft warm weight of my own body seemed to be all there was in the world. I climbed straight into the back seat and took my shoes off.

Sa'id was speaking to me, but I just curled myself up. I think I smiled at him. I hope I did. It was very hot in the car but I felt better because I felt on home ground. Damn, I was grateful to Eddie for reappearing to be our enemy, so that Sa'id and I could be on the same side.

But were Sa'id and I on the same side? Was it home ground?

I lay silent in the back and he stood by the open door. After a while my head cleared a little, and I sat up and said: 'So?'

He sat himself in the passenger seat, one eye still on the cafe.

'I've seen him before,' he said. 'It's a small town. We have spoken before.'

'What plan was he suggesting?'

He laughed. 'It doesn't matter. I am not listening to him.'

Wasn't he? I heard his laugh and felt my belief in him, my big, immediate, natural, irrational belief in him. It was still there.

'Are you doing good works?' I asked.

'For God to judge,' he said.

'What about Chrissie?' I asked. 'Could you tell anything?'

'No,' he said. 'Very complicated, those two. A lot of layers, a lot of lies.'

I closed my eyes and lay back. Sod Eddie, sod Chrissie. Sod this whole situation, except that I am with Sa'id.

What do I want from him? Do I know? Can I remember?

That he love me again, so that I can tell him? Yes – keep it personal.

It was easy to think of that. Easy to think of love, filling all gaps, smoothing all edges, allowing all possibilities, bearing all things, believing all things, hoping all things, enduring all things . . .

The longer I don't tell him . . . the longer I'm deceiving him. God preserve me I don't want to deceive him.

Am I afraid he will feel forced by my pregnancy?

Oh but he is forced. And that's not my doing, it's the force of nature. The nature of nature.

'*Habibi*,' I murmured.

He was there, I could feel him. I could feel his concern at my swoony state. Passing out is absolutely not what I usually do. Oh lord, he doesn't know that. He only knew me for a few weeks, a few weeks ago. How could he know me? How could he love me? This is an absurd and desperate situation.

I could go home again, I whispered to myself, inside my cloth and my miasma. (Away from Eddie, too.) I could go home, and never tell him. I could go home to Lily and this new person, this shrimp. I could, I said inside me, but I was absolutely unconvincing. There was amazing strength to my unconvincingness, given the weakness that suffused me in every other way.

He was giving me water.

'Don't be stupid, you're ill,' he said. 'We're going home now. The convoy's leaving anyway. We'll just go home. You sleep.'

During the journey I heard his phone ring several times; heard him speaking, in Arabic, English, French. Of course, he has a life. Luxor – the West Bank even – has many interesting inhabitants. The doctor at Qurnah is a sophisticated Copt from Cairo who amazed his friends by upping sticks (and books and music) to this dusty village twenty years ago. There are the archaeology lot; the pyramidiots in love with the temples; there are writers and poets and foreigners, addicts from all over who return again and again; the architect; the Frenchman who lives on the blue *dahabeyya* by the landing stage, and a dozen or more *khawageyya* wives of various kinds. Of course he has a life. And one in Cairo, too.

But I was very happy to be on the back seat of his car, wrapped up, being taken, my eyelids heavy moths, my legs molten Aswan granite. There's always the question with that granite – how did they get those great lumps from Aswan hundreds of miles down the Nile to the Osireion? Or hundreds of miles further, to Cairo? The size of the sarcophagi in the Serapeum – it's a mausoleum for bulls sacred to Serapis, a labyrinth lit by naked 1950s lightbulbs, great chambers off a deep passage, and within each chamber lies an Aswan granite block the size of a London bus, hollowed out, polished and carved: coffins for bulls. Mummified bulls. That's what I feel like – a mummified bull. They found one intact – who was it found it, Champollion? There were fingerprints in the sealant on the door of the chamber. From two thousand years ago. New, by this country's standards. The bull mummy is now in the museum of agriculture. Agriculture, I ask you.

No, I feel like Aswan granite. Heavy, helpless, and how did I get here?

I did wonder where – when he says home, does he mean the West Bank? I would like to wake in his house, on the flank of the sphinx mountains, on the verge of the Sahara, with a *gallabeya*'d boy bringing me sweet hot tea and a tin plate of newly washed apricots. The way droplets of water cling to the cheeks of newly washed apricots. I bet there's a word for that in Arabic . . . from the same root as love, or caress, or something. *Fil mish mish*.

There was a girl at school called Natasha, who talked too much, all the time, and Zeinab and I would piss ourselves laughing because *natasba* is the Arabic for to unplug. Which these days almost means its own opposite: unplug the radio, it shuts up; unplug a blockage, it pours forth. Both could have usefully been applied to Natasha.

It's not apricot season anyway.

After a while we pulled in. I didn't move, but I knew

he looked back at me. 'Dendara,' he said. 'We have to wait here, half an hour. You should eat.'

'Don't want to,' I murmured.

'You should eat,' he said. 'They've gone into the temple. Don't worry, it's a long walk back. It won't happen again. I'll see them when they come out. Come. You should get air.'

I so didn't want to stand up. He took my arm, and he pulled me, to help me up. It was the first time he'd touched me since last night, that dream sequence – but maybe that had been a dream. This wasn't. That line of ancient Egyptian poetry sprang to my mind – 'He brings a blush to my skin, for he is tall and lean.'

As I came to standing every atom of my body started to fall towards him, to home in on him, to gravitate. My conscious instruction came like a voice from beyond the grave, telling my body to stand the fuck up and stop that. My body was not inclined to listen, it was inclined to him. My brain fought through this physical mutiny – I couldn't think of the word. I was thinking menagerie. Stand the fuck up on your own feet.

Sa'id took my arm and led me quite firmly to a café, sat me on a wooden divan under a worn and sunbleached tented hanging. I lay down and hid my face; he sat on another divan across from me and ordered water, coffee, eggs and bread. The smell of hot butter revived me and he stared at me as I wolfed a scorching mess of hot yellow omelette from a thick black iron frying pan. He was leaning back again: that you-probably-think-I'm-relaxed-but-I-most-certainly-am-not pose. As he had been last night when he said: 'You want my help. Do you want my love? Do you want to marry me and have my babies?' He watched me eat as he had once watched me walk. And I felt, as I had felt then, that I was putty in his hands. But now I felt that he might not give a damn that I was putty in his hands.

'What's wrong with you?' he said. 'Is it just our lost love, or is it Eddie? Or something else?'

I glared at him for not more than half a moment, and then I stood up and shouted: 'Our love is not lost. You don't lose a love like that. You don't–' I couldn't say anything. It was coming out as a Barry White song. 'A love like ours doesn't die.'

Those were extremely delicious eggs.

'Sit down,' he said. I sat. Mopped up some more butter with turtle bread. Fabulous.

OK, I am strong. This weakness goes in waves. I must remember to eat.

'I want to dance with you,' I said. 'I want to hold you in my arms and touch your face and kiss you and fuck you and be with you forever and kill you if you ever leave me.'

Looking back, I suppose I was hysterical, feverish, or something. At the time I just looked at him, very straight, and thought, with the last little drop of sense and clarity left in my poor love-fear-and-pregnancy-pickled brain: Oh. Whoops.

His mouth moved, very slightly, and a muscle around his cheekbones hardened a little.

Well, I've done it now.

The mid-afternoon heat sat. A goat ambled by. The temple just was. The tattered hanging above me flapped, very gently, very slowly. Nothing here is going to let me off the hook.

'I know,' he said. Quite gently.

'I thought you probably did,' I murmured. Looking up, and not bearing to look at him, my eyes hid, and slunk off, to the right, past the sheltering piles of rock towards where Hathor gazed out, her six-times-four great faces looking out at me, kind and wise, and into the recesses of her own dark temple, roofed in stone, lined in stone, ornamented with the stars of the sky, the signs of the Zodiac, and the kings and queens of the human world. Cleopatra's temple. Temple of love and single mothers, rising from the desert, which had been half swallowed by the desert for generations, and reclaimed from it only a few generations ago, with the stillness of the desert forever rolling in to embrace it. And up on the roof, way in the distance, insects above Hathor's great multiple smiles, I saw Mr and Mrs Bates, standing against the sky. Like a lighthouse on a cliff, I thought. The captain of the ship knows that if he can see it he has moved in too close. Only I'm not moving. They are. I'm not too close: they are. Too close to the edge.

So in that flash I knew what was going to happen. Let me correct that: I knew something was going to happen.

I jumped up and called out something – her name, probably, not his – and ran like the wind up the dust path, past the ticket booth with its tourist police and soldiers, up the avenue of placid sphinxes, past the *gallabeya*-clad ticket collectors, shouting – them at me, me at Chrissie. Into the great dark hypostyle hall, the columns looming massy as cliffs above me, the dark corners, the rows of stone trunks, a petrified forest of immense stature: and inside, into the smaller chambers. Jesus – where are the stairs?

It's almost a joke, a moment of panic in an Egyptian temple. For a split second it becomes Hollywood – temple of doom. Hierogyphics bearing in on you, dark doorways looming, not knowing which way to go. But Hatshepsut outweighed Hollywood, fear can be genuine, oh lord it can. But I do know this temple – I have sat here and read the paper, lain about here, just for the pleasure of the place. This is a place I know. There are stairs to the roof to both east and west. Round to the right – cut through – dark doorway – past where you go to the trapdoor down to the crypt – find the right dark doorway – and the low sloping stone steps, more like the bed of a stream, worn down and down, a low grey gleam like pewter, only two thousand years, not so long. They used to take the goddess up on to the roof for her to be looked on by Ra. The passage is dark and cool; the walls an encyclopaedia of hieroglyphic carving. Up. Out into the clear blue blinding sky: first roof. Round. Past one and another little temple squatting on the roof of the great temple like baby frogs on their mother's back. I clatter up the external iron staircase, to the top, the high, wide stone expanse of the highest roof, the front, the field in the sky, supported by Hathor's heads below, and with the desert all around spreading out below. The heat of the sun like a god's breath. Clutching the iron railing as I pull myself up, the scene spreads before me. Chrissie is there, against the sky. Alone.

Behind me comes a hurly burly: tourist police, guides. They didn't like it one bit; they hurled themselves after me. Hatshepsut had been only weeks before. They were jumpy, and wouldn't you be? It was me they were after, because they didn't know what I knew. Not yet. They're at the bottom of the rackety iron stairs.

'Chrissie!' I called to her, and as I did her oxblood scarf billowed out against the clear blue sky in the breeze of the high place, and its movement seemed to drown my call.

I had a stitch. I went towards her, and then cut left, and went to sit, on the edge of this arena, not close to her, panting and panting. Her bag was at her feet. She stood on the ledge, on the two feet or so of edging stone from which any mother would warn her child. From thirty feet or so away, I watched her. We had a moment when only the boots on the staircase behind me disturbed us. She was looking out. Out, not over.

Someone else must have seen. Someone will be down there with him.

'Chrissie,' I called again . . . She turned round to me: Medea on the stern of her ship; Hera in one of her moods.

It was a face you could have put on a shield to turn your
enemies to stone.

She's going over too, I thought in a rush, and I was up
and with her, taking her in my arms, holding her as I hadn't
held her at his funeral, leading her to safety – of a kind.
Away from the edge.

But she's done it. She's been over the edge. It's done.

*

It wasn't at all clear what would happen next. The hurly
burly caught up with us; and started to babble and exclaim.
Sa'id was there, his arm round my shoulder for a second,
then gone. Chrissie was immobile in my arms, stiff,
stationary. I was thinking about my baby, my shrimp, saying
to it OK, sorry about that, I'll sit still a moment now –
did you get that adrenaline? I'm sorry if it was too much.
Soothing it. Singing to it.

Then Sa'id was squatting at the roof's edge just where
Chrissie had been standing, looking over. Not out, over.
Voices came up from below; he called back down. There
was a wailing from somewhere. Everybody else ran around
in circles. A young tourist policeman, with his dusty indigo
uniform and white spats and cheap-looking submachine
gun, stayed by us. He stood weight on one leg, hip tilted,
cuddling his gun. He reminded me of Hakim: tender.

After a while I asked him what was happening. I spoke
to him in Arabic though Chrissie showed no sign of understanding anything so it made little difference to her, and I

think it was her I was trying to protect. He said he thought the man was dead. He murmured a prayer, his eyes full of shock and sadness, but his stance pure and immutable duty.

Did anyone see what happened?

Sa'id came back to me, shaking out his trousers. His pale eyes were hot and distracted.

'Dead,' he said. 'Absolutely dead. He's broken, down there.'

For a moment I was laughing.

Remembering Harry telling me that day in the café near Scotland Yard: Eddie's dead, and I was so – so blown apart because – apart from anything – I thought I had contributed to his death with my wallop on his head. And I had wept. And now.

I laugh.

But so swiftly that nobody notices.

Then I stood and walked quickly to the edge where Chrissie had been. Squatted. Looked over.

He was a distant small pile of limbs and linen. The proportions of him were wrong, and the angles. I hadn't seen Janie when she flew through the air and landed dead. I'd been lying broken myself. But death is visible from a long way off.

People stood around him. His hat had abandoned him. I looked for it, and made it out, lying alone off towards the ditch full of ancient rubble and palm trees that used to be the sacred lake.

No one was touching him.

I remembered my leg when it seemed dead. The weight,

the pain, the cold damp grey-yellowness of flesh. Broken.
What a word that is.

What had I said to Sa'id? Bind it up, and it will heal?
Some things heal.

Some things can't.

I found that I was crossing myself, which is not something I often do.

When I returned Sa'id was in my position, holding
Chrissie.

'Did you see what happened?' I asked him.

'I wasn't looking,' he said. 'I was following you.'

I thought about that for a moment. I realized that I
would have to think about it again.

'We should take her down,' I said.

He carried her. Remembered Harry at the funeral,
supporting her in her fur coat and stillettos. Oh Chrissie.

*

We gathered at the doorway of the hypostyle hall.
Seventy-two vandalized faces of Hathor stared out and
down and back and away. I wrapped my scarf round Chrissie
as she was starting to shiver. Sat her on the step for a
moment. The policemen were talking to each other. Radios
crackling. Sa'id was talking to one of them. The policeman
was saying that he didn't understand.

Sa'id, his face like a blade, came to where I was sitting
with Chrissie. He looked down at us for a moment, then
squatted down by me.

'How are you feeling?' he said.

'Capable,' I said, but guardedly.

'Capable of what?' It was the same kind voice, but the blade was in it.

I looked into his eyes. I still only want to kiss him; that is still, even here, even now, all I want.

'You know everything I know,' I said. 'I didn't see what happened.'

'But you ran – you set off like a . . . you ran.'

'We're not going to give a judgement here,' I said.

He snorted. 'What, wait until you have got your story straight?'

Oh, no. No, Sa'id.

'Is that what you think? Is that what you think?'

'It could look like that,' he said. 'I don't know what to think.'

I tightened my arm around Chrissie, wooden doll beneath my embrace.

'I think she had every reason to . . .'

'So did you,' he said.

'Stop it! Stop it! I'm telling you . . .' I was angry. Oh my god was I angry. This had not crossed my mind.

'She may have. Maybe she did. Maybe he fell. Maybe she was going to and changed her mind. Maybe he was trying to push her. I didn't see.'

'You ran to her because you thought she would? Or because it would distract attention?'

A dark and utter fury took my heart.

'Sa'id,' I said, 'fuck off.' And went to the policeman, who found the taxi driver, who, after some toing and froing and fussing and talking in quiet, intense voices, drove us, together with two police vans, back along the stripes of the land and the river and the sky to Luxor. I don't know what Sa'id did. I held on to Chrissie all the way, and managed to ascertain that we were being taken to the hotel, where a doctor would come, not to the police station. So that was OK.

THIRTEEN

The Winter Palace

When Amun Ra first got pissed off with humanity, as creator gods tend to sooner or later, he created a lioness called Sekhmet, and sent her into Egypt to eat everybody. Which she did, with great pleasure. After a while Amun Ra got over his pique, and told Sekhmet she could stop now, but she had acquired a taste for blood and didn't want to stop. So Amun Ra sent his servants to make gallons and gallons of beer, and they stained it red with the red clay of Elephantine, the island at Aswan, and they went to where Sekhmet slept among the reeds and poured the beer into the fields around her. When she awoke, she thought the beer was blood left over from her previous rampages, and drank it greedily. Then, of course, she was drunk, and she lay down to sleep again and Amun Ra's servants picked her up and carried her to their master.

Sekhmet, he said, you may not eat people any more. But because you have been my loyal servant, I will give you a greater power over mankind: you will be Hathor, goddess of love, and all humanity will be your victims.

Which was running through my mind in several directions at once as I sat with Chrissie under the huge red chandelier in the hall of the Winter Palace Hotel, waiting for the policemen to say it was all right for us to go upstairs.

So far, no one had seen. Chrissie and Eddie had been by the south-west corner of the roof. The guides were mostly inside. The few visitors were inside. My panic and dash had distracted the people at the teashop. The guards and tourist police had been gathered at the front. Nero, Caesarion and Cleopatra were carved on the walls, what could they know? And Hathor stared out below, oblivious to what went on above her.

Chrissie wasn't saying anything. She hadn't said a word since I had taken her in my arms on the roof of the temple, under the huge sky. I didn't even know if she had gathered that he was dead. And I didn't know what had happened up there.

I didn't know. I just remembered the look in her eye when she said, 'Oh is he now', to the news that he was alive.

When we went upstairs to our rooms the doctor came, and gave her something, I don't know what. I wasn't, despite my best attempts to be strong and capable, fit to judge or observe or have an opinion. I was only strong and capable at all because she wasn't and someone had to be. We put her to bed, then when the doctor had gone I ran a bath in her bathroom, and put myself in the beautiful hot water to sing to my baby, and then I lay down on the other bed in her room, and if I slept I didn't notice, but I didn't notice anything else either. I think I slept. I may have cried.

I came to myself around eleven, wide awake, frightened, hungry. Chrissie was sleeping, breathing shallow. Face calm. What is she going through now? I didn't want to leave her but I couldn't stay. The balcony called me to come and look at the river, and across the river, to the layers of purple and silver that make up the Nile night. I wouldn't go. I didn't want to look.

I wanted to go to the bar and drink vodka martinis and listen to the terrible piano player. I wanted, a little of me wanted, now that he was dead, to think about him. Just for a bit. I wondered, briefly, where they had taken him.

In the end I left a note for Chrissie, went to my room and got dressed, and went down through the chill of the evening to the garden behind the hotel, where 100-foot palms and fluffy dollops of mimosa stood around on the green smooth lawns like English people at a garden party. Glass globe lights like beached moons hung along the edges of the winding paths: way down at the bottom the swimming pool gleamed silent and blue. Orion above, and the moon, filling out, and every other star. Orion is Osiris. I sat on a bench near the small aviary, and listened to the rustling, murmuring sounds of sleeping pigeons.

From beyond this visitors' oasis came the sound of the town, lively with the inverted timetable of Ramadan. I had never before this trip stayed in such separatist institutions. How come, on a Ramadan night, I can't smell frankincense? I am cut off from an Egypt united in Ramadan, and I am cut off from Sa'id.

'Fuck off' is a fairly ambivalent message.

And I had left. Which I think I had promised I would never do. Maybe I hadn't promised him, but . . .

I suppose, because his mother left, it is all that much worse.

Oh, well done, Angeline. Well spotted. Deep psychological insight there.

A young man emerged out of the dusk, as they do. Did I want anything, he wondered. Yes, I said, I want food. The restaurant has only just closed . . . but then he said, you wait, madame, and I just sat, as I had been sitting, and in fifteen minutes or so he came back with a plate of beef and vegetables. Food. Bloody marvellous. He waited until I had finished, and then took my plate away again, saying as he left that there was a man asking for me, should he tell him where I am?

A quick clutch in my heart as I feared and then realized – yes! – that it could not be Eddie. Followed by the slow clutch, that it can only be Sa'id.

'Yes,' I said.

I'd tell him. That was all. I can't carry on trying to control this situation. If he thinks I planned with Chrissie to kill Eddie, then fuck it. I can't help what he thinks. I can just tell him: that I didn't. And that I'm pregnant.

How could he think it? How could he?

Ha ha. My outrage was just not taking off. I was simply incapable of being angry with Sa'id for thinking so badly of me – why? Because he was right, up to a point. I probably would have been capable of killing Eddie. Certainly anyone could have died in the chaos that surrounded and informed him and me. After all, I hit him over the head with a poker. I could very well have killed him then. And Sa'id knows it, and actually he probably doesn't think the worse of me for it. This is still a land of blood revenge, after all.

What I wouldn't be capable of was planning it, of doing it on purpose: plotting with Chrissie that she should lure him up there, and I should panic and divert attention just at the right moment. Nor was I capable of trusting her enough, even if I was inclined to plotting murder – and anyway we didn't know Eddie was here, and it was pure coincidence Chrissie meeting people who knew him, and anyway why would I have dragged Sa'id along?

Stop it. You're not being called on to defend yourself. If Sa'id accuses you, then defend yourself. Don't leap up to greet your misfortunes. I just have to talk to him, and then . . . OK things aren't so great. But they're not as bad as they might be.

And Eddie is dead.

Having been through it before, when he wasn't dead, my reaction this time was muted in comparison. Muted, but deep. I opened my eyes wide to the cool night and put my hands to my face. So he's dead. Good.

At that moment the lad reappeared, leading a taller figure behind him. Why is he leading him? As if Sa'id needed showing around.

I turned my face away. I didn't know where to look, how to look. My face didn't know what shape to take.

But at least he had come.

So when I did look up at the figure in moonshadow before me, I was kind of smiling. But it wasn't Sa'id. It was Harry.

Curiously, this was almost the most shocking thing to have happened. Harry, in Egypt? Does not compute. It was as if he had walked in on me naked, or —

'Where's Lily!' I cried.

'With Brigid,' he said. 'I told her I was coming to get you and she was fine, she was pleased.'

I stared at him. Confused, on several levels.

'How?' I said.

'What?'

'How did you tell her? How did you get here?'

'I flew.'

'But I talked to you this morning.'

'Wonders of modern technology,' he said. 'I flew. It happens.'

It seemed too quick. I felt that Luxor was farther away than that. It somehow threatened the integrity of this other life, my Egyptian dream. (There's a song that they play on the plane, called 'My Egyptian Dream'. Patriotism and handsome young people, shots of the pyramids in the video.) I didn't like Harry being here in Egypt.

'What are you doing here?' I said.

'You needed me.'

That shut me up for a moment.

'No, I didn't,' I said.

'Yes, you do.'

'Oh bollocks,' I said.

'Would *you* leave you alone and pregnant in the same town as Eddie Bates, bent on saving a madwoman?' he asked.

'Shut up with this pregnant thing,' I snapped. 'I'm fine.'

He sat down beside me on the bench. 'It's nice here, isn't it?' he said. I turned my head to look at him. What's he playing at?

'I saw my mum pregnant five times, Angel,' he said. 'I have nephews and nieces and I know where they came from. I know that pregnancy exists and that a pregnant woman, being busy on another level, needs stuff from those around her. I'm not casting aspersions on your ability to deal with stuff, I'm just accepting reality.' He breathed the night air. 'I recommend it,' he said.

'I don't need you,' I said. 'Anyway, Sa'id's looking after me.'

Harry said nothing. Just glanced around him, noting absence. A movement which spoke volumes.

We sat in that loud silence for a few moments.

'Will you come inside? I'm getting cold,' he said. I

assumed that he said *he* was getting cold rather than wasn't *I* getting cold in the same way that I would use that trick with Lily. But I was getting cold, and we went in, leaving the cold night scent of mimosa on the air behind us.

*

The bar was still open. The pianist was playing 'New York, New York'. Harry took one look around, ordered a martini, and then laughed at it when it came because it was so bad (90 per cent vermouth and full of ice). I had hot chocolate, which came tasting of cinnamon and cardamom and almonds. We went to the other end of the room, to an overstuffed leather sofa under a shelf full of Edwardian entomological encyclopaedias and volumes by E. Wallis Budge, by a dark wood fireplace. Green baize and low lighting. It could have been a library in an English country house, except that it so obviously wasn't. Memories of colonialism crept through the walls like rot.

'So?' said Harry.

'What?' said I. If Sa'id and I can't help understanding each other, Harry and I can't help misunderstanding. And if we don't, we pretend to.

Oh no, that's not true. That's the past. Don't fall into it again. The difference is that Harry and I, having mislaid our initial God-given understanding and passed through a period of incomprehension and lies, have learned to understand each other again. The truth is, we have healed, Harry and I.

'Fill me in,' he said. 'How come you're hanging round

in gardens in the middle of the night all alone, when the last I heard you're scared to death, grabbing Chrissie and leaving on the next train? Where's Chrissie? Where's Eddie, for example? Where's Sa'id, even, but perhaps we can come back to that.'

He doesn't know.

'Have you talked to anybody?' I asked him. 'Since you got here?'

'Like who?' he said. 'I came straight here and asked for you.'

At that moment there was a movement at the bar. Where previously the barman had been lounging, half asleep, suspended in time, waiting for us to finish but not really caring either way, there was now a conversation. Unlikely, at this hour, in this quiet tourist season, in Ramadan. I looked up. It was the small policeman from years ago, from when Nadia and I went to Dendara, and we were being pointed out to him.

'Eddie is dead,' I murmured to Harry. 'He fell from the roof of a temple out in the countryside. Chrissie was with him. It's unclear exactly what happened. She's upstairs, tranquillized.'

He turned to me in astonishment. His eyes were alight.

'You look happy,' I said.

'Jesus fuck,' he said. 'What the . . .'

'I don't know, I don't know,' I said. 'I just want to go to bed. There's a policeman coming to talk to us.'

Harry looked up to see a small man wearing a suit and

a polite expression. He made a respectful gesture towards
Harry and introduced himself. Shezli.

Harry introduced himself as DI Makins, slurring the DI
slightly, neither hiding nor emphasizing his police identity.
He's covering himself, I thought. So that if they don't pick
it up he can remain anonymous, and then if they say later,
'Why didn't you tell us you were a policeman?', he can
say, 'I did tell you.' Keeping his options open.

'And Madame Gower,' said Shezli to me. I agreed that
I was.

'Is your friend sleeping?' he asked.

'I believe so,' I said. 'The hotel doctor gave her some
pills. She was in shock, I think. I was just going to bed
myself.'

'I wished to say, we will wish to speak with Mrs Bates,
and we will wish instruction for the body. We have no next
of kin for Monsieur du Berry.'

They don't know she's his wife.

'Perhaps she will be able to speak to you in the morning,'
I said. Shall I disassociate us? We never knew him anyway,
ask those Germans. Shit, and what about Hafla? The missing
link – she knew him as both Eddie Bates and François du
Berry. No, do nothing before you've thought about it. 'I'm
sure she will be better after a good night's sleep.'

'Tell me what happened, please,' he said, but he didn't
sit down, so I gave him a short version. They were up
there, I got worried, I ran, he was on the ground.

Shezli had a thoughtful face at the best of times.

'Do not leave Luxor, please,' he said, politely. 'I will wait on you in the morning.' And he left.

Harry's eyes were narrow and I could see his brain ticking.

'Eddie was here,' I said, 'had been for about a week. Hafla, this Turkish girl that he has known for ages, in London as well, a dancer – she was here with a German couple. Chrissie met Helmut, the German guy, here in the hotel. So she met Eddie – I don't know when. Yesterday or today. Today they went on this day trip – Eddie and Chrissie. The Germans were meant to go but they didn't show up. I don't know where Hafla was. Sa'id and I were following them – honestly, it was the only thing we could do. I'd wanted to warn Chrissie that Eddie was here, or just take her away, or something, and the next thing there they were together. So we were waiting and wondering what to do while they visited this temple and the next thing they were on the roof, and I had a kind of a flash that something was going to happen, and I ran up, and when I got up there he was dead. Down below.'

'Did she push him?' he asked. Well of course he would. He's not a fool.

'I don't know.'

'Does anyone think she did?'

I looked up at him.

'You?' I said.

'I wasn't there.'

'Nor was I,' I said.

He gave me one of his looks. A kind of 'don't try that' look.

'I don't know if she did,' I said. And then, 'I'm not sure it matters.'

'Death of a bastard is still death, Angel,' he said. 'It's still death.'

'He made her have four abortions,' I said. 'What's that? Isn't that death? And he's officially dead anyway – officially, he's someone else. Someone who doesn't actually exist.'

'Pushing someone off a roof and killing them is murder,' he said.

I stared at my chocolate.

'I know,' I said.

'What does Sa'id think?'

'He thinks I – he is not certain that I didn't panic at just the right time in order to distract attention, so that nobody would see if she pushed or not. Can I go to bed now?'

'Does he?' said Harry. And looked at me.

And I looked back at him.

'No, I fucking didn't!' I started to shout, but he put his hands on my shoulders and said, 'I know. I know.'

I was heaving great sighs. Huge sighs.

'Go to bed,' he said.

'What about you?'

'What about me?' he said.

I had meant, where was he going to sleep, was he booked in, because if not he could have my room because I was going to sleep in with Chrissie anyway, to keep an eye on her. But it became, for a second, one of those swift-passing moments of sexual tension. Those times, lately, when he's said, 'Can I come too?' and that kind of thing.

We kind of acknowledged it as it flew by. There was a tender tiredness in his eyes as he accepted the offer of my room. I went to the front desk to clarify the changeover. I wanted Lily.

As we parted in the corridor, I said to him: 'Do you want Chrissie to face a murder trial in a foreign country?'

He pulled his lips inside his mouth and bit them.

'Either we tell Shezli or we don't,' I said. 'We have to know what we're saying.'

'We have to know what she's saying too,' he observed.

'I don't think she'll lie,' I said. In fact I was sure she wouldn't. This pure new honest self she'd been after. She had many years of dishonesty that she had been fighting off. I didn't think she would be capable of changing direction now. She was all or nothing for the truth. If she'd killed him she'd be proud of it.

At his funeral. In the back of the ambulance in her fur coat, shouting to me, 'He wasn't yours to kill, I would have killed him myself . . .' Something like that.

Oh god.

'Let's talk first thing,' I said. 'You, me and her.'

'Not necessarily a good thing,' he said.

'What?'

'She knows me as one of her husband's louts. Remember?'

244

Prompted, I did remember. Undercover Harry, working for Eddie.

'But . . . you're one of the people she wants to apologize to. You know – the AA apologies. She said so.'

'Oh. Well. That might be useful.'

'Couldn't she be allowed to know the truth now?'

'Ideally not,' he said, placidly.

I queried him with my eyebrows.

'Least said, that kind of thing,' he said.

'Did Eddie ever find out you were police?' I asked, curious.

'Nope,' he said.

'But . . . couldn't Ben have told him?'

'Ben didn't know,' he said.

That floored me. 'But . . .' I was remembering the afternoon when Harry turned up with four men in suits and carted Ben away to face his fate . . . though actually now I come to think of it, it was the four men who did the carting, not Harry. 'Gosh,' I said. One of Chrissie's words that I seem to have picked up. 'But – risky, though.'

'Yes,' he said. Calmly as ever.

Then Harry waited by the door while I went into my room to get my toothbrush and stuff. And to check my messages. There were none. A country and western lyric: 'Since my phone still ain't ringing, I assume it still ain't you.'

I slept well, which was absurd under the circumstances.

FOURTEEN

'Well, I woke up this morning,

with a black snake in my room,
I woke up this morning,
with a feeling of impending doom . . .'

I woke late, about nine. This particular morning's *musa-hourati* and muezzins and chromatic variations had passed me by as I slept oblivious. I didn't feel too bad, physically. But there was a black snake there all right, winding round the feet of my bed, giving me dirty looks, like 'I'm going to get you'.

Chrissie was sitting up in the bed next to me, white as her sheets, looking somehow catatonic, stretching. Her arms were very thin. She looked over to me and smiled.

'Good morning, Chrissie,' I said, kindly.

'Oh, my days,' she said, in a slightly gaspy way. 'Oh, my days.'

'Tell me something?' I said, sat there in my single bed

beside her like the neighbouring girl in the school dorm. It seemed unseemly to have this conversation before we were even properly awake, but Shezli might appear at any moment. She looked over to me with a sort of daft girlish expression on her face. Gentle but overwhelmed.

'I don't think I pushed him,' she said. 'I really don't think I did. I thought he might push me . . .' She fell silent. Smiled up at me again. 'I don't think I would've done that. Am I arrested?'

There was something wrong about her.

No love, I thought — you're deflated. You're retarded. You're . . . half of her wasn't there.

I believed her. Yesterday I'd been sure she'd done it. I could admit that, now that I felt she hadn't. And I wasn't leaving her here.

I was glad to know that I knew where I stood, that I knew what my next job was. Regarding her, my job was to find the most efficient way of getting her out of Egypt and into some kind of helpful and comforting place in England. This seemed to me absolutely clear. The girl needed help.

'What happened before?' I asked. 'You were in the car . . .'

'He was there!' she said. 'Well, he was there and we got in the car together and he said he was so glad and he loved me and all that. He was their friend. They didn't come. They changed their minds. He'd come because he heard I was there. Said he loved me. He was lying, of course. He hates me, I know that. But he's so vain. Doesn't know I'm different now. I am different, aren't I?' She said this not smugly but beseechingly. 'What's going to happen now, Angeline, because I don't think I can do anything – I'm telling you now because I don't know if I can even think. Don't know how long I'll be able to. Don't let me drink, will you. I'm feeling very odd.'

She lay down again. She was shaking. I kissed her forehead and rang for breakfast: eggs and toast, *omali* (named after Shagaratt ad Durr's murderer), coffee, fruit salad, yogurt. If only I could send her back to London with Harry, know she was safe. But we're meant to leave today. If Shezli lets us.

I knew why I was looking after her. Why I was so loyal. It was to do with Janie. Something to do with sisterhood. Eddie's victim women: Janie, Chrissie, and *not* me. To do with the complicity we all have in what he made us do. Janie wouldn't have whored herself unless he had offered the opportunity. I wouldn't have knocked him out, or fucked him, unconscious. Chrissie wouldn't have aborted her children, turned to drink, sent all those poisonous letters, been a bad mother to Darla, or – who knows – pushed him off the roof of the temple. I'm not suggesting that this excuses us. Just that it explains something. He ruined people. Helped them to ruin themselves.

But he wasn't going to ruin me.

He's dead. Oh, I'm glad.

I went in to wake Harry. He was up, in the bathroom. I checked the phone as I waited for him, but the little red light was not flashing. No one had called me in the middle of the night, making any midnight declarations, demanding or offering any midnight explanations.

Harry came out with his towel round his waist, rubbing his hair. Very relaxed we were, breakfast in our rooms and nine o'clock showers. Until, as his arms came down, I saw my name, flying across his bicep, as it had been all these years, as if it belonged there. I tore my eyes from it. And from the rest of him. Went and sat modestly in a chair, slightly averted.

'How is she this morning?' he said.

'Well,' I said, 'she's lost it a little. She's gone a bit wobbly round the edges, if you see what I mean. Out of focus. But she's compos enough to know that she's wobbly. She says she didn't push him. I believe her.'

He said nothing.

'I think . . . Harry, I really think that we should not mention her connection with Eddie, but just take her home. If we can – if the police don't suspect her. The problem is we don't know what the Germans are saying, or what Eddie said to them, about her, and . . .'

'Angel,' he said, his voice quite quiet. 'I'm a police officer.'

'Yes, but . . .'

'In London, in Luxor, on Mars, I'm a police officer.'

His voice held the authority that I didn't often hear, but which when I did made me understand how come he was an inspector at the age of thirty-eight.

'I didn't mean that,' I said.

'What *do* you mean then? Because it sounds very much as if you are suggesting that we withhold evidence in a possible murder case.' He didn't say it accusingly. More as a quiet observation, just wondering if I'd noticed.

Oh god, so it did. Oh shit.

'But there is no case, as far as we know,' I said, optimistically.

'But if my Egyptian colleagues knew what I know, there would be.'

'Harry, in the normal run of things I would absolutely agree with you,' (and I half did anyway) 'but look at this situation, look at it . . . It's too much, Harry,' I said. 'There's no tidy way out . . .'

'It's not for us to find a tidy way out,' he said. 'That's not our responsibility.'

Is this Gary Cooper? Or is it Jobsworth?

'Have you just metamorphosed into some corporate robot?' I asked. 'Are you suggesting that we just hand her over, tell them we think she killed him and bugger off? Is that what *you* mean? Because this whole mess is a result of what your colleagues thought was a good way of sorting things out and I didn't notice any of them being sticklers for the bloody law. We are a little bit beyond that, aren't we? What purpose, exactly, would we be serving by announcing that an already dead man has been murdered? Jesus, Harry, it's enough of a fucking mess, if we can simply take her away then maybe one life at least can be salvaged . . .'

'There's right and wrong, love,' he said.

'And there's eight million shades of grey along the way. Please. Let's keep it simple even if it's not necessarily entirely true. Given that the truth can't be proven anyway. Maybe he fell. Maybe he was trying to push her. Or maybe he jumped – one last twisted fucking Eddie Bates trick. He knew it was all up and decided to be nasty to his wife one more time. Just to ruin her all the more completely. To frame her. Who knows? Is a court going to find out? Do you want an international incident about this? Englishwoman of uncertain sanity sentenced to death in Egypt for murder of gangster husband formerly thought dead? It's bollocks, Harry. Bollocks.'

The shutter rattled in the light breeze. A car honked outside. Beep beep, and another honked in response.

'I've found,' he said, after quite a long pause, 'that you have to be quite simple about right and wrong. It's wrong to kill people.'

My heart agreed with him. My head said no. Or was it the other way around?

'We can't make it simple, Harry, because it's not. All we can do is not make it more complicated. I can't desert her. If you can, then . . . then do.'

He looked a question at me.

'Go,' I said. 'Just leave. Do nothing. It won't be on your conscience, or your record, or whatever it is you're worrying about. Leave it to fate.'

'Fate and you,' he said.

'He could have died when I hit him with that poker,' I

said. 'But you carried on protecting me, even though I did that to him. Fate decreed that he didn't die then. My luck. And he did die now. Fate. Chance. Chrissie's luck. The world's good fortune that he's gone. Fair karma, because he escaped his due punishment that he got sentenced to by a court of law. If you can't be involved, just go away. I won't hate you. I'll see you back in London.'

'You're asking me to say nothing.'

'Say it back in London if you have to. Say it to Oliver, and get some backup or sanction or something. Just don't pitch her into it here, now. Please.' I thought that was a good offer. A good idea.

'And don't pitch me in, either,' I said. 'I want to go home. I don't want to be up as her accomplice.'

He stared at me. Picked his clothes up and went back into the bathroom. Came out fully dressed, and saying, 'I'll talk to you later,' walked out.

'Harry!' I shouted after him. 'Where are you going?'

But he was gone, and I couldn't tell if any of my words had got through. All I knew was that his had got through to me. But at the same time: if Chrissie had killed Eddie, she had done me a great service, and I would be indebted to her for the rest of my life.

*

Chrissie was still in bed. The breakfast lay untouched on the side table. I ate half of it and then went to close the shutters against the Nile and what lay beyond, but as I tried to I leant against them and felt tears fill me up inside. Where was Sa'id?

*

Our flight to Cairo left at four thirty, our flight from Cairo to London at eight the next morning. There was no way, other than the four-thirty flight, for us to make tomorrow's flight. Harry's direct flight back to London left today. Presumably we could get on that. Presumably Harry was going to get it . . .

I called the hotel travel desk and learnt that yes, the direct flight left at six, and there were places. Five minutes later I was wondering whether the Germans had spoken to Shezli yet – the later it became before he contacted us the more likely it seemed – and how the hell I could get them to tell me what they had said, and what the hell to do about Hafla, when the phone rang and Shezli said, still very polite, that he thought he had requested that we not leave Luxor.

'We are booked on a flight this afternoon,' I explained, terribly nicely. 'I was just seeing about a later flight to make more time for you in case you needed it.' I wondered if he could perhaps see us sooner rather than later, if he still wanted to talk to Chrissie, as she was upset and keen to get home, and my daughter was expecting me, too, and our holiday was due to finish today . . . I was my best tourist self. Not a word of Arabic, not a hint of anything out of the ordinary.

'You may come now to the manager's office,' he said.

'We'll only be a moment,' I said.

I roused Chrissie and dressed her: a long sundress, a decent jacket, sunglasses optional. She looked pretty ropey. I forced a cup of coffee down her, and a bit of bread. 'Come on, darling,' I said.

'You're being very nice,' she said.

'Shut up now,' I said, kindly, and took her shoulders in my hands. 'Listen. When you were with Nina and Helmut, did you meet a girl called Hafla? A Turkish dancer, who was giving Nina lessons?'

'She wasn't called Hafla. Her name's Fatma. She was a bit snotty.'

'That's the one. Where was she yesterday?'

'Oh. She's gone away. She was going to meet someone somewhere – I don't know the name of the place, I heard it but it meant nothing to me. I'm terribly sorry. I'm terribly sorry about all this. Terribly, terribly sorry . . .'

'Did she know you, when you met?'

'Know me? How could she know me?'

'Of course she couldn't. Now stay with me, love. Listen: did Helmut and Nina call Eddie Eddie or François? Did they know you were his wife?'

'Oh – oh gosh. Oh. I don't know. They . . . they never mentioned Eddie. I was amazed – God, Angeline, when he turned up yesterday . . . They did talk about a François. Earlier. But yesterday I didn't see them. Eddie gave me their apologies. I might have thought it was rude of them but I wasn't thinking about that, of course, not that they would have known, of course.'

It actually didn't make any difference that they hadn't been there. Fewer witnesses, so that was good. Less opportunity for fuss to be made. But he might have told them she was his wife. He must have enquired about her to work out that she *was* her. And no Hafla. That was good.

I thought of asking Chrissie to ring Helmut and see if he let anything drop. Then I thought of the promptness with which Shezli learnt of our travel plans, and concluded that the hotel telephone system was not exactly secure.

I made the decision. It was a risk, but it was worth it. We would proceed as if the police did not know who she was.

'Chrissie, the policeman wants to talk to you. Be as upset as you are. Tell him what you know, what happened. But sweetheart: don't say you're his wife. They know him under the fake name. François du Berry. A man you met yesterday morning, through your mutual friends Helmut and Nina. Answer as little as possible. Let them say what they know. Say as little as possible. Then probably we can go. All right?'

She started to cry. I held her a little, and mopped her up, and jollied her along because that was girls like her were brought up with, and I wanted her to feel safe. As safe as possible. As I steered her down the stairs, my gullet was rebellious. Was it sickness, or panic? Or was it just lost love again, back to provoke me?

*

I saw through the doorway that Shezli sat in the hotel manager's office as if it were his own. Not that I was given much chance to notice, because even as I started to enter I was courteously steered one way and Chrissie the other: her into the room, me on to a sofa outside. I sat, and I amused myself by flexing my pelvic-floor muscles like Chrissie's yoga book suggested, and I tried to quell the fear. Didn't work.

I just sat. Flex. Quell. Flex. Quell. Like a chemist's shop shelf. Shampoo, indigestion pill, shampoo, indigestion pill. Ha ha ha. Another thirty seconds got through. What was she saying? What were they asking?

The longer it takes the worse it is. It only takes three minutes for her to give her version. What's taking so long?

I couldn't stay there. If I couldn't participate, protect her directly, then I was wasting time, displacing, procrastinating when I had no tomorrow to procrastinate to. She'd be no better off for me sitting on my arse out here when I could be trying to make sense of my own predicament.

I stood, and said to the bumfluff cop who had diverted me to the sofa in the first place: 'I must go, I have some business to attend to. I will come back. Look after her.' And I left, and I went out the door, and down the filmstar staircase, and across the first side of the Corniche, and across the flowerbeds in the middle, and across the other side of the Corniche, and along to the *ma'adeyyah* landing place. A small boy in charge of a small motorized iron barge (*Nefertiti*), lined with floral chintz cushions, tried to win my custom, but I had had enough of the special expensive tourist ways; I wanted to be united with Egypt now, to be as near as a *khawageyya* can be to a *bint balad*, a daughter of the country. At the very least, crossing on the public ferry. I had to laugh at myself for being confused about my identity here. An Englishwoman fretting about who she feels she is in relation to Egypt when the Egyptians live with the questions every day: are you urban or country, modernizing or traditional, religiously liberal or fundamentalist, veiled or bareheaded, *gallabeyas* or trousers, open to the West or protectively nationalistic? Where, along the lines that connect these poles, do you place yourself? Where do you get chucked by fate and circumstance? How frequently, and with what pain, do you get moved? To what can you cling? An Egyptian novelist, Waguih Ghali, wrote years ago that the reason Cairo looks cosmopolitan is not because of the foreigners, but because so many Egyptians feel and act like strangers in their own land. Unsure which way to go. Something Sa'id said, a while ago: 'How do you think it feels for a nation to sit where it has always sat, knowing that you all think *we* are on *your* edge?'

I noticed that the bumfluff police lad was accompanying me, but at a more than decent distance. I caught his eye and smiled at him; he looked away quickly. I didn't mind.

So I crossed the Nile. I looked out as I went for kingfishers, because I always do, but there weren't any. Around me thronged the populace: the women wrapped up in black, carrying packages, black eyes and green checking me and quiet comments sneaking out, with giggles and nudges. The men-*gallabeya*'d, trousered, busy with their business. No one eating, as they would be doing any other time of year. A handful of animals. Some fuss with a bicycle which had caught against someone's crate of chickens, resulting in some friendly joshing about how if they can't even hold it upright how do they intend to ride it? The bicycle owner squatted down and kissed the bamboo chicken crate: 'Look,' he said, 'they're not upset now.' A few years ago we would all have been squashed in between cars and taxis. No cars, not any more, because of the bridge.

The great ancient ark slid turgidly across, awash with greetings and gossip and the exchange of news. Beneath its strong and rusty hull slid the river, which was today the colour of amber, iron and almonds. I looked north towards Qus, Qft and Qena, to Dendara and Abydos, to Sohag, Assyut, Al Minya and Beni Suef. And Cairo, and the Delta, where the stem of the Nile swells into the lotus bud, and to the Mediterranean, the great sea that Allah put there for a purpose to separate the Muslims and the Christians. And I looked south, towards Esna and Edfu, Kom Ombo and Aswan, the dams and Lake Nasser, drowned Nubia, dead cataracts, Abu Simbel, Wadi Haifa, Sudan, Shendi, Khartoum, where the Blue and the White Niles came together out of Ethiopia and the mountains of the moon. Up there is where the giraffe (from the Arabic: *zarafa*, lovely) was caught that Muhammed Ali sent to the King of France in 1826. I daydreamed about the little giraffe, sailing down the Nile and across the sea to Marseilles, strange and beautiful to the French. I listened to the rackety babble around me, let the sun shine on my face. None of these people would seem that out of place on the Uxbridge Road. How out of place am I? I don't feel it.

London is my home only because it was, like for the newly hatched orphan geese, the first pair of Wellingtons I saw. My blood is English. But my heart and mind and inclination take me anywhere. Anywhere. Specially right here, among these people who know perfectly well that I don't belong here, but would welcome me anyway. For a moment I saw myself, surrounded by my books and my CDs, in white Nubian pyjamas, living in Sa'id's white marble-floored house, looking out from cool shade, through the window towards the tumbling yellow ruins of Ramses's funerary temple, Ozymandias, King of Kings, visible from our bed, and the palms arching and swaying in a mass down by the river. Saw myself crossing every day to the market, gossiping with these women. Saw Lily tapping away at bits of alabaster and making the workmen laugh as they showed her how to do it.

Stopped myself. Education? Language? Asthma? Harry? The heat, the hideous melting inferno of the heat, in the summer? Putting myself – and Lily – *entirely* in his hands? Flies, dirt, poverty, whatever? Ageing parents alone at home who've already lost one daughter? A man who doesn't even know I'm pregnant yet? Always being the *khawageyya* – the outsider. Always. Even if I were to become *Umm Ibn Sa'id* – Mother of the Son of Sa'id.

Stop it. This may be a subject for thought, but it is not a subject for fantasies about black curls and white pyjamas and the view of the Ramesseum.

And then when we landed something happened which made me feel quite ill.

Among the passengers was a European woman of fifty-odd, Scandinavian perhaps. Nice-looking, well-dressed, exchanging a few phrases of tourist Arabic with the people around her, friendly, cheerful, looking slightly excited. At the landing stage she was noisily hailed by a young man, I mean young, early twenties, skinny, dark, moustached, good-looking. Newly washed and pomaded. Her name was Ingrid. 'Inaga-reeda! Inagareeda!' he called. He fought through the throng to get to her, and when he did, kissed her loudly, publically, pretty much sexily. She quivered in his embrace, half embarrassed, very pleased. He grinned triumphantly. The gaggle of women I was sitting with looked, kissed their teeth, caught each other's eyes and made their opinion quite clear. His mother would be ashamed. His father would be ashamed. He should be working for a living, not . . . And that woman. But she's our sister now, she's a guest, she likes him so much . . . too much. But he should be ashamed. What's wrong with the fields and the workshops if he wants to make money? What's wrong with work? Times are hard now, but things will get better, *insha'Allah*, and look at him, in public, in Ramadan, selling himself like a . . . for all to see.

They were married, this couple. He put her in the car

(did she pay for it?) and got in beside her, playing with her fingers, smiling up at her under his little moustache. She just fluttered with delight at him.

These women, in public, are as quiet as water in a *zeir*, a water pot. I know what they'd be saying in Cairo though. (She's not bad-looking, for a meal ticket. Ah, but what grandchildren will his mother have? Well, there's a miracle we don't expect. Not for lack of trying, by the look of it. Why would we want to look?)

And they went on their way. I stood staring after the car.

That is not us, I said. No one would see that in us. If he were here with me now no one would be kissing their teeth that way, no one would say that of Sa'id. It's not the case, it wouldn't even look like it was the case. That is nothing to do with us.

But how could that woman not see, not hear? Is she looking at other couples and saying, 'That is not us'?

And that man – he knows. He must know. And yet so public – he must not care. Or – no, I know what it is. He thinks he's clever. He thinks that he's a *ga'dda*, a big clever fellow to have got such a catch, and that they are just jealous.

This morning's black snake seemed to have followed me across the river. It seemed to be laughing at me from the middle of the road. I felt slightly winded.

I went up the hill a little to see if I could get some juice, and stopped to get my breath. When I looked up a young lad was trying to catch my eye. He was making a slightly odd face at me. I had noticed him in the crowd on the boat, noticed him noticing Ingrid. Oh my god, he thinks he's giving me the eye.

'*Ramadan karim*,' I said to him. He melted away. The snake laughed and laughed.

Within five minutes I was hitching a lift to the *fabrique* in the cab of a pickup truck full of gas canisters. The driver kept hawking and spitting out the window on to the road. I tried to imagine that he was being devout, not swallowing, but he wasn't, he was just being disgusting.

'Tourist?' he grunted, grinding his gears as we turned right past the colossi of Memnon.

'*Bint el Araby*,' I said. Daughter of the Arabys, literally. Friend of the family, loosely. Though saying it gave me a bit of a turn. Daughter of the Arabs. He grunted again, and spat a bit more.

When we got there he wouldn't take any money. Any friend of the Arabys was, he implied, a friend of his. He waited for a while, I think wanting someone to see that he done this favour for their friend, but no one came out and he went off again, bearing my thanks and leaving me as ever in two minds about this country. And wondering, what do I mean, 'this country?' I lived here. This country used to be, to some degree at least, mine. The fruit of this country is within me.

*

I suppose I had hoped that Sa'id would come out, alone, by some miracle, and by some miracle it would all be all right. As it was there was no one out the front except the figures painted on the low white wall, sun-bleached multi-colour against the whitewash, tomb-painting-style ancients striding and offering and smiling their enigmatic smiles. I stood for a moment at the verge of the low flattened dunes of glistening white alabaster dust which surround the building for several yards all around, by-product of gener-ations of carving and grinding and polishing. I had a moment of alabaster reverie, breathing in the powder of crystallized peach, fractal ginger, oily green. I looked up to the two dark basalt hounds that guard the entrance, and considered walking into the shop. Decided against. Perhaps he is in there selling ashtrays to Dutch people. Perhaps Hakim will jump on me like a puppy. Oh no, he's gone to Aswan. Went round to the side instead, where a whitewashed alley leads into the courtyard. Went in.

It was Abu Sa'id who was sitting on the divan, in the shade, resting. My feet were quiet on the alabaster dust of their territory, but he heard me, and looked up. His face was a little more seasoned than ten years ago, a little darker, a little tougher. Though I had seen him only two and a half months before, it was his face from longer ago that was in my memory. The white hair above his ears was a little wirier, his beard a little wispier. His eyes carried their wisdom a little slower, his mouth could have been cut in rock. And he smiled, and his smile lifted his face like a fountain lifts water in a still pool. It was Sa'id's smile, the one Sa'id had not been giving me, and it was the cool water for which I thirsted. A line of poetry came to me: '*waka'anaha bardu al-sharabi*, it is as though she were the very coolness of drink itself.'

'Angelina,' he said, and he held out his hands and stood, and I made him sit again, and said, 'Abu Sa'id,' and the name in my mouth, carrying his son's child, seemed to me so full of respect: Father of Sa'id, I said, mother of Sa'id's child. Umm Ibn Sa'id. I wanted to tell him. I wanted so badly to tell him. This kind man. This first of the family that I knew, this host to me and my sick friend all those years ago when Sa'id and Hakim were children and Sarah was still a ghost, and Mariam moved through their house like a fish in dark waters.

'I am glad to see you here,' he said, and I knew that he was, that he remembered every curious thing about our curious brief friendship from years before. But does he know what has happened since? And if so, what does he think of it?

The smile was broad and brown and calm. What he said, however, knocked me sideways. 'You funny modern woman,' he said. 'You come yourself for your groom? Have you no one to send? Have you come to ask me for yourself?'

I think my jaw may have dropped.

'Abu Sa'id!' I think I said.

'Oh!' he exclaimed. 'Abu Angelina! Maybe! Who

knows? Do you want my boy? My big stupid beautiful boy. But . . .'

'What?'

'Will you take him away?' he asked.

'I don't know if he wants me, Abu Nil,' I said. The old nickname, Father of the Nile, not Father of Sa'id, was easier for me. 'I don't think he would let me take him anywhere he didn't want to go.'

'We can do without him,' he said. 'Don't let him pretend that we can't. Hakim will be sensible very soon. Don't let him claim to be indispensable here.'

'I'm too old for him,' I said.

'Love is ancient and timeless,' said the father.

'I have a child already.'

'Your dead sister's child. It is right that you take her in.'

'I live far away.'

'This is the modern world. We fly like birds, north to south, south to north.'

'I am a Christian.'

'I don't think that you are. And – Christian is not a bad tradition. You have one God. You have love and charity.'

'You and Sarah couldn't do it,' I said, knowing as I said it that I was pushing my luck.

I swear he curled his eyebrow as he paused, and looked, and laughed, and said: 'Hope springs eternal. I still believe in *el infitah*. At least between individuals.' The *infitah* was Egyptian government policy in the mid 1970s. Open door. Foreign investment, Western cultural influences, that sort of thing. Around the time Sa'id was a child. Then: 'I have seen my son these weeks. What he lost when you left, he needs. He will do as I say. He knows I am right.'

Suddenly it was not quite right. The surge of support I had felt turned into . . .

'Please don't tell him what to do,' I said. 'Please let him make up his own mind. Please . . .'

'Of course,' said Abu Sa'id. 'But whatever I do, he will be aware of what I want. He is my son.'

Family is here. Here is family.

'I am so sorry,' I said, 'about the . . . trouble that I brought . . .' I was echoing the words Hakim used when he came to stay with me in London. I tried to change the tune. Hakim had brought me very little trouble, really. 'I am sorry the police were here.'

'Oh, those boys often come to visit. They are not a problem. They did not suspect my sons of anything. And Hakim brought his own trouble on his own head. That is not your fault. We do not blame you. For anything.'

'Sarah seemed to,' I murmured, thinking even as I said it that I shouldn't.

I sat on the divan, and he sat with me, and took my hand, and held it, very kindly. I wished I could put his hand on my belly and whisper within to the shrimp: this is your grandfather. Instead I led the warmth of his touch up my arm and down inside me to the child.

'I used to blame her a lot, too,' he said. 'Now not so much. Now I understand better.'

'Have she and Sa'id been . . . are they?' I asked.

'I believe so,' he said. 'I believe so. Talking. And Hakim is all in love with her and with England. And says as Sai'd went to Paris so he must go to London. He wants to be English now. I told him Sa'id earned his own money to go and study.'

I hadn't known that.

'Sa'id will be back soon, *insha'Allah*,' he said.

Oh. He's not here.

'Where is he?' I asked.

'Your friend telephoned for him this morning. He went to meet him. I don't know where.'

My friend?

Which friend?

'Ari?' said Abu Sa'id.

Harry!

'Oh,' I said. Merely filling a gap with a noise, in order not to be rude. 'Oh,' I said again, because I didn't know what to think of that bit of news.

Abu Sa'id was watching me. 'Is that good for you, little one?' he said, and I shook my head, more in surprise than in the negative, and then sighed. It became the sort of moment which normally would have been rescued by the ordering of tea or the offer of food, but it was Ramadan, and none of these easy let-outs were available.

'Stay till he comes,' he said. 'I must go in now. I'll send you some tea,' and he shuffled off. I wanted to call him back. I wanted to ask him about Sarah, about their life and their separation, about bringing up his sons, and why he is talking now so easily about them leaving him?

'Abu Sa'id,' I called. He turned.

'I'm sorry about . . . Hatshepsut,' I said.

He was silent a moment.

'No one has slept,' he said, 'since then.'

He moved through the mosquito nets into his room, disappearing from the sunlight into the shade.

*

I lay back on the divan under the shade of the whitewashed wall, my feet tucked up under me, with the muffled banging and singing of the men in the workshop behind, and the high morning sun shining so hot just beyond me, and the fresh cool smell of the mint in the tea which arrived in a moment brought by one of the boys – Omar, I think was his name. Normally, I would have dozed. But with Abu Sa'id's words in my ear I could not. I rested my head, and let all that had happened ebb and flow in my mind, hoping, and praying, that confusion might subside and clarity might rise to the surface.

FIFTEEN

Ezwah

When I looked up, they were both there, standing over me, looking down at me. Harry, in ancient Levi's and a faded grey-green t-shirt, very tall, very out of place, very calm. Sa'id, in a white *gallabeya*, as spotless as only people from very hot countries can manage, very harmonious, very cool, very detached. Me, in a daze, very hot, very dopey, very confused. Clarity had not risen. The green canvas under my cheek was damp even in the shade. The noon sky glowed azure (from the Arabic: *azraq*) behind them and I could not see their faces.

My first thought on seeing them surprised me so much I had to close my eyes again. Through the heat and against the sky, I thought: 'Why can't I have both of them?'

Closed my eyes. What?

'Why can't I? Two children, two fathers, why *can't* I have two husbands? Why not?'

Knock that thought back. Think about it later.

I opened my dopey eyes properly and tried to sit, and scratched my head with both hands, vigorously, and squinted. Brigid once said that trying to wake me is like trying to wake a haystack. I felt like a haystack. A hot and slightly winded haystack, a haystack confused by . . . I know I like Harry. But . . . I stared at the two of them.

'What's happening?' I said. Meaning: with them, in the world. Thinking: to me, inside. Enough. Think about that later. It's nothing. It's just – of course Harry's gorgeous and a good thing, I've known that for years. Nothing's changed. Silly. Shut up.

They looked at each other. What have they been up to, the two of them together without me?

'You go,' said Harry.

In return Sa'id gestured Harry to sit. Omar appeared, and hovered. Sa'id told him to bring coffee. Harry sat gingerly, his long legs unaccustomed to folding as far as the low seat required. Here, out of hotel-land, in Egypt proper, he looked – not lost, but thoroughly . . . other. Other to Egypt. Though thoroughly himself. It made me think how other I must be, here. However at home I may feel. Remembered the scene when the *ma'adeyyah* landed.

Harry kept glancing at Sa'id. Of course he hasn't seen him in Egypt before. Let alone in this thoroughly Egyptian garb. I smiled. Harry will be going through that moment, when you see the person who was a cosmopolitan foreigner in London become utterly at home when they are at home, therefore more foreign to you, and you realize, suddenly, that you are the foreigner.

I curled my feet up on to the divan and leant forward to hear.

'I spoke this morning to Shezli,' said Sa'id. 'He . . . he has been with Chrissie. Chrissie has told him everything she could think of.'

This was not particularly good news.

'And what did she think of?' I asked, quietly.

'She told him that du Berry was Eddie,' said Harry.

'Which he already knew,' said Sa'id.

'And that she was his wife,' said Harry.

'Which he already knew,' said Sa'id.

'And that you knew him,' said Harry.

'Which he already knew,' said Sa'id.

Oh.

'How . . . Well, where does that leave us?' I asked. 'Where the . . .' It was too hot for this.

'He knew du Berry was . . . wanted. The rest he got from Hafla,' said Sa'id. 'She danced here some seasons, before, I don't know when. He spoke to her this morning and she told him du Berry was really an Englishman called Bates. She is heartbroken, apparently. And he was talking to colleagues in Cairo, and heard about the fight at the Semiramis, about Angeline – about me. So when Mrs Bates is up there with du Berry, and you are in the teashop with me, of course, soon he rings me.'

'And?'

'I have invited him this afternoon. We will talk it through.' I shook my head again, trying to loosen the tangle that was building up inside it.

'And Chrissie?' I said.

'She's back in her room, at the hotel. The doctor has seen her again, he will make a report. They think she may be mad with what has happened.'

'Did you see her?' I asked Harry.

'I saw her,' he said. 'She didn't see me.' I smiled.

'Did she say anything about . . .'

'She didn't confess, no.'

I sat a moment, letting it sink in, waiting to see if any ramifications would float to the surface, wondering briefly if ramifications float. A ram probably wouldn't, a fortification wouldn't. Oh shut up.

Sa'id was watching me. Harry was watching him.

'So?' I said.

They exchanged glances again.

'So it is up to Shezli, knowing what he knows, to decide whether anything happened which needs to be . . . taken further,' said Harry. 'He needs to decide whether to speak to his superiors, to the people in Cairo, to the British police. The embassy hasn't been informed yet, though they'll have to be. Du Berry had a British passport. He has to decide whether to keep you and Chrissie here in the meantime . . .'

'I *can't* stay,' I said.

'Sweetheart,' said Harry.

Sa'id looked at him.

'Lily . . .' I said.

'Of course,' said Harry.

I interrupted him. 'No,' I said. 'She's all that matters.'

Harry raised an eyebrow.

Sa'id said, 'All?' with a little smile.

At that Harry stood up and enquired after the bathroom. And gave me just enough of a look. And went into the house.

Sa'id took a moment or two after he left, and then said: 'Perhaps this is not the right time . . . but quite apart from Chrissie and Eddie Bates, all you want is to go home to Lily. Is that it?'

'No,' I said. 'That's not it.'

'That is what it comes down to,' he said. 'It did before, it does now.'

'No,' I said. 'No, there is more.'

'No doubt,' he said. 'But what?' Still cold. His beautiful pale eyes just looking, not giving a thing.

Do I tell him now? Can I tell him now?

I was going to. But what I said instead was: 'Do you want me?'

He looked at me a while longer.

'That is several questions, none of which I can answer, though each has several answers,' he said. 'I'm sorry, we should not be talking about this now. Not just because of Ramadan, but because it is pointless, until we know what will happen.'

'I was meant to be leaving today,' I said.

'You come, you go,' he said.

'I came back again,' I said.

'You go again.'

He caught my eye, and we giggled. Briefly.

'I want to say to you, though,' he said, 'I cannot tell Shezli what to do. But if this goes wrong, if you are to be charged, or to be kept here for months while this is sorted out, while all these institutions deal with this disgusting mess that has been brought about around this wicked man, and if your life or liberty is to be sacrificed to the mess and the institutions, if you like, I will take you across the desert into Libya, and I will take you to Paris and bring Lily to you there; I will get you new passports and new lives if need be. You won't be able to return to Egypt, maybe not to England either, I don't know. I will take you to Argentina. There are places. I will stay with you or leave as you wish. As you wish,' he said.

I closed my eyes and all the shapes stood out against the sun inside my eyelids. An idea hurtled through my head, a little comet trailing possibilities. Did Harry tell him about the baby?

'That's not real,' I said.

'So far.'

'Why do you say it?' I said.

Silence. Closed eyes. Heat. A donkey brayed in the distance.

'*Habibti*,' he said. '*Ya habibti*, it's as real as anything else,' he said.

Ah. Harry didn't say anything. A baby is as real as it gets.

'What do you mean, my love?' I asked gently.

'Ah, my love,' he said, teasing me a little, but even at this doubtful moment the words were beautful in his mouth.

'Yes, my love,' I said, firmly and luxuriously, offering him the word from my lips like a piece of fruit or a kiss. He's circling me, and avoiding me, and diverting me. He is like sand under the wind. I'll just wait.

And then he said: 'I *am* in love with you.' He said it thoughtfully, confirmingly, not quite surprised, not quite convinced.

I sighed, a long breath out.

'Why?' I said.

'Because you are fresh water to me, you are my skin, you are my own. For no reason. No proof. I tried to believe that I loved your blonde hair and your free ways, which would be easy, because they are not important things. But I don't, not specially. I love your heart. That's all.'

So there we have it. He loves. Confessed on the divan in his father's courtyard. I shivered.

Now, presumably, I should tell him.

I looked at him. His face was unutterably sad. Something else was going on.

'I fear for us, Angelina,' he said. '

Why?'

'Oh, we have plenty of problems, you and I. Where would we live?'

'At the surface of the water,' I said.

'What?'

I quoted: 'A bird and a fish may fall in love, but where would they live?' I can't remember where it's from, but it had been on my mind. He smiled at that.

'Would you ever stop romanticizing me?' he said.

'I don't romanticize you!' I squawked.

'Yes, you do. You love me for my blonde hair and my free ways. I know you do.'

'I do love your blonde hair and your free ways,' I said, smiling at the thought of his black curls and the delicious arabesques of his mind, 'but not only.'

'I have seen you romanticize me. I've seen you admiring my *otherness*. Look, now — I see you wondering whether I am wearing this . . .' he gestured his *gallabeya* with two hands, 'to put the distance between us, to frighten you off, or to appeal to you, when you know in fact I am just wearing it. I must tell you: I am not other to myself and I will not be other to my wife.'

Wife.

'Yes, you will,' I said. 'You're a man. She's a woman.' She.

And then he turned his face away and he said: '*Habibti*, do you want to hear this? Do you want to know my heart?'

'Yes,' I said. Gung-ho westerner that I am, I'm all for knowledge. He took my hand for a moment. The touch of him ran up my veins like salmon racing up river, quicksilver direct to my heart. And he put it down again.

'I don't want to love you,' he said. 'I don't want to leave Egypt, my father, my brother. I don't want my children to be what we have been, not one, and certainly not the other. And, and . . .' He turned back to me. For a second I remembered him sitting in the cloud of my white duvet at home, waking up after we had first made love, looking so happy, so golden, so young. He looked ten years older now. 'Do I sound sulky now? I am not sulking. I am torn . . . And there is something else, I don't know if you will understand this. I don't want to give myself and my life to a woman who . . .'

'Who what?'

'Who sleeps with a man and then leaves.'

There was something apologetic in his face. He didn't want to offend me. Or hurt me. There was something more. 'Who sleeps with a man,' he said.

'With you?'

'Yes. Not only.'

'Are you saying I shouldn't have slept with you?' I was steady. My voice was steady. Saying these unspeakable things.

'How could I say that?' he said, and in his eyes now I saw what I had seen the first time I saw him in London: the knowledge, the naked understanding we shared. The unavoidable, that is ours. Nemesis: that which is unavoidable, which is yours.

'But you're saying it.'

'I'm saying, you slept with Harry; you slept with Eddie; you slept with me . . .'

'I wouldn't say sleeping with is exactly what I did with Eddie. You can't compare those things . . .'

'I would like to say that I respect a woman's freedom, her freedom to do these things. But it doesn't matter — if I do or if I don't. My heart does not accept it. It is not the same for you as it is for us. You will do it again. It is your freedom. I don't judge it but I would not be able to bear it.'

'No woman should have the freedom to do what I did to Eddie. And . . .' my brain and heart were jostling each other here. Looking so steadily at that which makes me shake '. . . no woman should be in that position.'

'I know it is different,' he said. And there was a silence.

'What?' I said.

'Harry?'

'*Abl ma teshoufak enaya*,' I murmured. What I saw before my eyes saw you. I seemed to have forgotten the wild thought I had had when they were standing together above me. 'And you know,' I said, gathering my argument, as if argument was likely to do any good, 'you slept with me too,' I said.

'I didn't leave,' he said.

'You let me leave. And I came back. And I'm here now. And if you want a virgin, you know, you can have one, but it won't be me. I am me.'

He clasped his hands gently, his head low, as if in prayer. He shrugged.

'You're doing it again. You're leading me into danger,

and then making it all right. You're doing it again.'

That's what he said after the fight at the Semiramis. I still don't know if it's meant to be good or bad.

'You said,' he said, and thought for a moment. 'You said: Bind it up and let it heal.'

'I did.'

'It doesn't heal.'

'You haven't tried.'

'It doesn't heal.'

'Why not? Because your parents didn't? Are you afraid that I am like your mother? I'm not. I've healed before, I'll heal again.'

'Not what?' he said. 'Not what, of my mother? In what way are you different from any . . . free-wayed – I'm sorry, I don't like that phrase but now it has stuck . . . any free-wayed northern woman who comes here and leaves again?'

'And in what way are you different from any handsome man who fucks a tourist girl and waves bye bye? If we're pretending not to know each other, then how do I know you didn't, oh, fuck me for revenge on Englishwomen, because of Sarah? Please, Sa'id, we were beyond this before, why are we going backwards?'

'We weren't so serious before,' he said.

'I was serious. I was very serious.'

He looked at me again, thoughtfully.

'I know you were. I know you think you were. But . . . "*jada al-hawah bilfata wma la 'iba*",' he said. Love is a serious thing for a man, not a sport. I know that poem. Bassar, eighth century. What do I remember of the poem? It's about a girl who leaves.

'I don't think it's the same for you,' he said. 'I don't think serious means to you what it means to me.'

Is he patronizing me?

'Why?' I cried. 'Simply because I'm a woman? Because I'm English? Are you telling me I don't know love?' He shook his head.

'I know you know love,' he said. Oh, I knew he knew I knew love. He knew it, too. He began to smile, a slow curling smile, the one which grows and grows until the tip of his tongue appears and curls to touch his upper lip, and he looks at me sideways.

'Kiss me,' I said.

He snorted, quietly.

'No.'

'Bite my neck then. Hold my hand. Nibble my ear. Love me. Adore me.'

He started laughing. I laughed too. For a moment, we were just laughing. Then we stopped, and silence sat with us.

After a while he said: 'I know you weren't involved in his death. I was willing to think you were because I would think almost anything that would put a distance between you and me. I'm sorry, it's my protection against you. It was unkind. And I'm sorry I didn't come to see you last night.'

'*Ya habibi*,' I said. Oh my love. This would make me sad, and I wasn't interested in sadness. I had too much going on. This was just something to be got through because I knew he was wrong.

'If it goes right for you,' he said, 'and Shezli says you can leave, you will go home to London, and you will think about it. You may think that you want to be with him.'

'Who?' I said stupidly.

'He loves you. He is your child's father. You loved him before. We are very cool, aren't we, he and I, working together for your protection? But once you're safe, you know, we might fight like dogs for you.'

'But you don't want me,' I said.

'I don't want to want you,' he said. 'Different thing.'

He shook his head.

'Stupid, stupid,' he said. 'Anyway, first we must save you.'

We stared at each other a while. I couldn't but smile at him.

'This is too much talking,' I said. If he is not going to have faith in our ability to love each other, then how can we love each other? And is that what he's saying? Each thing we say has seven routes leading on from it, and as we converse we can only take one at a time. This conversation is a hydra. All I know is he is saying some terrible things and some wonderful things.

He stared at me. He was still leaning back. You will lean forward, you bastard, you will, you will.

And I still haven't told him the important thing.

*

Harry came back with Shezli, who he had encountered in the shop, with Abu Sa'id, while lurking to give Sa'id and I our privacy. Sa'id and I untwisted our eyebeams just in time. I could tell by the way Harry prowled that he knew it was all happening.

I moved over on the divan and Shezli sat beside me. Omar pulled over the other divan for Harry and Sa'id. Abu Sa'id positioned himself silently behind his son. I tried to gather up my self-possession, dignity, discretion and *savoir-faire*, which seemed to me to have been flung like lingerie around the courtyard floor by my conversation with Sa'id.

Shezli started, in Arabic, with courtesies. Sa'id responded in the same Luxori dialect, soft and southern. Of course; you don't speak with your own people in someone else's dialect.

Then Shezli stared at his shoes for a while. I was grateful for the time.

'I am in the sad position,' he began in English, 'Of knowing more than I like to know. So now I must know everything. Madame Angelina.'

'Sir,' I said. Which surprised me too. I suppose I wanted him to know I was a goodie.

'Are you married to Sa'id el Araby?'

'No,' I replied. Not, I think, giving anything away.

'Why did they think in Cairo that you were?'

I told him what I had told Mr Hamadi. He nodded.

'And why did you know Mr Bates?'

Keep it simple.

'Through me,' said Harry.

'And who exactly are you, sir?'

'Harry Makins,' he said. 'Detective Inspector. Metropolitan Police.' Pulling his authority on over his body like a garment, a little reluctantly, but recognizing the necessity. Like a jumper he didn't want to feel cold enough to need.

Shezli looked at him with his mild eyes. 'British police?'

'Yes,' said Harry.

'And why are you here?'

'Miss Gower alerted me – let me know – that Eddie Bates was here, and I came to give her any assistance she and Mrs Bates might need. Mr Bates was a very irrational man.'

'Irrational,' said Shezli.

'I believe you know what kind of man he was,' said Harry.

'Yes,' mused Shezli. 'And are you here as policeman?'

'If necessary,' said Harry.

'Do you have authority?'

'If necessary.'

'As police, are you glad that Mr Bates is dead?'

Harry didn't smile, but I could see the smile he didn't smile.

'The whole force would be grateful for the events that chanced to happen, if they didn't believe him to be dead already. It makes things very simple from our point of view.'

Another little pause, a musing and settling. Possibly also a going-over of the English, a checking that he had understood.

'Madame,' he said.

'Yes.'

'Do you believe your friend killed her husband?'

'No,' I said.

'Why not?'

'Because she said so. She is trying very hard at the moment to build herself a good and normal life. She has had many problems with him, and believed them to be over when he was said to be dead. She wants to be safe with her child. I don't think she would risk that now.'

'She believed her problems over when he was dead?'

I'm not falling for that one.

'Yes, but killing him would bring many more problems. Anyone can be glad of a death they would not go specially to cause.' Another digestive pause.

'If she wants no risk, why did she come to here, where he was?'

'We didn't know he was here. Had we known,' I said, with a sudden sense of effort, 'we would not have come.' And yet look how it has turned out. We are free of him. Not, however, free of his death.

I did remember that Chrissie had said, soon after she learned Eddie was alive: 'Safety is not the point.' But I also remembered how she had talked about her child, and getting strong, and making things right. And safety *was* my point. And my point on her behalf. 'And you? Would you kill him?'

'She was in the café,' said Harry. 'There is no question that she killed him.'

284

'She distracted witnesses with strange behaviour at an important moment,' said Shezli. 'Why?'

There have been enough occasions in my life when I have doubted my own motives, my actions, my responsibilities. Only through a lot of thought have I realized that I did no wrong in Janie's death, that I did no wrong in defending myself against Eddie with that poker, and that I did great wrong in fucking him, and not only to him. So it was easy for me to know I was telling the truth when I said: 'I had been worried to see them together in the taxi. I was sick. When I saw them on the roof I feared for her. I don't know why.'

'Feared for *her*?'

'Yes.'

'That she might be harmed?'

'Yes.'

'Or that she might harm?'

Ah well. Truth is so complicated, but lying is more so. I know, and knew, that Chrissie was a loose cannon.

'I didn't fear for him,' I said. Truthfully.

Then Shezli turned to Sa'id, and spoke in Arabic.

'How long have you known her?' he said. Clearly Sa'id had not told him the nature of our relationship. Whatever it may be.

'Sir,' I cut in. 'I speak Arabic.'

He looked at me. He saw that I told him that to show him that I was trustworthy.

'Why?' he said, and we continued in Arabic.

'Because I lived for a while in Cairo, about ten years ago. That was when I first came here, and first met Abu Sa'id.'

Shezli turned to the old man, who acknowledged my words.

'Do you vouch for her?' said Shezli.

'Of course,' said Abu Sa'id.

'And you?' he said to Sa'id.

'Of course,' he replied.

I was actually a bit reassured that he said that.

What, had I feared that he wouldn't?

Shezli sat in thought for a while. I told Harry what had been said. Shezli looked up. 'Policeman,' he said.

'Yes,' said Harry.

'What do you think?'

'Does it matter what I think?'

When he said that I knew we were still on dangerous ground. It sounded as if he were taking the question personally, not professionally. But then – yes, the British policeman in these circumstances might well wonder if it mattered what the British policeman thought.

'Yes,' said Shezli.

Harry was silent for a moment. I didn't look at him. I knew he would do what he thought right regarding Chrissie and me and our involvement, disregarding his involvement with me. I didn't want to make it harder for him, if he felt he had to land me in it. I knew that if he thought – personally, professionally – that Chrissie should face trial, and thus I should face being a witness, then he would say so. And I liked him the better for that. White hat Harry. Even though – no, because – he was doing me no favours. I like honesty.

So I had a bit of the flesh of my inner cheek between my back teeth as he spoke.

'There is no evidence,' he said. 'There is no case. In British law, there is nothing. We would have an inquest, it would say accidental death, perhaps misadventure. Perhaps causes unknown.'

Alhamdulilleh. But I found myself wondering. Did he really think that? Or was he saving us? Surely in Britain they'd have forensics up there analysing the angle of his shoe rubber and the speed of his fall in no time.

'What is misadventure?' enquired Shezli.

'When things go wrong, but it's nobody's fault.'

Shezli mused a little more.

'But that's British law. I don't know your law,' said Harry. He sat, imperturbable. I studied his face and I wasn't at all sure that that was British law.

'No witnesses,' mused Shezli, and looked at me again, as mild as ever. His head was narrow like that of a Sudanese.

'I didn't know he was here until the night before, when Sa'id told me,' I said. 'I didn't speak to Chrissie before she set off with him in the morning. She didn't know he was here until he turned up at the place where the convoy starts. I didn't see him before I saw him in the car, in the convoy. I was just looking for Chrissie to take her home, away from him.'

'Why didn't you see her? You were staying together, at the hotel?'

I . . . I said nothing. I was embarrassed. 'In the evening or in the morning? You didn't eat together?'

I . . .

'She stayed in my flat that night,' said Sa'id.

Harry glanced at me. Shezli's eyes opened wide.

There is a widespread belief in these parts that if a man and a woman are alone together there is always a third party present – the devil.

Maybe the devil pushed Eddie.

'She wasn't well,' said Sa'id evenly. 'She took the news badly that Bates was in Luxor. She fainted, and she slept.'

I did not like this. My sexual virtue weighed in with my trustworthiness. I saw how Harry was looking at me too. All these men accusing, defending, deciding, judging.

Shezli stared at Sa'id.

'It's Ramadan,' he said, in Arabic.

'Exactly,' said Sa'id, staring him right back.

Shezli looked to Abu Sa'id. He looked back, placidly.

Sarah's legacy to Sa'id slipped into my mind: this man will always be other to his own. She bore him, and left him here, always the half-English boy, but with no English person to help him with it. And Abu Sa'id will always be the man who married the *khawageyya*. Tainted – that's not quite the word – with the north.

'Well,' said Shezli.

'I don't think,' said Abu Sa'id, 'that he would have been
a better man to leave her alone, sick.'

'He could have returned her to the hotel,' said Shezli.

'She was not conscious,' said Sa'id. 'She was not well.
I don't think she is completely well now.'

Silence hung over us a little longer.

Shezli clicked his tongue on his teeth.

Harry looked at his watch.

'Don't leave yet,' said Shezli in English. 'I am sorry to
disturb your travel plans, madame. Policeman, when do
you leave?'

'This evening,' said Harry, 'but I'll stay on.'

'Call on me this afternoon.'

'Of course,' said Harry.

'I'll see you later,' he said to Sa'id. *'Insha'Allah.'*

'Insha'Allah,' said Sa'id, and they shook hands, and took
their open hands to their hearts, and shook again, each
with a hand to the other's shoulder. One of those curious,
specific and exclusive handshakes.

*

Shezli left, and Abu Sa'id left, and we three sat in silence.

'Thank you,' I said to them.

'It's not over yet,' said Harry.

'He doesn't want to deal with this,' said Sa'id. 'They
want to concentrate on the killers at Deir el-Bahri. He
doesn't want more bad news about Luxor in the European
press.' How coolly he mentions it now. None of the horror

he showed at his flat. 'I think we have given him enough to get out of it. And he is my *ezwah*. He will do what he can for me.'

'Are you using up your favours on me?' I said, with a little smile.

'I have plenty,' he said. Harry looked slightly amused by Sa'id's straight face as he said it. But it's true — he has plenty, *ga'dda* that he is. Remember the truckdriver who would not take money from me. No charge. And it may save my skin.

And at the same time, he is the Englishwoman's son. It says something for his character that he is both.

I don't want to take him away from this place which is his. He is the backbone. When the sons leave, the village dies. And it's usually the strong and the brave and the demanding who leave. I'm not saying Qurnah will collapse if Sa'id leaves. Just . . . when the sons leave, the village dies. He told me once that a million Egyptians left Egypt during the 1970s.

How angry he was when I didn't let him save me in Cairo. OK, *habibi*, save me. I don't mind. Save me.

I smiled at him, a big happy smile. '*Shukran, ya habibi,*' I said. Thank you, my darling.

He sighed and put his hands over his face.

Harry wanted to change the subject.

'Oliver doesn't know I'm here,' he said.

'Shouldn't you tell him?' I asked.

'I'm hoping I won't have to,' he said. 'If I do have to,

of course he'll wonder why I didn't tell him earlier. And why I didn't tell him about Eddie's death.'

I pulled myself to attention. There were other things going on in the world apart from me and Sa'id.

'Not that there's anything we can do,' he continued. 'Until Shezli sends down his verdict,' remained unsaid.

'We wait,' I said.

'Yup,' said Harry.

'Yes,' said Sa'id.

We waited a little. The sky stayed blue and the walls stayed white and the shadows may have crept round a little but nobody noticed if they did.

'I'll go and see Shezli,' said Harry.

Sa'id called Omar to drive him down to the landing stage.

Harry kissed me on the cheek as he left, his hand on my upper arm. 'Fucking tell him,' he whispered. 'It's not fair.' He didn't say on who.

*

Sa'id looked at me. I hoped that we might have an interlude during which the joy we took in each other's company might have a turn to flourish, but no.

'Lily is your priority,' he said. 'You will always put her above me. You assume this. You take it for granted. You assume London. You assume you are going home.'

'Don't cut me in half,' I said.

He smiled at that, and I saw clearly exactly how cut in half he felt, and had always felt.

'I assume,' he said, 'that I have some say in where I live.'

'At the surface of the water,' I said. 'Our problem is only geography.'

'I fear for us,' he said again. 'Why do you love me?'

'No reason,' I said. 'Why do you want a reason?'

'Why shouldn't I? Am I an unreasoning person? A romantic, unreasoning, stoical Arab?'

'And you assume,' I said, 'you assume that you can get away without ever facing your Englishness. Hakim is facing it. You won't.'

He smiled at me, and it was his beautiful smile. It *is* as if he were the very coolness of drink. *Al-sharabi.* The word drink doesn't quite have the same . . . coolness. Sweetness. *Sharbaat. Habibi sharbaat. Damoh sharbaat*, sugar blood, drinkable, sweetheart. Sa'id el-Sharabi.

Foolishness.

'Oh, how you steer me into waters where I don't want to go,' he said. 'Look how you do that. You're doing it again.'

'Anyway, maybe you will come to Brighton.'

He has a point when he says we can't talk about anything. How can we talk about this, and how can we not?

'Ah,' he said. 'The *gam'iyyaat* study.'

'What is *gam'iyyaat*?' I asked. 'You never explained.'

'There are a thousand different kinds. Credit schemes. The women run them, usually.' I looked expectant. It would be nice to talk about something else.

'You pay in a little money, every month,' he said, 'and

each person in turn gets a payout of all that everybody has paid in that month. You say when you will want the money, for a wedding, for extra lessons, for building, to extend your business or invest in equipment. If a crisis comes up you can say, can I have it now. So you can have the money before you would have saved the entire sum. No interest, so it is available to the devout, no collateral, no credit records, just your standing in the community, your neighbours' knowledge that you are honest. You don't have to borrow from your family, or the banks, there's no tax, it's accessible to almost everyone. Also the women can lie to their men about how much they are saving, so the men can't waste all the family money. They are beautiful. They are so simple, and they do what economic theory so often can't – they help people to live their lives.'

'Are they legal?' I asked.

'Not encouraged,' he said. 'But impossible to control anyway. Private. And there is this research project, and they need an economics graduate, and probably I know a lot of it already, but there is some comparative and analytical stuff to do, too, with equivalent enterprises in India and Latin America, and the mother says she has put me forward for it.'

'Are you going to?' See how cool I was being? Just asking?

'No,' he said. 'I'm not going back into her womb. But it made me think about what I might do. Maybe go to America and study the enemy.'

'Don't go to America,' I said.

'Ah, I'm not going to America,' he said, with a little laugh. 'I'm not going anywhere.'

How cool, how impersonal. Does he not realize that we are not exchanging news here, we are sealing our fate?

'Sa'id,' I said. 'What happened to Eddie's money?'

'Nothing,' he said, and looked to me with those pale, pale eyes. 'I don't know what to do with it. It's too much. I can't be responsible for it, and I have been unable to think clearly about what would be best . . .' It wasn't that he was accusing me, but only then did I realize what a big thing that had been to ask of him. Just offloading what I had been unable to deal with, and not thinking what it might mean for him.

'I thought of investing it, you know,' he said, 'and putting the interest to run a school or something. And also to adult literacy – you know to work in the public sector you must be able to sign your name for your pay cheque, even if you are the janitor or the watchman. So, if you have the price of a few writing lessons, you can become employable. And once you are employed, you pay back the price. Sweet and easy. I thought of sending it to your government with a note: here, have *this* for your Third World Debt.' He gave a bitter little laugh. 'But I have been unable to do anything.'

I was smiling at him. He caught me at it and shook his head.

Of course he realizes what we are doing. Of course he does. How we dance around each other. But when I was a dancer, I always danced alone. I'm not used to dancing with. And I don't like dancing around in this way.

'Stop it,' I said.

'Go and marry that man,' he said. 'Go and be an English family.'

'Stop it,' I said, and then I laughed, because he was being such an oaf, and irritating me.

'Why are you laughing at me, *habibi*?' he said. *Habibi* for a man.

I laughed some more.

'Stop that,' he said.

'Why?'

'The way your throat moves,' he said, with sudden tenderness, 'when you laugh . . .'

Oh lord, I've died and gone to heaven. If only for a split second.

'Sa'id, could you make up your mind? You're driving me mad.'

Our eyebeams twisted again, and we sat in silence.

He smiled and I melted, again, again.

Now, I thought. And swallowed.

'There is one more thing,' I said.

And as I started to say it Abu Sa'id came out, and sat down gently on the divan, taking over the conversation with the quiet authority of an unchallenged parent. He started off as he does from halfway through a conversation. Abu Sa'id starts off from a point which most people don't get to after twenty years of friendship.

'It is the Egyptian way,' he said, 'to recreate the family. Sa'id, if you are intending to recreate mine, I have one word for you. Don't let her go away. And if she does, go with her. There is the little family, and the bigger family, and the big family of Egypt, and there is the world and that is your family, too.'

And off he went again.

Sa'id didn't look at me. He was looking under his eyebrows towards his departing father. He said nothing about what Abu Sa'id had just said. Nothing pro, nothing con. Nothing at all.

The moment was gone. Abu Sa'id's words floated off into the blue. It was as if we hadn't heard them. If only, I thought, I could take Sa'id in my arms, this would be all right.

'Let's go for a walk,' I said.

He looked at me sideways. 'No,' he said. 'First we save you. *Insha'Allah*. The . . .'

It occurred to me that he hadn't eaten for hours. He was getting the Ramadan face.

'We have a lot to talk about,' I said.

'First we save you,' he interrupted. His face had taken on the condensed muscularity which means he has nothing to say, he has retreated. Then he stood, and said: 'Wait one moment.'

He disappeared, and returned with the holdall. The same one, full of the same money.

I looked at it.

He pushed it towards me. 'I'm sorry I couldn't help you.'

'I don't want it,' I said. 'Don't give it back to me. I don't want it.' The sight of it made me panicky. 'Please,' I said. 'I can't take it to England. What if I'm stopped? What if Shezli finds it? I don't want it. Please. Please don't look at me like that. Please don't do this hard polite thing. Please don't be sorry you couldn't help me. You have helped me so much . . .'

In a second, he was tender again. The hardness fell off him like scales.

'How?' he said.

'With Janie, with Eddie, with death and responsibility, with how to behave. With knowing myself. *Ya habibi*, I don't love you for nothing. I don't love you for nothing . . .'

He closed his eyes. Pain on his face.

'So what shall I do with it?' he said, very softly.

'Give it to Magdi Yacoub's children's heart fund in Cairo. Anonymously.'

'Meshi,' he said. OK.

We sat in our silence.

'Come,' he said after a while. 'I'll take you down.'

'I'll go back over,' I said. 'But I want to see you . . . I want to see you . . .'

'Be honest,' he said. 'You want to see me in England. You want to see me in England, two months ago, when everything was unreal.' Well, I laughed.

'Sa'id,' I said, 'I'm yours, I love you and I understand all this. All of it. Get used to it.'

He swore gently in Arabic. *'Bint el . . .'* Daughter of . . . what? A dog? Happiness? Both are common phrases. Shaking his head. 'Go away,' he said. 'Go away. Come on . . .' and he put me in the Merc and drove me down to the dusty landing stage, humming, and paid a small boy to take me on a boat back across the river, over to the bright lights strung like a necklace along the bank, and he looked as if he didn't know whether to laugh or cry. As I crossed over the river, looking back to see him turning and walking away under the arcs of the palms, an old song came to me: all the trees are laughing, they laugh with all their might, laugh and laugh the whole day through, and half the summer's night.

But in the car he had been humming a different melody: Umm Khal-thoum, of course. Not *'Enta 'Omri'*, You are my Life. *'El Atlal'*, The Ruins.

SIXTEEN

I don't think you understand

Halfway across the river I said to the boat boy: 'Take me back.'

'But Mr Sa'id said take you other side,' he objected.

'Take me back.'

He took me. A long skinny taxi driver was sulking in the café, looking utterly ready for *Iftar*.

'Would you take me to Deir el-Bahri?' I said. He stared at me.

'Hatshepsut closed,' he said. He didn't like to be asked.

'El Nobala,' I said. Tombs of the Nobles.

That seemed OK to him. *'Meshi,'* he said.

Up the road again. Past the colossi again. Stopped at the ticket office. I wouldn't need a ticket because I wasn't going into any of the tombs, but I didn't want to have to explain anything so I bought one. Turned right, and sailed past the *fabrique*. His car parked outside the front, the basalt hounds, the dust-coloured mosque across the way.

Heading up towards *el Qurn*, the horn-shaped peak at the top of the Valley of the Tombs of Nobles, for which Qurnah is named.

I jumped out at the end of the tombs. The driver said he would wait. Half an hour, I said. I waited until he had subsided and lost interest in me before I began to scrabble up the hillside to the right, following the route that Sa'id and I had taken two and a half months before, when we walked out here by moonlight, to be alone and to embrace. Up here on this hillside is the last place where Sa'id and I made love. That's not why I had come.

The afternoon sun was hot and the land was dry and difficult, but the climb was not long. Within fifteen minutes I stood on the prow of this particular sphinx-limb, looking down to the Temple of Hatshepsut in the valley below.

I have never much liked this temple. I like Hatshepsut herself, with her fake beard and her long poem in stone, but not her temple. It reminds me of Italian fascist railway stations, big and pale and stark and arrogant. See me? I'm here so fuck off. It seems to be trying to boss the mountain out of which it is carved.

Well, this day I couldn't see it. Even as I turned to look my eyes filled with tears and my legs gave way beneath me, and I found I was sitting on a bare hilltop and weeping. I turned my back on it. Wept.

After a while the taxi driver appeared in front of me. He stood a little way off, his eyes filled with tears.

'You have . . . family?' he said. Delicately.

'*La'ah*,' I said. No. '*Kolena wilet Adam we Hawa.*' I was just extending the family a bit. 'We are all sons of Adam and Eve.' Sons of Adam, in Arabic, means human beings. Including women and infidels. You know — what I am.

'Madame,' he said, holding his tears.

I wanted to say a prayer or something but I couldn't do a thing, so in the end I stood up and we walked back down together, taking care not to let loose stones on one another's ankles. He drove me back down to the landing stage and there was the *Nefertiti* boy, and I graced him with my custom and was wafted in isolation back to Luxor.

*

How does it go, '*El Atlal*'? The word actually means The Deserted Desert Camp, after the people have moved on. The classical Arab odes start there; they go on to lost love, the fineness of camels, the hardship of the journey . . . but this song is all about being drunk with love. Drink with me in the ruins . . . Has love ever seen drunkenness like ours, we built fantasies and dreams, we walked on a moonlit road and saw happiness jumping ahead of us; we laughed like children and leapt ahead of our shadows. Something about how his beauty offends beauty. And then: Give me back my freedom, let loose my hands; I gave everything, I held nothing back. You are making my wrists bleed. Umm Khalthoum sang that verse five times to Nasser in 1968; you can hear the applause on the recording. Crying out, the voice of Egypt.

And then — how did this love overnight become history?

And: We meet like two strangers, and each goes his own way. Don't say we willed it. Fortune willed it.

*

I rang him the moment I got to the hotel, from the foyer so I didn't have to see Chrissie or Harry.

'How are you?' I said.

'I'm hopeless,' he said. 'I'm mad. I'm mad in love with this woman, she's driving me crazy, I don't know what to do, she's just been here today and there's this other man she should be with, it would be so much better, it makes so much sense, and I don't want to ruin her life . . .'

'Why would it be better for her to be with him, if it's you she loves?'

'Oh, she loves him. She loves him. It's a different love. And they're older than me, they should be thinking of these adult things, they have a child. And they're both English, they could be at home together. She thinks she could live here, bring her child, desert the child's father . . . she couldn't live here. It would ruin her. She'd hate it. You know, foreigners can't swim in the Nile. Maybe in the middle, where it's fast-moving, if they splash about and get out again quickly. But if they go into the shallows, the still calm parts of the river, and stay there, they catch bilharzia, and they lose their strength and their own body fails them, they die . . . Do you know about Khaum Nakht?'

'No,' I said.

'Her mummy was found in the tomb of the two brothers. She died of bilharzia, and now research is being done in Manchester, using her tissues, tracing the development of the disease . . . we have so much to offer, you know.'

'So much to collaborate on,' I said.

'On some levels,' he said.

'Why not this one?'

Silence.

Then: 'I'm the grit in her oyster,' he said. 'I should just disappear . . .'

'The mummy's?' I asked, momentarily confused.

'Yours, *habibti*.'

'Pearl,' I said. A pearl on my tree.

He laughed, softly.

'We could live together in another place,' I said. 'Paris, or . . .'

'What, and add another culture to confuse your child? And then you and I have children, what are they? Where is their home? English Arabs in Paris?'

'Where I come from there are all kinds of cultures living together. English and Arab and everything you could imagine.'

'All in exile,' he said. 'All stateless. Homeless.'

'All building and contributing to their new homeland,' I said.

'Oh!' he said. 'Naive!'

'I am not naive,' I declared. 'I live there. Call me optimistic, but I am not naive. People do it. I'm not saying it's easy or simple, and certainly, what do I know, I'm white and English, but Sa'id, people do it. They land in it, stay in it, ebb and flow with it, suffer and survive, give and take, live and die. Who says life would be any easier anywhere else? I was born in the city everyone else comes to, *habibi* – my home is the most welcoming and most indifferent place in the world; we have the grandest theories and the most terrible failures, the best intentions and the worst tragedies, we have no ghettoes and yet our boundaries are strong – but they are mobile, they are flexible. In my home, everybody is other. Sweetheart – it is a long slow journey, but we are all building and contributing to this homeland. By surviving. By still being there. All of us. All of them. The whole world.'

'My world is here,' he said.

'I can't believe you're being so parochial . . .'

'Not parochial. Truthful.'

'But you've lived abroad, you've . . .'

'Exactly,' he said.

'What?'

'Multiculturalism is a luxury you can afford. We are clinging to our culture,' he said. '*Habibti* – multiculturalism is a Western idea.'

In all our conversations around these subjects he has never before stated it so starkly, nor applied it to me. Against me. So political, so personal.

I only wanted to be personal.

'Do you feel homeless, my darling?' I asked.

'No. This is my home.'

I closed my eyes and tried to look out through his. Absent mother. English blood. National service. Years in Cairo, years in France. Decline of great empires: the ancient Egyptian, the Arab. History of invasions: the Assyrians, the Greeks, the Romans, the Turks, Mamluk and Ottoman, the French, the British. Tourism and economic dependence. The violence of fundamentalists. All those languages. Seen through insecurity.

'Sa'id,' I said. 'Are we discussing our future, and how it might work? Or are you telling me we have none?'

He laughed again, so quietly.

'Why do you ask me?' he said. 'Do I know? Is it my decision? The future will come, *insha'Allah*, First we save you. Now go away.' And hung up.

I leaned back on the foyer sofa and listened as my blood rippled through my veins, and my muscles rippled up and down my body, and my child swam silently through his private salty sea. I wanted to roll over on to my front, and hold myself in my own arms for a while, and lay my head on my own shoulder. But I couldn't. So I went up to see if any of my compatriots were around. They weren't.

*

I found them down by the pool, on sunloungers. Together. I hesitated behind a cloud of mimosa, wondering what he had told her for it to be OK for him to be lying around with her. He wouldn't have told her he was a cop, so, what, who could he be being? Eddie's old running boy who's turned up here? What, by chance? Oh, sure. Or with Eddie? No, she wouldn't be lying around with him if that were the case. She'd be scared witless.

They looked for all the world like holidaymakers. Chrissie, in an orange bikini, was even reading *Captain Corelli's Mandolin* (though I had noticed on previous occasions that she sometimes had her AA handbook concealed behind this less-revealing fascia). Harry, in his ancient jeans, was dozing, lying back with his head sideways and his arms flung above his head, biceps like great peachstones under his white blue-veined skin. I could see part of 'Man is born free, and is everywhere in chains', snaking dark turquoise round his upper arm. Angeline was hidden, there on the other side. *Victory* was invisible.

I slunk through the palms round to the swimming-pool bar, and settled myself out of view. A waiter glided over to me.

'Madame?'

I asked him politely to go quietly and bring me that sleeping man over there. He looked only very slightly disapproving, but even so I whispered to him in Arabic, 'It's all right, he's my brother.' He giggled, and glided over.

Peering round, I could see Chrissie look up, and Harry rise, shrug to her, and follow the waiter over, pausing only to pull on his t-shirt. I was glad he did that. There's something unpleasant about half-naked bodies walking around in public in Islamic countries. Even bodies that are pleasing to look at, like Harry's. Even by pools built for westerners.

I watched him as he walked. He moves nicely. I teased him once about the silent way he lopes about. 'It's my training,' he'd said.

An image sprang into my mind: it lasted about three seconds. Sa'id, Harry, and me. I felt it, physically. It made me gasp.

Harry looked up.

I was thinking which one I would want where: which above, which below. Which in front, which behind. Which on which side of my neck. Whose hair, brushing me where. Four of those pointless, delicate male nipples. Two girdles of shoulder, held by bands of taut muscle. Two breathing ribcages, two beating hearts. All those limbs, all those buttocks, all those – oh please.

He was with me now, looking down at me. I swear I was scarlet.

But if I want both of them, I can't really want either of them.

'Hi,' I said tightly, but the images wouldn't leave my mind. A waist for each of my arms, a mouth for each of my ears, or one for the small of my back and one for my belly, two long backs, and four shifting shoulderblades, so many hollows of shadow around collar bones and between ribs. Four hands. Four arms, muscled with peachstone and rope, two honey-brown, two milk-white, one of them tattooed with my name.

I could picture both men, very clearly.

'Oh fuck,' I said.

'What?' he said.

'Nothing.' I couldn't look at him. Looking at his knees was bad enough. His knees, I remember, look like elephants' heads. All his joints are large in his long limbs. Big knots of sinew and bone. Such a surging physical memory of how we had been, together. Me and him. Me and Sa'id. I felt sick. Sick with lust.

He sat on the end of the neighbouring lounger.

'Are you all right?' he enquired.

'Yes,' I said, scrabbling for sense. 'What did you tell her?'

He grinned, his triumphant grin. He used to have a Triumph t-shirt – Triumph motorcycles, you know – and he'd wear that, and the *Victory*, and this grin, and he would look just the cockiest fuck you ever saw in your life. Actually this might be the same t-shirt, with the lettering finally faded away completely. It looked old enough. In my mind the whole shirt faded away. Oh lord.

He reached across his chest and hoicked up his left sleeve a little with one big-knuckled finger. There I was. Angeline. Dark tattoo turquoise on blue-white. Only a little faded.

'I told her I was your devoted ex-lover,' he said, 'reformed after an unfortunate interlude of crime, and desperate to regain your good graces and save you from a dreadful fate of single motherhood. I told her I had rung you, here, as a matter of course because I never normally let you out of my sight, and joined you as soon as I heard. I confided in her, deeply. She loved it. She wants to be fairy godmother to our rediscovered love. She told me all about Sa'id, and warned me of the terrible rivalries ahead, largely based on him being so good-looking and not at all some burning-eyed camel-driver, which was what she'd expected, but promised to be on my side because she doesn't want you moving to Egypt forever, she wants you to stay in London and be her friend. We're deeply bonded now. She wants to be our bridesmaid.'

My name, there on his arm.

'You're going to burn,' I said stupidly. 'You should put on some suncream.' It was the first thing that came into my head. I only said it because his body was on my mind, and I was trying to divert the direction my thoughts were taking with it. Fat lot of good it did.

'Good idea,' he said. 'Would you . . . ?'

The images flooded back, of both of them. But this one, the reality, the actual physical man of him, with his weight and his warmth and his concrete solidity, was right there, saying something that might require me, as an everyday courtesy, to put my hands on his warm, hard body . . .

I don't know if he saw the look on my face.

But I'm in love with Sa'id.

Enough already. I stood, and kicked off my shoes, ran to the pool and dived in.

*

Chrissie was squinting at me when I clambered out, pathetic with my dress clinging to my thighs and my eyelashes sticking together. It had worked. I felt nothing but cold and wet and stupid.

'What's that for?' she asked.

'Oh, sweetheart,' I said, 'don't ask. Are you all right?'

'No,' she said. 'I'm waiting to be charged with murder in a foreign land. I can't go home until strangers have decided what to do with me. I tried to ring Darla and I can't get through. *He* turns up,' she nodded towards Harry, 'which is really terribly confusing. The policeman took away my passport. I want to go to a meeting because if I don't I know there's a bloody bar in this hotel, and I have been imagining from your descriptions the large and very bad-quality martini that's waiting down there with my name on it. In Arabic. There's a limit to what a girl can take, Angeline, I'm sure you know that. But I'm . . . oh. I'm glad to see you. Did you tell him yet?'

'No,' I said.

'No!' said Harry. 'Jesus, girl, what's the matter with you?'

I looked up at him, looked at his face, and said, 'Oh please. Please, Harry.'

'This can't last,' he said.

'Things fall apart, the centre cannot hold,' said Chrissie. We both stared at her.

'Clearly it's time to get drunk,' she said. 'Harry, you must do it for us.'

'I don't think so,' he said.

'Did you see Shezli?' I asked.

'Elvis?' said Harry.

'Yes.'

'So did I,' said Chrissie. 'Little man, big power over me . . .'

I was watching her. Still wobbly, definitely.

'What did he say?' I asked Harry. Elvis indeed. But it made me giggle.

'More of the same,' he said.

I was putting myself down on a sunlounger, but it was useless. I was too wet, and the sun was heading west. It wouldn't be long till *Iftar.* Sa'id would be eating soon. Can I call him when he's eaten, when he's balanced again?

Balanced! I'm a fine one to talk.

Can I call him at all after what I've just been thinking?

'Go and get changed,' said Harry. 'You'll catch your death.'

I stood up again. Uselessly, and stood there, uselessly.

'Come on,' said Harry, and not for the first time in my life he took me by the arm and led me to safety.

*

'What's it been like, having my name on your arm?' I asked him in the corridor.

He looked at me.

'Well, there are situations where it doesn't help,' he said. 'Specially not *your* name.'

'Why specially mine?'

'When Amygdala saw you . . . she took one look at you and left me.' Amygdala was his girlfriend, last summer.

'When did *she* see *me*?'

'Queensway. That night. You were with Sa'id.'

'Oh.' I remembered that night. We'd been eating, they'd passed by, I hadn't seen them.

'I'd told her you were a horse I had won on . . . she didn't fall for it. Specially not once she saw you.'

I laughed all the way to the door. Then as he opened it he turned to let me pass, and he stood there, and he said, 'Well?'

'Well what?' I replied, in time-honoured fashion.

'Well why didn't you tell him?'

'The time wasn't right,' I said after a sulky pause.

He stepped into the room, and prowled around it a little.

'Do you want me to?' he said, not unkindly. 'I can call him now.'

'Don't you fucking dare,' I said.

'So?' he said. 'What?'

I stood there in my wet dress.

'It hasn't been possible,' I said. 'Believe me I've tried.'

'What are you holding out for?' he said. 'He loves you, he wants you, he'll have you, you want him, you love him, what the fuck's the problem? I wish,' he said, suddenly vehement, 'that you would get on with it.'

'He doesn't want to want me,' I said.

Harry looked at me.

'That's bollocks,' he said. 'That's just bollocky – that's nothing.'

'No, it's not,' I said, because I knew what it was. I could quite understand why he would want not to want me. He knows that I would stay here for him, if that's what it took . . .

Oh, but would I? Look at that list of potential problems again. Where would Lily go to school? How would she take to Arabic? How would living in the desert affect her asthma? How are the hospitals? What would the climate do to her eczema? A hundred and twenty degrees, sometimes, in the summer? There's no way Lily could bear a Luxor summer. And next June, when I give birth, *insha'Allah* – do I want to give birth here?

And my total and complete loss of independence . . . what kind of burden would I be on him, with no wings? The independent weigh twice as much, when they become dependent. There is a liberty for him in London that I could never find here.

And Mum and Dad. Friends. Work. Finance. Even if it were Cairo, not here in the desert . . .

And . . .

Harry? Lily's just-found father? After all we've been through? I tried to imagine telling Harry that Lily and I were moving to Luxor. It made my stomach shake. I wondered if he had thought of it, all the times he encourages me to talk to Sa'id. How could he not have? Or does he assume . . . as Sa'id thinks I do . . . that we would live in London?

Whether or not Sa'id believes I would stay, he thinks I would leave, later. Like his mother did. Like I did before. And he doesn't fancy that, and who can blame him.

And yet, and yet. It's so negative.

And yet that which I understand I must respect. Which put me in what I think is called a double bind. Or a triple. Thought of Chrissie's large martini. I'll have a triple bind, please, on the rocks.

Actually I'd rather not.

'Anyway, he won't do anything, or say anything, till I'm saved,' I said.

'Well, that I can understand,' said Harry.

'I think he doesn't believe in "mixed marriages",' I said, putting a self-conscious emphasis on the phrase because it's stupid.

'All marriages are mixed,' said Harry. 'Anyway, in that case he shouldn't have been shagging you without a Durex.'

'How tenderly you put things,' I murmured.

'Sorry,' he said. 'Sorry.'

I sat on the bed. 'No,' I said. 'It's true.'

'Have a bath or something,' he said. 'Go on.' He knows what my comfort thing is. Sweet. Tender, in his way.

I went and turned on the taps, pulled off the cold wet dress. Felt stupid.

'Do you want me to talk to him?' said Harry, from the bedroom. I thought about that a little.

'Why?' I asked.

'In case,' he said.

There was a great deal unspoken between us.

I climbed into the bath even though it was only an inch or so full. Just to do something, to make some change to a situation in which I was powerless. The water flowed in, hot, and the room started to steam.

'We could try another way,' he said.

'Another way of what?'

'Another way out.'

'Like what?'

'From London,' he said.

But we both knew there was no other way out of this mess. Not one as swift and effective as this would be. If it worked.

I tried to sink down into the water but there wasn't enough. A question which had been lurking in the recesses came floating out.

'Hon?' I said.

'What?'

'What you said this afternoon, about British law . . . Is that true?'

'Pointless question,' he said.

'I'm asking it anyway.'

I could feel his silence through the bathroom door.

'Get to the point then,' he said.

I thought about that for a moment. It pleased me.

'Did you lie to protect me?'

I waited, thinking it was just another of those silences. But no answer came.

A while later I murmured: 'Poor Chrissie.' My mind had wandered on.

He laughed, quietly.

'What?'

'I love your ridiculous sympathy,' he said.

Yeah, well.

*

She came and knocked at the door about half an hour later. Harry called her in and she entered shyly.

'I didn't know . . .' she said.

He smiled at her. I could tell, though I was still in the bath, topping up hot water. I think he'd been reading.

'Says it all,' he said.

The bathroom door was still open, the steam creeping around.

'Should we eat?' she said.

We didn't answer, so she ordered a bucketload of room service, and we sat, and we ate. We were all very quiet. All of us knew there was absolutely nothing we could do.

*

When Chrissie went to bed, I sat for a while with Harry, still not saying much. There was a very deep fatigue about, part calm after a storm, part calm before the storm. Part calm in the eye of the storm. The windows were open and the rivery smell had crept across the Corniche and all the way up to the room.

'You remember when Eddie died before?' he asked suddenly.

'Yes,' I said.

'Does it feel different this time round?'

'Yes,' I said. 'But I don't know why . . . Last time, I suppose, it was a shock. This time I'm used to the idea. Last time, even though he was the danger, it felt dangerous that he was dead . . . in case I had done it. Of course it's dangerous this time too. But last time I thought I might have contributed, and this time I know I didn't.'

'Even though last time there was no question of legal proceedings, and this time there is?'

'Evidently I mind more about being innocent than I do about being thought innocent.'

'So far,' he said. 'It could go very wrong, this.'

'If it does I will just throw myself on the mercy of . . . whoever seems to have any mercy.' I'm not thinking about it. There's nothing I can do.

He grunted.

'How about you?' I said.

'What?'

'Him being dead?'

'Ah.' Silence, for a while. 'You spend years chasing someone, catch them, have them swiped from under your nose, then they die anyway. There's that. And there's him, himself.'

'Your ex-boss.'

'Yes.'

'Well?'

He wrapped his long arm around himself again, to scratch his back. 'He was a corrupter, a bastard, a mad person.'

'Did he corrupt you?'

'In a way.'

Harry had grown so much more communicative in recent years that I had almost forgotten how reticent he could be when he was uncomfortable: his umms, and pauses, and diversions.

'How?' I asked.

'Have you forgotten?' he asked.

I tried to think of what I might have forgotten.

He seemed a bit amused that I couldn't think of anything. Bemused too.

'All the lies I told you? Not telling you I was a copper, letting you think I was working for him, telling you he was dead . . .'

'You thought he was dead . . .'

'Not telling you when I learnt he wasn't . . .'

'You couldn't have – well, you could have, but . . .'

An echo of our old joke – I *could* tell you, but then I'd have to kill you.

'I deceived you, a lot,' he said. Sitting on the bed, leaning forward, elbows on his knees, hands hanging heavy in between. Looking up at me under his brow with his muddy green eyes. 'I did. I'm sorry.'

'Doesn't matter,' I said. 'I trust you.'

We sat a while longer. The moon sailed by outside. The world carried on spinning. The river flowed on.

*

Later I went out for a walk. Strolled up the Corniche, past the great Temple of Luxor, its columns huge in the night, and hanging above it the green lights of the mosque of Abu al-Haggag, perched above the great court of Ramses II, twinkling away above his massive monuments to his own self-importance. The Ramadan children's funfair twinkling along too. Up to the right past the Brooke Animal Hospital, listening for the soft breath of the retired *calèche* horses, smelling the warm smell of it, mixed with frankincense, and the hot oil of the felafal stand up on the corner by the police station. Past the man who sells clay pots: yellow ochre, moth grey, burnt brown, powdery dry, every desert colour in rows on the streetside.

I went over to the felafal stand and ordered myself a sandwich. The felafals were still sizzling away in their iron pan over the gas burner, not quite ready yet. We stood about and waited, and chatted.

'Tell me,' I said, because I was in that kind of a mood, 'do you think a *khawageyya* and an Egyptian can marry and be happy?'

That perked them up.

'You want a husband?' cried the felafal man. '*Ya* Ahmed! Come here!' He summoned an array of his friends from around the place. 'OK: this is Ahmed, this is Yussuf, this is

Ali, this is – well, his name means Scarabeo, scarab, because he pushes shit – excuse me – and this is Boutros, he's a Christian, you know Copt. You are Christian? OK. But no, they won't do. Ahmed is too fat.' (He was quite fat.) 'And Yussuf is too stupid, and Ali can't afford another wife, and Scarabeo is too dirty – marry me! You like me?' he grinned, most appealingly. 'I'm very nice! But do I like you? I don't know. Can you cook?'

The others were joining in – objecting to his descriptions of them, assessing my charms.

'Can you cook?'

'Prove it!'

'Well, these are ready,' I said, looking at the crispy little felafal bouncing in their hot oily bed. Someone handed me the cross between a sieve and a ladle that they use for taking them out.

'You do the bread,' I said to the felafal man ('Ah, she's bossy!' said Scarabeo) and he neatly split the pittas open while I checked who wanted pickles and who wanted tahina and who wanted hot sauce, and in moments everybody had their sandwiches.

'Not bad,' he said. 'Now put on a new lot.'

I turned down the gas, swiftly squished little patties out of the tacky green and white gloop of beans and parsley in its tin bowl, slid them hissing into the oil, watched as they started to turn golden, filling the air with the scent. God, this smell, if you haven't eaten since *Imsaak* . . .

'OK,' said the felafal man. 'You can marry me.'

I laughed. We all laughed. I started to eat my delicious sandwich.

'It's not you she wants,' said a policeman lounging on the periphery. 'Sa'id el Araby will fry you like one of your felafals if you try to marry her.'

I stopped laughing. Then started again.

'Goodnight, boys,' I said. Walked off, eating, laughing.

'Don't go!' they called behind me. 'Stay with us! Stay in Luxor! You can marry Sa'id, we don't mind!'

There's a lot of sugarblood around here.

*

Later still I went and sat on the cold balcony outside Chrissie's window. Looked out over, to the mountain beyond, and tried to think of his mind, but I couldn't see into it any more. Remembered moments of connection. Ran through moments of joy.

'It doesn't heal,' he'd said. And I'd said, 'It can.' Because I have healed so much. He doesn't know healing. He resists it. How reluctant he was to let the wound of his mother heal. He sees perfect, and he sees broken.

That's all. He sees us as broken. I saw him, swiftly, as an idealistic boy.

Went to bed in the end. Lay there like nothing, holding on to my hip bones. Wanted Lily so much that I might have rung her.

SEVENTEEN

A little touch of someone in the night

Harry was touching my shoulder, in darkness.

In my sleep I rolled over, as if to roll into the embrace of the man who is always beside you when you sleep.

'Sa'id's on the phone,' he said softly. 'It came through to the other room.'

I stumbled through. Harry stood there by the window, towel round his waist, his torso long and grey in the pre-dawn. Pre-*Imsaak*, even.

*

'Forgive me,' said Sa'id. 'I can't say this to your face.' I felt he hadn't slept.

'What?' I said, standing half naked.

'I have a . . .'

His voice was all . . . all impossible.

'What?' I said.

There was a long silence.

'What?'

Nothing.

'I'll meet you,' I said.

'No,' he managed.

'Where?'

'No.'

'I'll be on the pontoon.'

'No,' he said.

'I'll be there,' I said.

I dressed against the morning chill. Took his scarf: the huge, thick, white one. White on white. The one which had . . . that one. Harry was leaning in his doorway as I padded down the corridor; I took his hand for a moment as I passed and for a split second I wanted to throw myself into his arms, on to his mercy, at his feet. Didn't. Walked out, down the filmstar stairs, and on to the Corniche, beneath the ilexes and the palms in the fairy-light necklaces, neon colours against the dark lapis blue sky, and across the main road and its flowerbeds and over to where the pontoons stretched out into the river, where obsidian covered the surface of the water, and the colours of night lay unmoving. Behind the Winter Palace the stripey thing was imminent: green, and gold, and crimson. Indigo, and pearl, and crawling darkness. To the west, on the mountain, the strange echo.

Pearl. Does he really think he is grit in my oyster?

I sat on the wall with my back to the dawn and my face to the river. The fairy lights hung in the trees above me, gleaming, jewel-like artificial fruit among the dark and sober leaves. Orion – Osiris, to the ancients – hung above them.

A little while later he came up beside me and touched me on the shoulder, and left his arm lying along me as he leant on the wall.

'Sweet sweet darling,' I said.

'Yes,' he said.

'What is it?'

Silence.

'*Habibti*,' he said, after a while.

We're sitting on the fucking Corniche again.

But my heart lifted to it, because he had used the female endearment.

The silences were long, though.

'You can go,' he said. 'You and Chrissie, all free, all done, if I ask him.' He paused. 'Not if I don't. He is waiting for me to say.'

'Not?' I said. 'Why would you not?' There were, after all, a few possible reasons. Maybe in some mad way I wanted him to use this to keep me in Egypt. To refuse to let me leave, even though it spelt misery for me. As if he were a crazy possessive lover, to whose passion I could succumb.

And how curious, that he is giving me, as a great gift, the freedom to go, to leave him, when all that I want is to be with him. To stay, or to take him with me. I haven't yet done my job, the thing I came for, and yet I am grateful that I can go, grateful to him for arranging it . . . something is wrong here.

'Oh no,' he said. 'I'll do it. I'll do it. But will you do something for me?'

'Da enna ashilak ala ramoush enaya, ya habibi,' I said. It means, I'd carry you on my eyelashes, my love. I'd do anything for you, you know that.

Fool! Herod to Salome, Isaac to God, every myth and legend, every fairy story: first lesson, don't promise until you know what you are promising.

He closed his eyes and smiled, and the smile drifted away.

'Don't come back,' he said.

Silence. Mine.

'Leave me,' he said. 'Leave me alone.'

'No,' I said.

He shrugged. Hands wide.

'Habibti,' he said.

Silence.

'There is a flight to Cairo at nine tonight. Get your tickets.'

Silence.

'I know you understand,' he said. 'Don't . . .'

'I wasn't going to,' I said. Why is not a question I ever need to ask him. 'But listen. I know that *you* understand.'

'I know what I am losing,' he said.

'No, you don't.'

And I couldn't tell him. I know I should have. I knew I should have earlier. But I couldn't. 'Forgive me,' he said.

He didn't look at me. Just walked back down to the pontoon. I heard the engine of the boat. Sat, until the cannon went for *Imsaak*. The gates of heaven open at this hour, they say. Angels come and go. There goes one.

Nothing more, after this. Too late. The fast begins.

And what is my fast? What am I renouncing now? What am I called upon to renounce?

You're not meant to lie, during Ramadan.

Him. But not forever, whatever he may say. I have his child.

Love. But not all love. Love is still with me. Hold to that.

I am losing a pearl. Or maybe, a tree is losing me.

I sat most of the day in the same place on the wall. After a while the felucca men stopped offering me their services, though it occurred to me that floating on beauty, suspended in time (like travelling, like being broken, incapable, in traction, protected from the necessity of action, but among beauty) might be a good way to spend this impossible day.

My mind was full of what I must give up.

Harry came out and offered me things, this or that. Brought me water. Chrissie came and talked to me, but I don't know what she said. I was madder than her that day. I thought about Janie a lot, and about what Harry had said in London, about me wanting things to die since I had faced death, about not being able to give myself to things or claim anything as my own. He couldn't say I haven't tried here. Oh god, but he could . . . When he appeared the next time he did.

I was sitting looking out over the Nile, thinking about figs, and he put his arms around me from behind, two arms folded round my neck, resting on my shoulders, his chest warm against my back. I rested my head against his arm, and he rested his face against the side of mine, temple to temple. When I had first found him again, after Ben Cooper had sent me to chum up with him in order to chum up with Eddie, I had gone to a nightclub we used to frequent, and spotted him, and manoeuvred myself in front of him, and he had slipped his arm around my waist from behind. Our first touch in ten years.

'Sweetheart,' he said.

But I was busy looking over the water.

'What's going on, Angel?'

Only Harry can call me Angel.

'We can go,' I said. 'He's arranged it. Shezli will let us leave, because Sa'id wants him to. Which he does. He wants us to go. He wants me to go. He said. He said . . .' and I gulped a little as I repeated his words, 'he would have Shezli do this, if I promised not to come back.'

Harry's arms tightened a little bit.

'But you haven't told him,' he said.

'How can I tell him now?' I cried. 'How can I tell him? He's made it clear, I can't – how can I?'

He put his large left hand on the top of my head. I felt he was holding my brain in place in my skull.

'How can you not?'

'I can't.'

'Is that pride?' he said. 'You didn't make the situation. You're letting him control it when he's not fully informed.

You are — you are exactly doing what I said before. Life-denying. Literally. Denying to him the existence of his kid. Think onwards a little. Take it forward. Will you never tell him? Will this child have no father? Because of the way you love each other now? You've known each other a few months . . . you have years to come.'

He never ceases to surprise me.

I turned round in his arms and pulled away.

'Do you want me to be with him?' I cried. 'Do you know what it means? He won't come to London — I would come here. I would stay here. And Lily. Do you want that?'

He looked me straight in the eyes. Touched his teeth with his tongue. Closed his eyes briefly. His Mongolian face: all cheekbones and inscrutability. DI Makins gives nothing away.

'I spoke to Shezli,' he said. 'Our passports will be at the airport. We get them when we're on the plane — nine o'clock, to Cairo. Then overnight to London. We're not to leave the airport when we change.'

'He thinks of everything,' I said bitterly.

'Go and talk to him again before we leave. He loves you.'

'He says you love me.'

This time he turned away. Then: 'Every time I look at you I see him with his hands in your hair, murmuring in your ear, "Why is he looking at you like that?"'

I thought about that for a moment.

'You are not free to be loved,' he said.

And I thought about that.

'I'll go and pack,' he said. 'Please don't stay here. Come in, or go over. I'll go with you.'

'Not going,' I said.

I stayed.

*

An hour or so later he came out again.

'He's young,' he said. 'He's young. Don't blame him.'

'I don't blame him.'

Silence sat with us.

'What do you want from him?' he said.

Strangely, I found I couldn't answer. What does a woman want from a man?

'There's one thing I know,' he said, conversationally.

After a bit I said, 'What?'

'The opposite sex,' he said, 'is opposite. A foreigner is even more opposite. He is as opposite as you can find, the most opposite, and so the most attractive. He is, forgive me, a dusky stranger . . .'

'He's not a stranger . . .'

'Yes, he is. Take it from me, he is. I know he's a good bloke and your heart's desire, too, but he is also a slinky Arab love god. He just is. He can't help it, any more than you can help being a blonde bombshell. Maybe what he is for you is the other side of the coin. But you can never get both sides of the coin, you turn it over, and the first side has disappeared. And again, if you turn it over again. I remember you talking about Egypt and Islam and stuff, so close and yet so far, the other side of our own Mediterranean, our missing thing, the religion which shares half the prophets of our religion, the language which is so alien and yet so connected, the place where culture lived when it deserted Europe a thousand years ago, the place where so many things we share were invented, all that stuff you've told me about . . . I think you feel an obligation, a desire to close the circle, join the gaps . . . you want this to succeed in order to prove that it can succeed, but you know . . . if you two are free just as a man and a woman, and not as the stereotypes you might be to each other, then you are as free to fail as you are free to succeed. You are not obliged, for any political or cultural reason . . .'

The egrets were beginning to buggle buggle da, the light to change.

'But I love him,' was all I could come up with.

'Of course you do,' he said. He let that sit for a moment. 'I think what I'm saying is – all that stuff, cultural differences, history, religion, gender – you can't ignore them just because you disagree with the interpretations that have always been put on them. They still exist. You just have to find your own way of dealing with it. We all do. Like – um, racism. You can be against it; doesn't mean all races are the same. Branches on a tree, trees in a forest. Men and women – equal, but not exactly the same. Got baggage.

Habits. Assumptions made about us, by us. I'm not being very clear here. Or, say, Ramadan. I'm as infidel as they come, but I still get woken by the bloke with the drum in the middle of the night. I'm affected by the fact that no one round here eats all day, and that affects their mood. So, I mean, you and Sa'id have these things going on, you have to deal with them, here they are.'

I murmured.

'If it doesn't work out for you two, it doesn't mean that East and West hate each other forever. You've had some unity. You've made this kid. It's not like the end of the possibility of harmony between nations. It's just a broken romance and another kid with a complex domestic life. Nothing you haven't dealt with before.'

Brutal sod sometimes, Harry.

I brought my legs up on to the wall, sat crosslegged.

'What do you want?' I asked him after a while.

'For you to be safe, and all to be well,' he said.

I smiled at that.

'Oh, don't ask me,' he said, with the tiniest snort of exasperation. 'I'm biased.'

After a bit I said, 'Why am I talking about this with you, not him?'

'Good question,' he murmured, and then raised his head suddenly, and said quite firmly: 'If you won't talk to him, we're to go home, babe. Deal with this from home ground.'

'Home is where the heart is,' I said, with a little laugh.

His face changed quickly, his eyebrows solidifying, his cheekbones turning firm.

'Bollocks,' he said. 'Are you going to stay here, against his wishes, alienated from him, deserting Lily, and have Chrissie face a murder charge, and you face whatever comes in its wake? Pregnant? On your own with that psychotic woman? Are you? Love is great, Angel, but there's love and there's bollocks. This is bollocks. Listen,' he said. 'All that stuff with Eddie. All the stuff with Ben, with Janie, with Preston Oliver . . . I can see how you have had to do things you wouldn't want to do, how you have had unpleasantness forced on you, and you have fought it and dealt with it, my god, like a fucking ten-armed warrior goddess, but if you volunteer for this, Angel, if you volunteer for this danger with the same gusto you have managed to face unavoidable danger with up till now . . . Sweetheart,' he said. 'Come home and stay sane. Or stay here and lose it. That's your choice.'

He stopped suddenly. He seemed surprised to have found himself at so final and presumptuous a conclusion. For a moment he seemed to weigh where he had found himself, and at the end of the moment he found himself to be right. He looked at me to confirm his arrival at that point of view.

'Jesus,' he said. 'I try so hard not to . . .'

'Not to what?' I said.

'Not to invade you, not to boss you, lose it, throw chairs out the window at you,' he said. 'Make demands on you. Require things of you. But Angel.'

'What.'

'Oh god, I'm about to quote Merle Haggard.'

'You can't. I'm the one who quotes country and western lyrics at ridiculous moments.'

'So do I.'

'No you don't.'

'Yes I do. Maybe it's just one of the many stupid things we have in common.'

I snorted a little.

'Well get on with it, then,' I said.

'I know you are an independent-minded woman. I try to respect that even when you're being a fool. But. I was going to say,' he said, glancing away and back swiftly, with a self-conscious but fuck-it-so-what smile, 'and I know it's flawed. But. "Don't confuse this gentleness with any sign of weakness in your man."'

'You're not my man.'

He smiled again, wider, and harder.

'Tell him about his child,' he said. 'And see if it changes his point of view. And if not, we go home. That's all.'

*

I just sat. My fantasies were spinning around me. I tell him, now, and he's happy, and we go and live in Paris and Harry comes at weekends for Lily; she gets a Eurostar season ticket . . . He takes the job in Brighton and we all go and live by the sea, Sarah becomes my best friend . . . we move to Cairo, and Lily goes to the American School . . . oh no, Sa'id wouldn't like that . . . and spends holidays with Harry . . . I take up archaeology again, get a job on the Tomb of the Sons, or in Alexandria on Cleopatra's palace that they found in the bay . . .

They all started with me telling him, and him being happy. But I haven't told him, and he's not happy.

These fantasies are based not on orientalizing, but on the basic fantasy that he wants me.

But it's not a fantasy. He does want me.

But he's sending me away.

But he loves me he said so.

*

At about five he came. Presumably word had seeped across the Nile that his *khawageyya* girlfriend was sitting on the Corniche like a colossus, and about as unlikely to move. He took my arm and helped me down from the wall, and we walked along a little further, past some building sites, quiet now, with the end of the day and the suspension of . . . everything, after Hatshepsut . . . and down to another landing stage, and he peered at the moored feluccas in the declining daylight and said: *'Ta'ali.'* Come.

He found one, and unloosed its painter, and said, 'You will have to be my crew, can you crew for me?'

'Yes,' I said. 'I can do anything for you.'

'No,' he said. 'You can't do anything for me except what I have asked.'

'So why are we here?' I asked.

The wind was low. There's never wind at dusk. It was

cold anyway. Him regal in his dark lapis-coloured scarf, me in the white one. Yes, he wrapped it tighter around me. The big canvas of the sail flapped loosely against the white-painted mast.

We drifted out. He leaned back against the bulwark and steered with his beautiful bare foot, as they do, as he had done the night we had first arrived from Cairo. He held his arm out to me. I sat by the mast and I refused him.

'What's going on?' I said.

'A moment,' he said. 'An interlude.'

'What interlude?' I asked.

He said nothing. Sailed us on up river, not far, and then drew into a reedy bank and moored the boat on to a branch of a tree, the sail still up, creaking slightly in the remains of the breeze. Some birds cackled at the outrage. Egrets were hanging like handkerchiefs, white, clean and triangular in the creeping dusk.

'Between joy and sorrow,' he said, though it was good fifteen minutes since I had asked the question.

'What, drink with me in the ruins?' I said. 'We are already in sorrow.'

'You can go home,' he said finally. 'I have spoken to Shezli. It's done.'

I was just looking at him.

'Don't come back,' he said.

Silence all around me.

'I get no say,' I said.

'I know what you'd say. You've said plenty. You love me,

335

you'll stay here forever, you'll bring Lily, Harry can come and go, you'll do what is needed.'

'What's wrong with that?'

'I'll believe you,' he said, with a bitter little laugh. 'So no, you get no say.'

'Shut up,' I said. 'I can't talk to you. This is unspeakable.' Then: 'What if I say no?'

'You can't,' he said. 'It's Chrissie's life.'

'And mine,' I said.

'Maybe.'

'Oh, it's my life all right . . .'

The river air trickled down my spine. Loneliness and fear gathered over me like vultures.

'You want rid of me so much?' I asked.

'Yes,' he said.

'I had no idea it was so bad.'

'Nor had I,' he said.

'You blackmail me, bully me, betray me. After all this.'

'Yes,' he said.

'But you love me.'

'Yes,' he said.

'And you think you can make me hate you.'

He smiled at that.

'I don't care what you think of me,' he said.

'I'm not talking about what I think of you. I'm talking about how I feel about you. I won't hate you,' I said. 'I understand.'

'Don't understand,' he said.

'Can't help it.'

Silence all around, and the sun slipping westward into the desert, into Libya.

The cannon went. *Iftar.* Green and crimson and gold across the sky, darkness entering my heart. A swift dusk.

He opened a little bag he had with him. Took out a small package: dates. A bottle of water: Baraka. It means blessing. Two flat breads. Two tomatoes. A twist of paper with *do'a* – salty spices. A knife. He washed his hands in a handful of water, opened the bread, sliced a tomato, handed me the food. Poured water into a cup. In Ramadan you don't drink from the same vessel. At any time, if a man and a woman drink from the same vessel, the last to drink will follow the first for the rest of their life. If you drink the water of the Nile you will always return. We ate. We drank. Contributed our silence to the great silence of *Iftar.*

After a while his arm rose in the air between us. He wasn't looking at me. Found the back of my neck. Took hold of it, his hand.

'Whether or not you understand,' he said, 'there are some things I want to say to you. I owe you this. I don't mean to be unkind . . . You know . . . I love my country. There are things I want to do. It is only right here, at home, that an educated man can speak to, or for, the people of his country. Do you know we were expelled from the Arab League because we sucked up to the US? Yes – they moved the headquarters from Cairo to Tunis. And do you know how the rest of the Arabs looked at us during the

Gulf War? We were trashed. For the keenness with which our government turned on an Arab country. Not Saddam Hussein. I'm not defending him, God forbid. But the people of Iraq. We lost Nasser, we lost Sadat, whatever you think of him, we lost the Six Day War, we lost Suez, we lost Sinai, for a while . . . We have been too dependent on outside things, economically, politically, culturally. We have been losing ourselves . . . we have been offered blind adherence to tradition or blind devotion to innovation and consumerism. This is no choice. We are not blind . . .' He drifted off for a moment.

'I saw it, *ya habibti*. What I saw . . .'

For a moment I didn't know what he was talking about.

'River of blood,' he said. 'It was, a river of blood. Murdered children. Women. A young man from Qurnah, I knew him, a policeman . . . we brought a wounded woman to the *fabrique*. This English girl, five years old. You think I didn't think of Lily? And now everyone is being arrested, questioned, sacked, everyone is blaming everyone else. Wild accusations, wild fears. Desperation and igno- rance has turned brothers to this.'

His hand was still on my neck, heavy.

After a long while I said: 'But should this divide us? This division that belongs to others?'

'It belongs to me too,' he said. 'This is my home. Could I know you would be safe here?'

His name: el Araby. The Arab. There are two famous el Arabys: the poet, and the nationalist hero.

'So I *am* punished for being English,' I said.

'No, no, *habibti*. If I wanted to punish you I could do far worse. I am letting you off.'

I put my arm up and gently touched his hand where it lay on my neck. His eyes were on me.

'I don't want you,' he said. 'I don't want what you bring. You are desirable, ah . . . But I don't.'

Night edged in around us.

'Don't come back,' he said, and his hand trailed down, and round, and touched my throat, where I had laughed. 'Don't come back,' more quietly. A pause. A long pause. As if he was checking to make sure that I knew what this was, or rather what it wasn't. Then a hand on my cheek, an arm round my waist. Buttons, one two three four five six seven all down the front of my dress. I didn't help him. I considered stopping him. His warmth: his body. His pauses. My nemesis. A lifting of my hips towards its own.

The cushions slid down between the keel and bulwark underneath us as we slipped down. Ungainly and immutable. His breast, his collar bone, his leather *hejeb* and the smell and taste of him. The cold of the river, our warmth. Don't come back, he said. The slow movements of the felucca in the water, a slow echo of the rhythm of our movements.

I mean it, he said, punctuating and making me gasp. Go away. I love you. Go away.

The moon was rising; it threw some silver on his face, but only his eyes were light.

At some stage I turned him over, took his arms above his head and kissed him, covering him, laying my cheek alongside his, my body over him. Shivering with the cold, the pair of us.

Don't, he said. You know why.

But it's love, I said.

I know, he said, I know that. And turned me over in turn and fucked me till I wept. He tried to pull away, his gesture of manly responsibility, but I stopped him, just whispering the age-old phrase of a hundred possible meanings, it's all right. He didn't know why it was all right, but he accepted it, trusted me, couldn't stop then anyway. And he kissed me till I melted, and fucked me again, and held on to me in the rising moonlight until I stopped shaking, and wrapped me in his arms, his hair, his scarves, his love. I was mortally cold. My cheek against his and our breath melding, the sweat of our bodies slick and cooling. He had a strand of my hair in his mouth. I said nothing when he took it and bit through it, his teeth gleaming, nothing when he wrapped it around his forefinger, pale gold on dark gold in silver light. This is your father, I murmured, this is our love. Feel it, take it, have it. It was real.

But I didn't tell him, because it was too late.

*

He fell asleep, his hands in my hair. I lay a while, then extracted myself, watched him a while, kissed him a while, rearranged my clothing, buttoning my buttons, wrapping the white scarf around me. I spread the dark lapis scarf over him. He shifted, and murmured in soft Luxori: *khalliki jembi*. Stay by me. So many times he has said go away, and now, once, in his sleep, *khalliki jembi*.

I bent over and bit off one of his black curls, gnawing against the grain of it, and tucked it into my bra. I turned to leave, to clamber gently from the boat, but I couldn't. I slipped down beside him again, and lay alongside him a while longer, and another line of poetry came up from the depths, a Bedouin poem, about – oh, about all this. The love which doesn't just slip into place. The love which has no place into which to slip. 'He reached your arms, stretched on the pillow, forgot his father, and then his grandfather.'

And then remembered them again.

I was woken by a noise. Don't know what. I was alone.

Raised myself up like the Lady of Shallot: out flew my web and floated wide, the curse has come upon me, cried . . .

Considered casting off and floating down to Cairo to die.

We shouldn't, perhaps, have done that. Making love makes love, as Chrissie said. Creates it, feeds it, replenishes it. Fucking leads to kissing. And if we are to kill it we shouldn't be feeding it.

A phrase from *'El Atlal'* came to my mind: 'Don't say we willed it. Fortune willed it.'

It's all my fault, I thought, I shouldn't have left him last time. Should've thought.

Thought of Lily. Thought of Nippyhead.

Thought of Harry.

Clambered out, very gently, on to the bank. Scrambled up to the road. I dare say he was there somewhere in the darkness, in the trees, watching me.

*

It took me half an hour or so to walk back to the Winter Palace. I didn't hurry.

I saw Shezli in the foyer. 'You're free to leave, madame,' he said.

'I know,' I replied.

'Your friend is in the bar,' he called after me as I drifted by.

Harry was sitting on a barstool, his long back curved and his head resting on one huge hand, patience and . . . something else . . . in his posture. I moved into the room and sat up on the stool next to him. Without looking at me he ordered me a hot chocolate.

After about fifteen minutes, he said: 'It would never have worked. No shared history. I bet he doesn't know who Reg Varney is.'

About three minutes later he said: 'Sorry. That was a bit heartless.'

Then, 'So what did he say?'

'I didn't tell him.'

Harry was silent. I realized he was smiling.

'Then you don't love him,' he said. Statement, not question.

'I do,' I said.

'Not really,' he said. 'How could you not tell him, if you loved him?'

'I . . .' I said.

'Oh, of course you love him, a great poetical love like a song and your heart and your soul and dreams and passions and he's everything, he's – oh, yes, I know, I know. But you don't love him for . . . for the shared past and the imminent future. For being safe and all being well. For real. For reality. For dealing with reality. Look – here you are with me. Not him. Me. You could have changed everything by telling him, including quite possibly him sending you away, but you didn't do it. I'm taking you home, he doesn't know you're pregnant. You and I have been sorting out the problems, you and he have been gazing at the sunset . . .'

'That's not fair. It was him who sorted things with the police . . .'

'I know. I know. But that is . . . immediate, drastic and finite. Like how you and he are together. I'm talking about the stuff that goes on and on. Like children. Don't feel bad about it. It's all right. He can still be the dad, some kind of dad. You'll work something out. But you don't love him. You don't, or you would have told him. You would have. You couldn't have not told him.'

I was looking into my frothy chocolate.

'You don't want him, you don't trust him, you don't love him. He's turned you down, you've turned him down. Angel,' he said, and he bent his head a little; 'I'm gloating, I know I am. I'm sorry. I'm just very fucking happy.'

343

I sat for a while before I looked over in his direction.

'What are you saying, Harry?' I asked.

He looked at me sideways along the bar, and didn't grin.

'I'll give you time to wash his sperm off you before we go into that,' he said.

I stared at him.

He stared at me.

'Go on,' he said. 'We must leave any minute.'

'It's not washable,' I said. 'It's taken root.'

'I know,' he said gently. 'I know.'

I stared at him for a moment longer. And he leaned over towards me, and kissed me.

Our first kiss had been at a bar. A million years ago. We'd met three minutes earlier, he'd been the first to break away and my knees had given way beneath me.

Kissed me like yesterday, like forever.

*

Upstairs, when we were collecting our bags, the phone rang. Harry answered.

'No,' he said. 'No.'

I watched as he hung up. Blinked. I knew who it was. They're both leopards, I thought, and they can both read my mind, and they both know where to go. It's just Sa'id is going somewhere I can't join him.

*

Chrissie slept all the way to Cairo, and all the way to Heathrow. During one brief waking period she said to Harry: 'Thank you for talking the policeman out of it. I don't know how you did it, but thank you.'

I looked at them across the plastic seatbelts and nasty little trays. Harry shrugged.

'Mr Shezli told me,' she was saying. 'He'd got hold of the idea Harry was a policeman, and told me I was very lucky to have such a man on my side, and that between him and Sa'id they'd convinced him. He told me that. Said I should be grateful. Well I am. Even though I don't quite understand how you go from being Eddie's thug to being the kind of man who can talk foreign policemen out of prosecuting me.'

'Oh, I've never been a thug,' said Harry. 'I'm too skinny.'

Chrissie smirked at him. Jesus, does she fancy him? My immediate, animal reaction was 'Oy, woman, lay the fuck off'. I considered that a moment. Laid my hands across my belly. Hello, little one, I said inside.

Eight weeks ago, flying home from Cairo, I had wept all the way. Tonight I was silent, feeling parts of me slipping into place.

*

For a moment, by mistake, I got the Umm Khalthoum channel. She was singing a song called *'Fakkaruni'*: 'They Made Me Remember'. 'They spoke to me again of you, reminded me, reminded me . . . They took me back to the past, with its joys and its sweetness . . .' I listened for a moment or two. There was a line I wanted to hear. 'And I remembered how happy I was with you, and oh my soul I remember why we came apart.'

Ah.

Then the opening of '*El Atlal*'. '*Fakkaruni*' is an Abba song compared to '*El Atlal*'.

I turned it off.

*

Somewhere over the eastern Mediterranean, Harry said: 'How old is he? Twenty-six?'

'Why?'

'Same age I was when I lost you,' he said.

*

Somewhere over France I said: 'Harry.'

'Mmm?'

'I fucked Eddie.'

A pause. I hadn't thought about saying it. It just came out and got said.

'I know,' he murmured. Another pause. 'He told me. All about it.'

'Oh!'

'With some relish.'

'Sorry,' I said.

'And I know you wish you hadn't.'

I bowed my head. Said nothing.

Then: 'But I told you . . . I let you believe that we hadn't . . . that we weren't . . .'

'Well, you weren't, were you? That was – I gather – it was one mad thing, wasn't it? Not exactly a romance.'

'No.'

'Don't worry, Angel,' he said. 'He got us all in various ways. And now he's dead. And we're not.'

Echo of Sa'id: God has taken him, leave them to it.

And that's the truth.

EIGHTEEN

Sekhmet

At Heathrow, Harry put Chrissie in a cab to Chelsea, straight to an AA meeting. Then she was going on to her shrink. Energy returned to her. Alongside, I think, a realization of what she had escaped. A kind of realization. She wanted to come back to mine afterwards; Harry murmured to her perhaps not.

He and I stood in Arrivals, surrounded by people, under ugly overhead lighting, eyes sandy with sleeplessness, bags around our feet. Did he have to go to work? I didn't want him to leave.

'Let's get the tube,' he said, and headed off.

'We could have shared Chrissie's cab,' I said.

'No, we couldn't.'

'Why not?'

We were jostling through the crowd, getting separated. He was pushing ahead, clearing a way for me.

'I've had it, Angel,' he said, over his shoulder.

'What?'

I lost him for a moment. Caught up with him and a degree of calm at the entrance to the tube, as he bought our tickets.

'What?' I said.

He manhandled us through the barrier.

On the platform, standing in front of a sign saying 'Piccadilly Line' he said: 'I'm fed up. I'm fucking fed up with this . . .'

'What!'

'Jesus,' he said.

'OK,' he said.

'Haven't you noticed?' he said. 'That I am completely fucking in love with you, as much as I ever was, more than I ever was, just, just . . . For fuck's sake, Angeline!'

My jaw dropped. It did. He put out his finger, and raised it.

'Let's go home,' he said. 'Come to bed with me. Sorry about the decent interval and all that, but let's just . . . let's. Now.'

'We can't now,' I said, stupidly. 'We're on a railway platform.'

'Then let's,' he said, 'when we get home.'

I looked at him. He's so tall.

I stepped up on to the wooden seat against the wall, and looked him in the eye.

'Harry,' I said.

'Hello,' he answered.

I stared at him. Harry.

'Not yet,' I said.

He gave me a suspicious look.

'Now what?' he said.

'January 30th,' I said. 'Come to dinner. Will you?'

'And till then?'

'As usual,' I said. 'Just, how we've been.'

'We've been a lot of things,' he said.

'Please,' I said.

'Why?' he said. In a kind of 'I know you're up to something' voice.

I felt a bit wobbly. He saw it. I didn't know why I had to do this but I had to.

The long slow stare he was giving me. Tipping his head back a little because I was taller than him now. The look came up under his eyelashes.

Well, I kissed him. The arms went round me, and he lifted me, and after a while he put me down.

He started to smile. 'So, what, am I on a promise then?' Eyes locked.

'I . . .' I said.

'What, kiss me now and then not for a month?' he said. Quoting what I'd said to him, all those years ago, in that bar.

'Only three weeks,' I said.

'January 30th.'

'January 30th.'

'I'll put it in my diary.'

'You do that.'

'I will,' he said, not taking his eyes off me.

I shook my head quickly. Felt another seismic shift.

*

He took me home, and then he went back to his flat, and then we met for lunch and, talking, we were almost late to go and get Lily. She roared out of the classroom into my arms. Then remembered to be angry with me for staying away from her and scrambled down me, and went to Harry instead. Then remembered that he'd gone away too and stood between us, looking puzzled, until I fell on my knees in the school corridor and gazed at her, level eye to level eye. She agreed to look quizzically at me.

'Hello, girl,' I said.

'Did you bring me a present?' she asked.

'Yes,' I said. Seizing the moment as I had so remarkably failed to do over the past days.

'What?' she asked, pleased, peering to see if I had it concealed about my person. Which of course I had, in a way.

I smiled and found my smile had gone very wobbly round the edges.

'Baby,' I said.

She didn't grasp it at first.

'What baby?'

'Our baby,' I said. 'Ours. Baby boy or baby girl.'

She looked at me, and carried on about her business.

There was a small problem with her scarf, and some rationalization required of the school bag and the lunchbox. We walked home through drizzle, the three of us. Made tea. Offered the chammy-leather camel, the Egyptian equivalent of a donkey in a sombrero, that Harry had brought for her. He left, and as he did I thought – he's left, he's coming back. She and I had a bath. Read stories: *Bluebeard*, *Five Minutes' Peace* and a chapter of the *Big Friendly Giant*. Now there's an ideal man. Lay in bed.

'Did you get it in Egypt?'

'What?'

'The baby.'

'Yes,' I said. Truthfully.

She cuddled very close to me and looked down at my belly.

'Is it a real baby?'

'Yes, my darling.'

She thought a while. Curiosity and shyness fighting it out across her golden face.

'Did someone put their little sperm into you?' she whispered at last.

'Yes.'

Eyebrows very low; mouth thoughtful.

She whispered. 'Did you want him to?'

'Yes,' I whispered back.

More consideration.

Kissed me a few times on my cheeks.

'You'll still be my mummy,' she said.

'Forever.'

'And Harry will be my daddy.'

'Forever.'

'And a baby.'

I was waiting for her to ask whose little sperm it was. But she didn't. Just drifted off to sleep in my arms, and half murmured, 'I suppose it's Nippyhead, hello little Nippyhead,' which made me so happy I wept, and I couldn't stop weeping, but it wasn't like last time I came back from Egypt and couldn't stop weeping. As soon as she was asleep I went and rang Harry, and we talked for three hours.

*

I didn't say anything to anyone about Harry. For all it was so old and so strong there was something very new and delicate going on. Anyway I hardly saw him. I was just with myself, and with Lily. Very calm and quiet. Towards the end of January I told my mum I was pregnant. And who by. 'You do like things complicated,' she said, which I felt was less than helpful as remarks go, so I ignored it. Dad kissed me and said he was glad because he could see that that was what I wanted, and he found it simplest to take my lead.

Brigid said: 'That will be one hell of a nice-looking baby.'

Zeinab kissed the tips of each set of her own fingers in turn, and said: 'Life is long, *insha'Allah*. He'll be back, but you'll already be happy and it will be too late. And then it will all be all right anyway, because it has to be, *insha'Allah*. I'll be the Egyptian auntie for you in the mean-time. I'll sing to it.'

Lily made a little bed out of a matchbox lined with tissue paper, and put it in a shoebox and wrote Nippyhead on the lid in wobbly five-year-old's handwriting. She said: 'This is good because now there will be someone to come with me to your funeral.'

*

A few weeks later, a gloomy no-light English winter day, I was in the Syrian grocer's on the Uxbridge Road, buying a chicken for dinner, and salad and spuds and bread and olives and a kind of Lebanese broad bean salad for which I had developed a passion. There were biscuits and cakes everywhere, sugar and apricot, pistachio and syrup. *'Eid Mubarak!'* the boys and the Arab customers were saying to each other. *'Eid Mubarak'* on a sign up on the wall behind the cash register. *Mubarak* from the same root as *baraka* – blessing. It was a Friday. There was a lot of toing and froing at the mosque across the road too. (No dome or minaret here. Just a big old Shepherd's Bush house, turned into the house of god.) *Eid el Fitr.* January 30th. End of Ramadan. Lily told me all about it on the way home from school. Her class had all drawn *Eid* cards for each other. She'd kept hers for me. Happy *Eid*.

Harry arrived late, bearing roses, a pound of sugar almonds and two bottles of Pinot Noir.

'Full of iron,' he said. 'Very good for you. Is she asleep?'

'Yes.'

'Thank Christ for that,' he said, and dumped his gifts on the table. 'Come on.' He reached for my hand. That long lean arm with my name on it.

'Come on what?' I said. Amused by his urgency.

'Come on and –' Then he sat down suddenly. 'Oh lord I'm scared,' he said.

'Don't be scared,' I said.

'Why not?' Gave me one of those little grins. 'Makes it sexier.'

'We don't need anything to make it sexier.'

'Nor we do,' he said. Calming down. 'Nor we do.' Leaning back in his chair. And he looked over at me, that slow, insolent, cocky look.

'Anyway I'm not scared,' he said. 'I'm incredibly fucking happy.'

'So am I,' I said.

'Get your kit off then.'

I snorted. 'Harry!'

He fixed me with his eyes. God, he was laughing.

'Get your kit off, you gorgeous beautiful fucking angel woman of my life,' he said.

'Steady on,' I said, trying to stand, wanting to get near him, falling over my own feet.

'No,' he said. 'Won't. I will not steady on. OK. Yes, I will. OK. If that's what you want. We have plenty of time after all. Steady on, right now. Look. Steady.' He opened one of the bottles of wine to prove it.

LOUISA YOUNG

'I don't think it's a verb,' I said. 'To steady on.' I took the bottle to pour him a glass but the glass was upside down and the wine poured on the floor. 'Oh fuck.'

'It's that word again . . .' he said. 'There's that word . . .'

'I love you,' I said. Surprising myself. 'I love him but I love you . . .'

He was up and his arms were around me. 'Shhh, shhh,' he said, holding my head on, not quieting me but comforting me, just comforting me. 'I know. I know. It's so simple for us. I know everything. It makes it so much easier . . . Oh. By the way. Happy Eid.'

I opened my eyes to look at him.

'Everything,' he said.

I love you. I kept saying it. He was kissing me. Kissing me, kissing me, kissing me.

After a while: 'Oh my god,' he said, 'you smell the same. Ten years and you smell the same.'

'It's more than ten years,' I said.

'I don't give a fuck how long ago it was. Oh! Do you remember the last time?'

I thought a second.

'It was the night before you threw the chair at me,' I said.

'Nope. That morning.'

'Was it?'

'Definitely. I remember.'

I drew away from him.

'Was it good?'

'It was extremely fucking good. It was always extremely fucking good.'

'No, it wasn't,' I said. 'It wasn't extremely fucking good that time you . . .'

'Shut up,' he said. 'Shut up and kiss me.'

'Oh! Macho!'

'Shut up and fuck me.'

'You fuck me!' I retorted.

Silence.

Hanging there.

'OK,' he said. 'I will.'

*

There's a way of telling when your girlfriend's relationship is going to last: for the first time in all the time you've known her, she doesn't tell you how the sex was.

*

In the morning Lily woke us with hands full of sugar almonds, and climbed into bed between us. 'This is nice,' she said.

*

Five months less a day later, on June 30th, Harry and Lily and I were watching England versus Argentina when just as David Beckham kicked Simeone in the back of the knee an audible pop popped through the room, and I began to flood. And continued. They both took me to the

hospital in the Pontiac, ruining the white leather uphol-
stery, and I was four days in labour. Harry stayed with
me throughout, and Mum came and took Lily home to
our flat, and brought her twice to visit me as I cavorted
around on gas and air and pethidine. There was a tape
machine in the labour room, and I played Khaled, Hank
Williams, Aretha Franklin, *La Bohème*, the Bach cello
suites, and *Nirvana Unplugged*. No Umm Khalthoum. At
one point though I found myself singing *'Enta 'Omri'*, and
translated it for the midwives and they giggled; I pulled
on the gas and air as if it were a recalcitrant shisha, I saw
Sa'id's face and heard his voice and felt his hands in my
hair . . . and while I was sad that he missed this I knew
he would not miss everything, that I had done what I
could, that I would continue to do so, and that I would
do better than I had done. If he wanted to be a father to
her we could work it out. Work something out. Strange
to divide in half the roles a man has in a woman's life,
strange to have two men play the same role, albeit in
very different ways (and play it I knew he would). Strange,
necessary and possible.

Harry's phrase was in my mind: 'For you to be safe, and
for all to be well.'

In the end I had an emergency caesarian, and thought
of Cleopatra as a surgeon whose name I will never
remember rummaged inside me and pulled a dark golden
girl out of the slice across my belly, black hair plastered
across her head, pale eyes gazing serenely. Harry was there,

all scrubbed up in green, with a mask. He and Lily wrapped her in a big white scarf when she came home with us five days later. I wanted to call her Sekhmet but everyone told me this was a temporary madness. OK, Shagaratt ad Durr, I said, but they laughed in my face. I didn't like her much at first: I just looked at her and thought, 'What are you? What the hell are you?' Harry spent a lot of time with her then. He liked her from the moment she appeared. It took me until I was starting to walk again. Not long, in the scheme of things. 'Family man,' he said. 'It's good. I like it.' He took to playing Sly Stone on his car stereo.

On her birth certificate it says Aisha Jane el Araby Gower. Lily got her new birth certificate at the same time: Lily Makins Gower. We had a birth certificate party on the balcony: Harry, Chrissie, Zeinab, her husband Larry and the boys, Brigid and Caitlin and their boys and Maraidh and Aisling and Reuben, Adjoa and her mother, Mum and Dad, Fergus, Liam from the Winfield, Dizzy Ansah, who'd passed on the message to Harry two years ago that I was looking for him, because Harry ran into him in Portobello. Not Preston Oliver.

Harry said: 'You paid for my child, I'll pay for yours. Shut up. You know it's fair. Anyway they don't pay us badly.'

Lily would glare at her and say: 'She's *my* mummy, you know. My mummy.' One time when she was saying that I said to her: 'Do you know who her daddy is?'

'Harry?' she said.

'No,' I said.

359

LOUISA YOUNG

'Oh, stupid me,' she said. 'Sa'id, because you got her in Egypt.'

'Mmm,' I said.

Later I asked her what she thought of that.

'Will Sa'id come back?' she asked, after some thought.

'Perhaps,' I said. 'But not to live with us.'

'She can borrow my daddy,' she said. 'Do you remember when I was about two or something I wanted to borrow the baby's daddy if you had a baby? Well, she can borrow mine.'

That was a good moment.

'But if we have two daddies now, shouldn't you marry one?' she asked. 'You could you know. They're both very nice. But Sa'id doesn't have to come back to stay. Harry is nearer. Then me and Aisha could be bridesmaids and we could have another baby.'

Another! Harry's and Janie's, Sa'id's and mine, Harry's and mine. The mathematics of the biology pleased me.

Mother of three! Jesus fuck.

*

She was lying in her Moses basket by Lily's bedside, both of them asleep, as I wrote this letter on the kitchen table. Harry was not there that night.

(He'd said, as he left for work that morning, 'I'll give you a ring later.' 'Yippee yippee!' Lily had yelled. We'd looked at her quizzically. (You see how easily I use 'we'.) 'You're going to marry my mummy at last! You are you are, you said you'd give her a ring!' We laughed and laughed.)

This is the letter:

Sa'id *habibi*,

Don't say a word. I'm not coming back. But sweet-heart, sweetest of hearts:

This is neither an invitation, nor a rejection. It is something I tried to tell you, but time and circumstance – and you – forbade. Forgive me, if forgiveness is needed. Your daughter may come. I'll tell her who you are. I will bring her up to love you, and to love Egypt. Lily says: she can borrow my daddy. She is proud to have a daddy to share, so proud to have a sister. I think of you every day, not only because her eyes are the colour of palm-tree tips at dawn. She is beautiful, and loved. She smells like *ornali*. She is yours.

I am sorry you have not had this time with her.

I close no doors, I send love. I am not wasting away for you.

Looking at it now, it seems, what, sentimental? Self-indulgent? But it was part of the process.

NINETEEN

Iftar, Eid, the end

Simon Preston Oliver accepted the Luxori police's version of Eddie's death. François du Berry had fallen from a high place; nobody had seen. Why shouldn't he accept it? He never learnt that Harry had been there.

Chrissie's still dry, still precarious. She went to a clinic for a while. Still not saying what happened on the roof. I don't give a toot. Why would I?

Eddie was buried at the Protestant church in Cairo. I don't think anybody went. After all, he was already dead.

Janie's money is still in the box. As Aisha gets older I may try and buy a house. With Harry's income and my deposit we could have a garden, a bedroom each for the girls.

In the interstices of motherhood I am reading a lot. My brain, curiously, has come back to life. I am reading Jung, Frances Yates on *The Art of Memory* and a lot of archaeology reviews and journals. I think I may be going to do a PhD. Not on anything Egyptian. That's not what it's about.

I don't see Sarah, why should I? Or perhaps, how could I? I don't rule it out though.

I love having a girl in each arm. I love having both of them in bed, feeding one, reading to the other, Harry cooking dinner. It has actually happened, once or twice.

A month after I wrote to Sa'id, a letter came, with a package.

The letter, in his small and elegant handwriting, that looks like Arabic even when it is in English, said:

Dear Angelina,

I am glad I didn't leave you all day and all night on the Corniche, for if I had, all the felucca men in Luxor would have looked at our girl when she comes here and said ah, yes, her mother is that mad English woman who sat all day and all night on the Corniche . . . I am glad to have a child, in your city of all nations, and with such a mother. Part of me, you know, was sad that I couldn't give myself to your multicultural life. I am glad in some way to give my child to it. I will be glad to come, when you invite me, not before. Four requests. One: I have set up a bank account. The bank will write to you. I know what you are like for not using money. Use it – don't deny me this. Two: marry him (if you haven't already). If he ever fails you, come back to me. Three: send a picture. Four: kiss her for me.

Sa'id.

Lovely man, I thought. But my heart did not lurch when I read it. I pictured him at forty, me fifty, the girls teenagers, meeting in a restaurant on the shores of an Italian lake, eating, talking, getting over a small nervousness, remembering a fundamental faith, not regretting what didn't happen. Sharing an old knowledge, not having shared a life lived since then. Pictured myself helping Aisha to know the complexity of her history, as I have helped, and will continue to help, Lily. I didn't picture him at thirty, or thirty-five, reappearing, wanting me after all. Nor did I picture myself wanting him.

Inside the package, his *hejeb*. It smelt of him. Or maybe he had always smelt of it. I was about to put it to my nose, but then I felt very strongly that that would not be right. Instead I coiled the leather cord around it, and wrapped it up for her, to preserve what there was of him on it, so that if she ever needed it she could get that smell. It was not mine now, it was hers. I put it in a box with my Umm Khalthoum tapes, a curl of black hair and a very old sprig of mimosa.

'You sentimental old cow,' said Harry, disrespectfully.

'Don't mock,' I said, 'it's her heritage.'

'Her heritage is not dead in a box,' he said. 'Her heritage is going to crop up here one day realizing what a fucking romantic fool he's been.'

'Why romantic?'

'Can't square love and reality,' he said.

I smiled, because it was true, and I had already worked

it out for myself. And oh my soul, I know why we came apart.

'And if he does crop up?'

'He'll have to kill me,' said Harry.

I looked over to him. Thought for two seconds, then passed him the letter.

He was impassive as he read it. Put it down.

'Well, he's a good bloke,' he said. 'I always said so.'

'Stop it with that,' I said.

'Why?' he asked.

I busied myself with the box. Refolded the letter. Put it in the box with the *hejeb*.

'Can you handle it?' I asked. 'The fact of him?'

He looked up.

'Can you?' he answered.

'We have done so far,' I said carefully. 'One way or another.'

'We have, haven't we.'

'Mmm.'

'We're here now.'

'We are.' We were in the kitchen. Of course.

He was smiling.

'Angel,' he said.

Here we go.

'Yes?'

I looked over at him. He was slightly green.

'About that decent interval.'

I put the lid on the box. Let the past wash over me, and

away. Raised my eyes to the future, and knew what I wanted. The age-old notion was there with us. Before Sa'id, after Sa'id: me and Harry. Harry and Angeline. The things that used to scare me didn't scare me any more. Not one bit. The idea of a man and woman living together seemed to me charming, practical, full of possibilities. The idea – the reality – of his coming back, and being here, was – nice. Does this sound prosaic, compared to how things were with Sa'id? But Harry and I had been mad with love the first time round. Now we were sane with love. It's not prosaic. It's good.

'I thought you'd never ask,' I said.

'Really?' he said.

'No,' I said. 'I knew one of us would.'

He was looking at his hands.

'So?' he said, looking up.

'This is,' I said. 'This is a decent interval.'

He started laughing.

'Forgive me,' he said. 'I just kind of have to do this. We don't have to do it this way. But . . .' He was laughing like a kid.

'What?' I said.

He splatted his hand down on the table. Pushed something towards me. Small box. Inside, emerald ring. Dark like the green of his eyes. Yes, I have always had a thing for green eyes.

Then he leapt up as I took it in my hand and stared at it, and he came round the table and took my hands, box

and all, in his, and said, 'If that's how you'd like it, would
you like that? Would you?'

Would I?

'How long have you been carrying this around?' I asked
him.

He looked sheepish.

'How long?' I asked again.

'Don't be cross . . .'

'I'm not cross . . .'

'They looked like they needed the trade . . .'

'Who?'

'I got it in Luxor.'

God, how feelings can flood. They flooded. Inundation
of my heart. Harry, how you have dealt with all this, through
it all, patient, cool, generous . . .

If I say it was always Harry, that doesn't mean it was
never Sa'id. It was always Harry. And it was Sa'id – but it
is Harry. Look at him.

'Yes,' I said.

'What?'

'Yes. Just yes.'

'Yes?'

'Yes.'

Acknowledgements

My thanks are due as usual to Amira Ghazalla and Charlotte Horton, and quite particularly to David Brooks. And to Isabel Adomakoh Young, Emily Young and Hassan Elaraby. To Louis Adomakoh, Sue Swift, David Flusfeder, Clare Brennan, Nicola Dahrendorf, Al-Saqi Books, Jake Howard, Francesca Brill, Dominic Gill, Juan Carlos Gumucio, Caroline Gascoigne, Tom Whyte, Annabel Arden, Candida Blaker, David Jenkins, Anthony Sattin. To Nick and Sian Lezard, and to Nick Lezard's mum. To Abu Nagarr, Anwar and Captain Ziko. To Derek Johns, Linda Shaughnessy and the staff of A. P. Watt; my editor Rebecca Lloyd, Philip Gwyn Jones, Karen Duffy, Jon Butler, Humphrey Serjeantson, Becky Glibbery and the staff at Flamingo. To Alastair Niven and Catriona Ferguson at the British Council. To all the writers who knowingly or unknowingly have helped me not only with this book but with *Baby Love* and *Desiring Cairo*: Max Rodenbeck, Edward Said, Diane

Singerman, Wendy Buonaventura, Naguib Mahfouz, Ahdaf Soueif, Leslie Blanche, Albert Hourani, Robert Irwin, Deborah Manley, Geraldine Brooks, Andre Aciman, Lucinda Jarrett, Karin van Nieuwkerk, Margot Badran; and the dead ones: Flaubert, Herodotus, E. Wallis Budge, A. W. Kinglake, the Lady Travellers, the classical poets. Umm Kalthoum (RIP) and her songwriters and musicians; Ibrahim Nagui. Merle Haggard, Randy Travis and one of the Judds but I can't remember which. To my parents, my brother and my sisters. And to all the Sa'ids: Boris Romanos, Julio Segovia, Karaja da Cunha Jnr., Zed Zawada, Burt Caesar, Luis Angel Lopez Riou, Roberto Astori, Lola Omole, Younus, Ali, Daniel, Nathaniel, and now I come to think of it half the people on the list above anyway.

Louisa Young, 2000